The Long Shot

Stephen Leather

CORONET BOOKS
Hodder and Stoughton

First published in Great Britain in 1994 by
Hodder and Stoughton
A division of Hodder Headline PLC

A Coronet paperback

British Library Cataloguing in Publication Data

Leather, Stephen
The Long Shot
I. Title
823.914 [F]

ISBN 0-340-63237-2

Typeset by Avon Dataset Ltd, Bidford-on-Avon
Printed and bound in Great Britain by
Cox and Wyman Ltd, Reading, Berks

Hodder and Stoughton Ltd
A division of Hodder Headline PLC
338 Euston Road
London NW1 3BH

For Marie

The Long Shot

The tyres of the Boeing 737 bit into the runway, squealing like dying pigs and sending spurts of dust into the air. The plane taxied towards the terminal building which shimmered in the midday heat. In the First Class cabin the passengers began to unbuckle their seat belts before the plane had come to a halt. A dark-haired stewardess left her seat and went over to the occupant of seat 3B. She bent down and gave him her professional smile. "Mr Ahmed?" she said. The man continued reading as if he hadn't heard. "Mr Ahmed?" she repeated. He looked up and nodded. He was a typical First Class passenger: middle-aged, overweight and seemingly bored with the whole business of flying. He'd scarcely touched the inflight food and rejected the complimentary headset with an impatient wave of his hand. He'd spent most of the three-hour flight with his nose buried in the *Wall Street Journal*. "Mr Ahmed, the pilot has requested that you remain behind while the rest of the passengers deplane," she said.

The passenger didn't seem the least bit surprised by the request. "What about the people I'm travelling with?" he asked. The woman next to him was down on the manifest as his wife and, like the man, was travelling on a Yemeni diplomatic passport. A grey-haired older woman, apparently his mother, was sitting behind him, and on the other side of the cabin were his two young children.

All had Yemeni diplomatic passports.

"I'm sorry, sir, they're also to stay behind."

The passenger nodded. "I understand," he said quietly. "Will you tell my children while I explain to my mother?"

The stewardess went over to explain to the youngsters while Ahmed turned around and spoke to the old woman. Elba Maria Sanchez had grown accustomed to waiting in airliners while immigration officials took advice on whether or not her son should be admitted into their country. The family had been turned away from most of the countries in the Middle East, and previous safe havens including East Germany and Hungary had turned their backs on their old cohorts in their rush to embrace capitalism. Even the Sudanese had betrayed them.

The passengers shuffled off the plane. The stewardess asked Ahmed if he wanted a drink while he waited but he declined. He picked up a copy of *Newsweek* and idly flicked through it. "It's always the same," said his wife bitterly. "They should be ashamed of themselves, these people, they have no loyalty. After all we've done for them."

"Be patient, Magdalena," said the man, his eyes on the magazine.

"Patient! Ha! I was patient in Tripoli, I was patient in Damascus, I've been patient in virtually every airport in the Middle East. Face it, Ilich, no-one wants us any more. We're an embarrassment."

"Hush," he said quietly. "You'll upset the children."

She looked like she was about to argue but before she could speak a small, unimposing man in a dark suit appeared at the doorway. He carried a shiny black briefcase and he nervously rubbed his moustache as he approached

Ahmed. He introduced himself as Khatami, just the one name, and he didn't tell the passenger who he represented. There was no need. He suggested that they go back into the Business Class cabin where they could have some privacy and Ahmed followed him along the aisle. Ahmed's children looked anxiously up at him and he winked at them reassuringly. Khatami stood to the side to allow Ahmed past and then he whisked the blue curtain closed. Ahmed sat down in an aisle seat and Khatami took the seat opposite him, balancing the briefcase on his knees. Khatami seemed uneasy and beads of perspiration dripped down either side of his beakish nose. "Your passport, please," he said, holding out his hand.

Ahmed took his passport from the inside pocket of his Armani jacket and handed it over. Khatami flicked through the pages of the passport which contained a plethora of visas and immigration stamps. He read the name at the front of the passport: Nagi Abubaker Ahmed. The photograph matched the man sitting in front of him: a receding hairline, a thick moustache over fleshy lips, and jowls around the chin that suggested the man had lived a soft life with too much time spent in expensive restaurants. "You are Ilich Ramirez Sanchez?"

The passenger nodded.

"The woman travelling with you is Magdalena Kopp?"

Another curt nod.

"Mr Sanchez, I've been asked to put a number of questions to you before our Government decides whether or not it can accommodate your request for asylum." Sanchez said nothing. Khatami could see his own reflection in the darkened lenses of Sanchez's spectacles. It gave him an uneasy feeling and he took a large white handkerchief from his pocket and wiped his forehead. "You have been living in Damascus for some time, is that correct?"

"Yes," said Sanchez.

"From there you went where?"

"To Libya."

"The Libyans would not allow you to stay in their country?"

"You are well informed," said Sanchez.

"And from Libya you went back to Damascus?"

"That was the first plane out of the country, yes."

Khatami nodded, wiped his forehead again and shoved the handkerchief back into his top pocket. "Your assets are where?"

"Assets? I don't understand."

"You have money?"

Sanchez smiled. "Yes, I have money. I was well paid for my work."

"The money is where?"

"Switzerland, mainly. I also have one million dollars in my diplomatic baggage. I can assure you I will not be a burden."

Khatami smiled nervously. "Good, good. That's good." He looked down at his briefcase and noticed that he was gripping it so tightly that his nails were biting into the leather. He took his hands away and Sanchez saw two wet palm prints where they had been. "My Government is particularly concerned about your past, Mr Sanchez. Your, how shall I call them? . . . exploits . . . have been well documented, and have attracted a great deal of publicity. They want to know whether or not you have rescinded your terrorist past."

Sanchez sighed. "I am looking only for a place where

my family and I can live in safety. My past is my past."

Khatami nodded, keeping his eyes down so that he wouldn't have to look at his own reflection. "Then you no longer consider yourself a terrorist?"

"That is correct," said Sanchez.

"Ah," said Khatami. "That is a great pity. A great pity." He lifted his head and there was a look of hawkish intensity in his eyes. "It could well be in the future that we would have need of someone with your talents."

"I see," said Sanchez. He took off his spectacles, revealing brown eyes that were surprisingly soft and amused. "I would not have a problem with that. I think that whoever offers me sanctuary would have the right to expect me to perform a service for them."

Khatami grinned and nodded. He had expected the discussion with Ilich Ramirez Sanchez to be much more stressful. The man the world knew as Carlos the Jackal was proving surprisingly easy to deal with.

Jim Mitchell scanned the clear blue skies through the cockpit of his Cessna 172. It was a glorious day for flying. There were a few wisps of feathery clouds but they were way up high, much higher than the single-engine Cessna could ever hope to fly. To the north-west, about eight miles away, he saw the runway, almost perpendicular to the nose of the Cessna. The plane was perfectly trimmed and there was next to no turbulence so he needed only the barest pressure on the wheel to maintain his course. He turned his head to the right and caught his wife's eye. She smiled and winked at him and he grinned back. "Sandra, do you want to call them?"

"Sure," she said. She tuned the radio to the control tower. Mitchell watched her as she contacted the air-traffic controller, reported their position and told him that they were inbound for landing. She asked for a runway advisory and, through his headset, Mitchell heard the controller tell her that the wind was blowing right down the runway at about six knots. Perfect. At forty-five years old, Jim Mitchell was a decade and a half older than his wife and he never tired of looking at her. She smiled as she spoke into the microphone and she waved for him to keep his eyes on the outside of the plane. He glanced down at the sectional chart clipped to his leg. Their approach was taking them through a Military Operations Area, marked on the chart with a magenta border. Flying was permitted in the MOA, but it still made him slightly nervous. He peered through the windshield, scanning the sky in segments, looking for military traffic.

He felt a small hand on his shoulder. "Dad, Dad, turn around."

Mitchell twisted around to see his son Jamie holding their camcorder. The red light was on showing that Jamie was filming. Mitchell grinned and gave his son a thumbs-up. "Jim Mitchell, the fearless pilot," he laughed and Jamie giggled. The boy panned to the right. "Mom," he said, and Sandra looked over her shoulder.

"Don't use all the tape," she chided. "Save it till we get closer to Vegas."

"Oh Mom, don't say stuff like that, it gets recorded," Jamie moaned. He switched the camcorder off. "Now I'll have to rewind it." He sighed in the way that only a child can sigh and pouted. "I bet Scorsese never had this trouble," he said.

Sandra leaned back and ruffled his hair. He jerked away, refusing to be mollified. At eight years old he was getting to the "I don't want to be touched" stage, Sandra realised with a twinge of regret.

"I see the wind-sock," said Sandra, and Mitchell squinted, looking for the orange sock which would give him an accurate indication of the ground-level wind direction. He couldn't see it. His wife's eyesight was much better than Mitchell's, who was no longer allowed to fly without his correcting lenses. Another sign of old age creeping up on him, he thought ruefully. Mitchell reduced power and took the Cessna down to one thousand feet above the ground and joined the traffic pattern at the single runway. They were the only plane in the area and they were soon on the ground, taxiing up to a refuelling station.

Jamie filmed the plane being refuelled and then wandered off to get a canned drink from a vending machine. Mitchell put his hands on his hips and surveyed the sky overhead.

Jamie returned with his Coke. He took the camcorder out of the Cessna. "Okay, I want a shot of the two of you together at the front of the plane," said the boy, and he showed his parents where he wanted them to stand.

"Our son, the movie director," said Mitchell.

"It'll be a great loss to the real estate industry that he doesn't follow in his father's footsteps," said Sandra, smiling to show that she was joking. Real estate had given them an enviable lifestyle, even if Mitchell had to admit that it wasn't the most exciting of careers and that people tended to avoid him at parties. She stood close to him and he slipped his arm around her waist. Mitchell held his head high to conceal his growing bald spot and double chin from the camcorder, and sucked in his stomach.

Jamie panned across from the fuel pumps until his parents were in the centre of the viewfinder. They waved and grinned. He switched the camcorder off and climbed into the back seat of the Cessna while his father walked around the plane and checked the fuel tanks. Sandra told her son to put on a pullover. The weather in Phoenix had been unseasonably warm but the forecast had been for cold winds to the north.

Mitchell soon had the small plane up in the air. He headed west, his VOR tuned to the Needles beacon in Havasu Lake National Wildlife Refuge from where he planned to fly up to Vegas. There was little in the way of landmarks to navigate by once he'd flown over Highway 93, so he had to rely on his VOR. He would have preferred to fly at a slightly higher altitude, but Jamie kept insisting that they fly low so that he could look at the scenery, even if it was just sand, rocks and the many-armed cacti which stood like guardsmen on parade.

"Hey, Dad, what's that down there?" Jamie pointed down to the left.

Mitchell turned to look where his son was pointing but couldn't see anything. "What is it, Jamie?" he asked.

"There's someone down there. Cars in the desert, and some other stuff. Can we look?"

Mitchell squinted behind his sunglasses. The darkened lenses were prescription but lately he was finding they weren't as good at correcting his long-distance vision as they used to be. He checked his fuel gauges and saw that he had plenty to spare. With the VOR equipment there was no chance of getting lost, and it was supposed to be a vacation. "I guess so, son," he said, and put the Cessna into a slow, turning descent.

"Is this a good idea?" Sandra asked through his headset.

"We've plenty of time," said Mitchell. "And we're on a VFR flight plan, we can play around if we want."

"There!" Jamie shouted. "I think they're making a movie." He switched his camcorder on and began filming out of the side window.

"What is it?" asked Sandra. She was sitting on the right-hand side of the plane and her husband was blocking her view.

"I can't see," said Mitchell, putting the Cessna into a steep turn so that the ground whirled underneath him. The altimeter span as he took the plane down to two thousand feet.

"There are two towers down there, the sort they put cameras on," said Jamie excitedly. "I can't see what they're doing, though. I bet they're making a movie. This is cool. I wonder who the director is?"

Mitchell peered out of the cockpit. Far below he could see a wood and metal structure, about fifty feet high. It looked like scaffolding, and he could make out a figure on top of it. Chains or ropes tethered the structure to the ground. About half a mile away were a group of men standing on the ground in a line. Mitchell frowned. The figures were standing too still, and there was something awkward about the way they held their arms. They weren't cacti, but they weren't human, either. He levelled the plane off and pointed out the figures to his wife.

"They look like robots," she said.

"Or dummies," he agreed.

"There are real people over there, see?" She pointed to another group of figures standing several hundred feet away.

"I see them," said Mitchell.

"Let's go down lower, Dad," said Jamie, still filming. "It might be someone famous."

"That might not be a good idea, Jamie," said his mother, twisting around in her seat. "They might not want a plane buzzing overhead."

"Just one pass, Mom," implored Jamie. "Please."

"Jim, what do you think?" she asked her husband.

"One quick look wouldn't hurt," said Mitchell. "I must admit I'm a bit curious myself. They're miles from anywhere."

"Looks like I'm outvoted then," said Sandra.

Mitchell circled slowly as he lost height and levelled off at five hundred feet above the ground, several miles away from the two towers. Jamie trained the camcorder on the desert below. They flew around an isolated butte which rose majestically from the ground as if it had been pushed up from below. Jamie took the viewfinder away from his face and peered at the rocky outcrop. "There's someone on top of the hill," he said. He put the camcorder back to his eye and zoomed in on the butte. "He's lying down . . . I think he's got a gun, Dad."

"Are you sure?"

The Cessna had flown by the hill and Jamie couldn't see the man any more. "I don't know, I think so."

"There wouldn't be hunters out here, surely," said Sandra, the concern obvious in her voice.

"Nothing to shoot at except lizards," said Mitchell. "Okay, Jamie, keep your eyes open, we're only going to do

10

this once. Shout if you see Steven Spielberg, okay?" He cut back on the power and slowed the Cessna's airspeed until they were at eighty knots. Jamie panned across the activity below, zooming in on the three people on the ground and then tracking across to the two towers. Sandra shaded her eyes with her hands and peered down.

"Jamie, can you see what the men are doing on the towers?" she said. "They're not cameras they're holding, are they?"

Jamie concentrated his camcorder on the tower closest to the small plane. It was about half a mile away and seemed to be made of metal scaffolding and planks. "No, Mom," he said, "they're guns."

"Guns?"

"Yeah, like the guy had back on the hill."

Sandra turned to her husband. "Jim, I don't like this, let's go."

"You think maybe we should report it?" Mitchell asked.

"I don't know, I just think we should go. I've got a bad feeling about this."

"Okay, honey, no problem." Mitchell pushed the throttle full in and pulled back on the control wheel and aimed the small plane up into the blue sky. He looked at his VOR and saw that he was to the left of his original course so he banked the Cessna to the right as he climbed. The desert scrub seemed to slide below him.

Sandra settled back in her seat, glad to be away from the men with the guns. She closed her eyes and rubbed them with the back of her hands. She heard the crack of splintering glass and she jumped as something wet splattered across her cheek. Her stomach lurched as the nose of the Cessna dipped down and when she looked

11

across at her husband she saw that he'd slumped back in his seat, his head resting against the side window. Her first thought was that he'd had a heart attack or a stroke but then she saw that there was blood on his face and she screamed. His blood was all over her and there were bits of pink tissue and fragments of bone that looked like white wood shavings. She screamed and tugged on his shoulder, hoping that by shaking him she'd wake him up. His head lolled forward and she saw that the top of his skull had been blown away. His feet were drumming against the floor but she could see from the size of the wound that he was already dead, the kicking was just a nervous reaction. Something dripped down her face and she looked up to see thick globules of blood trickling down from the roof of the plane. She opened her mouth to scream again and blood ran between her lips, making her gag. Behind her, Jamie was screaming for his father.

Sandra wiped her hands across her face and felt the blood smear over her skin. Through the cockpit she saw nothing but the desert and she realised with a jolt that the plane was still diving. She reached for the control wheel and pulled back on it, feeling her stomach churn as the plane's nose came up. She was gasping for breath and her arms were trembling. She looked towards the attitude indicator but her husband's body obscured it, then suddenly his whole body swung away from the instruments as if he'd only been dozing, but she realised it was the deceleration forcing him back. The shaking in her hands intensified and she forced herself to keep her eyes on the instruments and not on her dead husband. The plane levelled off and she decided to accelerate away from the gunmen below rather than wasting time trying to climb. There was a loud crack

12

from somewhere behind her and then another and she yelled at Jamie to lie down across the rear seats. The rudder pedals abruptly lost their resistance as if the cables had been cut and the Cessna began to slide to the right, with the wind. More bullets thudded into the rear of the plane and she felt the control wheel kick in her hands. "Oh God, the fuel," she said, remembering the fuel tanks in the wings above her head. She began twisting the control wheel from side to side, jerking the plane around in the air. Mitchell's body swayed grotesquely, held in place by the seat belt. His blood was dripping everywhere, though thankfully his feet had stopped drumming on the pedals.

Jamie had followed her instructions and was lying across the back seats, sobbing into his hands.

"It's okay, honey, it's going to be okay," Sandra said, though there was no conviction in her trembling voice. Her mind was racing and she couldn't remember what the emergency procedures were. She closed her eyes for a moment and tried to picture the emergency transponder code. Seven Seven Zero Zero. She took her left hand off the control wheel and fumbled with the dials on the transponder, turning them to the four figures which would set alarms ringing at all radar facilities within range. The wheel jerked in her hand and pulled forward as the plane began to dive again. The engine started to splutter and the whole plane bucked and reared like a runaway stallion. Her hands shook as she keyed in the emergency frequency on the radio: 121.50 MHz. The control wheel began to shudder, making her shoulders vibrate.

"Mom, what's happening?" screamed her son.

"It's okay, honey. Stay where you are." The engine was coughing and the propeller blades became visible as a grey disc as they slowed. Black smoke was pouring from the left side of the engine cowling. According to the altimeter they were a little over a thousand feet above the ground and the vertical speed indicator showed they were dropping at five hundred feet a minute. She clicked on the radio microphone. "Mayday, mayday," she said. "This is Five Nine Four, position unknown, crash landing." She couldn't remember what other information she was supposed to give in a distress call.

The headset crackled but there was no reply. The altimeter was spinning and they were probably too low for anyone to pick up their signal. "Mayday, mayday," she repeated, then took her thumb off the microphone switch and concentrated on the emergency procedures. She pulled back hard on the control wheel to try to keep the nose up but it suddenly went slack and she knew she'd lost control of the elevators. The dive steepened and the airspeed indicator went above the red line. The plane was diving at its maximum speed but there was surprisingly little sense of movement. Sandra Mitchell became quite detached about her own imminent death. She kept pulling back on the control wheel, knowing that it was quite useless but wanting to do something. She took deep breaths. "It's all right, honey," she called to her son. "It's all right."

The ground seemed to get no closer until the last hundred feet and then it suddenly rushed up to meet her.

Cole Howard took the pack of cards out of his pocket and slid off the elastic band he'd used to keep them together. He scanned the first one. "Who was Barnum's partner in The Greatest Show on Earth?" he read. He thought for a while before turning the card over. The answer was J. A. Bailey. Howard sighed. The next question was "What is known as The Englishman's Wine?" Howard smiled. "Port," he said to himself. He turned the card over and his smile widened as he saw that he was correct. The telephone on his desk rang, a single burble that let him know it was an internal call. He picked it up as he continued to read the Trivial Pursuit card. "Howard," he said.

"Good morning, Cole. You busy?"

It was Jake Sheldon, Cole's immediate superior in the Federal Bureau of Investigation's office in Phoenix. "Nothing pressing, Jake," said Howard.

"Can you come up and see me when you've got a moment?"

"Sure thing. Now okay?"

"Now would be just fine, Cole. Thanks."

Howard knew that Jake Sheldon always relayed his orders as requests, often in a manner so abstruse as to cause confusion. A polite suggestion that an agent "come up and see me sometime" was as urgent a call as he'd ever make, even if his office was on fire. Agents new to the office had to be taken to one side and briefed on Sheldon's management techniques lest they confuse his deferential manner with laziness or complacency. Howard studied one of his cards as he waited for the elevator. "How many notes are there in two adjacent octaves?" Howard frowned, decided the answer was sixteen and turned the card over. "Fifteen," he read. He showed no annoyance at his mistake, he merely memorised the answer and went on to the next question.

Sheldon's office was as neat and formal as the man himself, his desk uncluttered, his college degree and legal qualifications lined up on the wall behind him in identical rosewood frames, the blinds across his window as straight as razors. He was wearing a dark blue suit and crisp white shirt, a uniform which he never varied. Sheldon was rumoured to have more than a dozen suits, each exactly the same in colour and style, which he rotated religiously. He looked as if he'd just stepped out of a clothing catalogue, and even though he was sitting behind his desk he still had the jacket on. He had the look of an elder statesman, a senator perhaps, with white hair, a soft voice and fleshy jowls. He closed a file on his desk when Howard entered his office and asked him to sit. "So, Cole, how's your lovely wife?"

"Fine, sir. Just fine."

"And her parents?"

"Great. Just great."

Sheldon nodded. "Give my regards to Mr Clayton when you see him."

"I'll do that, sir."

The pleasantries over, Sheldon handed Howard a videocassette and the file he'd been reading. "I want you to look into this for me, Cole. It's a strange one, a triple homicide, but there's more to it than that. A family were flying about sixty miles south of Kingman when their plane was shot down. Normally we wouldn't get involved in an incident of this nature, but it's what they saw before they were shot down that involves us. Put that into the VCR, will you?"

Howard took the cassette over to the VCR in the corner of the office, slotted it home and pressed the 'play' button.

He stood to the side and folded his arms across his chest. A woman's face appeared on the screen, distorted because she was so close to the lens. She was laughing and Howard could hear a small boy shouting: "Go on, Mom, make a face."

"Sandra Mitchell, a thirty-year-old homemaker. Her husband, Jim, is flying the plane. They were en route from Phoenix to Las Vegas."

The camera moved jerkily so that the back of the pilot's head was in frame. "Dad, Dad!" The pilot turned and gave the boy a thumbs-up.

"They were flying at about three thousand five hundred feet here, there's a map in the file which will show you their exact position. The local police are conducting a search of the area now, but it's going to take several days."

The camcorder panned across the cockpit windows giving them a view of the desert far below. Sandra's voice called out above the noise of the engine: "Don't use all the tape." There was a flicker showing that the video had been turned off and then there were two adults in the frame, the man and the woman standing proudly in front of their plane. It was a small Cessna, with one propeller. The man was holding in his stomach and his young wife patted him as if telling him there was no need.

. The picture flickered and then there was another view out of the window. There was no way of knowing how long it had been switched off. A sandstone butte filled the screen. There was a figure lying on the top, with what looked like a rifle in his hands. The camcorder wavered as the lens zoomed in and focused on a close-up. Then the camera angled down and far below amid the cacti and brush Howard could see some sort of a tower which had been built of metal scaffolding and wooden planks.

"At about two o'clock in the afternoon they saw this structure, and another just like it, and went down to take a closer look."

The picture swung from side to side as the boy struggled to keep the structure in sight. There was a man on the top and Howard saw that he was holding a rifle. The plane levelled off again and in the distance Howard could make out a group of figures.

The little boy played with the focus control, zooming the lens in and out on the figures standing below in the desert. It wasn't a pleasant effect and Howard averted his eyes for a moment.

There was a sudden cracking sound and then the woman began screaming. The camcorder swung round and Howard could see there was blood all over the front of the cockpit. The top of the pilot's head had been blown away. "My God," whispered Howard.

The boy began screaming and the picture lurched as if the camcorder had been thrown to the side and all Howard could see was the blood-spattered material of the seat cover.

"Mrs Mitchell also had a private pilot's licence and she took over the controls. Within thirty seconds after the first shot, eight more hit the plane."

Howard heard the small explosions as the bullets struck home, then he heard the engine splutter and cough.

"The engine went at about the same time, and we think the plane was between a thousand and fifteen hundred feet high at that point."

Howard heard the woman make a disjointed Mayday call, but there was no reply.

"She put out a distress call on the emergency frequency and set her transponder to the emergency code: that's how the local Flight Service Station got her position." Sheldon's voice was clinical and detached.

The engine noise died and the camcorder must have moved again because Howard could see the ground rushing up.

Howard listened as the boy began to scream and his mother tried in vain to calm him down. The last thing she said was "Please God, no . . ." and then there was a sickening crash, and the sound of metal grating and what sounded like the wind.

"At this point the plane is down and the occupants are dead. The camcorder continued to record for a further twenty minutes until it came to the end of the tape. You might as well switch it off now."

Howard leaned forward and pressed the 'stop' button. Just before he did he thought he heard the boy call out for his father but it could have been the desert wind.

"Luckily they didn't hit the fuel tanks. When the local sheriff got there the camcorder was intact. What you've got there is a copy we made. The original is in one of our labs in Washington." Howard sat down and toyed with the cassette as he listened to Sheldon. "The towers you saw in the video had been pulled down and set on fire by the time the sheriff got there. All the vehicles had gone. There's no sign of it in the video, but we suspect they also had a helicopter. The investigation you'll be leading is unusual in that we're not actually concerned about the victims in the case. All the signs are that they were merely innocent bystanders, in the wrong place at the wrong time. What we want to know is who those people were in the

19

desert, and what they were doing."

"So it's not a homicide investigation?" asked Howard. He couldn't get the woman's voice out of his head. Trying to reassure her son as the plane plunged to the ground. He shivered.

"Those men weren't shooting duck out there," said Sheldon. "They'd spent a lot of time and money setting up those towers, they were obviously rehearsing something. It was a practice run for an assassination. And only an assassination of the first rank would merit such a rehearsal."

Howard nodded. "The President?"

"Possibly. Or a visiting head of state. Someone with protection, someone they can't get close to. It wouldn't be a gangland hit, they prefer to get in close with a shotgun or a handgun to the back of the neck. It has to be political. And it has to be soon. Your job, Cole, is to find out who the hit is, and to stop it. Do that and you'll hopefully also catch the men who killed the Mitchell family. But that's secondary, you understand? Your first priority is to put a stop to the assassination."

"I understand. Do we have any idea who the men are?"

Sheldon shook his head. "The tape is being examined by our experts now. The camcorder is one of those new models with a high-powered zoom lens, which has very high resolution. Our lab will do the initial work on the tape, but I gather that they don't have the capability for the sort of analysis we might require. That's one of the reasons I want you handling the investigation."

"My father-in-law?"

Sheldon nodded. "Theodore Clayton's electronics company is one of the few at the forefront of this

20

technology which isn't based in Japan. His help would be invaluable, and the request might be better coming from a family member, don't you think?"

"I'm sure it would," Howard agreed. He knew exactly how much Theodore Clayton would appreciate a call for help from his son-in-law.

"I want you to act as FBI liaison with the local investigators, and to organise the analysis of the tape. Any questions?"

"You said it has to be soon. Why do you think that?"

"Whoever is behind this already has his assassins in place, and obviously has a specific venue in mind. The longer they wait, the greater the risk of the whole operation falling apart. I doubt if they're planning more than a few months ahead. It may be only a matter of weeks or days."

"What about targets? Do we issue a warning to the President's security people?"

Sheldon sat back in his leather chair, his palms face down on his desk like a pianist about to begin a concerto. "I'm sending a memo to the Secret Service's Intelligence Division in Washington, of course, but at this stage I don't want to go overboard. As yet we don't know for certain who the target is, and I don't want to be caught crying wolf. As soon as we know for sure who the target is we'll throw a cordon around him, but not until then. And there's no point in issuing a general warning – that would scare too many people needlessly and we'd run the risk of the snipers going to ground. No, Cole, you tell me for sure that it's the President and we'll sound the alarm."

Sheldon paused for a few seconds as if he was having second thoughts. He tapped his fingers on the desktop. "But I think it would be a good idea if you got hold of the

President's itinerary and see if there are any situations where snipers could get at him."

Howard left Sheldon's office with the tape and file. He wasn't looking forward to asking his father-in-law for help.

Mike Cramer looked at his watch, pulled open the bottom drawer of his desk and put his hand on the bottle of Famous Grouse he kept there. He took it out and weighed it in his hand. It was a powerful hand, the fingers strong and the nails neatly clipped. There was scar tissue over the first two knuckles and the skin looked as if it had been out in all weathers. It was the hand of a sailor, a hand used to doing manual work. It was shaking as it held the bottle and the whisky slopped against the glass. Cramer tightened his grip but that just intensified the trembling. He stood the bottle on the desk and looked at the label as he used his foot to close the drawer.

He looked at his watch again. Nine-fifteen. He'd only bought the bottle the previous evening in the off-licence down the road but already it was half empty. Cramer smiled to himself. There had been a time when he might have taken a more positive view and thought that the bottle was half full, but those days were long gone. He unscrewed the cap and lifted the neck of the bottle to his nose. He sniffed gently, the way a dog might test the night air, then he took a mouthful, swallowing almost immediately. Cramer wasn't drinking for the flavour, he was drinking to stop the shakes. He took another mouthful, then another, and then recapped the bottle and put it back into his desk drawer. He had an open pack of Wrigley's gum on his desk and he unwrapped a piece and popped it in his mouth.

The office was small and windowless. It took up a corner of a large warehouse and was little more than a plywood box with space for two desks, a photocopier, a filing cabinet, a small fridge and five steel lockers. On the wall above the filing cabinet was a chart and Cramer went over to look at it. Two groups were due to start at nine-thirty so he went to check the battle arena.

The warehouse had been built as a place to store goods before they were loaded on to ships on the Thames, back in the days when the east of London was a thriving docks and not just an offshoot of the City's financial district. As the shipping companies switched over to containers and the river traffic died off, the best of the warehouses were transformed into Yuppie flats and glitzy winebars, but this one was too run down to be remodelled and it had been left to decay. The two young Greek Cypriot businessmen Cramer worked for had bought the warehouse for a song at a time when property prices were falling, and they had turned it into a successful paintball venue where executives could work off their aggression by pretending to blow each other away with paint pellets instead of bullets. There were five floors in the building, linked by a staircase at each end. The new owners had installed fireman's poles and ladders then had added wooden walls, chain-link fences and other obstacles to make a battlefield which they illuminated with a computer-controlled light and laser system. The top four floors were used for combat, and on the ground floor was the office, along with a changing room and shower facilities, a shop selling paintballs, equipment and clothing, and a large practice area where the players could fire their

23

guns at targets. Cramer went into the shop and turned on the lights. There were no windows anywhere in the warehouse other than in the roof so everywhere had to be illuminated. Racks of sweatshirts and nylon protective clothing were against one wall with a display of goggles and facemasks lined up above them. In a case by the cash register there was a selection of the latest paintguns and cleaning kits. Cramer checked that there was change in the cash register, then went to turn the lights on in the practice area. As he walked across the concrete floor he heard the main door swing open and turned to see Charlie Preston walk out of the sunlight.

"Yo, Mike, sorry I'm late," shouted Preston. He was a teenager who'd started working at the arena on a Government-sponsored work experience programme but had stayed on as a full-time employee, more because he loved the sport than because of the money. Preston had once spent four weeks travelling across America in Greyhound buses and during the trip he'd acquired a collection of sweatshirts and an accent which he kept in shape by watching American movies. As he closed the door behind him, Cramer could see that he was wearing his Washington Redskins shirt and knee length Miami Dolphins shorts and had on a blue New York Yankees baseball cap. Cramer smiled. It was barely above freezing outside. The boy had style, all right. "No sweat, Charlie," he answered. "You see anyone out there?"

"Couple of BMWs just drove up. I guess that's them."

Cramer hit the light switches and the fluorescent lights above the practice area flickered into life. "Okay, can you check the arena lights program? We're going to use number six, we were having trouble with the searchlight on number five yesterday so I want to see if it's the programming or the light that's not right."

"Cool," said Preston. As he walked over to the computerised console which controlled the lighting system, two men arrived carrying nylon holdalls. They were both in their late twenties, well groomed and tanned as if just back from a Mediterranean holiday. One of them dropped his holdall on the floor.

"You in charge?" he called over to Cramer.

"Sure am," answered Cramer. "Which team are you?"

"We're the Bayswater Blasters. Is the other side here yet?"

"You're the first," said Cramer. "You're due to start at nine-thirty, right?"

Five more young men arrived, all dressed casually in jeans and sweatshirts. "They here, Simon?" one of them shouted.

"No, you sure they said they're still on?" the man in glasses replied.

"Sure. I spoke to their captain on Wednesday."

"Why don't you get changed while you're waiting?" Cramer suggested. "Have you guys played here before?"

They all shook their heads so Cramer showed them where the changing room was and gave them photocopied maps of the arena. When they reappeared ten minutes later there was still no sign of their opponents. Cramer watched them as they waited by the main entrance. They were wearing camouflage outfits and military-style boots and carrying futuristic paintball helmets and facemasks. They were all equipped with neck protectors, padded gloves and special vests to hold extra paintballs and had clearly spent a lot of money on their gear. Their weapons were also expensive. Their leader, the one called Simon, was carrying a Tippmann Pneumatics 68 Special semi-automatic which had been fitted with a twenty-ounce carbon dioxide constant-air cylinder and a large capacity bulk loader which would hold up to two hundred rounds. It would pack a punch, Cramer knew, and the TASO red dot sight meant it would be accurate, too, though he also knew from experience that most players who used semi-automatics just kept firing blindly until they hit something, relying on brute force rather than skill. The 'spray and pray' method.

Cramer looked at his watch. It was nine-forty. He went over to Simon and asked him if they wanted to start.

"Our opponents still aren't here," he said.

"You've booked it for the next two hours whether they come or not," said Cramer.

"Yeah, but there's no point without someone to fight, is there?"

"You could divide into two teams."

Simon gave Cramer a withering look. "You can count, right? There are seven of us."

Cramer raised his hands in surrender. "Hey, okay, I just didn't want you to waste your money, that's all."

Preston walked over, doing his impersonation of a Brooklyn pimp. "They ready?" he asked.

"No, we're not ready," snapped Simon.

Cramer explained that the opposition hadn't turned up.

"Bummer," said Preston.

Simon looked at his watch, a rugged stainless steel diving model, and made tut-tutting noises. Preston tugged at the peak of his baseball cap. "You could split into two teams," he suggested. He nodded at Cramer. "Mike here could give you a game, that'd make it four a side."

Simon narrowed his eyes. "We're a team," he said slowly as if addressing an imbecile. "We train together, we have a system, we can't just divide into two and expect to function. It just won't work."

"I'll take you on," said Cramer, quietly.

"What do you mean?" said Simon.

"I mean I'll give you a game. I'll take you all on."

Several of the men laughed. Simon looked Cramer up and down. The man in front of him was in his late thirties, a little over six feet and wiry rather than muscled, and looked as if he might be able to handle himself in a fight. But his deep-set eyes were watery and reddened, the cheeks crisscrossed with the broken veins of a heavy drinker and there was a strong smell of whisky about him that wasn't masked by the mint-flavoured gum he was chewing. Simon shook his head. "What? You against the seven of us? I don't think so," he said.

"Come on, Simon, give the guy a chance," shouted one of his team-mates.

"I tell you what," said Cramer, "I'll show you a new game. No enemy flags to capture, no teams. You go where you want to go, I'll come in and get you. I call it Hide and Kill."

"You against the seven of us?" Simon repeated.

"What, you don't think that's fair?" said Cramer. "How about if I tie one arm behind my back?"

Several of the team began laughing and Simon's cheeks reddened. "Okay, you're on," he said. "I tell you what, why don't we make it a bit more interesting? Why don't we have a bet on the side?"

Cramer chewed his gum and looked at the younger man. "How much were you thinking of?"

Simon shrugged. "How does fifty pounds sound?"

"Sounds fine to me."

Simon nodded. "Okay, so what are the rules?"

"No rules, no umpires. Everything is allowed."

"Headshots?"

"Headshots, physical contact, whatever."

Simon smiled. "Okay, Mr Cramer, you have yourself a game."

"Why don't you guys study the maps while I change," said Cramer, as he turned to go back to the office. Preston followed him. He closed the door behind them and leant with his back against it.

"Jesus, Mike, have you got fifty pounds?"

Cramer opened his locker and pulled out a pair of paint-splattered blue overalls. "No," he said. He pulled on the overalls and took a pair of plastic goggles from the top shelf.

"Do you wanna borrow my helmet?"

"No."

"Aw, come on, Mike. Their semi-automatics pack a real wallop, and you've told them that they can go for headshots."

Cramer went over to his desk and pulled open the bottom drawer. He took a couple of swigs from the bottle of Famous Grouse and put it back. There was no point in offering any to Preston, he drank only imported American beers. At the back of the drawer was his paintgun, an old single-shot Splatmaster. He took it out.

"You have got to be joking," said Preston, banging the back of his head against the door. "At least use one of my guns."

Cramer zipped up his overalls and slid the goggles on.

He checked the bolt action of the gun and that it had a full twelve-gram carbon dioxide cartridge. "This'll do just fine, Charlie."

Preston opened the door for him and they walked together back to the Bayswater Blasters who were fastening their gloves and neck protectors.

"Ready?" asked Cramer.

Simon raised his eyebrows when he saw Cramer's gun. "You're going to use that?" he said. He lifted his own gun, with its skeleton stock and laser sight. "Against these?"

Cramer winked. "Wanna raise the bet?"

Simon shook his head in amazement. "We're ready."

"Okay, there are four floors above here, you go up and pick your positions. I'll give you two minutes."

Simon put the helmet on and slipped the goggles down so that his whole head was covered. He turned to his team and signalled for them to move out. Cramer sighted down his gun at the back of the man's head and tightened his finger on the trigger. "Bang," he said, quietly.

"What lighting system do you want?" Preston asked him.

"Bare minimum," said Cramer. "Just enough so they don't fall and hurt themselves. And use the red lights, it'll screw up their laser sights."

Preston smiled. "Be gentle with them, Mike."

Cramer stood at the bottom of the stairwell and waited a full ten minutes before moving up to the first level. The stairs opened out into a large bare room off which led three doorways. Once he was satisfied that the room was clear he stood with his back against a wall for another five minutes, waiting for his eyes to get used to the gloom. There was no point in rushing. He wanted them to be over-eager because that way they'd be careless. He heard a footfall from somewhere above him and muffled voices. Cramer smiled. They had no patience, these game-players. Amateurs. He began to clear the first level, moving silently from room to room, his gun at the ready. There were twelve rooms on the first floor, linked by doorways but no doors. Several had furniture in, old tables and sofas, armchairs with the stuffing oozing from torn leather like purulent wounds.

He found his first opponent crouched behind a wooden chest, his gun aimed chest high at the doorway. Cramer ducked his head around the door jamb, saw the barrel of the weapon and his opponent's plastic mask, and pulled his head back. He took a deep breath then rolled through the doorway, hitting the floor with his shoulder and coming up with his gun at the ready before the man had a chance to aim. The red dot of a laser sight flashed across his chest but the guy's reactions weren't anywhere near fast enough. Cramer fired and the paintball hit his opponent smack in the middle of his mask, knocking his head back and splattering the plastic with green paint which shone blackly under the dim red overhead lights.

"You're dead," said Cramer.

The man sat back on the floor, resting against the wall. "Fuck," he said.

Cramer reloaded. There were only two rooms remaining on the first floor and both were clear. Three levels left, and six men to go. He doubled back to one of the rooms, which had a trapdoor leading to the second level. A thick hemp rope hung down and Cramer grabbed it. He twisted it from side to side and then set it swinging before rushing back to the stairs. He took the stairs three at a time on the balls of his feet, keeping close to the wall, his gun at the ready. He had to pass through one room before he reached the room where the rope was, and it was clear. He put his head close to the doorway and listened. He heard something rustle and he risked a quick look. The rope was swinging gently. In the far corner of the room one of his opponents was moving cautiously towards the trapdoor, his eyes fixed on the hole and the rope, the barrel of his gun pointing down. Cramer stepped into the doorway and shot the man in the chest. The man looked up, unwilling to believe that he'd been hit so easily. He put a gloved hand onto the wet patch of paint and looked at it. Cramer raised his gun in salute, then motioned silently that the man could go down the rope and wait for his friends.

Cramer chewed his gum thoughtfully. So far he'd been lucky. His paintgun could only fire a single shot at a time so he'd have real problems if he came up against more than one opponent. He could have borrowed Preston's gun but something about the team leader's attitude had got under his skin. He reloaded and ducked into the next room. Clear. He heard a cough from the room ahead and smiled thinly. Despite all the money they spent on the gear, the weekend warriors just didn't take it seriously. They got hit, they wiped off the paint and they played again. That made them careless because they knew that they'd always get another chance. Cramer had trained in a different school. He picked up a wooden chair and placed it at the side of the doorway, careful to make no sound as the legs touched the wooden floor. He placed his foot against it and then kicked it hard into the middle of the next room. It hadn't travelled three feet before it was peppered with paintballs. The guy had his finger tight on the trigger sending out a stream of the small spheres which burst in fountains of yellow paint whenever

31

they hit their target. Cramer bent low around the doorway, and aimed and fired with one smooth movement, catching the man dead centre in his chest. The man stopped firing and shook his head sorrowfully. "Dumb, dumb, dumb," he muttered.

"Can't argue with that," said Cramer, reloading.

He waited until the defeated opponent was going back down before moving ahead, knowing that the sound of footsteps on the stairs would be a distraction. Three down, four to go.

By the time Cramer had got to the top level of the warehouse there were only two opponents left. The top level was the most dangerous because there were several old skylights through which the sunlight streamed in, leaving no dark corners in which to hide. It had originally been one large storage area but had been divided up into a maze with eight-foot tall sections of plasterboard. Cramer's big advantage was that he'd memorised the layout of the maze, but that didn't count for much against two opponents. He stood at the stairwell as he steadied his breathing. Above the maze were thick oak rafters, supporting the slate roof and its skylights. The rafters were about ten feet above the top of the maze and would provide a perfect vantage point, but climbing up would expose himself. He decided not to risk it, not with fifty pounds at stake. There were four entrances to the maze, one on each side, and Cramer chose the one furthest from the stairs which he'd climbed. He went in low, checking left and right before standing up. He listened. There was a scuffling noise from somewhere off to the right but it sounded more like a scavenging river rat than a pair of Reeboks. He approached a junction and bent down so that his head was at waist level before looking around the corner. Nothing. He kept his gun moving, ready to lock onto any target, his left hand out for balance as he crept forward. He felt rather than heard the presence behind him and he twisted and ducked in one movement as a stream of pellets blasted into the wall where his head had been a second earlier. He fired and saw his paintball thwack into Simon's neck protector. Simon levelled his gun at Cramer and pulled the trigger, but before the first ball had left the barrel Cramer had launched himself to the side and into another section of the maze. The team leader was a sore loser and was refusing to acknowledge that he'd been hit. Cramer reloaded and kept moving. He could hear Simon behind him. He took a left turn and then a right, and was about to head left again when he almost bumped into the last remaining player. Cramer pulled his head back just in time to avoid a single shot and then he rolled forward and fired at the same time, catching his opponent in the chest. "Good shot," said the man approvingly and lowered his gun. Cramer moved to go around him but as he did Simon appeared from a side passage, paint still running down his chest. Simon's gun came up and Cramer grabbed the man he'd just shot, pulling him into the line of fire. Simon fired and bullets pounded into the man's chest, each exploding into a yellow flower of paint.

"Hey come on, Simon!" yelled the man. His team leader was so close that the shots hurt, even through the overall and vest.

Simon kept firing, hoping that one of the balls would hit Cramer. Cramer needed one hand to hold the man up in front of him so he couldn't reload. He pushed his human shield forward onto the barrel of Simon's gun and then grabbed Simon's arm, close to the elbow, twisting around to get him in a lock. Simon squealed and Cramer used his hip to throw him onto his back. The semi-automatic fell to the ground and Cramer put his foot on Simon's chest, pinning him to the ground. Simon was winded and he lay gasping for breath, unable to speak. Cramer's other victim got to his feet, his chest covered with yellow paint. "You bastard, Simon," he said.

Cramer calmly reloaded his gun and aimed it at Simon's chest. "Game, set and match," he said quietly, and fired. The paintball caught Simon just over his heart and exploded. Cramer walked away without looking back.

Preston was waiting for him downstairs by the office with the five members of the Bayswater Blasters he'd defeated earlier. "How did it go?" Preston asked.

"Piece of cake," Cramer said, removing his goggles. One of the men handed Cramer five ten-pound notes and he winked and accepted the money. Simon came down the stairs, his helmet still on, and went into the changing room without saying anything. The guy Cramer had used as a shield shrugged as if apologising for Simon's bad behaviour and followed him inside.

"Did you see him?" Preston asked.

"Did I see who?" replied Cramer.

"The guy who was looking for you. Old guy, said he wanted to see you. I told him you were in the middle of a game and he said he'd give you a surprise. Borrowed a paintgun and a helmet and went in about ten minutes ago."

Cramer frowned and spat his chewing gum into a wastepaper bin. "Old guy?" he asked. To Preston, anyone over the age of thirty was old.

Preston shrugged. "Grey hair, about your height, bit

bigger. He didn't give a name. Said he was an old friend."

"I guess I should see what he wants," said Cramer. He slid the goggles back on and reloaded his Splatmaster. He crept back up the stairs, wondering who his mysterious visitor was and why he wanted to play games rather than meet in the office. The first level was clear but as he passed beneath the rope and trapdoor he heard a footfall as if someone had suddenly shuffled backwards. Cramer smiled. He took the end of the rope and started swinging it, before running silently back to the stairs. It was going to be too easy, he thought. He moved through the first room on the second level, and stood for a moment by the open doorway. He heard a noise in the far right-hand corner and he moved immediately, stepping to the left and sweeping his gun around at chest height, seeking his target. He frowned as he realised that the room was deserted, then his heart sank as he saw the single paintball lying in the corner. Before he could move he felt the barrel of a gun jam up against his chin.

"Careless, Joker," said a voice by his left ear. Cramer shifted his weight and brought up his right arm, trying to grab his adversary but the man behind him swayed easily away and swept Cramer's feet from underneath him with a savage kick. Cramer hit the ground heavily and before he could react the man was on top of him and the gun was once more pressing into his throat. "Very careless."

Cramer squinted up at the facemask. "Colonel?" he said.

The figure pulled off his facemask with his left hand, the right keeping the paintgun hard up against Cramer's flesh. Cramer looked up at the familiar face of his former mentor. It had been more than two years since he had set eyes on the senior SAS officer. His hair was considerably greyer than last time they'd met, and cut slightly shorter, but the features were the same: eyes so brown they were almost black, a wide nose which had been broken several times, and a squarish jaw that gave him a deceptive farmboy look. Cramer knew the Colonel had a double first from Cambridge, was once one of the top twelve chess players in the United Kingdom, and was an acknowledged expert on early Victorian watercolours. "Good to see you, Colonel," said Cramer.

"You're unfit, Sergeant Cramer," said the Colonel with a smile. "You wouldn't last two minutes in the Killing House with those sort of moves."

"It's been a long time, Colonel. I guess I'm out of practice."

"You're out of condition, too. A few forced marches across the Brecon Beacons would do you the world of good." The Colonel stood up and offered Cramer a hand to help him up off the ground. "You sounded like an elephant on crutches, Joker. And you never, ever, enter a room without checking out all the angles. You know that."

Cramer rubbed his neck. "I can't believe I fell for the oldest trick in the book."

The Colonel slapped him on the back. "Have you got somewhere we can talk?"

Cramer took him downstairs and told Preston he was going to use the office for a while. Two more teams of paintball players had arrived and Preston was busy setting up a game for them. Cramer closed the door and waved the Colonel to a chair. He pulled the bottle of Famous Grouse from his desk drawer and held it out to the Colonel, who nodded. Cramer poured large measures of whisky into two coffee mugs and handed one to his visitor. They clinked mugs.

"To the old days," said Cramer.

"Fuck them all," said the Colonel.

"Yeah, fuck them all," said Cramer. They drank, and Cramer waited for the Colonel to explain why he was visiting.

"So, how long have you been working here?" asked the Colonel.

Cramer shrugged. "A few months. It's just temporary, until I can find something else."

"Security job didn't work out?"

"Too many lonely nights. Too much time to think." Cramer wondered how the Colonel knew about his previous job as a nightwatchman. He poured himself another measure of whisky.

"Money problems? The pension coming through okay?" Cramer shrugged. He knew that the Colonel hadn't come to talk about his financial status. "You ever meet a guy called Pete Manyon?" asked the Colonel.

Cramer shook his head.

"I guess he must have joined the regiment after you left. He was in D squadron."

Cramer looked at the whisky at the bottom of his mug. If the Colonel had bothered to check up on his employment record, he'd have been just as capable of checking the regimental files. He'd have known full well whether or not the two men had served together.

"He died a week ago. In Washington." He held out his empty mug for a refill. As Cramer poured in a generous measure of Famous Grouse, the Colonel scrutinised his face for any reaction. "He'd been tortured. Four of his fingers had been taken off. He'd virtually been skinned alive. And he'd been castrated."

Cramer's hand shook and whisky slopped down the side of the Colonel's mug. "Shit," said Cramer. "I'm sorry."

"That's okay," said the Colonel, putting his mug down on the desk and wiping his hand with a white handkerchief. "It was Hennessy, right?"

The Colonel nodded.

"Bitch," said Cramer venomously.

"Manyon was a captain, working undercover in the States, on the trail of Matthew Bailey, an IRA activist. We'd heard that he'd popped up in New York so Manyon infiltrated one of the NORAID groups there."

"Did he say he'd seen Hennessy?"

The Colonel shook his head. "No, but considering what happened to him . . ."

"Yeah, yeah, I get the picture. Jesus Christ, Colonel, the bitch should have been put down years ago."

The Colonel shrugged. "She's been underground a long time, Joker. And she has a lot of friends."

"I can't believe you let a Rupert go undercover against the IRA," said Cramer. "I mean, I've served under some bloody good officers, I can't deny that, but knowing which fork to use and what month to eat oysters in doesn't carry any weight when you're hanging around with the boys. They can spot a Rupert a mile away."

"He was an experienced officer, Joker. He'd been with D squadron for almost three years."

"How old was he?"

"Twenty-five."

Cramer shook his head, almost sadly. "After what happened to Mick Newmarch, I'd have thought the SAS would've learnt its lesson."

"I know how the NCOs feel about officers, but Manyon

38

was different. His parents were Irish, his accent was perfect and he knew Belfast inside out. His cover was faultless, Joker."

"So how did he get caught?" Cramer poured himself another whisky. He offered a refill to the Colonel but he shook his head. The question was clearly rhetorical and the Colonel didn't answer.

"How are you these days, Joker?" The Colonel looked Cramer up and down like a surgeon contemplating a forthcoming operation. Cramer wondered if he looked like a man who'd lost his nerve.

"I get by," Cramer replied. "Why do you ask? Is *Mars and Minerva* thinking of doing a feature on me? It'd be nice to get an honourable mention in the regimental journal."

"You sound bitter."

"No, not bitter, Colonel. I can't spend all my time looking back, there's no profit in that. I just want to get on with my life."

The two men sat in silence. Overhead they heard shouts and the sound of running feet. "You should let them try it with live ammo," said the Colonel with a smile. "See how they like it."

"Yeah," agreed Cramer. "They'd piss themselves stupid the first time they used a real weapon."

The Colonel looked at Cramer with unblinking eyes. "What about you? Could you face action again?"

Cramer started, the question catching him by surprise. He looked at his former boss, wondering if he was joking. "I'm Elvis, Colonel. You know that. Yesterday's man."

"You were right when you said the boys could spot undercover officers, Joker. We need someone who fits in, someone who doesn't look like he's just come off a parade ground. You know as well as I do that even when our men grow their hair and slouch around in torn jeans and Nikes, they still look like soldiers. Undercover work isn't our speciality." Cramer was already shaking his head. "We need someone who has lost his edge, Joker. No disrespect, but we need someone who doesn't look as if he can handle himself, someone who has let himself go."

"Thanks, Colonel. Thanks a bunch. You're really making me feel good about myself."

"I'm being honest, that's all. Have you taken a look at yourself recently? You reek of drink, you've got broken veins in your cheeks that have been months in the making, and you've a gut on you that'd do credit to a Sumo wrestler. No-one in their right mind would ever suspect you of being in the SAS."

"That goes for me, too, Colonel. Double."

"We want Mary Hennessy, Joker. We want to take her out. A hard arrest, a shoot-to-kill operation, whatever you want to call it."

"Revenge."

"That's as good a word as any, Joker. And you're the man who can get it for us."

Cramer finished his whisky and picked up the bottle. It was empty. Completely empty. He dropped it into the wastepaper bin by the side of his desk. "You're asking me because of what happened to Newmarch, aren't you? And because of what she did to me?"

"I'm asking you because you're the best man for the job. The only man."

Cramer shuddered. "I'll have to think about it."

"I understand that." The Colonel stood up and held out

his hand. Cramer shook it. "You know where you can reach me, Sergeant Cramer."

"Yes, sir," Cramer replied. The 'sir' slipped out naturally and the Colonel smiled. He left the office, leaving Joker deep in thought, staring at the empty whisky bottle.

Cole Howard caught the morning flight to Washington, DC. As he sat in the front row of the economy section he flicked through the pack of Trivial Pursuit cards he'd brought with him. "You like playing?" asked his neighbour, an elderly woman in a neck brace. "My nephews bought me a set last Christmas. I play it all the time."

"I dislike the game intensely," Howard answered. The woman looked shocked as if Howard had sworn at her and she buried her head in a magazine. Howard began to go through the cards, memorising the answers.

There was a queue for taxis when he arrived at Washington Dulles International Airport but he took the wait good-naturedly. The FBI laboratories were half an hour's drive from the airport, during which time he worked his way through another two dozen cards. On arrival, he clipped his FBI badge to his breast pocket and flashed his identification at the security guards at reception. He was told that the lab he was looking for was on the second floor. There he asked for Dr Kim. He wasn't surprised when a woman came out to meet him, because they'd spoken several times on the phone, but he was surprised at how young and attractive she was. She was Oriental, with waist-length hair which she wore as a single braid. She had razor-sharp cheekbones and a small, delicate mouth and oval eyes which narrowed almost to slits when she smiled. "Dr Kim," said Howard, as they shook hands. His hand seemed to dwarf hers. It was as delicate as a six-year-old's, with nails painted a deep red.

"Call me Bonnie," she said. "My lab's this way." Her high heels clicked on the tiled floor as they walked. Even with the heels the top of her forehead barely reached his shoulders, and Howard was only a little over six feet tall. She took him past several doors and into a long, thin laboratory which had white benches lining the walls and a small cubbyhole of an office at the end. On the benches in the lab were several IBM computers and racks of VCRs and monitors. One of the VCRs had been opened up and she'd been doing something with a circuit board and a soldering iron. The iron was still on and she pulled out the plug.

She poured him a cup of coffee from a percolator and sat on a swivel chair facing one of the monitors. She opened a drawer under the bench and handed him a pale blue file.

"These are prints of what I've been able to achieve so far," she said. "But I wanted you to see the video with me, too. I have some suggestions which might help."

Howard sipped his coffee as she started the video. By now he knew every second by heart, and he could watch it without emotion. He no longer grieved for the dying family, and he could listen to the woman's last words of comfort to her son without cringing inside. They watched it together, in silence.

"This is the original video," she said, "the same version you've seen in Phoenix. I've taken the signal on the tape and programmed it into the computer, then used it to boost the definition several-fold. To see it we'll need a very high-definition television monitor, this one here." She flicked a switch on a console and the video played again on a wider television screen. Howard could see the improvement immediately. Bonnie kept her hand on the pause button and as the camera panned to the ground below she pressed it. The frozen picture was much sharper than on a standard video-recorder, too; there was no fuzzy line or flickering. On the screen was one of the towers, and Howard could clearly see a figure with a rifle. The face was still blurred.

"The quality is much improved, but there are limits to what we can do with analog methods," said Bonnie. She let the video play on. "We can get better results by digitising the video and storing it on a CD." She patted one of the computers, an unimposing white box. "This is our image processor, which takes the video signal and digitises it. We call it a frame grabber. It can digitise images in real-time – about one-thirtieth of a second each – and save them into storage. Then we use a computer to handle and process the data. Once we've processed the images and cleaned them up, we can choose the frames we want on the monitor, and print them on a film recorder. That gives us much better definition. That's what's in the file – computer-generated pictures."

Howard opened the file and looked inside. There was a stack of more than twenty glossy eight-by-tens. He went through them. There were photographs of the towers, and close-ups of the snipers. None was clear enough to make out their faces, however.

"That's the best I can do with my equipment," Bonnie said as she saw his face fall. "Not much help, I'm afraid. Though you can see that they're better than the images we had on the screen."

"What have you done to them?" Howard asked.

"I tried neighbourhood averaging first, but that wasn't too helpful," she said. "Those pictures are after I used a technique called median filtering. I could probably enhance them more if I used pixel aggregation, but that's going to take me more time." She smiled as she saw the deep furrows appear on Howard's forehead. She took a sheet of paper and a pencil, and drew a square box with deft strokes. "Imagine this is a tiny piece of the screen," she said. "That unit is as small as you can go. It's indivisible. We call it a pixel. The camcorder in the plane was a Toshiba TSC-100, with a Canon 12:1 servo zoom lens, and it records 410,000 pixels with seven hundred horizontal lines. That's a lot more than the average camcorder, some have fewer than 300,000 pixels on the image sensor. He had some pretty specialised equipment."

Howard nodded. "He was a real-estate salesman, he used it to make videos of properties he was selling."

"Ah, that explains it," said Bonnie. "We're lucky he had it, because anything less powerful and we probably wouldn't see half the details we have. You can make that pixel as large as you want, it'll still be one unit. You'll just have a big pixel. What neighbourhood averaging does is to smooth out the image by taking an average of the colour and brightness of individual pixels in a predefined area. There was an improvement in the clarity of the images, but the edges blurred and we actually lost some detail, which was to be expected. Median filtering is a similar computer technique, but it uses a median value instead of an average value. It's a small difference, but a significant one. I ran through a three-by-three neighbourhood and then a five-by-five, right on up to a nine-by-nine. For the worst areas I'd

44

like to use the technique I mentioned, pixel aggregation. You choose a pixel which has properties you can clearly identify in terms of colour or texture and then you gradually move outwards, adding to it pixels of matching qualities, until you grow a defined region. That produces clusters of matching pixels, which can then be highlighted. I'm afraid it'll take me quite a while with the equipment I have."

Howard continued to go through the photographs as he listened to Bonnie's explanation, most of which went way over his head. One of the pictures showed a row of bald, naked figures. "What are these?" he asked.

"Yes, I'm quite proud of those," she said. "You could barely see them in the original, and the camera only picked them up once, but they're there all right. They're what the snipers are aiming at. Four dummies. The sort used in shop window displays."

Howard put two photographs on the bench. They showed two sedan cars and a large flatbed truck. "I didn't see these in the video," he said.

Bonnie nodded eagerly. "They were only there for a few seconds, when the plane was spinning. The quality isn't good, but you can see the colour and make. They're Chrysler Imperials, one blue, one white. The truck I'm not sure about. Could be a Dodge."

"That's good, really good," said Howard. He made a mental note to ask the Sheriff's Department about tyre tracks at the scene.

The next set of pictures showed a group of three people standing together, a middle-aged man with a paunch, a young man, and a woman. The older man was holding something in his hand. There was a magnifying glass on the bench and Howard used it to examine the object.

45

"It's a walkie-talkie, I think," said Bonnie. "I assume he used it to keep in contact with the snipers."

"Is there any way of magnifying the photographs any further?" Howard asked.

Bonnie shook her head. Her long braid swung from side to side like a rope. "I've taken it as far as I can," she said. "I can make the images bigger, but I don't have the software necessary for the sort of filtering that would make them any sharper. You should try one of the Japanese firms. Sony, or Hitachi. They should have the computers geared up for it. Or you could try firms working on artificial intelligence or robotics."

"Robotics?" queried Howard.

"Robotics companies are big on artificial intelligence, and that's the sort of expertise you'll need. The pictures can be cleared up further by the application of algorithms using what are called the Hough Transform and Fourier Transform, and I can tell you which experts would be able to do that. A computer with some form of artificial intelligence could compare adjoining pixels and correct for abnormalities based on an assumption of what it's looking for."

Howard frowned. "I don't follow."

"Well, if the computer knows it's looking at a face, it will know that an eye has a certain shape, so has a nose, so has a chin. It has to know whether a dark patch is a moustache, a nostril, or the pupil of an eye. It has to know that human bodies are made up of curves, but that mechanical objects are usually flat surfaces. If it's looking at a licence plate, for instance, it must know to look for numbers and letters and not abstract shapes. I'm sorry, Agent Howard, I'm not explaining this very well."

"Cole," he said, "please call me Cole. And you're doing just fine. Actually, I know someone who has access to the sort of technology you're talking about."

"Really?" she said. "Who would that be?"

"Clayton Electronics."

Bonnie raised her eyebrows. "They're good. Of course, their head office is in Phoenix, I'd forgotten. Why didn't you go to them first?"

Howard stacked the photographs together and slid them back into the file. "We wanted to keep it within the FBI as much as possible. You've seen the video, you know what the implications are."

Bonnie lowered her eyes and her cheeks reddened like a guilty schoolgirl. Howard wanted to ask her what was wrong but felt that she'd shy away from such a direct approach. He waited for her to tell him what was troubling her.

"I had an idea," she said, still avoiding his eyes. "Well, not my idea, really. It was my husband's."

"Your husband?"

She nodded and raised her head. "He's a mathematician. A PhD. He specialises in computer graphics."

Howard was bemused, but he listened attentively. Bonnie Kim was clearly very intelligent and anything she had to offer on the case could only be of help.

"I was explaining about the video, about the three men with rifles and the towers, and he said it would make an interesting computer model. You could program the co-ordinates of the men and the targets, and get a 3-D structure representing their positions."

Howard understood why she'd been embarrassed. She'd told her husband about the video, and was now worried she'd breached security. He wanted to tell her that it was okay, but he didn't want to interrupt her. Her eyes were shining with enthusiasm. "You work out the heights of the towers, you calculate the angles and distances to the target, and then you superimpose that model on all the different venues where the target is due to appear."

Howard tapped the file with his fingers. "He could do that?"

"He could do the preliminary work, sure. I haven't shown him the video, but if I did he could put together the model, he said. He'd need to know the exact time of day the video was shot, so that he could use the shadows to determine heights and so on, and he might have to go out to the site to make some measurements, but yes, he could do it."

"What about the venues? How would he get those into his computer?"

"You'd need street plans and the heights of the various buildings. He could customise a program for you, but it would take a lot of work to input the information. Once it's in, though, the program would produce a 3-D model of the area, and it could then superimpose the snipers and target on it. It would tell you if the snipers were preparing for that venue or not. And if the models do fit, it'll tell you exactly where the snipers will be. It's a brilliant idea."

Howard smiled. "It is. Your husband's a very clever man. We do have one problem, though. At the moment we don't know who the target is."

Bonnie's mouth opened, showing perfect white teeth. "Oh. I just assumed . . ."

"That it was the President?"

She nodded. "You think it's someone else?"

48

"Bonnie, we just don't know. But your husband's idea is a good one. We know the President's itinerary well in advance; if he can set the program up for us, I can bring in extra manpower to do the inputting."

"So I can tell him to go ahead?"

"Sure."

Bonnie positively beamed. "He'll be so pleased. He thinks it'll be like a detective story. He suggested I ask you to come to dinner with us, tonight. I'll cook, and he can go over the details with you."

It was an offer Howard couldn't refuse.

Andy and Bonnie Kim's house was a spacious single-storey ranch house in a quiet suburban road to the north of Washington. The grass was neatly cropped, the paths were edged with orderly flower beds and the Stars and Stripes fluttered from a white flagpole. Two cars were parked outside when Howard arrived: a Buick Roadmaster and a Cherokee Laredo, and when Bonnie Kim opened the front door and let him in he could see that the interior was just as all-American. It wasn't what Howard expected at all. He'd always assumed that Koreans stuck closely to their heritage, but the Kims seemed to want it made clear to everyone that they were Americans through to the core.

Andy Kim had a round, smiling face and a mop of black hair which was continually falling over his eyes. He was as tall as Howard, but much thinner, and his horn-rimmed spectacles gave him a bookish appearance. He shook hands with Howard and asked him if he wanted a beer. Howard said he'd prefer an orange juice and Andy led him through to the living room while Bonnie went to the kitchen. Bonnie had changed from her working clothes into a floral print dress with a white collar and she'd let her hair loose so that it flowed around her shoulders and down her back. She looked impossibly young and he realised that she probably adopted the more severe look in the laboratory in order to be taken more seriously. She'd lost the high heels too and now stood just a little over five feet tall.

Howard sat down on a long sofa and looked around the room. One wall was lined with bookshelves, a mixture of scientific books, romances and thrillers, all of them in English. On a coffee table were copies of *Scientific American*, *Fortune* and several computer magazines. The large-screen television was on but the sound had been muted. The Washington Redskins were playing.

"Do you want to watch the game?" Andy asked.

"I'm not a big football fan," replied Howard.

"Really? I love it. There's a lot of mathematics in football, you know?"

Bonnie came into the room carrying a bottle of Budweiser for her husband and a tall glass of orange juice for Howard. "Dinner's ready," she said, "come on through."

Before he'd stepped into the house, Howard had expected that Bonnie would cook Korean food for him and that he'd have to deal with chopsticks but having seen the interior he wasn't in the least surprised to see that Bonnie had prepared steak, french fries and ears of white corn. After the meal, Bonnie served them coffee and all three of them went into the study, a wood-panelled room with several workbenches which were stacked high with electrical equipment and computers. Andy sipped his coffee as he switched on one of the machines. "I've done a little preparatory work already," he said. "I hope you don't mind."

"No problem," said Howard, sitting on a stool and watching as Andy's fingers played across the keyboard.

"These graphics are really simple, but they'll give you an idea what I have in mind," said Andy. Two circles appeared on the screen, green on a black background. Andy pressed another series of keys and the circles were replaced by two figures, one a man with a rifle, another a standing figure. "Okay, suppose we have one sniper, and a target. And suppose the distance between them is five hundred feet, and the angle is ten degrees." His fingers tapped at the keyboard and the picture became three-dimensional, with a dotted circle above the target. "We know that the sniper must be somewhere along this line," Andy continued. "Now, if we superimpose the sniper's possible positions on a city plan . . ." Several square and oblong shapes appeared on screen in various colours. "I know, they don't look like buildings, but you get the drift," he said.

Howard smiled. "I'm trying," he said.

Andy flicked his hair from his eyes and pushed his spectacles higher up his nose. "Okay, so now we can see which of the buildings are the right height and position to contain the sniper. And you can tell which floor he must be on to shoot at the required angle. Now, with only one sniper there are several positions which satisfy the position requirements." He pointed to four positions on the three-dimensional map where buildings coincided with the circle. "But, if we increase the number of snipers, we restrict the number of options."

STEPHEN LEATHER

Andy bent over the keyboard and began pressing keys quickly. The shapes disappeared from the screen and he added two more snipers, each linked to the target with a dotted line. "With three points to work with, the positions become more fixed, each has a spatial relationship with the others, and with the target. This time we don't get a circle, we have a tetrahedron . . ." A three-dimensional four-sided shape appeared on the screen, like a knifepoint sticking into the ground. "Now it becomes much more difficult to fit this shape into the model of the city." He called up the coloured blocks again. "See, all three points representing the snipers have to be in the correct position. There is only one solution." He pointed to the three places where the sniper positions coincided with the buildings.

Howard drank his coffee. "How long did it take you to set this up?" he asked.

Andy beamed. "About three hours, but this model is really simplistic. A true working model will be much more complicated."

"But possible?"

"Of course."

"How long would it take?"

Andy shrugged. "The snipers and target model would take a few hours, but getting the measurements and angles is the hard part. I'd have to go out to the desert and I'd need to give the video a thorough analysis."

"You haven't seen it yet?"

"Of course not," said Andy. "Bonnie wouldn't dream of bringing FBI work home with her. She'd stay in the lab all night, but bring work home? Never."

"I can arrange for you to see it at the lab," said Howard.

"Okay, and I'll have to go out to Arizona. I'll need the best part of a day there."

"That's no problem," said Howard. "You can come back with me, tomorrow morning. You can watch the video when you get back. And I already have a list of places where the President is going to be. We can use them to see if your system works. Can I ask you something, though? What do you get out of this? I mean, the FBI will cover expenses, and I guess we could come up with some consulting fees, but there's still a lot of work involved."

Andy looked at his wife and she nodded encouragement. "What I'd like, if it's okay with you, is to do a paper on it, if it works. Most of my research is pretty dry stuff, all very academic, and this is a real sexy application of my computer modelling. It'd be a great paper, it'd really get people talking."

Howard thought about Andy's proposal. "We'd need approval of the text," he said eventually.

"Sure. No sweat."

"And we might want to hold out some of the details, you realise that?"

"It's the mathematics I'm interested in, mainly."

"And you've got to realise that if this goes wrong, we'll have to keep the lid on it. You might not get the chance to publish anything."

"I'll take the risk."

Howard nodded. "It's a deal, then." Andy grinned and Bonnie leaned over and hugged him.

* * *

Joker caught the afternoon train down to Hereford. He'd
lost his licence six months earlier after a police car had
pulled him over on the M25 with a blood-alcohol level
almost twice the legal limit. It was a sunny day, but cold,
and he was wearing a Navy pea jacket and black wool
trousers. He spent the journey deep in thought, his
shoulders hunched and his eyes focused in the middle
distance as he stared at the countryside which rushed by the
train window.

He'd vowed never to return to the SAS Sterling Lines
barracks and hadn't even replied to the Regiment's
invitation to attend its fiftieth anniversary celebrations in
1991. His time with the SAS had been one of the most
challenging, and exciting, periods of his life, but it had also
changed him forever. It went above and beyond being a
soldier: the SAS had taught him to kill, and part of that
training had been a dehumanising programme which left
him with a cold, hard place where his conscience used to
be. It was only after he'd left the Regiment that he'd
realised what he'd lost. What they'd taken away from him.

The daylight was starting to leach from the sky as he
walked away from the station and he thrust his hands deep
into the pockets of his jacket. He'd taken the day off from
the paintball arena, but he hadn't made up his mind yet
whether or not to work with the Colonel. There were things
he had to get straight in his head first, and for that he needed
someone to talk to. A friend. He kept his head down as he
walked, but his feet took him unerringly to a pub he used to
frequent, set in the middle of a row of brick cottages with
leaded windows and old, warping oak doors. There were
two barmaids pulling pints and wiping glasses, one of
whom he recognised. Her name was Dolly and she served

him with a smile but no hint of recognition, leaving Joker in no doubt as to how much he'd changed over the last few years.

He ordered a Famous Grouse, a double. Two young soldiers stood together at a video game in one corner of the bar, feeding it coins as they drank pints of lager. They had the crew-cuts and thick moustaches that marked them out as being from the Parachute Regiments, from where the SAS drew most of its recruits. It would also make them feel right at home in some of London's rough trade gay bars. Joker could never understand why they allowed the Paras to stick with their macho style once they joined the ranks of the SAS. The officers insisted that the men refrained from using military plates on their cars and that they dressed as civilians when moving between operations, yet they were so easy to spot that any terrorist worth his salt would have no problem in targeting them, on or off duty.

Joker drained his glass and signalled for another. Dolly put a refill in front of him. "Don't I know you?" she asked.

"I don't think so," he said, handing her a twenty-pound note. "Can you give me a bottle of that, to take away?"

She nodded, wrapped a bottle in a sheet of purple tissue paper and gave it to him with his change.

As Joker drank his second whisky, a woman appeared at his side and sat down on a bar stool. He saw her reflection in the mirror above the cash register: she was a bleached blonde with a washed-out complexion as if she'd spent too many years indoors. In the mirror she appeared to be about thirty-five years old but when Joker turned to look at her he saw that she was older. She was wearing a red blouse and a black skirt that was a fraction too tight. The two squaddies at the video game burst into laughter and Joker had the feeling that they were laughing at her. Relations between the SAS and the locals were strained at the best of times: the soldiers usually called them 'pointyheads' and treated them with contempt, while the local men accused the soldiers of stealing their women. The Saturday-night fights in the crowded bars of Hereford were legendary, as were the queues in the hospital emergency room afterwards.

The woman ordered a brandy and Coke and when she'd been served she raised her glass to Joker. "Down the hatch," she said, and he smiled. She had the eager-to-please look of a scolded puppy.

"Cheers," said Joker.

When she put the glass back on the bar it was smeared with lipstick. She nodded at the bottle in his pocket. "You need a hand to drink that?" she said. "I don't live far from here."

Joker felt a sudden wave of compassion for the woman. She looked as if she expected men to treat her badly and he didn't want to hurt her feelings. "I can't," he said, "I'm visiting a friend and he's a big drinker."

Her face fell momentarily, then she smiled. "Enjoy yourself," she said.

Joker drained his glass and left the warmth of the bar. He walked quickly, surprised at how much the temperature had dropped. He wondered if he was getting soft. The church was a brisk ten minutes walk away from the pub. It was built of grey stone with a slate roof and shielded from the road by a line of spreading chestnut trees. The wooden gate squeaked as Joker pushed it open and he walked slowly down the gravel path. He'd been to the church on more than a dozen occasions in his dress uniform: three times for weddings and the remainder for funerals. The churchyard was where the SAS buried its dead.

Joker followed the path around to the left of the church. The graves were immaculately maintained, the grass verges trimmed with military precision and there were fresh flowers in brass vases on many of the stone and marble slabs. As Joker's feet crunched along the gravel, the graves he passed sparked off memories and he shuddered. Two of his friends had died in an ambush on the Irish border, another had perished in a car bomb in Germany. Mick Newmarch was the only one he'd seen die.

There was a fresh grave to the left, covered with bouquets of flowers which had begun to wither. The stone was clearly new and it bore the name of Pete Manyon. Joker stopped for a minute and looked at the cards that were still affixed to the floral tributes. A wife. Parents. A wreath in the form of the regimental crest.

The stone on Newmarch's grave was brutal in its simplicity: it was a grey granite block into which had been carved the officer's name, rank, date of birth and the date he'd died. That was it. No words of condolence, no prayers for his soul. Just the facts. When it came time for Joker to be buried six feet below the ground, that was all the epitaph he wanted. The grave was set back from the path and Joker walked across the short-cropped grass, unwrapping the bottle of Famous Grouse. He took off his pea jacket, dropped it down next to the stone and sat on it. "Evening, Mick," he said.

He looked up at the darkening sky as he unscrewed the cap on the bottle. One or two of the brightest stars were already visible and it didn't look as if it was going to rain.

"It's been a while, Mick," said Joker. "I'm sorry I didn't get here sooner." He took a long, deep pull on the whisky and felt its warmth spread across his chest. He looked at the bleak stone monument. "Drink, Mick?" he asked. He poured a measure of the spirit in a slow trickle onto the lush grass and then took another mouthful himself.

Cole Howard picked up a copy of *Electronics Monthly* and glanced through it. He looked at his watch and pulled a face. He'd been kept waiting for fifteen minutes in his father-in-law's office, yet he'd arrived right on time for the four o'clock appointment. There were times when Theodore Clayton could be an out-and-out bastard. Clayton's secretary looked up from her word-processor as if she'd read his mind. "I'm sorry, Mr Howard, he's still on his call. He knows you're here."

"Oh, I'm sure he does, Allison. I'm sure he does."

He tried to read an article on a new Japanese microprocessor but his vocabulary wasn't up to it. He tossed it back on the table and watched the tropical fish in the tank by the secretary's desk. Brightly coloured fish weaved in and out of fronds of plants that seemed too green to be real and a stream of small bubbles dribbled up from a plastic galleon sitting on the gravel at the bottom.

At Howard's feet was a brown leather briefcase. All it contained was the original Mitchell video. Howard could have carried the videocassette in his jacket pocket but he felt more confident entering his father-in-law's office with a briefcase. It suggested status and authority, as did the dark grey suit he'd put on. Theodore Clayton always managed to make Howard feel as if he hadn't washed behind his ears that morning and that he was about to be scolded for the oversight.

He'd caught the first flight from Washington with Andy Kim, who was now out in the desert with the men from the Sheriff's Department who'd been first at the scene. Howard had wanted to go with them but he knew it was important to get the video to Clayton now that he knew the limits of the FBI's technology. He looked at his watch again and smoothed the creases of his trousers. After a while he stood up and walked over to a display case containing some of Clayton's kachina dolls. The religious figures, carved from the roots of cottonwood trees by the Hopi Indians of Northern Arizona, were extremely valuable, and some of them dated back to the eighteenth century. Clayton was an avid collector of Native American art, and he enjoyed putting it on show, more as an exhibition of his wealth than his good taste.

"Mr Clayton will see you now, Mr Howard," said the secretary. She stood up and opened the door for him. Howard knew that Clayton wouldn't even consider walking to the reception area to greet him, and that when he entered his office the man would be sitting behind his big desk. He was right. Clayton waited until Howard was halfway across the large expanse of shag-pile carpet before getting to his feet and he adjusted the cuffs of his made-to-measure silk shirt before stepping around his antique desk. Clayton's suits were made for him by a tailor in London's Savile Row who flew over every six months for fitting sessions and they cost more than Howard earned in a month. Clayton was as well groomed as a TV weatherman and had the chiselled good looks to go with the wardrobe: brown hair greying at the temples, the sort of teeth that only serious money can buy, a light tan which suggested business trips overseas rather than vacations, and just enough wrinkles to imply maturity and confidence.

"Cole, Cole, sorry to have kept you waiting for so long." Clayton's apology and gleaming smile seemed as artificial as the plants in the fish tank outside. He slapped Howard on the back and guided him to a sofa in the corner of the office.

"Oh, I know how busy you are, Ted." Howard sat down and put the briefcase on his knees.

"You said this was important?"

"Very," said Howard.

"FBI business, or is there a problem at home?"

Howard felt himself flushing involuntarily. "No, Ted, there's no problem at home."

Clayton put a firm hand on Howard's shoulder and squeezed. "Glad to hear it, Cole. Glad to hear it. So, what can I do for you?"

Howard opened the briefcase, took out the videocassette and handed it to the older man. "This is a recording of an incident out in the desert near the Havasu Lake Wildlife Refuge last week. A small plane was shot down by a group of snipers. We've gone as far as we can with our video equipment, and we need to know who the men are."

"Snipers in the desert? What in God's name would they be doing in the desert? Leaving aside the fact that it's a wildlife refuge, there's nothing worth hunting out there. I should know." Theodore Clayton was an avid hunter and had a large trophy room in the basement of his home, where he insisted on taking Howard at regular intervals. Howard hated the glassy-eyed stares of Clayton's victims but humoured him for his wife's sake.

"We think they were rehearsing an assassination," said Howard.

Clayton's eyebrows leapt up. "You're joking!" he exclaimed.

Howard shook his head. "I wish I was. There are three of them at different distances and heights from four dummies which we assume represent the target. We think the plane was shot down because they inadvertently stumbled on the rehearsal."

"Cole, this almost defies belief. Who on earth would go to the trouble of rehearsing an assassination in the middle of a desert?"

"The rifle sights have to be calibrated, the timing has to be practised. Assuming they're only going to get one chance, they'd obviously want to do a dry run somewhere secluded. They chose the site carefully. The only major highway anywhere near is 93 and that's the other side of the Hualapai Mountains."

Clayton held up the cassette. "And they recorded the whole thing?"

"No, one of the passengers had a camcorder. It survived the crash."

"Fortuitous," said Clayton.

"Depends on your point of view," said Howard, thinking about Mrs Mitchell trying to calm her son as the plane plunged to the ground.

"So, what is it exactly that you want me to do with this?"

"We can't make out the faces of the men in the video. There are three with rifles, and three more who seem to be organising the rehearsal. There are several vehicles there; we can see what make they are but we'd like to pick out the licence plates."

"You're not asking much, Cole!" laughed Clayton.

"Can you do it?" asked Howard.

"Depends," said the older man, walking back to his desk. "Depends on how detailed the tape is, depth of focus, quality of the lens. There's a whole series of factors at work. I'll have to get my people to take a look at it before I can give you a verdict."

"But you are doing work on this sort of tape analysis, aren't you?"

"We sure are," said Clayton, sitting down in his high-backed leather chair. "And the Government's picking up most of the bill, too, so I'd be more than happy to help out the FBI. It'll help us when it comes time for appropriations."

"What's Uncle Sam's interest in video technology?" Howard asked.

Clayton smiled and beat a tempo on the top of his desk with his palms. "It's not just Uncle Sam, Cole. Image processing is big business in medicine, physics, astronomy, biology, you name it, there's hardly a scientific field not involved. We've only begun to scratch the surface. The day's going to come when machines will read and analyse X-rays and Cat-scans, without any humans being involved at all. Diagnosis by machines. It's coming."

"That would explain why MIT would get involved, but not Clayton Electronics," pressed Howard, recognising his father-in-law's familiar evasion technique. He'd long ago learned that when Theodore Clayton was being flexible with the truth, his hands tended to betray his lips.

"Well, I can't deny there are certain military applications which we think will be particularly profitable," said Clayton. "But there's a big future in the commercial computer processing of satellite photographs – things like crop monitoring and weather assessment. And there are opportunities in all sorts of quality control operations – computers can make interpretations on the basis of mathematical equations and statistical moments, with none of the distractions that make human decisions so unreliable." Clayton's fingers were tapping silently on the desk blotter. He looked levelly at his son-in-law and his voice was as steady as a judge pronouncing sentence, but Howard knew that he was hiding something. "You tell me, whose judgment would you most trust – a computer which has a one hundred per cent record of accurate diagnosis of cancer from X-rays, or a radiologist who has just broken up with his wife and had his BMW vandalised?"

"No contest, I guess," said Howard. He wondered what Clayton was hiding. Howard crossed his legs and looked out of the window to the side of Clayton's desk. It overlooked the parking lot and he could see Clayton's pristine Rolls-Royce gleaming in the afternoon sun. Theodore Clayton hadn't got to where he was by working to help further the cause of medical science, he'd made a fortune on the backs of a series of multi-million dollar defence contracts including night sights, heads-up displays and computerised video surveillance equipment.

Howard realised that his father-in-law was talking to him. "Well?" said Clayton.

"I'm sorry, Ted, what did you say? I was miles away."

Clayton looked irritated. "I asked if you were all right for Sunday night."

"Sunday night?"

"You and Lisa are coming round for dinner."

Howard's heart fell. He hated going to his in-laws'

house, and he figured that his wife had been waiting for the right time to tell him. "Sure," he said, "we're looking forward to it."

Clayton stood up, leaving the cassette on the desk. "Good, good," he said. "Hopefully I'll have some news for you then."

Howard frowned. Sunday was five days away. He stood up. "Is there any way of getting the results faster?" he asked. "We don't know when the real thing is set to happen."

"I'll speed them up," agreed Clayton. He patted Howard on the back as they walked to the door. "I'll call you as soon as I have anything. By the way, haven't you forgotten something?"

"Oh, yes. I'm really grateful, Ted. Really grateful."

Clayton laughed. "No, I meant your briefcase. You've left it on the floor."

Howard felt his cheeks flush. "Thanks," he said through gritted teeth.

The Colonel handed Joker a bulky manila envelope and leaned back in his chair. Joker opened the package and slid the contents onto the Colonel's desk. On top of the pile was a British passport. He picked it up and flicked through it. The passport was three years old and featured a photograph that must have come from the SAS's files, the face thinner and the hair almost shoulder length. The name in the passport was Damien O'Brien and the date of birth was Joker's own. He looked at the visa pages: they were blank except for a multiple re-entry visa to the United States.

"I haven't travelled much," he said with a smile. He picked up three sheets of typed paper which had been stapled together and read through them quickly. "Ah, I see why," he said. "A labourer, some part-time bar work, and two convictions for drunk and disorderly conduct and one for assault. I'm not a particularly nice character, am I?"

"It's only cover, Joker. Nothing personal." The Colonel wrinkled his nose. The man sitting in front of him didn't appear to have shaved for a couple of days and he stank to high heaven. His clothes looked as if they'd been slept in and there were grass stalks all over his coat.

If Joker was aware of the Colonel's disdain for his dishevelled appearance, he didn't show it. According to the fake CV Joker had been born thirty-six years earlier in Belfast, had lived for his first twelve years in Londonderry and attended a Catholic primary school. The house, and the school, had both been demolished years earlier – the house as part of a development project, the school following an arson attack in which the records had been destroyed. Joker had used the road and the school in previous identities when going undercover in Northern Ireland and was familiar with both.

"We've kept most of the background close to your own between the ages of twelve and eighteen, so that you won't have too much trouble remembering it," said the Colonel. "From eighteen years on we have you travelling around, never staying much in one place. That's pretty much up to you – you can say you've been to Ireland, bring up your time in Scotland, use any background you feel comfortable with. There's a number there they can use if they want to speak to someone you've worked with. If anyone calls they'll be told it's a bar in London and they'll give you a glowing reference. The two bottom sheets are a summary of Manyon's last report."

Joker nodded and put the typewritten sheets back into the envelope. There were half a dozen large photographs on the desk and Joker picked them up. His eyes hardened as he looked at a woman in her mid-forties, dark brown hair lightly curled in a pageboy cut and her eyes moist. Another of the photographs was a full-length shot, clearly taken at a funeral because she was wearing black and had a handkerchief in her right hand. In the background he saw men in black berets and sunglasses and a coffin covered with the Republican tricolour flag.

"They're the latest pictures we have of Mary Hennessy, taken at her husband's funeral five years ago," said the Colonel. "You've seen her since, of course."

"She hadn't changed," said Joker, his eyes fixed on the picture. He could see a big automatic in the hands of one of the men standing by the coffin.

"She's certain to have altered her appearance by now. She could be blonde, a red-head, brunette, we've no way of knowing. Her hair could be longer, or permed, and she could be wearing coloured contact lenses. And she could have put on weight."

"No," said Joker quietly, looking at the woman's slim figure and shapely legs. "She was too vain about her looks. The hair, yeah, she might change that, but she won't change her figure and she won't risk plastic surgery. And even if she did, I'd always recognise her."

There was a photograph of her getting into a car, and another of her outside a large red-brick house. Joker recognised several of the men with her, all of them leading

IRA and Sinn Fein figures. The rest of the photographs were of Matthew Bailey. He was below average height with an unruly mop of red hair and piercing green eyes. He had a snub nose dotted with freckles and a deep dimple in his chin, as if someone had poked him with a finger and left an impression in the flesh, and a mole under his left eye. "Bailey is now twenty-six years old, and is responsible for the deaths of at least four members of the RUC," continued the Colonel. "The IRA sent him to the States about six months ago when Northern Ireland had become too hot for him. One of the FBI's anti-terrorist units almost caught him in Los Angeles four months ago trying to purchase a ground-to-air missile system but he was tipped off and disappeared for a while. Last month we received reports that he'd surfaced in New York and we sent Manyon in."

Joker looked up sharply. "Tipped off, you said? Who could've tipped him off?"

"You know as well as me that the US is full of Irish Americans who sympathise with the IRA, Joker. They don't see them as terrorists but as freedom fighters. And the law enforcement organisations have more than their fair share of Irish Americans. Every second cop in New York has an Irish name, just about, and they all wear the shamrock on St Paddy's Day."

"Are you saying we can't trust the American cops?"

"Cops, FBI, Attorney-General's Office, you're to steer clear of them all. There's to be no contact with the Americans at all. We can't afford to blow this, we'll only get one chance."

Joker held up a picture of Bailey and one of Hennessy. They could have been mother and son. "What makes you think they're together?" he asked the Colonel. "Did Manyon see them?"

"No. We had no idea she was there. It was only when Manyon's body turned up that we recognised her signature. The Americans don't even know – they're treating it as a straightforward murder investigation."

"They don't know Manyon was with the regiment?"

The Colonel shook his head. "No. His sister arranged to have the body brought back, and his cover held."

Joker put the photographs on top of the passport. He smiled when he saw there was a UK driving licence in the name of Damien O'Brien. He thought of his own revoked driving licence, suspended for a further two and a half years. His smile widened when he saw a thick wad of banknotes. He ran his thumbnail along one edge of the stack of cash and images of Benjamin Franklin flicked past. They were almost all one hundred dollar bills. "There's five thousand dollars there," said the Colonel. "We're also giving you two credit cards, one Visa and one Mastercard, in the name of Damien O'Brien. You can use those for purchases or for withdrawing cash, up to $300 a day on each one. You should use the cards wherever possible, they're keyed into a bank account which we'll be monitoring. Each time you use the cards we'll know within minutes where you are. I suggest you use them once a day; just make a small withdrawal so that we can keep track of you."

"What about back-up while I'm there?"

"You'll be alone," said the Colonel. "The last thing you want is a team following you around. This is completely solo, Joker. It has to be if it's going to work."

Joker put the money back in the envelope and slid in the photographs and typed sheets.

"What about a weapon?"

"That you'll have to get while you're there. The sort of company you'll be in, you won't have any trouble getting tooled up."

Joker rubbed his chin with both hands. He could feel the stubble from several days' growth scratch the skin of his palms. "And then? You still haven't told me exactly how you want me to take them out."

The Colonel smiled thinly. "That's up to you," he said, his voice almost a whisper.

Joker nodded. He understood why it was a solo mission and why there would be no contact with the Americans. "Colonel, it'll be a pleasure," he said. Joker wished that he felt as confident as he sounded. His last encounter with Mary Hennessy had left him shattered – physically and emotionally – and his enthusiasm for the Colonel's mission was tinged with an emotion he hadn't felt for some time. Fear.

Cole Howard drove back to his office after dropping Andy Kim off at the airport. The mathematician had spent the previous day in the desert with several men from the Sheriff's Department and a laser measuring device which Howard had managed to borrow from the County Highways Department. Kim had been keen to get back to Washington and begin running his numbers through the university's mainframe computer. He'd been like an excited child during the ride to the airport, bobbing his head backwards and forwards as he talked. Howard wished he

69

could have got the same enthusiasm from the young FBI agent who'd been assigned to help track down the vehicles used in the desert rehearsal. She was a twenty-five-year-old college graduate straight out of the Academy, a pushy woman with too much hair who'd seen *Silence of the Lambs* fifteen times and clearly decided to model herself on Hannibal Lecter rather than on Jodie Foster's character. She was tall, had backswept blonde hair and a sharp profile, with pale green eyes that always seemed to regard Howard with contempt. It was a look he was used to seeing in his father-in-law's eyes. Her name was Kelly Armstrong and she seemed to blame Howard for giving her the mundane job to do, even though the assignment had come direct from Jake Sheldon. Howard had wanted someone more experienced but Sheldon had insisted that he use the new girl, because tracking down rental cars didn't require anything more than a room temperature IQ. She hadn't smiled at him once, and her icy politeness annoyed the hell out of him.

She was waiting for him in his office. She looked pointedly at her wristwatch, an expensive gold Cartier, and pursed her glossy pink lips. Howard wanted to tell her that he was late because of Andy Kim, but he didn't want to give her the satisfaction of having to explain himself.

"Good morning, Kelly," he said, coldly.

"Cole," she acknowledged. "I've found twelve rental companies within fifty miles of Phoenix who rent or lease vehicles of the make and colour in the Mitchell video. In all there were eighty-three out on the day of the shooting." She looked at her notebook and flipped over a page with the sound of tearing cloth. "Seventy-nine have been returned, four are still out. All four are still within their rental agreements."

Howard nodded and sat behind his desk. He waved Kelly to sit down but she ignored him. "All eighty-three were paid for by credit card, and all went through without incident. No fake cards, no stolen cards. I've run checks on all the driving licences and other than a few dozen unpaid tickets and a guy who owes several thousand dollars in child support, there's nothing untoward." Howard opened his mouth to speak but Kelly continued. "I asked all the rental companies if they had rented out a blue and a white car at the same time, and none had. A total of eight had been involved in an accident of some form, but all were collision damage and all had the names and insurance details of the other drivers involved."

"Good work, Kelly," he said. "You've done a good job." She nodded and turned to go. "But . . ." he began and she tensed. When she turned back she was looking down her sharp nose at him like an angry bird preparing to peck out his eyes. She raised her left eyebrow archly.

"Those cars must have come from somewhere," he continued.

"Without licence plates it's going to be difficult to track them down," she said slowly.

"Difficult, but not impossible," said Howard.

"We're not even sure they're rental cars," she said.

"True, but it's unlikely they'd risk using their own vehicles."

"They could be stolen."

"That's also true. In fact, that's a good line of inquiry. You should check if any stolen cars match the description. But first you should start checking all the licences which were used to obtain the rentals we know about."

Her smile tightened. "I already told you that I'd done that."

71

Howard shook his head. "No, you said the licences were in order. Which they would be if they'd been stolen and not reported. Or if the licences were genuine but based on fake IDs. All you need for a licence is to pass the test and show a birth certificate. And birth certificates are easy to forge or you can get one for a dead child. What we've got to do is to contact the owner of each licence and check that they did rent the car. And ask them where they went."

"Cole, that could take weeks."

"If that's what it takes, that's what it takes," said Howard. "And if that draws a blank you'll have to widen the area of investigation. Go to a one-hundred-mile radius from Phoenix. And keep extending it, to Tucson and beyond if it's necessary. This is important, Kelly." The girl glared at him as if she was going to say something, but instead she just nodded and turned on her heels. Her expensive wool skirt swung from side to side like a filly's tail as she stormed out of Howard's office.

Mary Hennessy stood in front of the bathroom mirror and studied her reflection. She'd always wanted to be a blonde when she was a little girl. She'd driven her mother to distraction: each time a birthday came round she'd always ask for the same thing – blonde curls – and she'd sent innumerable letters up the chimney to Santa Claus until she'd reached the age where she realised that hair colour was genetic and not something that a parent could change. By the time she discovered that chemicals could alter her natural brown colour she no longer wanted to be blonde.

Now here she was, just about to turn fifty, with hair the colour of a mid-summer wheatfield. She turned her head from side to side, then bent forward to check the roots. The dye job was good for another week or so, she decided. She raised her head and smoothed the skin around her neck with her fingertips. It was, she acknowledged with a twinge of regret, beginning to lose some of its elasticity. She shuddered, remembering the turkey necks of old aunts who'd visited her house when she was a child and given her minty-tasting kisses and pressed sixpences into her palm. Soon it would be her turn to face the ravages of time, and she wasn't looking forward to it. Perversely, her hair looked better than ever: the blonde locks suited her and the light perm made it much fuller. It also completely altered her appearance, though it matched the photograph in the American passport on her dressing table.

She adjusted the neck of her polo-neck pullover and then took a houndstooth jacket out of the closet and slipped it on. With the black jeans the outfit was casual but businesslike, she decided. Just right. She collected her car from the hotel car park and drove to the airport.

Matthew Bailey was waiting for her in the cafeteria with a half-eaten croissant and a cup of cold coffee in front of him. He stood up too quickly when he saw her and spilled his coffee over the table top. Mary smiled. Bailey was almost half her age, easily young enough to be her son, but he'd made it clear on several occasions that he'd dearly love to get inside her pants. That was one of the reasons she'd dressed so severely, so that there was no question of leading him on.

"The plane was early," he said, mopping up his coffee with paper serviettes.

"I'm sorry, I should've checked," said Mary.

"Oh no, that's okay," he said. "I didn't m-m-mind."

Mary had noticed that Bailey developed a slight stammer when they were alone together. It was hard to believe that the slightly-built young man was responsible for the deaths of four RUC officers in Northern Ireland. He was a full two inches shorter than Mary, with unkempt red hair and a sprinkling of freckles across his snub nose. He had the sort of hair which was difficult to dye – he'd tried it once with black colouring and it had turned out dark green – so he'd changed his appearance by cutting his hair short, growing a thin moustache and wearing John Lennon-type spectacles. It made him look about nineteen years old, and he dressed like an all-American student in sweatshirts, baggy jeans, and baseball boots. She slid onto the seat opposite him. "How did it go?" she asked.

"No problems," he said. He looked around for somewhere to put the wet serviettes. "Do you want anything? Coffee?" Mary shook her head. Bailey put the serviettes in an ashtray. "I bought a ticket to LA on the Amex card and used it to rent a car at the airport and to pay for a m-m-motel there. I returned the car on the second day and put the cards in a wallet with a few dollars and dropped it in Central LA. I hung around to make sure it was picked up – a couple of black guys got it and I could tell they weren't going to hand it in." He grinned. "One of them started dancing up and down. You should have seen it, it was so funny. I paid cash for the ticket back here, and I've destroyed the licence."

"Good. That should do the trick."

"Do you really think anyone will be after us?" he said.

"I don't know, but it's better to be on the safe side. After we brought that plane down in the desert the place must have been swarming with cops. There's always a chance they'll find out about the cars from the tyre tracks, or they might manage to find someone who saw us at a filling station. If they find where we rented the car from they'll have a record of the two credit cards and licences we used."

"But they were in phony names anyway."

"I know, but by laying a false trail in LA we'll have them thinking we're on the other side of the country."

Bailey nodded and toyed with his cup. He obviously had something on his mind and Mary waited for him to speak. Bailey kept his eyes lowered. "We're still going ahead, then?"

"What do you mean?" she asked. She kept her voice low and even, though her heart had begun to race. The last thing she needed was for Bailey to get cold feet at this stage.

"I just thought, what with what happened in the desert and all, that you'd think about calling it off."

"Oh no, Matthew. Oh no. There's no question of us backing out now. Except for the plane, everything went according to plan. The rifles are all calibrated and we practised the shoot itself. We're ready to go."

"Okay," he said quietly.

Mary reached over and touched the back of his hand lightly. He flinched as if he'd received an electric shock and then smiled at her. "We're only going to get one chance at this," she said. "We've invested a great deal of time and money to get this far, surely you don't want that to be wasted?"

"But what about that Sass-man? Manyon?"

Mary snorted. "He didn't know what we were planning. You heard what he said, it was you he was following, that's all. He was just in the wrong place at the wrong time."

"Like the plane," said Bailey.

"Like the plane," she repeated. She ran her index finger along the back of Bailey's hand. "The SAS had heard that you were in the States, and they sent him over to investigate. He knew nothing."

"If he can find me, there'll be others."

Mary withdrew her hand. "Which is why you're going to Florida until we're ready for the final phase. Go to Disneyworld, hang around in the sun, enjoy yourself. This time of year Florida is full of Brits, no-one will find you there. We'll meet in Baltimore in four weeks." She slipped him a piece of paper on which she'd written a telephone number. "Call me at this hotel on April twelfth. I'll tell you where we're staying then."

Bailey didn't look convinced. Mary leaned forward over the table. "Matthew, I need you for this. I really do." She smiled as warmly as she could. "Matthew, you're with me on this, aren't you?" He nodded and she rewarded him with another smile. "It'll be fine, really. Now you disappear for a few weeks and contact me on the twelfth. Before midday." She stood up, bent down to kiss him lightly on the cheek, and walked away. She knew he was watching her go and she swung her hips just a little more than usual, hating herself but knowing it was necessary.

Joker flew into New York on the afternoon of March 17, stiff and cramped after eight hours at the back of a British Airways 747. World Traveller the airline called it, but to

Joker it would always be Cattle Class: tiny seats, no legroom and food as plastic as the smile of the stewardesses. He didn't realise the significance of the date until his Yellow Cab ground to a halt somewhere around 72nd Street. The cab driver twisted round and grinned. "Fucking Irish," he said in a thick accent which Joker guessed was Slavic.

"Huh?" said Joker, who'd been half asleep. Even the back of a New York cab was more comfortable than his British Airways seat and the driver had the heater full on.

"Fucking Irish," the driver repeated. "Today's the St Patrick's Day Parade and the traffic's not moving. It's going to be like this all fucking day. Today it's the fucking Irish, next week it's the fucking Greeks and next month, wouldya believe it, it's the fucking Puerto Ricans."

"No problem," said Joker. "I'm in no hurry."

"Whatever you say," said the driver. He began pumping his fist on the horn. "You English?"

"Scottish," replied Joker.

"Yeah? I'm from Turkey. Great fucking country, America. Fucking great." He continued to pound on the horn and swear at the traffic ahead. It seemed to Joker that the man's swearing vocabulary was limited to the one expletive and that he couldn't go for more than a minute without using it at least twice.

Joker looked across at the crowds walking by the shops. It was a cold spring day and most people were wearing long coats and scarves. The gutters were full of rubbish: old newspapers, squashed soft drink cans and empty cigarette packs. No-one seemed to care. A thick-set man in an expensive cashmere overcoat dropped a half-finished cigar onto the ground and it glowed redly until it was crushed by

77

a white high-heeled shoe. Joker's gaze travelled up from the shoe to a shapely leg that disappeared into a fawn raincoat. The woman was a brunette, her hair glossy and shoulder length. She brushed past a large black man who thrust a styrofoam cup at her and asked for change. The beggar shouted something after her but she showed no sign of hearing him and he waved the cup at a businessman who pretended not to see him. Eye contact seemed to be kept to a minimum as if acknowledging another's existence would only lead to confrontation. The beggar saw that Joker was looking at him and he grinned. He ambled over to the cab, put a hand on the roof and bent down.

"Got any change?" he mouthed through the closed window.

Joker shook his head. All he had were the bills the Colonel had given him.

"Fuck off, why don't you?" the cab driver shouted. "Leave my fare alone."

"It's okay," said Joker. "No problem."

"And get your filthy fucking hand off my fucking cab!" the driver screamed.

The beggar walked to the front of the vehicle. He was wearing a shabby grey wool coat, with the buttons missing, over brown trousers that were wearing thin at the knees and a stained green pullover. He was still smiling but there was a cold, almost psychotic, stare in his eyes. His neck muscles tensed and he reared his head back and then he spat a stream of greenish phlegm across the windscreen.

"You fucking animal!" the driver screamed. He switched his wipers on and they streaked the saliva across the glass. The beggar began to cackle, nodding his head backwards and forwards as he laughed. The driver pressed his windscreen wash button and thin jets of water crawled up the glass. "What the fuck is this city coming to?" the driver yelled rhetorically. The traffic began to move and the cab pulled away. Joker turned to watch the beggar and for a couple of seconds they had eye contact and he had a cold feeling somewhere deep inside as he realised that he didn't have too far to fall before he'd have to live on the streets himself and he wondered how he'd make out in a city like New York without a home, without money. After he'd quit his job as a nightwatchman on the Isle of Dogs, he was out of work for almost six weeks and he'd come close to being destitute. If his landlord hadn't agreed to wait for his rent, Joker knew he'd have ended up sleeping in shop doorways. He had no close family and no savings and he was all too well aware that there was no Government safety-net waiting to catch him if he fell. "Fucking animals," repeated the driver.

"Yeah," said Joker, not wanting to argue. "Can you drop me here?"

"I thought you said Thirty-seventh Street?"

"Yeah, I did, but I'm feeling ill. I'd rather walk."

"Okay, okay. Whatever you want. Just don't throw up in the fucking cab, that's all." The cab slammed to a halt and Joker thrust the fare through a small hole in a Perspex barrier that kept the driver insulated from his passengers. He opened the door and pulled his cheap suitcase after him. The outside air felt cold after the overheated cab interior so he walked briskly to keep warm. In the distance he could hear the wail of bagpipes and he headed towards them.

He found the parade heading down Fifth Avenue and stood among the watching crowds, the suitcase at his feet and his hands thrust deep into the pockets of his pea jacket.

A group of kilted pipers were playing Mull of Kintyre. The pipers moved on, followed by a huge float in the shape of the Loch Ness Monster on either side of which had been stencilled the name of a Japanese computer company. Across the thoroughfare was an imposing white marble and stone Gothic cathedral and as the float moved by Joker saw it was called St Patrick's.

Joker wondered how many of the spectators who were cheering and waving flags realised that the pipers and the monster were Scottish and not Irish. It didn't seem to make any difference, everyone seemed to be enjoying themselves. A gleaming fire engine rolled by, decorated with huge cardboard shamrocks and with the firemen all dressed in green. It was followed by a large float decorated like an Irish hill with large inflatable cows surrounding a huge yellow block with the word BUTTER etched into it.

Behind the float was a line of old American cars, all convertibles with big, sweeping fins and lots of chrome. In the back of each car were youngsters waving to the crowds and on the doors were printed cards with the names of what Joker supposed were television shows: *In Living Colour, Herman's Head, Roc.* They were getting the most response from the crowds, lots of shouts and screams and whooping noises and the occasional small child running over to get an autograph. What they had to do with St Patrick's Day, Joker couldn't imagine. There were lines of blue-uniformed policemen marching at attention, all with shamrocks pinned to the breasts of their tunics, and Joker recalled the Colonel's warning about the number of Irish-Americans who were involved in law enforcement. A clown in a bright yellow costume and a blue wig appeared in front of Joker, waving a bucket. A sign in the bucket detailed the charities the money was for but Joker just shrugged and said he didn't have any change.

"Yeah, right," said the clown dismissively and flopped over in his yard-long shoes to a group of children. Paper streamers were raining down from the skyscrapers overlooking the parade and one wrapped itself around Joker's neck. He pulled it off and dropped it into the street.

A float sponsored by an insurance company rolled by, decked out in green with a trio of fiddlers playing an Irish folk tune while half a dozen girls danced a jig. Joker picked up his suitcase and began walking through the crowds.

He'd been in New York a number of times before and knew that there were several small hotels off 37th Street, close to the East River. He made slow progress along Fifth Avenue because of all the sightseers. A marching band of young black girls in silver spandex outfits and tall braided helmets overtook him in a flurry of whirling sticks, followed by young boys in similar outfits blowing brass instruments and beating drums. He decided to get off Fifth Avenue and waited until there was a gap in the parade before dashing across. Once he'd left the route of the parade the streets were relatively quiet and after a twenty-minute walk he was outside the hotel he'd chosen: The White Horse. It had been formed by knocking together two brownstone houses and refurbished on the cheap with plasterboard partitions, plastic light fittings and thin carpets. There was a small reception desk beyond the main door where a Hispanic woman was talking on the phone. She raised her eyebrows when Joker walked in but carried on her conversation. Joker put his suitcase down and waited. Eventually she pushed over a registration card for him to fill in. The ballpoint pen she gave him leaked and there were blobs of ink all over the card by the time he'd finished. She picked up the card, read it, took an imprint from his credit card and handed him a key, all the time talking into the phone. She gestured at a staircase to her right as she cackled away in Spanish.

Joker's room was on the third floor, at the back of the hotel, where it overlooked an alley which was dark and forbidding even in the afternoon. A rusting fire escape wound its way down the building and Joker pulled open the window to take a closer look. It provided a back way out in an emergency but he was also well aware that it offered a way in for any intruder. He checked the lock on the window but he knew that it wouldn't deter an enthusiastic amateur, never mind a professional. An air-conditioner was set into the wall underneath the window but nothing happened when he switched it on. He kicked it half-heartedly.

A small bathroom led off the bedroom, containing a shower stall, a cracked yellow washbasin and a toilet. A piece of paper was wrapped across the seat along with a note telling him that it had been sanitised for his protection. He picked up a glass tumbler from the shelf under the bathroom mirror and went back into the bedroom where he sat on the single bed and opened his suitcase. He took out a bottle of Famous Grouse and poured himself a decent measure. He toasted his reflection in the window. " 'If I can make it here, I can make it anywhere'," he said, his voice loaded with sarcasm.

* * *

Howard sat in Theodore Clayton's outer office, his leather briefcase at his feet. His father-in-law's secretary kept flashing him sympathetic looks but Howard didn't show his annoyance. If Clayton wanted to play infantile power games, it was a small price to pay for the help the FBI was getting.

Clayton kept him waiting just ten minutes so Howard figured he'd got off lightly. Clayton also opened the office door himself and personally ushered Howard in.

"Sorry, Cole, I was on the phone to Tokyo."

"Tokyo?" said Howard, puzzled. "I thought you were competing with the Japanese."

"Product-wise, we are, but all the technology is the same and there are several firms over there who are interested in taking stakes in us. It's the latest way of doing business with the Japs – they call it co-opetition – a combination of co-operation and competition."

"Would the Government allow that?"

"What do you mean?" said Clayton, sitting behind his uncluttered desk. A photograph of Lisa beamed from a brass frame, next to a picture of Clayton's second wife, Jennifer. The two women were surprisingly alike – blonde hair, fair skin, blue eyes – though Jennifer was the younger of the two by more than five years.

"Your defence work? Surely they wouldn't want overseas investors to be involved."

Clayton snorted and shook his head. "You think the Government gives a damn? There are no boundaries where business is concerned, Cole. Money is the universal language, the common philosophy. I tell you, the best thing that could happen to this country's armed forces would be if we had Japanese-built jets flying off Japanese-built aircraft carriers, and we had our soldiers driving Japanese tanks and flying Japanese helicopters."

"And using Japanese atomic weapons?" asked Howard, his voice loaded with irony.

"You mock, my boy, but it'll come. I remember when the first Japanese motorcycles arrived in this country, and how we laughed at them. Sewing machines on wheels. You know what car I drive now? A Nissan, and there isn't an American car can match it."

Howard knew that Clayton was being economical with the truth – more often than not the industrialist was to be found behind the wheel of a Rolls-Royce.

Clayton opened one of his desk drawers and took out a cardboard folder. "Anyway, at the moment we're just talking about a share stake. That's confidential by the way. I'd hate to see you hauled in for insider trading." He smiled to show Howard that he was joking and passed him the file. "This is what we've managed to do with your video."

"I didn't expect you to move so quickly," said Howard, opening the file.

"I had a couple of PhDs who were dying to show me what they can do with the new $10 million computer I bought for them. I think you'll be impressed."

The top two photographs were of the cars, and Howard's heart sank when he saw them because there wasn't much more detail than in the ones Bonnie Kim had done for him. Clayton walked around behind him and put a hand on his shoulder. "Yeah, those were a disappointment, the angle was just too acute to be able to do anything with the tags. You'll be more impressed with the faces."

Howard put the car pictures on the desk. The next photograph was of the man who'd been holding the walkie-talkie. It was a close-up of his face, and it was a big improvement on the pictures Bonnie Kim had produced, though he doubted it was clear enough to make a positive identification.

"Pretty good, huh?" said Clayton.

The picture in Howard's hands had little of the blurring that had made Bonnie's prints so difficult to decipher. The man was middle-aged and balding, with a round, plump face and dark sunglasses, though his features were hard to define. "Much better," admitted Howard. "But still not quite good enough, I'm afraid." He handed the picture to Clayton. "It's sharper than our versions, but there isn't enough detail for us to get a match from file pictures. Is there anything else you can do?"

"Oh sure," said Clayton confidently. "That's just for starters. They did what your lab had already done, the median filtering thing, but they coupled that with a technique we use to remove the blur caused by motion. A large part of the blurring was caused by the movement of the camcorder, and isn't a result of the distances involved. My boys ran the images through a program which compensates for the speed of the plane."

"Did they try pixel aggregation?" Howard asked, remembering the term Bonnie Kim had used.

Clayton frowned. "I think so," he said. His fingers began to tap nervously on his blotter and Howard suppressed a smile. "I know they've a few more ideas up their sleeves, it's just that some of the techniques take longer to run. There are some quite complicated transformations involved."

Howard nodded but he felt that his father-in-law's explanation was somewhat disjointed and he wondered exactly how much of the technology the older man actually understood. He had the feeling that Clayton was trying to articulate ideas which he didn't fully comprehend. He studied the face in the photograph. The features were flabby as if the man was used to living well and disdained physical exercise. The skin was olive coloured and Howard wondered if the man might be from the Mediterranean or the Middle East. The dark glasses hid the eyes and the nose was still pretty much a blur. The man could have had a moustache or it could just have been a shadow. Some of the photographs were full-length shots of the man. It was difficult to get an idea of how tall he was, but he was certainly broad in proportion to his height, with wide shoulders and an expansive girth.

The pictures of the younger man were slightly clearer. He had short, reddish hair and was wearing spectacles with small, round lenses. There was a picture of the three figures together and he was the shortest of the three, smaller even than the woman. The images of the woman were the least helpful – she was shading her eyes with her hand in most of the shots and in all but one of the pictures all that was visible was her blonde hair and the bottom of her face. Howard doubted that even the FBI's photographic experts would be able to produce a match from their files for any of the pictures but he felt that Clayton was hoping for a more positive reaction. And gratitude. "These are good, Ted. Really good. Let's hope that your men can improve them even more." He passed quickly through the pictures of the dummies and on to the photographs of the snipers. They all had their faces close to the telescopic sights on their weapons and Howard's heart fell.

"What's wrong?" asked Clayton, leaning forward.

"The snipers," said Howard. "I guess I was expecting more."

"I know what you mean, but the computer can't picture what isn't there; it has to have something to work with. They're still much better than the originals."

"Oh sure, they're a big improvement. But I doubt if we'll be able to get an identification from them. There just isn't enough detail."

Clayton walked around Howard's chair and stood behind him. Howard flipped through the photographs on his lap. He showed Clayton one of a sniper in the kneeling position. "Can you get a close-up on the rifle this guy's holding?"

"That's the sniper who was furthest away from the targets, isn't it? We're working on close-ups now. Incidentally, that's one hell of a shot he's trying to make. It must be two thousand yards."

"I know," said Howard.

"You're right, though, it's like no other rifle I've ever seen." Clayton pointed at another photograph, also of a sniper with a rifle. "I think this is a Horstkamp, a German model. I actually have one in my collection. It's a big gun, you could bring down an elephant with it. But this other one, it's got a completely different profile. You should get your weapons experts to have a look at it. It might be easier to identify the weapon than the man."

Howard nodded as he looked at the rifle. His father-in-law was right, the rifle was unusual.

"By the way, don't forget about Sunday," said Clayton.

"We'll be there," said Howard. "We're looking forward to it."

He left the office with his briefcase under his arm and a sick feeling in the pit of his stomach.

Joker flicked through the cable channels of the television in his room as he drank his way through the bottle of Famous Grouse. There seemed to be an unending stream of glitzy game shows, old situation comedies and Seventies police shows, punctuated with advertisements that insulted his intelligence. He waited until eight o'clock before leaving his room. Lights were going on around the city and the brightest of the stars were managing to make their presence felt in the darkening sky. He put up the collar of his pea jacket and hunched his shoulders against a biting wind that had begun to blow from the East River.

The file which the Colonel had given him to read in Hereford had included Pete Manyon's last report. Manyon had been hanging around an Irish pub on the Upper East Side called Filbin's while he was tracking Matthew Bailey, and Joker figured it was as good a place as any to start.

Filbin's wouldn't have looked out of place in a Dublin back street. It had small, leaded windows, a dark oak door and inside were wooden beams which ran the length of a narrow, smoke-filled room with a group of Formica tables and rickety wooden chairs at the far end. There was draught Guinness and Tennents lager and as impressive a range of malt and blended whiskies as Joker had ever seen. The bar itself ran for a good thirty feet, an edifice of polished wood and brass with no stools to get in the way, just a thick brass rod running along the bottom so that the hardened drinker's position could be assumed with the minimum of effort. Joker stood with one foot on the rod and leant on the bar. He took off his wool hat and thrust it into his coat pocket. A small, pixie-like barman walked over, polishing a glass, and asked Joker what he was having.

"Do you have a Grouse?" Joker asked in his soft Irish accent.

"Aye, I have to work on St Patrick's Day, but other than that I'm okay." The barman said it deadpan, with no trace of a smile. He finished polishing the glass, put it in the gantry behind the bar and grinned impishly at Joker. "Seriously, it's a Famous Grouse you want?"

"If it's not too much trouble," said Joker. The barman poured a measure of whisky into a glass. "Make it a double," said Joker.

The barman didn't ask if he wanted ice but placed the glass and a jug of water in front of him, recognising a serious drinker. Joker thanked him and paid for the drink.

"The name's Shorty," said the barman.

"Aye, it would be," said Joker. He carried his whisky over to a table and sat down. On the wood-panelled wall behind him were several framed black and white photographs of unnamed boxers. There were a dozen men in the bar and most of them appeared to be construction workers in jeans and heavy jackets, drinking pints of Guinness and speaking in Irish accents. Joker eavesdropped as he sipped his whisky, letting their accents and the rhythm of their speech wash over him. It had been almost four years since Joker had been in Ireland and he knew his accent would be a little rusty, though his cover story would allow for that. He tried to work out where the men were from by their accents: he was certain one was from Londonderry, and two were from the South, but his ear wasn't as acute as it used to be. He knew that an Irishman could often tell to within twenty miles where a countryman came from just from the sound of his voice.

Two teenagers appeared in front of Joker. They were both wearing green T-shirts and had green scarves tied around their heads and one of them was carrying a green bucket. The taller of the two held his bucket out and Joker saw that it contained coins and banknotes.

"Anything for the cause?" the teenager asked. His accent was north Belfast, harsh and nasal, and he had the aggressive tilt to the chin that Joker had seen on countless teenagers standing on street corners in Northern Ireland, youngsters who used the power of the IRA as a way of intimidating others. They weren't politically committed, they often had no idea what the ideas and the aims of the IRA were, other than that they wanted British troops out of Ireland, but by joining the organisation they could escape the boredom and hopelessness of the dole queue and gain some measure of self-respect. And a chance to skim a few pounds off the money they collected "for the cause".

Joker took out his wallet. Behind the bar, Shorty polished a glass and watched.

"A dollar buys a bullet for the boys," said the second youth.

Joker put a five-dollar bill into the bucket.

"Thanks, mister," said the boy holding the bucket.

"Don't mention it," said Joker, smiling.

The two teenagers swaggered off and waved the bucket in front of the construction workers. Joker had seen such IRA fund-raising in Belfast drinking holes but had been surprised to see it so openly in the United

States. He wondered if the Americans who poured cash into the IRA's coffers knew where their money went. Irish-Americans had a romantic view of the IRA: free-wheeling freedom-fighters battling an oppressive army which had no reason to be in their country. Joker knew what the flipside was. To him the IRA meant cowardly ambushes, bombs in crowded shopping centres and teenage soldiers shot in the back. Ceasefire or no ceasefire. He drained his glass and went to the bar for a refill. Shorty poured him another double Grouse and gave him a fresh jug of water. "I see you're contributing to the cause," he said conversationally.

"Will the money actually get there?" Joker asked.

"Oh, sure enough," said Shorty, an evil grin on his face. "If they tried ripping off the boys in here, they'd lose their kneecaps before you could say Gerry Adams." He chortled and put the clean glass back on the gantry. "I've been trying to place your accent. Where in Belfast are you from?"

"I moved to Scotland when I was a bairn, and I've been in London for a few years," said Joker.

"Aye, I could tell that, right enough," said the barman. "What brings you to the Big Apple?"

"Spot of bother with the taxman," said Joker. "I thought I'd see if I can get work here for a while, until things have cooled down."

"Yeah? What do you do?"

Joker shrugged. "Bit of everything. I've been a brickie, I've done some bar work, I pretty much take what I can get."

"You got a Green Card?"

Joker laughed and raised his glass in salute. "Oh aye, and a return ticket on Concorde." He leant against the bar and

91

chatted with Shorty, all the while keeping one ear tuned to the Irish construction workers.

"How do I look?" Cole Howard asked, adjusting his tie in the dressing mirror.

"Are you going to wear that tie, honey?" said his wife, standing behind him. Howard sighed. Obviously that had been his intention, but equally obviously Lisa didn't approve. She went over to his wardrobe and pulled out a blue silk tie she'd bought for him several Christmasses ago. "Try this," she said, handing it to him. Howard had to admit that she was right. It looked much better with the dark blue suit he was wearing.

Lisa didn't say anything but she stood next to the dressing table and waited for him to comment on her dress. It was a new one, pale green silk, low over the shoulder and cut to just below her knees. She'd fastened her long blonde hair back in a pony tail, a look which he knew her father preferred. Daddy's little girl. Around her neck was a thin gold and diamond necklace, a present from Theodore Clayton. "Fabulous," he said.

"Are you sure?" she said.

Howard could never understand why Lisa was so insecure. She was beautiful, well-educated, a terrific mother to their two children, and the daughter of one of the richest men in the state, yet she constantly sought approval. "Really," he said, stepping forward and taking her in his arms.

She laughed and pushed him away. "You'll mess my make-up," she said.

"You don't need it," he said, trying to kiss her again.

She slipped out of his arms. "Later," she said. "I'll check on Eddy and Katherine."

Howard gave himself a final check in the mirror and then went downstairs where their babysitter, the teenage daughter of one of their neighbours, was watching *Star Trek*. "Hiya, Pauline," he said.

"Hello, Mr Howard," she said, her eyes still on the screen. She was a pretty girl, but still at the gawky stage, knowing that men were looking at her in a different way but not sure how she should handle it. It would be another ten years or so before his own daughter reached that stage, but he was already dreading it.

"What's Captain Kirk up to?" Howard asked.

Pauline looked at him, raised her eyebrows and sighed. "That's *Star Trek*, Mr Howard. This is the *Next Generation*." She shook her head sadly and turned back to the television, her skirt halfway up her thighs. The girl was fifteen years old and she dressed like a hooker, though Howard knew she was getting straight A's at High School. Howard wondered how he'd handle Katherine when she began wearing make-up and high heels and wandered around the house without a bra. And the boys, standing on the doorstep with sweating palms, queuing up like dogs around a bitch on heat. So far Howard reckoned he'd done a pretty good job bringing up his two children, but they were still at the stage where they thought he was the bravest, smartest and kindest human being on the planet. Apart from their mother, of course.

Lisa came down the stairs, one of her many fur coats slung over her shoulders. "They're asleep," she said to Howard. She gave Pauline the rundown on where they'd

be, where the food was and what to do if there was an
emergency, then went out to the Jaguar. The green XJS was
Lisa's, another gift from her father, but Howard drove.
Theodore Clayton lived a half-hour's drive away from their
house, on an estate in Paradise Valley, to the north of
Phoenix. Howard handled the car well, though he drove it
only when Lisa was with him. She would have been quite
happy for him to use it every day, but he never quite felt
comfortable at the wheel. It felt too much like Clayton's
car, and he didn't like being beholden to his father-in-law.
As he drove he was aware of his wife looking at him. He
smiled. "What?" he said.

"Nothing," she said.

"Go on, say it. You were going to say something."

"Always the FBI agent," she said.

"But I'm right, right?"

They sat in silence for a while, both watching as the
Jaguar swallowed up the miles of road. "Daddy will
probably ask again, you know?"

"He does every time we go around," agreed Howard.
"He won't take no for an answer."

"He's used to getting what he wants," said Lisa. She
flipped the sun visor down and checked her make-up in the
vanity mirror.

Howard knew she was nervous, as she always was when
she was visiting her father. Howard had learnt from
experience that it was the worst possible time to start an
argument with her. Eventually she broke the strained
silence, and her voice was softer. "And if he does ask
again?"

Howard shook his head slowly. "The answer's going to
be the same, Lisa. I'm sorry, but that's the way it is. I like

doing what I'm doing. I like being with the Bureau. I wouldn't get the same satisfaction as your father's head of security."

"You'd get a lot more money, though," his wife said. It was a discussion they'd had many times, and they'd both expressed their views so often that they talked about it almost on auto-pilot, as if the words no longer had meaning.

"I know, I know," said Howard. "Maybe in the future; we'll see . . ."

"That's what you always say," said Lisa.

"But at least I'm not saying never," said Howard. "I'm just saying not right now." Howard's stomach tightened as he drove off the highway and onto the single track road which led to the Clayton estate. White fences seemed to stretch for miles, enclosing paddocks where sleek Arabian horses stood proudly, their heads turning to follow the Jaguar. The first time he had seen the Clayton house he'd stopped his car and checked the directions Lisa had given him. He'd been going out with her for three months and while it was clear she had money she'd never given him any hint of the magnitude of Theodore Clayton's wealth. They were both students – he was studying law and she was an English major – and most of their time was spent either in bed or hitting the books, and there had been little time for discussing their families. Howard had never forgotten how nervous he'd been the first time he'd driven his clapped-out Ford Mustang up to the front of the house, and how dry his mouth had been as he'd rung the doorbell. The wait for the door to open had been one of the longest in his life and it had taken all his self-control not to run back to the car and drive off. Even now, more than a decade later, he had the feeling that he didn't belong and that the door would be slammed in his face.

The house had been designed in the style of Frank Lloyd Wright, a two-storey home which curved around a teardrop-shaped pool. The twelve-bedroom house was made from stone ground on the site which blended perfectly into the desert setting, and had huge windows that took full advantage of the magnificent views of Camelback Mountain. It was a short drive to the Paradise Valley Country Club, where Clayton was a leading light, and he was only minutes away from Arizona's finest golf clubs. To the left of the multi-million dollar home were stables which were twice the size of Howard's own house, and a garage which contained Clayton's collection of old British sports cars.

Howard parked the Jaguar next to Clayton's Rolls-Royce as Lisa checked her make-up again. Jarvis, Clayton's butler since before Lisa was born, opened the door for them and took them into the impressive drawing room where Theodore Clayton was waiting with Jennifer, his second wife.

Lisa's mother lived in Connecticut, supported by five-figure monthly alimony cheques. Howard liked the first Mrs Clayton, whose only mistake had been to grow old, and he and Lisa visited her with the children every few months. But he could see why the industrialist had traded her in for a new model. Jennifer had long blonde hair, perfect skin and the firm figure of a cheerleader. She was wearing a tight white dress, cut low at the front to show her ample cleavage and the large diamond pendant which nestled there. She was, Howard had to admit, absolutely gorgeous, but there was a cold, predatory gleam in her eyes. Often it appeared that she looked right through Howard, as if only men with net assets of more than a million dollars were visible to her ice-blue eyes. She would be absolutely amazing in bed, Howard decided, but her performance would be in direct proportion to the wealth of her lover. It was the money she'd make love to, not the man. Clayton and Jennifer made a perfect couple, and like the horses outside it was as if they were posing for the effect: he with his right hand in the pocket of his blazer, she with her head tilted to tighten her jaw and show off her flawless neck. Clayton stepped forward and hugged Lisa while Jennifer watched with flint-hard eyes. When Clayton released his daughter and shook hands with Howard, Jennifer and Lisa embraced warily with little warmth. They complimented each other on their dresses and their jewellery while Clayton watched them with obvious pleasure. After all, thought Howard, he had paid for it all.

The rest of the guests arrived shortly afterwards: the owner of a local television station and his trophy wife, a white-haired oil man from Texas and a companion young enough to be his granddaughter, and a lawyer from Phoenix who, apart from Howard, was the only one there with a wife close to his own age.

Dinner, as always, was perfect, cooked by Clayton's personal chef and served in the dining room by Jarvis and two maids in black and white uniforms. On the walls were several of Clayton's Navajo rugs, some of them more than a hundred years old. The best of Clayton's collection was on loan to Phoenix's Heard Museum and the Museum of Northern Arizona in Flagstaff. Clayton took great delight in telling his dinner guests how both museums had recently asked him to lend them more. With the top quality rugs worth upwards of $75,000, Howard reckoned that the industrialist was as interested in their investment potential as he was in their artistic quality.

Clayton loved Maine lobster and he took obvious pride in telling his guests that the crustaceans had been flown in from the East Coast on his private jet that morning.

Over coffee the conversation turned to a recent court case where a serial killer had used a camcorder to record the gruesome deaths of his victims and had then sent the tapes to local television stations. Several had refused to show the grisly tapes, but others, including the station owned by the man at Clayton's table, had aired them. When the subject came up, Clayton smiled and nodded at Howard as if to reassure him that he knew the tape of the snipers was to be treated as confidential.

The lawyer suggested that the tapes were evidence of a crime and as such shouldn't be made public as they could prejudice a later trial, an argument which Howard considered valid.

Clayton screwed up his napkin and dropped it on the table in front of him. He nodded fiercely. "This is the video age, and I'm not talking about the rubbish they show on MTV. There are about twenty million camcorders in this country. We're getting to the stage now where there's a camcorder on every street corner. Every time there's a major disaster the camcorders get there first, we're seeing them at crime scenes, plane crashes, car crashes, street fights. They're being admitted in courts as evidence and used in insurance claims, but no-one has really thought through the ramifications of what it means."

He lifted his wine glass to his lips and sipped. No-one interrupted. Clayton liked to sit and pontificate after a good meal, and his guests knew better than to try to spoil his enjoyment. Clayton slowly put the glass back on the starched cloth and gently ran his finger around the rim. He fixed his eyes on the lawyer.

"Eyewitnesses can be cross-examined and their veracity can be challenged, and as you and Cole know, no two witnesses ever see the same thing. That's all going to change. Before long everything that happens in public is going to be recorded on tape, and the video recording will take precedence over all other forms of eyewitness evidence. It started during the LA riots in 1992 and the wave of prosecutions which followed. The camcorder is the silent witness. If you can show a jury a video, they'll believe that over everything else. It's the old truism: a picture is worth a thousand words. When Kennedy was shot, there was one black and white film of it, lousy quality and taken well away from the event. When Reagan took a bullet there was a videocamera there to record it. The next time they try to hit a President, there'll be half a dozen camcorders there, and that's not including the networks' Death Watch cameras. Imagine what that'll mean. Imagine what the Warren Report would have looked like if there had been half a dozen camcorders close to the motorcade in Dallas. Cover-ups become impossible. That's what the video age means. The age of truth."

He looked at Howard as if to make sure that he was listening. "But tapes can be altered, events can be faked," he continued. "And the Government is only now beginning to realise the inherent problems in allowing juries to believe what they see. We're one of several companies working on analysis of video tape, both in terms of improving the quality of recordings and in determining their fidelity."

Howard began to realise that there were other uses for

the technology Theodore Clayton was developing. He knew how keen the CIA and FBI would be to use camcorders to identify trouble makers at civil rights demonstrations, and there were certain to be those in the darker corners of the Pentagon who'd love to be able to use phony videotapes in all sorts of covert operations. Howard knew how easy it would be to blackmail someone who was a threat to Government interests, or how the right sort of tapes could be used to usurp an uncooperative head of state. The hi-tech manipulation of videotape would work both ways: in the hands of the unscrupulous it could become the greatest propaganda weapon of all time. It was already happening to a small extent in advertising, with Coca-Cola using images of long-dead Humphrey Bogart, James Cagney and Louis Armstrong to sell their products. It wasn't too much of a leap to manipulate news broadcasts. Howard remembered the black and white videos he'd seen of 'smart bombs' seeking their targets in the Gulf War, released to the television stations to show how well US technology was performing. True or fake? Howard had no way of knowing, and nor did the viewers. But everyone believed what they saw. Clayton was predicting not an era of truth, but a time of deception and lies, when no-one would be able to trust the evidence of their own eyes.

"So what are you saying, Ted?" asked the lawyer. "Are you saying that anything that's captured on tape should be in the public domain?"

"I think that's happening already," said Clayton. "The most popular shows on television are the so-called reality shows, the ones that follow around police and rescue workers doing their jobs, showing them making arrests and pulling victims out of car wrecks. The public can't get enough of them."

"Maybe the public needs to be protected from its blood lust," said Howard quietly.

"And who'll be the judges of what they should see?" asked Clayton. "Who'll be the censors? The FBI? You want to go back to the Hoover days?" He raised his hand to silence Howard before he could reply. Theodore Clayton preferred to answer his own questions. "No, the floodgates have been opened, I'm afraid. There's no going back."

"And what lies ahead?" asked the television producer.

Clayton grinned. "Ah, Ross, if I only knew. If only I knew." The two maids began clearing the table and Jarvis carried a large gold-inlaid mahogany box over to Clayton. It was his deluxe Trivial Pursuit set, a game he loved with a passion and which he insisted his guests play after wining and dining them. "Everyone ready for a game?" Clayton asked cheerfully.

"Terrific," said Howard as Clayton lifted the lid of the box and took out the board. Lisa kicked him under the table, but not too hard. She knew how much he loathed game-playing.

Kelly Armstrong sashayed into Howard's office unable to control her excitement. Howard was sipping a cup of hot coffee and he put it down on his desk and looked at her with an amused smile on his face. He was still feeling pleased with himself after his and Lisa's victory at Trivial Pursuit the previous evening. It was the first time Clayton and his wife had ever lost, and Howard had been unable to stop grinning all the way home. He was still smiling when he woke up that morning. It would take a lot to spoil his day. "Yes, Kelly, what is it?" he asked.

"I've found the firms that hired the cars!" she gushed. "Two firms, one leased a blue Chrysler Imperial three days before the plane was shot down, another leased a white Imperial two days before. Both cars have been returned."

"Well done," he said, sitting back in his chair. "Do they still have them?"

"The blue one is out with another customer, the white one is still available. And it hasn't been cleaned yet! I've told them to hold it for us."

Howard stood up. "That's the best news I've heard today," he said. "How did you find the companies?"

"Like you said, I contacted all the home addresses of the drivers who'd rented the cars. Two used fake addresses – one of the streets didn't even exist, and both were recently issued licences."

"And the credit cards?"

"Same addresses as the licences. Both cards were recent and are tied to bank accounts here in Phoenix. I'm applying to have access to the account records. With your say-so, of course."

"Of course," said Howard. "Go for it." He handed her copies of the photographs which Clayton had given him. "Then go out and talk to both rental firms. Show them these photographs, see if they recognise anyone."

Kelly scrutinised the pictures. "These are from the video?" she asked.

"They've been computer enhanced," said Howard. "I'm expecting to get improved pictures later this week." As he and Lisa had left Clayton's house, the industrialist had slapped Howard on the back, congratulated him on his unexpected victory at Trivial Pursuit and whispered that his researchers had been working on the tape over the weekend and had made considerable progress. They'd be in touch before the week was out, Clayton had promised.

"Where are the rental companies?" Howard asked Kelly.

"Both here in Phoenix," she said. "There's something else. One of the men wasn't American, the woman who rented out the blue Imperial said she thought he had an accent: Scottish or Australian."

"Interesting," said Howard. He sat down again. "Good work, Kelly. I'll make sure Jake Sheldon gets to hear what a help you've been on this."

Her green eyes widened and a red glow spread across her cheeks and Howard knew without asking that she'd already spoken to Sheldon. Howard's smile tightened and he picked up his coffee. "Thanks, Kelly," he said. He watched her buttocks twitch under her skirt as she left his office and he imagined burying a long, sharp knife between her elegant shoulder blades.

Cole Howard knew that he needed a briefing from someone with sniping experience, someone who could give him an idea of what sort of men he was up against. His office at 201 East Indianola Street was on the fourth floor and immediately below was the Treasury Department of Alcohol, Tobacco and Firearms. Howard knew one of the agents in the department, a fifteen-year veteran called Bradley Caine. Howard rang Caine's extension but got the engaged tone, so rather than wait he took the stairs down and stood at the agent's door until he'd finished his call. The two men shook hands and Howard dropped down into the chair opposite Caine's desk. Caine was a former soldier and he still wore his hair military-style. He was forever suffering from migraine headaches and swallowed aspirin like M & Ms. Without going into details, Howard explained that he needed information on snipers and their weaponry. Caine unscrewed the top of his bottle of aspirin and tossed two into his mouth, swallowing them dry.

"There's a guy in the Phoenix SWAT team, Joe Bocconelli, let me give him a call," said Caine. He held out the aspirin bottle to Howard, who shook his head.

"A bit early for me, Brad," said Howard, with a smile.

Caine shrugged and dialled Bocconelli's number. He put the call on the speaker-phone so that they could both hear him.

Bocconelli's first thought was that Howard needed someone with a military background and Caine nodded in agreement. Bocconelli said that only a very, very special sniper could have shot down a plane with a rifle and he suggested that Howard check with the Marines, or the Navy SEALs. According to the sergeant, there were only about a dozen men in this country who could make a two thousand yard shot and that most of them would be in the military. Bocconelli recommended a sniper who lived in Virginia, not far from the Quantico Marine Corps Air Station where the Marines trained their snipers. Bocconelli had explained that the man, Bud Kratzer, was a former Marine Captain who had retired in 1979 after twenty years' service, most of it as a sniper. He now worked as an independent consultant, selling his military skills to police SWAT teams around the country, and was a frequent visitor to Quantico where he was treated with a respect which bordered on reverence. Bocconelli also said he was on retainer from several counter-terrorist organisations but that details were understandably sketchy. Howard knew Quantico well. The FBI's Academy was there, and so too was its Behavioral Science Unit, the office responsible for psychological profiling of hunted criminals, especially serial killers. Howard scribbled a reminder to himself on a notepad that if all else failed the BSU might give him a clue as to the sort of men who might be involved in the assassination.

Back in his own office, Howard telephoned Kratzer who said he'd be in Washington the following day and that he'd be more than happy to chat with him. Howard had hoped that the former Marine would fly to Phoenix but he said it was out of the question, much as he'd wanted to help. He was going straight from Washington to Germany for a two-week training session with the Kampfschwimmerkompanie, the German equivalent of the Navy SEALs.

Howard caught the redeye flight and he washed and shaved in the men's room at Dulles Airport. Kratzer had suggested they meet at the FBI's headquarters and Howard had readily agreed because visiting Washington would give him a chance to see Andy Kim and find out how he was getting on with his computer simulations. Howard had phoned ahead and arranged for an interview room to be available and given Kratzer's details to reception so that his clearances would be ready.

Kratzer was on time and Howard went down to the

reception area to meet him and escort him up to the interview room on the third floor. He was a big man, not what Howard had expected at all. He'd assumed that snipers were lean, anxious-looking men, the sort who could sit silently for hours in one position before pulling the trigger. Kratzer looked as if he'd be more at home with a pint of beer in one hand and a pizza in the other. He was about six feet six inches tall, and had the physique of a linebacker who'd spent too much time on the bench. There was something amiss with his hair and it took Howard a few minutes to realise that he was wearing some sort of toupee or hair weave and that it was a slightly different colour from Kratzer's own hair. His hair was grey at the sides and back and black on top and Howard had to fight from staring at it.

Kratzer had huge fingers, as massive as bananas: they looked too big to squeeze into a trigger guard. His hands were clenching and unclenching as if he were exercising. "Joe Bocconelli gave you my name, you said?" he asked as they rode up in the elevator.

"Yeah, he's a member of the Phoenix SWAT team. He said he'd been in one of your training programmes a couple of years back."

"Can't say I remember," said Kratzer. "But it was good of him to put you on to me."

The elevator doors hissed open and the two men walked along the corridor to the interview room. "Good of him? Why do you say that?" asked Howard.

"Well, the FBI is going to pay me for this, isn't it? A consulting fee?"

"Well . . ." said Howard, who hadn't expected to be asked for money.

"Because I'll tell you right now, Bud Kratzer doesn't do anything for free. I put in twenty hard years with the Marine Corps for shit money, and now it's payback time. My skills are my pension, and I have to squeeze it for every cent I can. Capish?"

"Loud and clear," said Howard. "Though I was sort of hoping that you'd do it as a public service."

Kratzer stopped and looked at Howard as if to see if he was joking. Suddenly he burst into laughter and slapped Howard on the back. "Hell, and I thought you FBI guys had no sense of humour."

Howard took him along to the interview room and held the door open for him as he tried to guess how much money the former Marine might be talking about. The room contained a large desk and several chairs and Kratzer slid into the largest. He looked at a chunky gold watch on his wrist. "Okay, my meter is running, let's get on with this. What do you want to know?"

"Snipers," said Howard, "I want to know what sort of men they are."

Kratzer leaned back in his chair and looked up at the polystyrene-tiled ceiling. "A sniper is the most cost-effective killing machine there is, and at the same time he's one of the most maligned," he said, speaking as if he were delivering a speech to a large auditorium. "During the Second World War, to kill one enemy soldier the Allied Forces had to fire about twenty-five thousand rounds. In Korea our soldiers had to shoot an average of fifty thousand rounds and by the time Vietnam came around that had jumped to two hundred and fifty thousand. Just think about that, Special Agent Howard, a quarter of a million bullets fired just to kill one VC. And that doesn't include all the bombs we dropped on them. Now, take the sniper. When I was in Nam, our unit averaged 1.5 rounds per kill. For every three bullets we fired, we killed two Victor Charlie. The sniper's the surgeon of the battlefield. He goes in with his rifle, takes out an assigned target, and returns to his base. It's the cleanest form of combat there is. No innocent bystanders get hurt, there's no fallout, no dangerous hardware left behind. Snipers are the élite."

Kratzer lowered his eyes and looked at Howard. "But the generals don't see the sniper as a saviour, they see him as belonging to the dirty tricks department. I've had it said to me by some of our most respected military minds that the snipers are cowards of war, that they shouldn't even be used. These are the same generals who want to spend billions on nuclear weapons. They're prepared to kill civilians on a scale undreamed of, but they don't want to remove one enemy from the battlefield with a single shot. I can see you frowning. You don't follow me?"

"I follow you, but I don't see what point you're trying to make."

"The point is that snipers have to believe in themselves totally. They have to know that what they are doing is right." He reached into his jacket pocket and pulled out a paperback book. He threw it onto the desk in front of Howard who picked it up and looked at the cover. '*Marine Sniper*', it said, and underneath, '93 confirmed kills'.

"You want to get inside the mind of a sniper, read this," said Kratzer. "It's the biography of a guy called Carlos Hathcock, a gunnery sergeant who served with the Marines and did two tours in Nam. A couple of publishers have been after me to write a book like it, but I've never gotten around to it."

"Ninety-three kills?" queried Howard.

"Confirmed kills," said Kratzer. "Those are the ones with witnesses. I got eighteen myself, but I was in Nam towards the end, when we weren't interested in winning. Read that book and you'll have a good idea of how a sniper thinks. The first kill you'll read about is a twelve-year-old boy. The kill he's most proud of is a woman."

Howard looked at the cover: a painting of a man in a bush hat with a rifle pressed to his cheek, his face smeared with camouflage make-up.

"Long Tra'ng the VC called him, because of a white feather he wore in his hat," Kratzer continued. "He was just a kid in Nam, but he was an amazing shot. He once plugged a VC at twenty-five hundred yards."

"Do youngsters usually make the best snipers?" asked Howard.

"Not necessarily," said Kratzer. "They need to be experienced with guns, so country boys are best, especially ones from poor families who have to hunt to supplement the cooking-pot. An empty stomach is the best incentive there is, right?"

"Right," agreed Howard.

"But there's a lot of technical stuff to learn as a military sniper. It's one thing to hunt rabbits with a shotgun, quite another to nail a VC at a thousand yards. It's only with age that you get that experience. I was in my late twenties when I was in Nam. Hathcock was twenty-five, I think. But it's not a skill you lose. There's some stamina involved, but once you've got the technique, and providing you can maintain the level of concentration needed, you could be a world-class sniper well into your forties."

"I was thinking about what you were saying about

conscience. Doesn't it get harder to pull the trigger as you get older?"

Kratzer smiled. He picked up a match off the desk and began to pick his teeth with it. "I'd have no hesitation at all," he said. "I went down on bended knees and begged them to send me to the Gulf. I'd love to have blown away a few ragheads."

Kratzer's eyes widened. Howard had seen the same hungry look in his father-in-law's eyes when he was discussing his latest hunting expedition.

Howard held up the book. A soldier who could kill at twenty-five hundred yards sounded like just the man he was looking for. "This Hathcock, is he still in the Marines?"

Kratzer shook his head. "Bit of a sad story, really. He had to leave the Marines for medical reasons a few months before he'd put in his twenty."

"What was wrong with him?"

"Multiple sclerosis, I think. Shakes all the time. Ironic, isn't it? His main claim to fame was that he could lie perfectly still and shoot a bullet thousands of feet with almost perfect accuracy. Now he can't even lift a beer to his lips without spilling it. There's a lesson there for all of us: when it comes down to it, all you've got is yourself to depend on. You can give your all to an organisation like the Marines but if you're no more use to them, out you go. I tell you, when they call me in to help with their sniper training, they pay through the nose. I'm not giving them the chance to kick me in the balls, no sir."

Kratzer sounded bitter and Howard wondered if he'd also been put under pressure to resign from the Marines. Howard hadn't had much experience with snipers, but it seemed to him that there was something not quite right about Kratzer. He was too overbearing, like a television evangelist.

"What's involved in making a shot of two thousand yards or more?" Howard asked.

"You need a gun that packs a real punch, for a start," said Kratzer, still working at his back molars with the matchstick. "A lot of snipers in Nam used Model-70 Winchesters, .30-06 Springfield calibre, but I wouldn't be happy shooting one beyond a thousand yards. Sometime in the late Sixties, 1967 I think, Marine Corps snipers began using the Remington 700 with an M-40 scope. They used the same 7.62 ammo that the M-14 rifle used but it had more than its fair share of problems, not the least being it wasn't really up to taking the sort of hard knocks a rifle gets out in the field, and neither the stock nor the barrel were camouflaged. The boys at Quantico ended up modifying it to come up with the M-4OAl. It had a modified stock of pressure-moulded fibreglass and a twenty-four-inch stainless-steel barrel with a large diameter. I'll tell you, Agent Howard, with that weapon you could hold your shot group inside a twelve-inch circle at almost fifteen hundred yards. If you were up to it. But for the really long shots we'd use the M-2 .50-calibre machine gun, it's got a stable trajectory for almost three thousand yards. The bullets are so much bigger, you see, 700 grains, so they get more momentum. You could fire one of those babes well over two thousand yards, and with a ten-power telescopic sight like a Lyman or a Unertl you'd have a high degree of accuracy. Maybe not as accurate as the M-40Al, but close. Certainly enough to hit the target and, with the man-stopper bullets, that's all you'd need."

Howard nodded. He had the computer-enhanced

photographs of the Arizona snipers in his briefcase but he wanted to get a general idea of how snipers operated before showing them to Kratzer. "Joe said that only military-trained snipers can make the really long shots."

"Damn right," said Kratzer. He took the matchstick from his mouth, examined the moist end and then chewed it again. "SWAT teams don't have the space, not in the urban environment. But in a war zone, the further you are from the target, the better. You don't want the enemy to hear or see you."

"And long shots create special problems?"

"Sure do. Gravity and wind. When you shoot at point-blank range they're relatively unimportant, but over long distances they're as vital as the type of gun and ammunition. Do you want the short explanation, or the detailed one?"

Howard felt like asking for a price breakdown first, but instead he told the former Marine that he wanted as much detail as possible. Kratzer swung his legs up on the desk. His shoes gleamed as if he'd spent all morning polishing them.

"A bullet is just like a baseball being thrown through the air," he said. "As it travels, gravity pulls it down, so to throw a long distance you have to throw it up and along. It follows a parabolic path, moving up to a peak and then down as it travels through the air. A bullet is the same: the path it travels depends on its initial velocity, the rate it loses velocity, and the distance it has to travel. Over one hundred yards, a 650-grain bullet will probably fall about six inches. So to hit the target you'd have to aim six inches high. And over that distance the bullet's velocity would probably fall from twenty-eight hundred feet per second to about twenty-six eighty feet per second. Over five hundred yards the drop would be about eighty-two inches. Almost seven feet. And the bullet would slow to twenty-one hundred feet per second. Still not much of a change in the velocity."

Howard nodded. He scribbled the numbers into his notebook because he knew he'd never remember them.

"Now, suppose you're trying for the really long shot. Two thousand yards, say. Over that distance the bullet will slow to under a thousand feet per second, about one-third of the velocity it had as it left the barrel of the rifle. And the drop is of the order of two thousand inches."

"Two thousand inches?" said Howard, in disbelief.

Kratzer smiled, pleased by the FBI agent's response. "Uh-huh. That's one hundred and sixty-seven feet," he said, "give or take."

"So you're saying that the sniper would have to aim one hundred and sixty-seven feet above his target?"

"It's not quite as simple as that, because like I said, the bullet follows a parabolic path. And you'd have to take into account if the target was above or below the sniper. But that's the basic idea. Is that what you're after, a sniper who's planning a two thousand yard hit?"

Howard nodded and Kratzer's eyes widened. "You know that it'll take a bullet four seconds to travel that distance?" Kratzer asked. "Four full seconds. He'd have to be sure of his shot, he'd have to know that his target wouldn't move. Even at a slow walk the target could easily get out of the way." Kratzer steepled his fingers under his chin. "It'd be one hell of a long shot," he mused. To Howard, the man sounded almost envious.

"So any sniper attempting such a shot would probably have a number of practice shots first?" asked Howard.

"Absolutely. He'd be crazy not to. But not everything can be planned in advance. A sniper has to be able to calculate the wind velocity in the field at the instant he shoots: he looks for drifting smoke, the movement of grass or the waving of tree branches. There's a sort of Beaufort scale for wind. A wind under three miles an hour, you wouldn't feel it but it'd make smoke drift. Between three and five miles an hour and you'd feel it on your cheek. Between five and eight miles an hour and you'll see leaves on trees moving all the time, between eight and twelve and dust is raised from the ground, and a wind of between twelve and fifteen miles an hour will make small trees sway. Those figures are pretty accurate."

The words were rattling from Kratzer's mouth like bullets, as if the man was charging by the word rather than the minute. Most of the numbers went right by Howard.

"Now, say the range is one thousand yards. You multiply the wind velocity, say it's four, by ten, the range in hundreds of yards. That gives you a figure of forty. You divide that number by a constant, in this case it's ten, and that gives you the number of minutes of angle you have to take into account as the windage factor. Four. You understand about MOA?"

Howard frowned and shook his head.

"MOA is Minute of Angle," explained Kratzer. "It's a measure of the accuracy of a weapon. Basically, if a rifle has one MOA it means that over a hundred yards a test firing will give you a grouping of about one inch. For serious sniping, one MOA is the minimum. Okay, so two clicks on the scope compensate for one minute of angle. Eight clicks puts you right on the target if the windage factor is four. Now, I've made that sound simple."

Howard smiled ruefully. "Yeah, right."

"Back in Nam we either did the sums in our head or used charts we carried with us. These days there are pocket calculators that can work it all out for you."

Howard tapped his notebook with his pen. "It seems to me that there's a dehumanising effect in all this," he said. "The sniper becomes so focused that he's no longer aware of what he's shooting at. The target almost becomes abstract."

Kratzer nodded enthusiastically. "That's probably true," he agreed.

"So to what extent would a sniper concern himself with the nature of the target?"

"I've killed three women, and it doesn't keep me awake at night, if that's what you mean." Kratzer seemed proud of the achievement.

Howard opened his briefcase and handed the photographs to him. "I'd like your opinion on the weapons being used here. And if you recognise any of the faces, I'll not only be amazed, I'll be eternally in your debt."

Kratzer studied the faces. "I see what you mean," he said. "These were taken with a hell of a long lens, right?"

"Something like that," said Howard.

"These three guys were all shooting at the same target?"

"Yeah."

Kratzer tossed one of the pictures back to Howard. "This one was furthest away, right?"

Howard was impressed. The man had picked out the sniper who had been two thousand yards from the dummies. "How did you know?" he asked.

Kratzer grinned. "That there is a Barrett 82Al semi-automatic rifle. Short recoil operated, magazine-fed, air-cooled. Takes .50 calibre ammunition. If my memory serves me well it has a maximum range of more than seven thousand yards but for sniping you wouldn't go much beyond two thousand. It's American made, the firm is based in Virginia, I think."

"It looks almost futuristic."

"Yeah, they used one in the movie *Robocop*. Remember when the terrorists blow up a car with one shot from a rifle? That was a Barrett. It's one hell of a weapon."

"Does the army use it?"

"Yeah, all the armed forces use it. It was responsible for a lot of long-range kills in Iraq and Kuwait during Desert Storm. The UK uses them, too, and they've got them in France, Italy, and Israel, I think. The company'll give you more details, I'm sure."

Kratzer took the photograph back and studied it again. "There's a sniper in the Navy SEALs, name of Rich Lovell. He's an expert shot with the Barrett. I'm not certain, not a hundred per cent, but this might be Lovell. The face isn't clear, but there's something about the way he holds his head when he uses the scope. That could be him."

Howard noted down the name and Kratzer told him where the SEALs were based. They were one of the units happy to pay the former Marine for sniping coaching. "What about the other two weapons? My father-in-law said that one of them might be a Horstkamp."

Kratzer looked at the photographs for some time, chewing the inside of his lip. Eventually he passed over one of them. "Well, I'll be honest, I'm not as sure as I am about the Barrett, but that could be a Horstkamp. It's a much more traditional shape so it's hard to tell. It's used by some SWAT teams, and it's reckoned to get one MOA accuracy beyond one thousand yards."

Howard nodded. "It's German, right?"

Kratzer shook his head. "They're made in Wisconsin, designed and built by a guy called Klaus Horstkamp. They're sort of made-to-measure, so if it turns out to be a Horstkamp it shouldn't be too hard to get a list of owners." He reached over and took the photograph back. "Wait a minute," he said. "See the slots on the muzzle break?" He showed the picture to Howard and pointed at the barrel. "The basic Horstkamp has holes here, not slots. The slots are only on the company's sniper version."

"And the third rifle?"

"No way of telling. Standard profile, it could be any one of a dozen makes."

"Okay, two out of three is better than I expected," said Howard. "Earlier you said that ammunition is important?"

Kratzer nodded. "Factory ammunition isn't consistent enough for really long-distance sniping requirements, so the men you're after probably reload their own. That gives them a much greater degree of control. Both the Barrett and the Horstkamp use .50 calibre ammunition, the sort that's used by the Browning machine gun. It's readily available and I doubt you'll be able to track them down that way."

Howard settled back in his chair and put his notebook back in his pocket.

"Have I been of help?" Kratzer asked.

"A big help," said Howard.

"Do you have a card?"

"Sure," said Howard. He took out his wallet and pulled out one of his business cards. As he handed it to Kratzer a Trivial Pursuit card fell onto the desk.

"You into game-playing, Agent Howard?"

Howard flushed and picked it up. "I hate the game," he said, "with a passion."

Kratzer waved the business card. "Okay if I send my invoice through you?" he asked.

"I guess so," said Howard. "Can you give me an idea of how much it'll be?"

Kratzer sighed. "I usually charge by the full day," he said. "Twelve hundred."

"Twelve hundred dollars a day!" said Howard.

"Plus expenses," said Kratzer.

"Jesus Christ," said Howard. He could only imagine what Jake Sheldon would say when he saw Kratzer's invoice.

Kratzer looked at his watch. "Look, we've only been talking for half an hour, and I'm going to be claiming expenses from the Germans for most of today. I'll invoice you for two hundred dollars, okay?"

"Sounds like a bargain," said Howard, thankfully.

Joker slotted his Visa card into the automated teller machine and keyed in his PIN number. He took out $300, looking quickly over his shoulder to check that he wasn't about to be mugged, and slipped the cash into his wallet. If ever he needed to begin a life of crime, Joker decided he'd start out by hanging around automated bank tellers with a knife. They were a mugger's paradise. The machine spat out a receipt and Joker pocketed it. He had yet to be convinced of the value of the daily withdrawals from a security point of view. He could see how it would allow the

Colonel to know where he was, but it wouldn't help if he got into trouble. He wondered how long it had taken the SAS to realise that Manyon was missing. He wondered, too, what Mary Hennessy was doing to him as the men in Hereford scrutinised the bank records.

He walked to Filbin's, his head down in thought. A black woman with a small child stood in front of him and held her hand out for money. Her eyes were blank and lifeless and the baby was snuffling and coughing. The woman looked as if she was in shock and was making small, rocking movements on the balls of her feet. Joker averted his eyes and stepped around her but was suddenly hit by guilt and he went back. He took ten dollars of the Colonel's money and handed it to her. A skeletally thin hand took it and she mumbled thanks, but didn't look at him. Joker had never in all his life seen so many street people or been asked for money so frequently. It seemed that he could barely walk a hundred yards down any New York street without being asked if he had any spare change. There were men with handwritten signs saying they were homeless, or dying of AIDS, women with sickly children, beggars with dogs, others just lying in doorways with hands extended, palms upward, like heart-attack victims. Joker shuddered.

Filbin's was almost empty, midway between the lunchtime rush and the early evening clientele, and Shorty was the only barman on duty.

"How's it going, Damien?" the barman asked. "Usual?" he added, before Joker could reply. Joker nodded and Shorty placed a double Grouse in front of him. "Any joy?"

Joker shook his head. "Couple of places said they might have something next week, but nothing definite. Cheers." He raised the glass, saluted the barman, and drank half the whisky. He'd told Shorty that he was looking for work and the barman had taken a sympathetic interest in his search. He leaned across the bar conspiratorially, even though there were only two other customers present. "Look, Damien, I might be able to put a little work your way."

"That'd be great, Shorty."

The barman raised a hand. "I'm not promising, you understand, but we're short-handed at the moment and one of our lads is going back to Ireland. I'll have a word with the boss, if you like."

"Would I?" said Joker. "Shorty, you're a lifesaver. You know I haven't got a social security number?"

"Don't let that worry yez," said Shorty with a Puckish grin. "Half the lads who drink in here are in the States illegally. You'll be paid in cash, under the table. No names, no pack drill, know what I mean?"

Joker nodded and finished his whisky. He pushed the empty glass across the bar and Shorty refilled it. "There is one thing, though, Damien. You're going to have to cut back on your intake while yer working, okay?"

Joker grinned and raised his glass to the diminutive barman. "Sure, Shorty. Whatever you say."

Kelly Armstrong flashed her FBI credentials at the young woman behind the reception desk. The name on the badge pinned above the woman's right breast said Tracey.

"Are you Tracey Harrison?" asked Kelly.

"Yes, miss," said Tracey eagerly. "You're the lady from the FBI I spoke to yesterday?"

"That's right. Is there somewhere we can talk?"

"Sure. Just let me get someone to cover for me." She disappeared through a door and returned a few moments later with a middle-aged man whom Kelly took an instant dislike to. He looked her up and down with an expression she'd seen a thousand times before and knew that he was wondering how someone with her looks could be working for the FBI.

"You're a Fed?" he asked, his gaze hovering around her breasts.

"Special Agent Armstrong," she said, holding out the ID.

"Never seen a Fed like you before," he said, looking at her legs.

"I'm sure," she said, tartly. "I'd like a few moments with Miss Harrison, please."

"It's nothing I can help with?" he said. "I'm her superior."

Kelly wanted to laugh in his face because superior was the last description that came to mind: he had a flabby body, pale, flaccid skin and greasy, slicked-back hair and he reminded her of the Italian baker who was always trying to pat her on the butt when she was six years old. Before she could reply, Tracey spoke up. "It's about the cars I rented, Wally."

Wally could barely conceal his disappointment. "Maybe I should sit in on it," he said.

"That won't be necessary," said Kelly. "Can we speak in private, Miss Harrison?"

As Kelly followed Tracey out of the reception area she had to walk by Wally and for an awful moment she flashed back to the sweet aroma of freshly-baked loaves and cakes and the floury smell of the Italian's thick forearms as he twiddled the ends of his moustache and waited for her mother to look the other way before trying to touch her. Kelly looked at Wally, her eyes blazing, and he took an involuntary half-step backwards. Kelly smiled. "Thank you, Wally," she said. "We won't be long."

The office was light and airy with a window which overlooked the car park. The two women sat down and Kelly opened her briefcase and took out a notebook. "The forensic people were here this morning?" she asked.

"That's right," said Tracey. "They've left it a mess, too. Will they come back and clean it? Everything is covered in that white powder they use for fingerprints."

"I think you should leave it as it is for a while," said Kelly, "we might need it for evidence."

"Yeah, that's what the men said, but they couldn't tell me how long it would be."

"I'm sorry," said Kelly. "But I can tell you that we really appreciate your help." She took out a big white envelope and slid out the computer-enhanced photographs which Cole Howard had given her. "Can you look at these for me, see if you recognise anyone?"

Tracey went through the pictures one at a time. She looked up, frowning. "They seem a little out of focus," she said. "Can't you make them any clearer?"

Kelly laughed. "Tracey, you wouldn't believe how much time and trouble we've gone to in order to get to this stage," she said. "I'm afraid that's the best we can do."

Tracey handed back the pictures of the woman. "It certainly wasn't her, it was two guys I saw." Then she passed over the photographs of the bigger man. "He's too big, they were normal build, and younger." She studied the

122

three photographs left which were all of the man who had been standing next to the woman. "Yeah, this could be one of them. His hair was more red than this, though."

"That could be because of the enhancement process," said Kelly. "What about the shape of his face, his build?"

"I think so, yes," said Tracey. "I mean, I can't say for certain, but I'm reasonably sure."

"Was this the one with the accent?"

"That's right. Justin Davies."

"Scottish, you said. Or Australian."

"Well, I've been thinking about that since you called. I'm really not sure what sort of accent it was, you know? They all sound the same."

Kelly nodded. "I know exactly what you mean," she said. "You know the accent is different, but you're not sure how."

"That's right, absolutely," agreed Tracey.

"I thought of a way that might help," said Kelly, taking a tape-recorder out of her briefcase. "I've brought along some recordings of different accents, and I'd like you to listen to them."

Bonnie Kim was waiting for Howard in the reception area of the FBI's Washington research centre and she took him along to her laboratory where her husband was hard at work on one of her computers.

"Cole, good to see you again," said Andy, pumping the FBI agent's arm in a hearty handshake.

"I didn't realise you were working here," said Howard,

sitting down on one of the stools in front of the workbench.

"We thought it best," explained Bonnie. "In view of what the video shows, we felt it should stay on FBI property."

"My professor said he was quite happy for me to work here for a while," added Andy.

"Did you tell him what you were working on?" asked Howard.

"Only that the FBI had an application for my computer modelling. I told him that it was classified at the moment but that I should be able to get a paper out of it in the not-too-distant future."

"Good," said Howard. "How's it going?"

Andy pushed his spectacles up his nose. "I've almost finished the sniping model," he said. Bonnie stood behind him and put a hand on his shoulder.

"He hasn't left the lab in two days," she said.

Andy smiled and shrugged. "The hardest part was the measurements," he said. "That laser measuring device you got from the Highways Department was a godsend." His hands moved across the keyboard. For the first time Howard noticed how small and delicate they were. The computer monitor cleared and three yellow dots appeared, each about the size of a dime. "These are the snipers," Andy explained. "To get the complete image on the screen I'm using a scale of about three hundred feet per inch." He punched more keys and four blue circles appeared in a row on the far right of the screen. "These are the targets," he said. "For the purposes of the model I'm assuming it's the figure second from the right which is the assigned target. They're so close together that over the distances we're looking at it won't make much difference which of them it is. Okay?"

"Sounds fine to me, Andy." Howard watched as thin white lines joined the yellow circles to the blue circles. "Again, I'm making another assumption here and that's that the bullets go straight from the rifles to the target. You probably know that that's not actually the case and that they follow a parabolic path, but for what we're doing that doesn't make any difference. There you have it." Andy sat back from the screen while Howard looked at the geometrical shape formed by the seven circles and three lines. Andy smiled and flicked his unkempt hair from his eyes. "It doesn't look much different from what I did for you on my micro at home, does it?" he said.

"That's just what I was thinking," said Howard.

"You've got to remember that it's not the shapes and colours that are important – it's the distances and the angles. What you're seeing here is an accurate representation of what went down in the desert."

It sounded to Howard as if the mathematician was trying to justify all the hard work he'd put into the project, so he smiled reassuringly. "I understand, Andy. So where do we go from here?"

"Now we have to input the locations where you think the target might be, using the same scale. Actually, that's not so important because we can change the scale pretty easily once it's in the computer's memory. For an example I've done the White House and the area around it." He took a floppy disc and slotted it into one of the disc drives. The computer made a growling noise as the information was transferred to the main hard disc. "Okay, so this is my representation of the White House," said Andy, his fingers stabbing at the keys. A small line-drawing of the

President's home appeared on the screen, surrounded by lawns. "Now, I'll reduce that to the same scale as we used for the snipers, and bring in the roads and buildings within a two thousand yard range." The image changed and as it shrank in size it seemed more realistic. It looked like an architect's drawing, and Howard appreciated how much work had gone into it. He understood why Andy hadn't gone home in two days.

"Okay, now I'll superimpose the model of the snipers on the White House," said Andy. "I'll put the four figures in the Oval Office, but I can tell you now it doesn't make any difference. You'll see why in a minute."

He hit more keys and the circles and lines appeared over the line-drawings. Andy turned away from the screen. "See, no matter how we rotate the snipers around the White House, at no point do all of them coincide with buildings in the vicinity. I can say for a fact that they weren't practising to shoot the President in the White House."

Howard watched the circles and lines slowly pivot around the building. Only once per revolution did one of the small yellow dots intersect with a building, and when it did the two others were suspended in space. "Andy, this is terrific," said Howard. "Really terrific." He leant forward and studied the screen. It would work, he realised. It would actually work. "How long did it take you to input the buildings?"

Andy took off his spectacles and rubbed his eyes while Bonnie stood behind him and gently massaged his shoulders. "That's the sticking point," he said. "It took me twenty-four hours of solid programming." He saw Howard's face fall and held up his hands. "I know, I know, we don't have the time. I'm working on a way to speed it up, using a scanner, so that the computer can take in the maps and floor plans itself and reduce them to scale."

"What about getting them directly from the city's Zoning and Planning Department? Won't they have their own records computerised?"

Andy slapped his forehead. "Of course!" he said. "Why didn't I think of that?" He looked at his watch. "I'll get onto it right now."

"Use my name, and if there are any problems tell them to check with Jake Sheldon's office in Phoenix," said Howard.

"Wait a minute," said Bonnie, "which cities do we concentrate on?"

"Good point," said Howard. "Washington is obviously the place to start. I'll get in touch with the Secret Service and see if I can get some sort of itinerary."

Bonnie stroked the back of Andy's neck. "But first you must go home and sleep," she said.

He shook her off. "No, this is too important. I've got work to do. I'll sleep tonight, once I've spoken to City Hall."

Matthew Bailey put his feet up on the chair opposite his own and sipped at his Budweiser as he watched a boat disgorge a group of scuba divers onto the quay. The divers were a mixed group: half a dozen young men with military haircuts, a handful of Oriental tourists with underwater video cameras, a middle-aged couple with matching wetsuits, two pot-bellied balding guys who seemed to be instructors, and a stunning blonde girl who wore a bikini several sizes too small and who was not exactly oblivious to the lustful looks she was attracting.

"Prick-teaser," he whispered to himself, though his thoughts were on Mary Hennessy and not the blonde on the boat. He put his glass down on the white circular table and ran his finger slowly around the rim. On the quay below, the divers were washing their gear in a large black plastic tank of water. As the blonde bent over, her breasts almost sprang free of her bikini top. "Bitch," murmured Bailey. He ran the back of his arm over his forehead and wiped the sweat from his brow. It was in the low nineties and his white skin didn't take kindly to the sun. He hadn't wanted to leave Mary Hennessy but she had been insistent and Bailey found it difficult to oppose her in anything. He'd done as she'd said and headed for Orlando, even visited Disneyworld, but had soon grown bored.

He'd hired a car using another of the licences supplied through the IRA's New York contacts and headed south, driving through Miami to the Florida Keys, the line of tiny islands hanging from the tip of Florida like a string of pearls. He'd booked into the Marina del Mar Hotel in Key Largo, the largest of the islands and the one closest to the mainland, and spent his days at Gilligan's Bar, drinking and brooding. There had been something different about Mary when they'd met at the airport, something in the way she'd smiled at him and touched his hand. Bailey had lusted after her for months, but she'd always kept the relationship on a purely business level. However, in the cafeteria he'd felt for the first time that there was the possibility of something sexual between them. Bailey felt himself grow harder under the table and he closed his eyes and squeezed his thighs together as he remembered the way she'd swung her hips as she'd left his table. God, she had the greatest figure: long, shapely legs, tight buttocks, a trim waist and breasts that he ached to touch. He opened his eyes again and saw the blonde leaning over to pick up a weight belt and dip it into the water tank. Her breasts swayed forward and from his vantage point on the balcony Bailey could see her nipples. The girl looked up suddenly and saw Bailey watching her. She smiled, and leant forward further to give him an even better view. Bailey grinned and raised his glass to her. "Prick-teaser," he mouthed, knowing that she wouldn't be able to read his lips from down on the quay. She averted her eyes, pulled the weight belt clear of the water and began to pick up the rest of her gear. One of the instructors rushed to help her.

The blonde must have been about half Mary's age, but she didn't come close to her in desirability, Bailey realised. All the girl had in her favour was a young body whereas Mary had experience, confidence, and a natural sexuality that turned heads wherever she went. The instructor placed a proprietary hand on the blonde's shoulder and her laughter wafted up to the balcony. Bailey drained his glass and a waitress in white shorts and halter top appeared at his shoulder and asked if he wanted another. Bailey shook his head. Three of the weak American beers were more than enough.

Bailey walked back to his room, feeling rivulets of sweat trickle down his back under his cotton shirt. When he opened the door to his room, cold air billowed out and chilled his perspiration. He'd left the air-conditioner switched on, knowing that if he didn't it would be like returning to an oven. He closed the door behind him and drew the blinds. He put his sunglasses on top of the television set and stood at the end of the double bed, closing his eyes as he breathed in the chilled air. Images of Mary Hennessy filled his head: her soft brown eyes which glistened when she laughed, her tanned, muscular legs, her fine, shining hair, now dyed blonde, her pert nose and perfect white teeth. And her firm, inviting breasts. Bailey arched his back and ran his hands down the front of his shorts. He could feel how hard he'd become and he gripped himself. He shuddered and dropped down onto the bed, pulling down his zipper as he whispered Mary's name to himself, over and over again.

Cole Howard read the book Kratzer had given him on the flight back to Phoenix. The lack of emotion when the sniper described the kills was chilling. Howard had never had to draw his FBI weapon in anger, and despite all his training he knew that when the time came for him to fire his gun his mind would be in turmoil. He'd seen the damage bullets could do to human flesh, and the emotional problems suffered by agents who'd had to pull the trigger. Howard knew that he didn't have what it took to be a sniper, he cared about people too much. A sniper had to be cold and mechanical. A killing machine.

The cab dropped Howard in front of the nondescript brick building which housed the FBI's offices. There was no indication from the outside that the building housed the bureau and other federal agencies. Howard paid the fare and got out of the cab. He looked up at the tinted-glass windows. Reflections of clouds scudded across the dark glass. An unshaven man in a stained T-shirt was sitting on the porch of one of the ramshackle wooden houses opposite. He scratched his expanding stomach and drank beer from a bottle before wiping his mouth with the back of his hand. Howard's throat was dry and he massaged his neck.

When he got back to his office there was a message on his desk asking him to go up and see Jake Sheldon. He found Kelly Armstrong already in with the director, her legs neatly crossed showing shapely calves and expensive high heels. She flashed him a condescending smile and then turned back to Sheldon.

"Take a seat," said Sheldon, waving Howard to the chair next to Kelly. Kelly moved her chair sideways as Howard sat down as if distancing herself from him. "Kelly was just filling me in on your progress," Sheldon continued. Howard smiled tightly. The computer-enhanced pictures were spread out across Sheldon's desk.

"The young one, the one without the radio, used the name Justin Davies on a credit card and driving licence when he booked a rental car," said Kelly. "His prints were in the car and on the rental agreement he signed. We're running the prints through our files now. The other credit card and licence were in the name of Peter Arnold but there were no prints on his rental agreement, or his car. His was the car that had been cleaned."

"And we can definitely place those cars at the scene?" Howard asked.

Kelly nodded. "Forensics had made casts of the tyre tracks they found close to what was left of the towers and we have a match with the rental cars."

Howard nodded thoughtfully, barely managing to conceal his annoyance. Kelly should have reported to him before briefing Sheldon. "Were the car hire people able to identify any of the photographs?" he asked.

"No, the pictures from the video were too blurred to be of any real help," Kelly said.

Sheldon turned to Howard. "Did you have any luck with your sniping expert?"

Howard nodded. "It looks as if we're dealing with military-trained snipers. And I've a possible identification of two rifles involved."

"How will that help?" asked Sheldon.

"Snipers have favourite weapons, it seems," said Howard. "And one of the rifles, a Barrett it's called, is quite unusual. I've got the name of a SEAL sniper who is an expert with that weapon. I'm planning to approach all the armed forces for any snipers not accounted for."

"It's a pity we can't do more with the photographs," said Sheldon. "From what Kelly tells me, even the improved ones your father-in-law has supplied aren't clear enough to make a positive identification."

"He tells me his researchers should have something more for me sometime this week," said Howard. "We're also tracking down the credit cards used to hire the car, right, Kelly?"

"Already in hand," said Kelly. "The Justin Davies credit card was used to buy a one-way ticket to Los Angeles on US Air and for a number of purchases since. We're concentrating the search in California."

Howard gave them a rundown on his meeting with Andy Kim and Sheldon agreed to contact the Washington office and request that as many computer programmers as possible be seconded to the laboratory. "We're going to need more manpower here in Phoenix, too," he added. "I'm going to get McGrath to help Kelly out on the credit card side," Sheldon said to Howard. "Do you need any help?"

Howard thought for a moment, then shook his head. "I can handle it," he said. "Though I'd like to make contact myself with the Secret Service's White House office."

Sheldon agreed. "Let me speak to them first," he said. "The Secret Service is always a bit touchy where protocol is concerned. I'll get someone to call you." He leant back in his chair. "Right, let's get to it." He smiled warmly at the two agents, though Howard had the distinct impression that it was meant more for Kelly than for him.

Joker pulled the metal tab on a can of Guinness and sipped the dark brew as he watched the game. Gaelic football took the most aggressive aspects of soccer, rugby and all-in wrestling and was played as much for the physical contact as for the score. The lunchtime matches in the park in the Bronx were a magnet for New York's Irish community, and for those native New Yorkers who appreciated the finer points of grown men knocking the shit out of each other. It was a warm day and Joker had unbuttoned his pea jacket. Birds were singing in the tree branches overhead and he'd actually seen people smiling in the street as if they realised that summer wasn't too far away. Joker walked over to a wooden bench and sat down next to a man in a blue anorak who was reading a newspaper. The man looked up as if defending his territory and Joker smiled and raised his can.

"Do yer mind if I sit here?" he asked. The man shook his head and went back to his paper. Joker concentrated on the game. Most of the shouts he heard, from the players and from the spectators, were Irish, and he saw several bottles of Irish whiskey being handed around.

Joker wasn't due behind the bar at Filbin's until three o'clock and so he'd decided to leave Manhattan and cross to the Bronx. It was a pleasant enough borough in places and in some ways it reminded him of Glasgow, struggling to outgrow an image of deprivation and poverty which it no longer deserved. He'd spent most of his teenage years in Glasgow, and learnt to love it despite its rough edges, but it seemed that whenever he talked about the city to those who had never been there, the talk always turned to the Gorbals and the razor gangs. Joker had grown tired of explaining that the decaying tenement blocks of the Gorbals had long been torn down and that the bad guys in Glasgow now carried automatic weapons like bad guys everywhere.

Joker took a mouthful of Guinness and swallowed slowly, enjoying the taste and feel of the thick, malty brew. Joker had read that pregnant mothers used to be given a half pint of the Irish stout when they were in British hospitals, it was so full of vitamins and goodness. As he drank he looked over at the paper his neighbour was reading. It was the *Belfast Telegraph*. Joker began reading the headlines and the man looked up, an angry frown on his face. Joker looked away. He stood up and walked around the pitch, scanning faces and listening to accents, trying to pick up any information which would give him a lead to Matthew Bailey's whereabouts. He recognised two men from Filbin's; he didn't know their names but the tall one with a black, bushy beard and thick eyebrows drank vodka and tonic, the other, red-faced with a paunch that drooped over his belt, preferred Guinness with an occasional malt whisky. One of them waved him over and he joined them. They both knew him by name and they chatted like old drinking buddies. Joker had another can of Guinness in his coat pocket and he offered it to them. The Guinness drinker accepted with a mock bow while the other bemoaned Joker for not carrying vodka and tonic with him. "What sort of fockin' barman are yez anyway?" he laughed.

Joker confessed that he'd forgotten their names and they introduced themselves: the Guinness drinker was Tom, the other was Billy. As it always did when strangers from Belfast met, the conversation soon turned to the basics: where you went to school, where you lived, and who your family were. The answers to the three questions identified your religion, your politics, and your social standing, and woe betide the Protestant who supplied the wrong answers to a gathering of Catholics, and vice versa. Joker's cover story was as ingrained as his real childhood, and he had no trouble convincing the two men that he was a working-class Catholic who'd left Belfast for Glasgow while still a teenager.

"What brings you to New York?" Billy asked.

"I was being paid under the table for the past couple of years, and the taxman got on my case," said Joker, watching the teams run back onto the pitch. "Thought I'd lie low for a while."

"Aye, it's in a terrible state, the British economy," said Tom, wiping white froth from his lips with the back of his hand. "Mind you, it's not so great here. Yer wuz lucky getting the job at the bar, right enough."

"Yeah, that was a break," Joker agreed. "Friend of mine

called me some time back, saying it was a good pub to hang out in." He took a long pull at his Guinness and kept his eyes on the pitch as the game restarted. "Maybe you know him. Matthew Bailey."

Both men shook their heads. "Can't say the name rings a bell," said Tom.

Billy leant forward conspiratorially. "Was he one of the boys?" he asked. He moved back and held up a hand. "Not that I'm prying, yez understand. It's just that sometimes we have visitors who are a mite flexible about their names and origins, if yez get my drift."

"Aye, I know what yer mean," said Joker. "Better forget I asked. The telephone number he gave me has been disconnected, so I guess he's moved on." He stayed drinking and chatting with the two men until two-thirty, then wished them well and headed back to Manhattan. On the way to Filbin's he used his Visa card in an automatic teller machine, withdrawing another $300 and slipping it into his wallet.

Cole Howard's phone rang. "Agent Howard?" asked a crisp authoritative voice.

"Speaking," said Howard. He had the photographs of the snipers spread out on his desk in front of him.

"My name's Bob Sanger, I'm head of the Secret Service's Intelligence Division. I've just been speaking to your boss; he said we should make contact."

"Sounds good to me," said Howard. "Where are you?"

Howard heard Sanger snort as if suppressing a laugh.

"At the moment I'm about thirty thousand feet above San Bernardino en route to Andrews Air Force Base," he said. Howard was surprised. The line was perfectly clear as if the call had been placed from the next room. "Can you get to the airport by ten-thirty?"

"Andrews?" said Howard, confused. He heard the snort again.

"No, Sky Harbour International," he said, referring to the main international airport in Phoenix.

Howard looked at his wristwatch. It was just after 10 a.m. "Sure," he said. He'd been assuming that he'd have to fly out to Washington to meet with the Secret Service representative. The opportunity of seeing him in Phoenix was a bonus.

"Come along to the General Aviation terminal, ask for me there," said Sanger.

"Which plane will you be on?" Howard asked, reaching for a pen.

Sanger made the soft snorting sound again. "Don't worry, Agent Howard," he said. "You'll have no trouble finding us."

The line went dead, leaving Howard wondering what the Secret Service man had meant. He collected his car from the office parking lot and drove quickly to the airport, parking in front of the General Aviation terminal. As the electronic doors hissed open to allow him into the terminal building, he saw a line of airport workers and passengers standing in front of the large picture window which overlooked the tarmac. As he walked up to them he realised with a jolt what they were looking at. Standing alone was a majestic Jumbo Jet, resplendent in a blue and white livery with the gold and black presidential seal on its belly. Air

Force One. The spectators stood in silence, awed by the glistening symbol of Presidential authority. The plane was in pristine condition as if it had just rolled off the Boeing assembly line. Howard stood behind two baggage handlers and watched as a team of overalled workers busied themselves refuelling the jet. They were being supervised by two men in dark suits wearing sunglasses and carrying walkie-talkies.

Howard frowned as he studied the plane. The President had no official visit scheduled for Phoenix that he knew of, and the FBI would have been informed as a matter of course. He headed for the doors which led to the tarmac. His way was barred by two more Secret Service agents, wearing matching sunglasses and black suits. Howard identified himself before reaching slowly into his jacket to pull out his ID. Both agents tensed and the one on the right, the younger of the two, began to move his hand towards his waist. Howard smiled and slowed his movements, opening the wallet and showing his FBI credentials.

The older agent carefully checked the ID. "Are you carrying, sir?" he asked. Howard shook his head. The agents relaxed and stepped to the side. The younger pushed open the door for Howard, his face unsmiling.

"Bob Sanger's waiting for you on board, sir," said the older agent. "Have a nice day."

As Howard walked across the tarmac to the gleaming jet, he heard the younger agent talking into his walkie-talkie. There were half a dozen agents standing at various points around the plane and several looked at Howard as if they were checking him out. They had earpieces from which wires disappeared into the collars of their jackets. A gust of wind blew the back of one agent's jacket up around his waist and Howard caught a glimpse of a machine pistol in a nylon holster in the small of his back. Even Howard, an eight-year veteran of the FBI, felt nervous under the scrutiny of the stone-faced men in dark suits.

The giant plane epitomised the power and the glory of the United States of America, both in its sheer size and its technological superiority, and it pulled at his insides the way the National Anthem and the raising of the Stars and Stripes always did. It was more than patriotism, more than pride, it was an instinctive reaction that he couldn't have controlled if he'd wanted to. He felt as if he should salute the plane, or bow his head in reverence.

A flight of stairs led up to the main hatch and another Secret Service man stood at the bottom, a walkie-talkie in his hand. He motioned for Howard to go up the steps. They seemed to go on for ever and Howard began to truly appreciate the immense size of the plane. Yet another agent waited at the top of the stairs and he led Howard down a corridor to a large meeting room with eight white leather seats surrounding a boat-shaped mahogany table. A man in his mid-forties was sitting in one of the high-backed chairs, a walkie-talkie and a computer printout on the table in front of him. Unlike the rest of the Secret Service agents, he wore a pair of delicate pince-nez eyeglasses and had hung his jacket over the back of his chair. As Howard entered the room the man looked over the top of his glasses like a college professor disturbed in the middle of correcting papers. He smiled and removed the spectacles. "Agent Howard?" he asked. Howard nodded and the man stood up and shook his hand, introducing himself as Bob Sanger. He waved Howard to one of the empty seats as the agent closed the door, leaving the two men alone.

"Is the President here?" Howard asked, his voice almost a whisper.

Sanger smiled and shook his head. "No, he's on the back-up plane today. This is SAM 28000, it's been in for repairs to one of the communication systems, so the President has been using SAM 29000 for the last few weeks. They're identical, though. In fact, right now the President is probably sitting in the duplicate of my chair."

Howard looked around the plush room. "I can't believe I'm having a meeting on Air Force One."

Sanger sat back in his chair. "Strictly speaking, it's only Air Force One when the President is on board. At the moment this is just a Boeing 747-200B with a presidential paint job. The President is due to visit Los Angeles in a couple of weeks and we've been putting the security teams there through their paces. As you can imagine, we're still nervous about LA, after what happened in 1992."

Howard nodded. He looked out of one of the windows and saw the refuelling teams move away from the plane. One of the men in overalls waved goodbye to a Secret Service agent but he was ignored. Several of the agents walked up the stairs to the plane, talking into their radios.

"We're dropping into Dallas for a threat assessment meeting with the head of security there, and then we're onto Washington," Sanger continued. He saw the look of alarm flash across Howard's face. "Don't worry, Agent Howard, you're not coming with us. The pilot's under instructions to hold until you leave the plane. Do you want a coffee?" Howard shook his head. "Okay," continued Sanger, "let's get down to business. Jake tells me you think there's going to be an attack on the President."

"He told you about the video?"

"He did. Do you have it with you?"

Howard took it out of his jacket pocket and held it out to Sanger. The Secret Service man pointed to a television console and VCR and Howard went over to it and slotted in the cassette. Sanger removed his glasses and the two men watched the video in silence. When it had finished Sanger began polishing his glasses with a white linen handkerchief. "Have you identified the snipers yet?"

"No, but we think they are military-trained. Navy SEALs, maybe."

Sanger raised his eyebrows. "What makes you think that?"

"The types of weapons they're using, and the distances involved."

Sanger nodded. "Okay, I'll run through our quarterlies for you, to see if we've any military snipers."

"Quarterlies?" said Howard.

"We keep a close eye on anyone who has ever threatened the President; it's our equivalent of your Most Wanted List, but it's a lot longer. We've about five hundred names on it at the moment, and our agents visit them every three months. That's why we call them quarterlies. We've a watch list too, with approaching ten thousand names on it, but they're not visited on such a regular basis. What we do is cross-check the names on the lists with hotel registers and company payrolls in the areas where the President is due to visit. If we get a match, we interview them and if necessary remove them for the duration of the visit. We'll check the watch list for your snipers, too, of course, but to be honest they're generally all talk. It's the quarterlies we worry about."

"I doubt if the men we're looking for would have written

141

threatening letters," said Howard. "They seemed too professional for that."

"I agree," said Sanger, "but until you give us a name or a photo to go on, there isn't much else we can do."

"We're working on better pictures of the snipers," continued Howard. "We've some computer experts trying to digitally enhance the video." Howard leant forward. "There is another reason I wanted to make contact with you. We might have a way of identifying where the snipers plan to carry out their hit." He briefly explained Andy Kim's scheme as Sanger continued to polish his spectacles.

Sanger appeared impressed. "That's one hell of an idea," he said. "Our computer boys might want to take a look at his program."

"I'm sure he'd be more than happy to show them," said Howard. "He's very keen to help. What he needs now is the President's itinerary for the next few months. We already have his official functions, but we need a more detailed itinerary: every appointment, every route, even the private functions. If Andy can program them into his computer model, he can see if there are any scenarios which match the rehearsal."

Sanger put his glasses back on and looked at Howard over the top of the lenses. "How secure is this Mr Kim?" he asked.

"He's a mathematics PhD at Georgetown University. His wife works for us as a computer researcher. Andy Kim is okay."

"He'd better be," said Sanger. "We wouldn't want the President's itinerary getting into the wrong hands, would we?"

Howard smiled. "I'll take the responsibility," he said.

Sanger also smiled, but there was little warmth in it. "I'm glad to hear that, but responsibility isn't the issue. The President's safety is. Who else but Kim is involved?"

"His wife. And we're seconding four or five of our programmers to work with him. The itinerary won't leave our labs, all the work will be done there."

"The lab is in Washington?" asked Sanger. Howard nodded. "I've a suggestion," continued Sanger. "Why don't Kim and the programmers move over to our offices in the White House? We've all the computing power they could need. I presume all his programs can be put on disc and brought over?"

"I suppose so," said Howard. "That could work."

"Good," said Sanger. "That's agreed, then. Anything else I can help you with?"

"I have a question," said Howard.

"Shoot," said Sanger. He grinned. "If you'll forgive the pun."

"Are you planning to beef up security?"

"Because of what happened in Arizona? The straight answer is no. Not because we don't take the threat seriously, but because the President is already the most protected man on this planet. Every city he goes to is swept clear of potential trouble-makers before he even sets foot there, no-one gets near him without being checked by one of our agents. We have helicopters overhead, we have our men on the ground, and we have an intelligence network second to none."

Howard listened to the Sanger lecture, but all he could think of was the attempted assassination of Ronald Reagan when he was President, shot by a boy for no other reason than to impress a Hollywood actress, despite being surrounded by the men in black sunglasses. He felt that Sanger was being too dismissive of the snipers, but knew that he still didn't have enough information to press the panic button.

"You know how many death threats the President of the United States receives each month?" Sanger asked. Howard shook his head. "It never amounts to fewer than three figures," said the Secret Service chief. "Some are written, some are phoned in, some actually walk into the White House and start shouting. We investigate them all, but we don't pull the President out of the public eye each time there's a threat. He'd never attend a public function if we did."

"But this is different," said Howard, "this is being planned like a military operation."

"That's true. But you can't yet say when or where they're going to strike. And from what Jake told me, you're not even sure that the President is the target. Am I right?" Reluctantly, Howard agreed. Sanger sensed Howard's reluctance and he leaned forward. "Only a madman would think it worth killing the President," he said. "There is nothing to gain – the Vice-President's policies wouldn't differ one iota from the policies of the incumbent. This is not a JFK situation."

"And a madman wouldn't be able to plan an operation of this complexity; is that what you're saying?"

"That's it exactly. The sort of assassination attempts we've seen in recent years have all been the lone madman type, either attention-seekers or psychopaths. There have been no organised assassination attempts, no conspiracies. That's the reason for my scepticism. Who would want to kill the President? The Russians are our allies now, even

Castro is looking to build bridges. The Iraqis, the Iranians, all our old enemies are keen to start trading with us again. No, I believe a major hit is being planned, but I don't think for one minute that the President is the target." He held up his hands. "I'm not saying I won't offer you every facility; I'd be a fool if I refused to help. But unless you give something harder, I won't be cancelling any of his appearances."

"That's understood," said Howard. He knew that the Secret Service man was right. Crying wolf wouldn't help anyone's long-term career prospects.

"Having said that, if your computer model does indeed match any of the Presidential venues, well, that's a whole new ball game. Look, I'll be in DC tonight, call my office tomorrow and we'll arrange for Kim and your programmers to come over. The sooner we get started, the better."

Sanger stood up and held out his hand. The two men shook. "Do you smoke?" Sanger asked. Howard said he didn't but Sanger handed over two packets of cigarettes and a book of matches, each with a large Presidential seal on them. "Take these anyway," he said, "souvenirs of Air Force One."

As Howard stepped off the stairway and onto the tarmac the men in black suits were walking back from the terminal, looking at their watches and whispering into their walkie-talkies. The huge jet engines began to whine and by the time he was starting his car the 747 was rolling majestically down the taxiway.

* * *

The two men sat in the darkened room, watching the television monitor. The picture was black and white, though the image was being recorded in colour. On the table next to the video-recorder were two large reel-to-reel tape-recorders, the tapes hissing slightly as they passed over the recording heads. One of the men, tall and thin with sandy hair and a sallow complexion, was lounging in a deck chair and holding a pair of headphones in his lap, while the other, overweight with slicked-back black hair, stood behind the camcorder on its tripod and looked down its long lens, through the Venetian blinds at the street below.

Everything was automatic, all the men had to do was to replace the videotape every eight hours and to change the audio tapes every ninety minutes. Most of the time there was only one man in the room, but it was just before three o'clock in the afternoon, the time when they changed shifts, and Don Clutesi, the man at the window, had decided to stay on for a few minutes to chat with Frank Sullivan.

The camcorder was trained on the bar across the street from the apartment block they were in, and had been for the last three months. The electronic eavesdropping devices were a recent addition: one had been inserted into the telephone by the men's room, the other was inside a power socket behind the bar. Both had been installed by FBI technicians after they'd engineered a power blackout of the whole block one Friday afternoon.

Sullivan took off the headphones. "That's the new guy," he said, looking at the monitor. Clutesi squinted at the figure walking along the sidewalk, his shoulders hunched and his hands thrust deep into the pockets of his sailor's pea jacket. "His name's O'Brien, Damien O'Brien."

"Irish?" asked Clutesi.

"British passport, but born in Belfast. We're running the details through our London liaison office."

"Green card?"

"No, tourist. He came in through JFK on March 17 and INS gave him a six-month B2 visa. He shouldn't be working."

Clutesi chuckled. "Was he expected?"

"Apparently not. He visited the bar a few times as a customer and then Shorty hired him as a barman."

"And we've nothing on him?"

"Not as Damien O'Brien, that's for sure. And we haven't got a match with any photographs yet. We're trying to get a new face from the Academy to go in and get a glass for prints, but it's taking time to arrange."

Clutesi nodded. "Yeah, but those Paddies can smell a Fed a mile off. We need a youngster, someone fresh. We can't rush it." He watched as the man in the pea jacket pushed open the door and went inside, then turned round to face his colleague. "What do you think?"

Sullivan shrugged. "Could be on the lam from the Brits. We'll know soon enough." He slid the headphones back on and leaned back in the deck-chair.

"I'm going," Clutesi mouthed, pointing at the door. "See you tomorrow." Sullivan gave him a thumbs-up. He was listening to Shorty tell a particularly dirty story about two Protestant farmers and a sheep.

Andy Kim drove the red Cherokee Laredo up to the barrier and wound down his window. "I can't believe this, I really can't believe this," he said to his wife.

"I know, I have to keep pinching myself," Bonnie whispered. She giggled, but stopped abruptly when a guard appeared at Andy's window, a clipboard in his hand.

"Andy Kim and Bonnie Kim," said Andy, before the guard could speak. "We're expected. We're supposed to go to the West Wing."

Bonnie leaned over and showed her FBI credentials to the unsmiling guard. He nodded and consulted his clipboard and then waved to a colleague to raise the barrier. "Park in bay 56, someone will meet you there," he said brusquely and handed them both temporary visitor badges.

Andy nudged the vehicle down the driveway and wound up the window. "Friendly," he said to Bonnie.

"They're not paid to be friendly, I suppose," she replied.

They both looked to the left as they headed slowly down the driveway. The White House gleamed in the afternoon sun as if it had been freshly painted. The grass surrounding the building seemed unnaturally green, like Astroturf, though the operating sprinklers suggested that it was the genuine article. "My parents brought me here as a kid, just after they got citizenship," said Andy. "We queued for two hours in August, so they could see the house where the President lived. 'Our President' they kept saying, as if he was their personal representative. They were so proud that they could finally call themselves Americans." He saw the bay where they were to park and he edged the car between a convertible white Saab and a black Lincoln. "We were herded through the public rooms like sheep, they barely gave us time to see anything because of the lines outside." He switched off the engine and looked across at his wife. "They'd have been so proud of what we're doing now.

Actually working at the White House, helping the President."

Bonnie wanted to take her husband in her arms and squeeze him. His parents had died in a car crash shortly before his seventeenth birthday and she knew that the thing he missed more than anything was not having them there to see how successful he was becoming and how all their financial sacrifices had paid off. He wanted so badly for them to be proud of him, but the drunken driver at the wheel of the overloaded truck had robbed him of that. "They'd have been proud," she said, reaching over to hold his hand.

"I hope so," he said. He held her gaze for a moment and then winked. "Come on, let's get to it."

They climbed out of the four-wheel drive vehicle and Andy began pulling the cardboard boxes off the back seat. They'd brought several hard disks, Bonnie's CD and back-up copies of all the programs they'd been using. As Andy stacked the boxes on the asphalt, a thin young man with a military hair cut and pockmarked cheeks, wearing a blue blazer and grey slacks, walked up. He introduced himself as Rick Palmer, a former Army programmer on attachment to the White House, and he helped them carry the boxes. He'd spoken earlier to the Kims to ensure that there would be no equipment compatibility problems, but this was the first time they'd met. He took them through a side entrance, past a uniformed guard who scrutinised their badges. "I'll have personal IDs fixed up for you by this evening," Palmer promised as he took them to the sub-ground level of the West Wing. They walked by signs identifying the White House Communications Centre and the Situation Room. Palmer pushed open a door with his shoulder and led the Kims into a white-walled office. "This is home," he said, placing the boxes he'd been carrying onto one of the four desks in the room. Each of the desks had an IBM computer and a telephone. "It was part of the secretarial pool but Bob Sanger had it requisitioned for you. Well, for us, actually, I'll be working with you."

"Great," said Andy.

"We've another five programmers coming," said Bonnie. "We'll have to bring in more desks. And terminals."

"Let me know what you need," said Palmer. "These terminals are hooked into our mainframe, I'll take you along to see it later. I think you'll be impressed." He rubbed his hands and nodded at the CD which Bonnie was unpacking. "Okay, let's see what you've got."

Cole Howard flew from Phoenix to San Diego and drove a rental car south to Coronado. It was warm and sunny and he had the windows down as he drove along Highway 75. The buildings which housed the Naval Amphibious Base were south of the town. Across from the base were more buildings and as Howard drew closer he could see an obstacle course made up of various log structures like half-finished mountain cabins, and beyond it a long ribbon-like stretch of beach. A group of men in white T-shirts and shorts were running along the beach with what appeared to be a telephone pole held above their heads.

The rating who checked Howard's credentials at the gate looked to be about sixteen years old, tall and gawky with a bad case of acne. He cross-checked Howard's name with a list of approved visitors and directed him to the visitors' car park.

Rich Lovell's former squad leader was a big man, well over six feet and built like a heavyweight boxer. When he shook hands with Howard, the FBI agent felt like a child being gripped by an adult. The features on his egg-shaped head all seemed larger than life: big blue eyes, a wide forehead and thick lips which covered gleaming, chunky teeth. His name was Sam Tucker and he spoke with a slow, Texas drawl. He was wearing immaculately pressed khakis and a dress blouse with his single bar ensign tabs on his collar. He took Howard through to a cramped office and waved him to a chair.

"I mentioned you were coming to my XO, and he said he'd like to be present, Agent Howard."

"XO?" said Howard.

"Executive officer," explained Tucker. "Lieutenant Walsh. I said I'd call him when you arrived."

"Sure, that's fine by me," said Howard.

The ensign picked up the phone and called the lieutenant. After saying "Aye-aye, sir" crisply a few times he replaced the receiver and stood up. "XO said you might appreciate an orientation tour, and then he'd like to see us in his office."

Howard nodded. He told Tucker that he knew little about the work of the Navy SEALs and he'd appreciate the background. They decided to use Howard's car and they drove out of the base and across Highway 75 to a cluster of concrete buildings which Tucker said housed the SEAL training centre. They parked and Tucker led the FBI agent to the Phil. H. Bucklew Centre for Naval Special Warfare and into the main hall. Tucker waved at a collection of photographs on the walls. "These are all the classes that have graduated from Coronado," he explained. "You've chosen a good time to visit. We're halfway through Hell Week."

"Hell Week?"

"Yeah, the first phase of SEAL training is a seven-week conditioning programme – mainly running and swimming. The fourth week is where we push them to their limits – we call it Hell Week. If they get through Hell Week, they've a good chance of making it. By the end of Hell Week, two out of three have dropped out."

Howard's jaw dropped. "That's one hell of a cut," he said.

"It's worse than that," said Tucker, grinning. "Only one in five actually graduates from the full twenty-six-week course. We only take the best of the best. You can easily spot the ones who have still to pass Hell Week – they're wearing white T-shirts. Once they're through Hell Week they wear green."

The two men walked through to a central courtyard of asphalt. "We call this the Grinder," said Tucker; "it's where we do our drills." He took Howard over to a brass bell which was fixed to a post. "All the men are volunteers," he said. "Any time they want to drop out, all they have to do is ring this bell."

"How tough is the training?" Howard asked.

"By the end of the first phase we've worked them up to running four miles in under thirty-two minutes, swimming a mile in the bay without fins in seventy minutes, a two-mile ocean swim with fins in ninety-five minutes, and they can swim fifty yards underwater. We keep them going twelve hours a day. The academic work is tough, too, we teach them first aid, reconnaissance and lifesaving."

"I saw some men running with a telephone pole on the beach."

"That's right, we do a lot of log work. It builds team spirit. Same with the IBS, we make them take the IBS with them wherever they go."

"IBS?"

"Inflatable boat, small," said Tucker. "It weighs almost 300 pounds and is twelve feet long. The men have to carry it wherever they go and make sure it's not damaged or deflated. Teamwork's probably more important in the SEALs than any other branch of the services. Your life can often depend on the man next to you. One mistake when you're a hundred feet underwater in a war zone and you're dead."

"Rich Lovell, was he a good team player?" Howard asked.

Tucker shaded his eyes with one of his big, square hands. "XO said we should wait until we get to his office before we discuss the reason for your visit, sir," he said.

Howard nodded and realised it wasn't worth pressing the ensign. "There's another SEAL base in Virginia, right?"

"That's right, at Little Creek. SEAL Teams One, Three and Five are here, Two, Four and Eight are at Little Creek."

"With SEAL Team Six?"

"The Mob, you mean," smiled Tucker. "They're a law unto themselves. Even their manning levels are classified. They train separately, and they report directly to the Secretary of Defence and the White House."

"Counter-terrorism, right?"

"That's it, and other dirty work. They were originally taken from SEAL Two, but now it's only their admin which is at Little Creek. They spend a lot of time playing with Delta Force. You interested in Six?"

Howard shrugged. "Just curious. You read about them occasionally, I just wondered what they were like."

"Mad bastards, most of them," said Tucker. "You wouldn't want your sister to marry one."

"I'll remember that," said Howard. "What's the operational set-up here?"

The ensign headed towards the tallest building in the compound. "The basic unit is a platoon, twelve enlisted men and two officers. A platoon has two squads of six men each with an officer. I'm a squad leader. Each SEAL Team has fourteen platoons, plus a headquarters platoon."

They reached the building and Tucker led Howard inside. "This is our dive tower, which allows us to train our divers down to a depth of fifty feet," the ensign explained. They watched a group of SEALs practising swimming up from the bottom without their tanks. "Our motto is 'The only easy day was yesterday' and that's the truth," said Tucker. "It was the hardest six weeks of my life, believe me." Tucker looked at his watch. "XO'll be waiting. We'd better go."

They drove back to the camp and Tucker led the way down a battleship-grey corridor to the executive officer's office, which was several times larger than Tucker's own, and considerably tidier. Walsh was in full naval uniform, with not a speck of lint on the dark blue material. He was a complete contrast to the squad leader, about five feet nine with swarthy skin, dark, hooded eyes and a clipped New York accent. He seemed eager to help, and sat back in his chair with his fingers steepled under his chin as Howard explained that he was trying to track down Rich Lovell. As

154

he talked, Tucker stood with his back to the wall, almost at attention.

"Can you tell me what the FBI's interest in Lovell is?" asked Walsh.

"At this stage we're just making preliminary inquiries," said Howard.

"Which is as polite a way of stonewalling as I've heard," said Walsh, with a smile. "Anyway, as Ensign Tucker has already told you, Lovell left SEAL Team Three some eighteen months ago."

"How long was he with the SEALs?"

"Twelve years."

"On what basis did he leave?"

"I don't follow you," said Walsh.

"Honourable discharge?"

"Ah, I see what you mean," said Walsh. "The decision to leave was his; can I put it that way?"

"Which is as polite a way of stonewalling as I've heard," said Howard.

Walsh laughed, and Tucker smiled. "*Touché*," said Walsh. He fingered a class ring as he studied the FBI agent. "Seaman Lovell left with an honourable discharge, but we didn't try to dissuade him from leaving. You know that he was a sniper?" Howard nodded. "Lovell was trained in all aspects of SEAL work: underwater demolition, parachuting, reconnaissance, the works. But his speciality was sniping. He was the best sniper in the SEALs. He served with distinction in Operation Desert Storm, but he found it harder to function efficiently in peace-time."

Howard nodded. "There wouldn't be much use for his skills, I suppose," he said.

"That's the case with all our men," said Walsh. "Ensign

Tucker gave you the tour, right?"

Howard nodded.

"We give them the most testing training exercises you can imagine," Walsh continued. "We keep them at the peak of their abilities, but we can't give them the real thing. It's not like the British SAS, they can keep their skills sharpened by taking on the IRA. The Germans have the Red Army Faction and what's left of the Baader-Meinhof gang, the French have to deal with Basque terrorists, the Italians have the Red Brigade. We don't have home-grown terrorists, during peace-time our men are like Formula One racing cars with the engine running and nowhere to go."

"And Lovell couldn't cope with it?"

"Ensign Tucker can brief you on that better than I," said Walsh. "I've only been with SEAL Three for eighteen months." Walsh looked over at the ensign, who nodded curtly.

"In my opinion, he was finding it progressively more difficult to cope," said Tucker. "Snipers are a breed apart. It's like no other form of warfare. Killing in the heat of battle isn't difficult, Agent Howard. The body's self-defence mechanism takes over and you kill without thinking. It's kill or be killed. It's easy to stab a man in the stomach if he's coming at you with a knife. But a sniper kills from a distance, he's usually in no danger himself, yet he gets to see the victim close up. The sniper looks through his scope and sees the eyes of his victim. You have to be a special sort of man to kill like that and to stay sane. Seaman Lovell, like all of our snipers, underwent regular psychiatric evaluation, and it became clear from them that he was no longer performing effectively. That's not to say he wasn't as accurate or as effective a sniper. He was. If anything, he was getting better."

"So what was wrong?"

Tucker sucked air in through clenched teeth. "I think he missed it."

"Combat?"

Tucker shook his head. "The killing. Combat we could offer, even if it was make-believe, but we couldn't allow him to kill."

"But how was that a problem?" asked Howard.

Tucker smiled tightly. "Shooting targets wasn't enough for him any more," said the ensign. "He'd developed a taste for hunting humans. He kept talking about it, describing kills he'd made, relishing the details."

"War stories?"

"More than war stories, much more," said Tucker. "He was becoming obsessive. Don't take it from me, take a look at the psychiatric reports."

Howard looked across at the lieutenant. "Can that be arranged?"

"I'll have the BUPERS file sent to you," said Walsh.

"BUPERS?" Howard felt that he was constantly having to ask the SEALs to explain their jargon. Like most groups, they used a verbal shorthand to exclude outsiders. He understood, and didn't object, because that was exactly the way FBI agents and cops operated.

"Sorry, it stands for Bureau of Personnel. Their file should have everything you want."

"What sort of operations was he involved in? You mentioned Desert Storm?"

Tucker took a step forward. "Lovell was in one of two platoons of East Coast SEALs who were sent into Kuwait prior to the invasion by the Allied Forces. He recorded

STEPHEN LEATHER

twenty-eight confirmed hits, but much of the time he was working alone and so many went unrecorded. He claims to have killed more than fifty, most of them high-ranking Iraqi officers."

"What weapon did he use?"

"Barrett Model 82," said Tucker.

"Was it after Desert Storm that he began to have psychological problems?"

Tucker looked uneasy. "I think it would be safer to say that Desert Storm opened a door for him, and he didn't want to close it. It was the first time he'd actually killed a man with his rifle."

"And he enjoyed it?"

"I don't think enjoy is the right word. It was a challenge, a way of testing himself. And after the Gulf War, he no longer felt his abilities were being tested to the full. On his return to California he made several requests to be transferred to Seal Team Six. He was refused. There isn't much love lost between SEALs on the West Coast and those on the East Coast. That's when the psychiatrists began to express concern about him continuing on active service."

"Was he especially close to anyone in the SEAL unit? Someone I could talk to?"

"His dive buddy was Lou Schoelen, another sniper," said Tucker.

"Can I see him?"

"He quit, about two months after Lovell left."

Howard wrote the name down in his notebook. "Can I see his BUPERS file, too?" he asked Walsh.

"Of course," said the Lieutenant. "There's no indication that the two resignations were connected, though."

158

"You said he was a sniper. Did he also use the Barrett?"

Walsh looked at Tucker, who shook his head. "No, Schoelen preferred a Horstkamp."

Howard's ears pricked up at the mention of the rifle type. "What sort of man is Schoelen?" he asked.

"A bit of a loose cannon," said Tucker, "but a damn good SEAL. The only real blot on his record was his phone-hacking. He was originally trained in electronics by the Navy and he used his specialist knowledge to abuse the phone system. The phone company caught him selling little black boxes which let you dial around the world for the cost of a local call and they wanted to prosecute. We managed to persuade them to let us handle it internally." He grinned. "He suffered on the Grinder, believe me."

"Is there anyone else Lovell was close to?"

"Not really," said Tucker. "They were both pretty much lone wolves. Like I told you earlier, normally we stress teamwork in the SEAL units, but snipers are always loners. It goes with the territory."

"How good a sniper was Lovell?"

Tucker shrugged. "He was the best I've ever seen. He can consistently hit a target at two thousand yards with his Barrett. Probably further, it's just that it's harder to find ranges beyond that distance. He claimed to have taken out an Iraqi colonel at more than three thousand yards in the desert. There were no witnesses, though."

"Three thousand yards?" said Walsh. "I never heard that. That's damn near two miles. No sniper can make a two-mile shot."

"That's what he said, sir," said Tucker. "And he rarely exaggerated."

"Was Schoelen as good a sniper as Lovell?"

"Almost. I mean, he's a world-class marksman, but Lovell is something else."

Howard took the photograph of the sniper with the Barrett rifle from his pocket and handed it to Walsh. "I know the quality isn't very good, but is this Lovell?"

Walsh held the picture at arm's length and slowly brought it closer to his face. He squinted his eyes, frowned, and shrugged. "That could be anyone, Agent Howard," he said.

"Yeah, I'm sorry, it was taken from a long distance away and we've had to blow it up."

Walsh handed the picture to the ensign. "Is the face in shadow or is that a beard?" Tucker asked.

"We think it's a beard," said Howard.

"Lovell didn't have a beard, not while he was here. We don't allow facial hair, it gets in the way of the mask. But he could have grown it after he left, of course." He narrowed his eyes as he scrutinised the photograph. "I can tell you one thing, that's definitely a Barrett in his hands. There's no mistaking its profile."

"Yeah, that's what put me on to him," said Howard. "I showed it to another sniper who recognised it and said that it was Lovell's favourite weapon." Howard rubbed his chin. "This might sound a crazy question, but I don't suppose he took his rifle with him, did he?"

The two SEALs laughed. "I hardly think so," said Walsh.

"Out of the question," agreed Tucker, "but you can buy them through most firearms dealers."

"Do you have any idea what he's doing now?" Both men shook their heads. "Do you think he might be selling his skills?"

"What, you mean as a mercenary?" asked Walsh.

"Yeah, that sort of thing."

Walsh and Tucker looked at each other, then back to the FBI agent. "It's possible," said Walsh.

"Would he be concerned about the nature of the target?"

"I would say not," said Walsh.

Howard looked at Tucker for confirmation. The ensign nodded in agreement. Howard paused, tapping his pen on his notebook. "This last question is hypothetical, and I wouldn't want it repeated outside this room. But I have to know exactly what I'm up against, I have to know what Lovell is capable of." Both men stared at Howard, waiting for him to finish. "If he was paid enough, would Rich Lovell shoot the President?"

"Jesus Christ," whispered Tucker.

"Based on what I've read in his file, I would say it's a possibility," said the lieutenant.

"Oh yes," said Tucker. "Definitely."

Rich Lovell's BUPERS file listed his last address as an apartment block on the outskirts of Coronado, a ten-minute drive from the SEALs training compound. Howard sat in his car, read through the file, and examined the photograph of Lovell. The former SEAL had an unnaturally thin face as if giant fingers had pinched his head at birth. He wasn't surprised to find that Lovell no longer lived at the apartment. His knock on the door was answered by a teenage girl with dilated pupils and the spaced-out stare of an intravenous drug user. A Grateful Dead record was playing in the background. Realising that the girl would probably freeze if she knew that there was an FBI agent on her doorstep, Howard slipped his credentials back into his pocket and told her that he was an old friend of Lovell's. In a slow, faraway voice she told him that Lovell had left a year ago, that she'd never met him and that mail had stopped arriving about six months earlier.

"Did he leave a forwarding address?" Howard asked. He heard a voice from within the apartment and a bearded man appeared at the girl's shoulder. He also had blank eyes and smelled like he could do with a bath.

"Who are you?" he asked, sticking his head forward.

"He's a friend of that guy who used to live here," the girl explained.

"He looks like a cop," said the man.

"A lot of people say that," said Howard.

"Yeah, well he doesn't live here any more," the man said and moved to close the door.

Howard put his foot against the door and kept it wedged open. "Did he leave anything behind?"

"No," said the girl.

"That's a cop's question," said the man, pushing harder.

"If I was a cop, I'd be in there with a warrant," said Howard, coldly. "And if you don't stop behaving like an asshole I'll make sure they do pay you a visit." The man mumbled something incoherent and moved away. Howard smiled at the girl. "Who's your landlord?"

"Why?" she asked, frowning.

"I just want to know if the landlord has a forwarding address, that's all."

The furrows on the girl's brow deepened as if she was having trouble understanding him, then she nodded. She left the doorway and disappeared back into the apartment. Howard slowly pushed the door open with his foot. The apartment was a mess, with clothes strewn across the furniture and dirty plates and fast-food cartons piled high on a table. The bearded man was sprawled on a sofa, one arm across his face as if shielding his eyes from what little sunlight fought its way through the grimy windows. The girl returned with a piece of paper torn from a notebook on which she'd scrawled a number. She thrust it at him and closed the door.

According to the BUPERS file on Lou Schoelen, Lovell's diving buddy lived with his parents in a section of Coronado best described as belonging to poor white trash. The house was a single-storey building which was badly in need of repainting. A rusting Ford pick-up was standing in the driveway, its tailgate held closed with string. The untidy lawn, which was parched and turning brown in places, was surrounded by a chain-link fence. On the fence was a large, handwritten sign warning 'Beware of the Dog'. Howard slowed his car as he drove by and a large Rottweiler sitting on the grass stared at him. Howard decided not to go knocking on the door, instead he drove to a telephone booth and called the number in the BUPERS file. An old woman answered and Howard guessed it was Schoelen's mother. Her accent was Germanic and she spoke slowly as if she had trouble forming sentences. Howard told her he was an old friend from the Navy and Lou had always insisted that he drop by if ever he passed through Coronado. The woman was apologetic and said that her son was working in California and that she wasn't expecting him back for at least three months. Howard asked if she had a number for him but she said he was moving around. When she asked for his name, Howard pretended not to hear her and hung up. He had several more quarters so he called Lovell's former landlord from the public phone. He wasn't surprised to find that Lovell hadn't given a forwarding address.

Before catching the plane back to Phoenix, Howard telephoned the office to tell Kelly about Lovell and Schoelen and to give her the names and account numbers of the banks into which the Navy had paid their monthly salary cheques. He doubted that the two men would have been foolish enough to continue using the accounts, but he couldn't afford not to check. It was surprising how often it was the little things which ended up with a name being crossed off the bureau's Ten Most Wanted list.

"Bad news about the Peter Arnold and Justin Davies credit cards," she said.

"What's the problem?" asked Howard.

"I asked for a breakdown of the purchases and they've just arrived. Gold jewellery, television sets, video-recorders, stereo equipment. Not the sort of things that a terrorist would buy."

"But exactly the sort of shopping list a homeboy with a stolen card would have," said Howard.

"Just what I was thinking," she said. "Sheldon says we should just pull them in."

"I agree," said Howard. He told her when he'd be back in the office and hung up. He ran a hand through his hair, mentally cursing Kelly Armstrong. It seemed that every time he left the office she took the opportunity to go running to see Jake Sheldon. She was one hell of an ambitious woman and Howard had the feeling she didn't care overmuch who she had to step over to get to the top.

He made one final call – to his wife. She wasn't at home

and so he left a message on the answering machine telling her which flight he'd be on and that she wasn't to worry, his car was at the airport and he'd drive himself home.

Mr Oh handed the old woman a receipt and wished her a good day. As she carried the Nintendo game system out of the shop, Mr Oh saw the two black youths standing at the window, looking in. They were pointing at a portable CD player, the latest Panasonic. They were wearing brand new black leather jackets and expensive Reeboks and had lots of gold chains and bracelets. They looked too young to be pimps, thought Mr Oh. More likely they were drug dealers. He sighed and waited for them to decide if they were going to buy or not. Mr Oh didn't like his customers much, even though he depended on them for his livelihood. He didn't have enough capital to open a store in the more prosperous areas of Los Angeles so until he could amass enough savings he was restricted to the black areas to the east of the city. Premises were relatively cheap, though security was a problem. Mr Oh had been robbed at gunpoint twice, and now he kept a small automatic taped under the counter.

His wife sat behind another counter at the far side of the shop reading a Korean newspaper. She glanced up at the two teenagers as they walked into the shop and then she returned to her newspaper.

"How can I help you?" asked Mr Oh.

One of the teenagers nodded towards the window. "Yeah, we wanna see the boom box in the window, the one with the CD player."

"It's $649," said Mr Oh.

The teenager thrust his chin forward. "We've got money," he said. Mr Oh went to the window display. "These fucking Koreans, they've got a real attitude," said one of the boys.

"Yeah, you don't get no respect, that's for sure," said the other.

Mr Oh snorted. He wanted to tell them that respect was something that had to be earned, and that it was hard to respect people who did nothing more productive than hang around on street corners, sell drugs and shoot each other. Mr Oh hated East Los Angeles with a vengeance. His shop had been looted during the 1992 riots and he had given serious thought to moving to the East Coast, where race relations weren't as heated as they were in LA. If his eldest daughter hadn't been in her second year of law school the family would have probably moved. Eventually he had decided to stay put, to refurbish the shop and restock it, but he had never got over the bitterness and resentment. The people who came to his store had to be tolerated, that was all. He carried the CD player over to them and put it down in front of them. "This latest model, very good," he said.

"Yeah, right," said one of the teenagers.

"We'll take it," said the other, handing over an American Express card.

Mr Oh took the plastic card over to his cash register and swiped it through his card reader. As he waited for confirmation that the card was good he looked at a special bulletin of names and numbers by the side of the register. His eyes widened when he saw the name Justin Davies. He checked the number on the card and it matched. His palms began to sweat. He pressed the cancel button on the card reader and called his wife over. The teenagers looked across at him.

"There a problem, man?" one asked.

"No, no problem," said Mr Oh. "Machine slow today, that's all." He spoke to his wife rapidly in Korean, asking her to handle the transaction while he phoned the police from the back office. Mrs Oh smiled at the men as she swiped the card a second time.

The Colonel's private line buzzed and he picked it up, motioning to the bulky sergeant that he could go. He waited for the soldier to close the door behind him before speaking. The man on the end of the line didn't identify himself, and neither did the Colonel.

"Our friends in the Big Apple have been asking questions about Damien O'Brien," said the voice.

"Nothing worrying, I hope?" said the Colonel.

"Seems routine," said the voice. "Surveillance pictures, passport details courtesy of INS, and a set of prints, taken off a Budweiser bottle of all things. General request for information with a copy to the RUC and a request that we cross-check with CRO."

"It's good to see them on the ball," said the Colonel. "When will they get their reply?"

"Thought we'd sit on it for a day or two. Pressure of work, you know."

"They'll understand, they've had their own cutbacks to deal with."

"Sign of the times," said the voice. "Thought you'd appreciate the call, anyway."

"Absolutely," said the Colonel. "Hopefully that'll be the end of their interest."

"I would hope so," agreed the voice. "I'll keep in touch."

The line went dead and the Colonel replaced his receiver, a tight smile on his face. So far, so good.

The phone on the bedside table rang, startling Cole Howard awake. He grabbed at the receiver but before he could reach it, Lisa answered it on one of the downstairs extensions. Howard squinted at the clock-radio. It was seven-thirty. He rubbed his eyes and groaned. Lisa had a golf game at eight o'clock and as usual she'd slipped silently out of bed without wakening him.

He heard her walk down the wooden-floored hallway and stop at the bottom of the stairs. "Cole!" she called. "It's Daddy!"

Howard picked up the receiver. "Good morning, Ted," he said.

"Still in bed?" asked Clayton. Theodore Clayton made it a point of principle to be at his desk before anyone else in his company. He claimed it was because he could get more work done in the early hours, but Howard suspected it was because it gave him the opportunity to go through his employees' offices.

"Late night," lied Howard. "What's up?"

"My computer guys have something they'd like to show

you. Seems they've made something of a breakthrough using one of their programs."

Howard sat up and ran a hand through his messed hair. "Great. Where do I go?"

"Come to our labs. I'll arrange for your clearance, just tell the gate you want to go to the Image Processing and Research Labs, they'll tell you where to go. Ask for Jody Wyman."

Howard repeated the name. "This morning?" he asked.

"If you can make it," said Clayton. "Cole," he said, his voice almost hesitant. "When you meet Wyman, don't be put off by the way he looks, okay? You have to make allowances for his appearance and his attitude. He's a creative type, right?"

"Right," said Howard, intrigued. An hour later he was walking down a white-walled corridor which seemed to be pulsating from the sound of a Led Zeppelin track being played at full blast. Clipped to his breast pocket was a visitor's pass which gave him access to the section where Wyman worked and nowhere else. Sensors embedded in each door detected a magnetic coding on the pass and it had been explained to him that all sorts of alarms would ring if he tried to pass through a door without it or if he entered an unauthorised area.

He found a door with a plastic plate with two names on it: Jody Wyman, PhD, and Bill McDowall, PhD. The pulsating beat was coming from behind the door, and Howard knocked hard. The door swung open and the music billowed out, along with the distinctive sweet smell of marijuana. Howard saw two men standing with their backs to him, rocking their heads backwards and forwards and strumming imaginary guitars. Their laboratory was almost a carbon copy of the one Bonnie Kim worked in, though it seemed to have more equipment. Like Bonnie Kim's it had no windows.

Howard stepped into the laboratory and closed the door. The two men failed to notice him. Their whole bodies were rocking in time with the music. They began a synchronised side-step and then as one they turned round, eyes closed, fingers strumming, mouths open, hair flying. A joint was smouldering in a glass ashtray next to a laser printer. The track came to an end and the two men opened their eyes, looks of rapture on their faces. They appeared to be in their twenties but looked like refugees from the hippy era: sweatshirts, Levis which had faded at the knees, and leather sandals. Both had several days' growth of beard.

Their eyes widened as they realised they weren't alone in the lab. One of them began to speak but before he could say anything the next track began and Howard couldn't hear him. The other man rushed over to a CD player and switched it off. "Sorry," he mumbled. "We gotta have a Led Zep injection or we can't get any work done."

"It's sort of like brain flossing," said his colleague. He squinted at Howard. "Er, who are you?"

"Cole Howard," said Howard. He waited a beat. "Of the FBI."

The guy who'd switched off the CD player looked guiltily at the ashtray. The other man stepped forward, his hand extended. Howard noticed he was wearing a mood ring. He hadn't seen one since the Sixties. It was green, but Howard couldn't remember what that signified. "I'm Wyman," the man said. "How's it going?"

As they shook hands, Howard saw the other man frantically stub out the joint and toss it into a wastepaper bin. "This is Bill McDowall," said Wyman. "He's been helping me with the video."

Howard shook hands with McDowall, whose hands were hot and sweaty. "It's a pleasure," said Howard, holding McDowall's gaze just long enough so that he'd know that it wasn't too bright an idea to be smoking pot when expecting a visit from the FBI.

"You want a Bud?" asked Wyman, opening the door to a refrigerator and taking out a can. When Howard refused, Wyman popped the can and took a sip.

"What about a coffee?" asked McDowall. "It's from a machine, I'm afraid."

"Coffee would be good. Cream, no sugar," said Howard. McDowall fumbled in his pocket then shrugged shamefacedly. "No change," he said. Howard dug into his pockets and handed over some quarters. As McDowall wandered out into the corridor, Wyman pushed a chair in front of a computer terminal and motioned for him to sit.

"Clayton showed you the pictures we did already?" Wyman asked. Howard nodded. "I think you're gonna be pleased with what we've done," said Wyman. His fingers played across the keyboard. "We've left it all on the computer, it'll only take us a minute to print out the pictures you want." He switched on a large monitor and a picture flickered onto the screen. It was the middle-aged balding man who was holding the walkie-talkie. Howard's face fell. The quality appeared no better than the photographs Clayton had given him.

"This was the stage we were at before the weekend," said Wyman. Howard felt a wave of relief wash over him. "We went pretty much the same route as the guy you used."

"Girl," corrected Howard. "Bonnie Kim."

"Okay. Well we did the neighbourhood averaging thing, but then we took it further by running a few pixel aggregation programs through the blurred areas. That gave us some more definition, but as you probably realised, the improvement was marginal at best."

"Clayton said you'd compensated for the movement of the plane," said Howard.

"Yeah, that was the main improvement; I'm surprised the Kim girl didn't try it."

"She was pushed for time," said Howard. He felt a sudden urge to protect Bonnie Kim from the man's snide comments. "You said you'd taken it further?"

Wyman brushed his hair behind his ears in a feminine gesture that was at odds with the facial hair and bitten nails. His fingers began pecking at keys. "We used a version of the Hough Transform, and the Fourier Transform. Did the Kim girl tell you about them? They detect relationships between pixels."

"I'm not sure," said Howard.

Wyman grinned. McDowall returned carrying a plastic cup of coffee. Howard took it. He noticed that it was black but didn't say anything. McDowall leaned against a bench and watched Wyman stabbing at the keyboard.

The screen went blank and then the picture of the man with the walkie-talkie appeared, but this time it was as clear as if he'd been photographed from six feet away. Howard was stunned. "My God," he breathed.

"Pretty good, huh?" said Wyman.

"How did you manage that?" whispered Howard, moving closer to the screen. The picture was as sharp as any he'd ever seen on a television. The man had black hair which was receding, and a thick, black moustache. If the

172

FBI had the man on file, there would be no problems in obtaining a match and a positive identification.

"I told you he'd be impressed," Wyman said to McDowall. He turned to look at the FBI agent. "I'm not surprised that your people didn't know about this stuff – most of it is classified. We've been developing it for the military and it requires huge amounts of computing power. The program effectively analyses every single point on the picture and carries out several complicated calculations for it. We set it up on Friday and had it running over the weekend."

"Don't forget to tell him about the spatial-domain program," said McDowall.

Wyman turned around in his seat, grinning. "You think he'd understand? Jeez, man, I barely understand it." The two men sniggered like schoolchildren.

"We could explain about the spatial masks we generated from the frequency-domain specifications," said McDowall. He giggled girlishly.

"Yeah, right," laughed Wyman. Howard resented being the butt of their humour, but he knew he needed their specialist knowledge. "How many did you do?" asked Howard. He sipped his coffee and then pulled a face when he realised it had sugar in it.

"About a dozen," said Wyman. "We picked out what we thought you'd want the most – the guys on the ground and the snipers. But if there's anything else you want you can let us know and we'll have it within a couple of days." He pecked at more keys and the picture of the balding man was replaced by the young man with glasses. It was as sharp as the first image.

"Amazing," said Howard, under his breath. Wyman

went through the rest of the pictures he'd worked on: the woman, the snipers, the vehicles, the towers. All of them were perfectly in focus and the detail was phenomenal. He could clearly see a small, crescent-shaped scar on the cheek of one of the snipers. On the original video the sniper had been little more than a blur.

Wyman sat back in his chair, grinning proudly. "You should see some of the stuff we get," he said. "They make your video look like a Hollywood movie."

"Who else do you do this for?" Howard asked.

Wyman grinned. "Military, CIA, DEA, you name it, they all want what we're developing," he said. "They just don't know it yet. We can pick a face out of a crowd at several thousand yards. We did some work for the LAPD after the riots . . ."

"Yeah, but they wouldn't let us near the Rodney King video," interrupted McDowall, sniggering. "I never understood that."

"Yeah, the video tape doesn't lie," sneered Wyman.

Howard frowned. The two computer experts were clearly on a different wavelength, possibly a different planet. "I don't follow you," he said.

The two men looked at each other as if deciding whether or not to let him in on a dirty secret. "What do you think, do you think he'd appreciate it?" asked Wyman.

McDowall shrugged. "He's a Fed. He might tell."

Wyman grinned. "We could delete the evidence. If a tree falls . . ."

The two men laughed again. Eventually Wyman stopped giggling and waved Howard over to another terminal. "We shouldn't be showing you this, but it might give you an idea of what video and computer imaging is capable of," he said.

"You'll understand why you can't believe the evidence of your own eyes any more. And why we think it's so funny whenever anyone says that video can't lie. Jesus, they go and watch *The Terminator* and accept that the special effects are computer-generated, then they see a news video and they automatically believe that it's the truth. It's yet to sink in that you can't believe a photograph or video any more. They're too easy to fake."

"Yeah, what about the Caroline Perot pictures, remember them?" said McDowall. "Ross Perot pulled out of the presidential race in July 1992 after he heard that pictures of his daughter were being circulated. We were given them to analyse. They were fakes, but good. Really good work." He grinned at Wyman. "So good that we had a pretty good idea where they came from."

Wyman nodded. "Didn't matter whether they were fake or not. Perot knew that the great unwashed just believe what they see, especially when it's printed in the supermarket tabloids." He pressed a few keys and a picture flickered onto the screen. There were two men on the screen, one in a dark blue suit, the other in a military uniform. The two men embraced and shook hands. It was George Bush and Saddam Hussein. Howard's jaw dropped and he looked at Wyman.

"It gets better," said Wyman.

Howard looked back to the screen. A woman in a dark blue shirt and jacket walked into the room and Howard immediately recognised Margaret Thatcher, the former British Prime Minister. She kissed the Iraqi dictator on the cheek, then all three stood facing the camera, smiling and nodding.

"It never happened," said McDowall, walking up behind

Howard and putting a hand on his shoulder. "But it sure looks like it did, doesn't it?"

Howard shook his head thoughtfully. "That's dangerous," he said.

"In the wrong hands," agreed Wyman.

"In any hands," said Howard.

"It gets better," said McDowall, nodding at the screen.

The scene changed from an office to a bedroom, and the three world figures were naked on a king-size bed. Howard grimaced and leaned over to switch off the visual display unit.

"So, Special Agent Howard, I guess you want prints of them all," said Wyman. "The snipers, I mean. Unless you want a few prints of our little threesome. I could put you in there with them if you want."

"The snipers and the people on the ground will do just fine," said Howard.

"I can give you close-ups of the faces, if you want."

"Sounds good," said Howard. "I'd like duplicates, too."

McDowall walked over to a large printer and switched it on while Wyman pounded on the keyboard. A few seconds later the printer made a humming noise as it processed the first print. Wyman crushed his empty beer can and threw it into the wastepaper bin. "So, what sort of music does an FBI Special Agent listen to?" he asked.

Mary Hennessy took a cab from Baltimore–Washington International Airport to the city. It was a hot day but the driver, a big black man wearing mirrored sunglasses, hadn't turned the air-conditioning on. Instead he'd opened all the windows and the draught blew Mary's blonde locks backwards and forwards across her face. It was a pleasant feeling and she closed her eyes and moved her head from side to side, letting the breeze play across her face.

"You Australian?" the driver asked over his shoulder.

"British," she replied. She hated having to hide her Irish origins but knew it was necessary.

"Yeah? I can never tell the difference," said the driver laconically, his elbow resting on the open window. There were three lanes of highway heading north to the city and all the traffic was sticking religiously to the 55 mph speed limit. There was none of the lane switching and aggression she associated with driving on European roads, everyone seemed quite content to cruise along in their own lane. "First time in Baltimore?" the driver asked. He didn't pronounce the 't' in the city's name. Bawlmore.

"That's right," said Mary. She looked out of the window at the lush, almost tropical, vegetation which lined the side of the road. Years ago, in what almost felt like a past life, she'd gone on honeymoon to the Far East and had stopped off in Singapore for two days. The climate and the rigid adherence to the speed limit reminded her of the island republic.

"You here to see your man?"

Mary frowned. "My man?"

The driver laughed, a deep-throated rumble that vibrated through his body. "Yeah, your Prime Minister. He's coming here in a week or so, didn't you know?" He watched her in the driving mirror. Mary shook her head. "Yeah, he's going to a Bird's game," he said. "Stopping off on the way to Washington, I guess."

"What's a Bird's game?"

He laughed again. "The Orioles," he explained. "They're our baseball team, and Maryland's state bird. We're coming up to the ball park on our right." Mary looked over to the right and saw the stadium looming up like a modern-day coliseum. "We had your queen here in 1990. She went to a Bird's game in the old Memorial Stadium, north of the city. Don't know if she enjoyed it much." He laughed. "Your man's going to throw the first pitch," he continued.

"Really?" replied Mary.

"Uh-huh," he grunted. "The President's going to be there and everything." He laughed throatily. "Last time the President was here he threw the first pitch – and they measured it at 39 mph. He never lived that down. I mean, there's ladies' softball teams with faster throws than that, know what I mean?"

"Yes," said Mary, even though she only understood half of what the man was saying. The stadium was brick-built with huge arches that gave it a cathedral-like form. Overhead were huge banks of floodlights. The building looked brand new.

"Built in ninety-two," said the driver as if reading her thoughts. "It's a great ball park. You should go while you're here in Baltimore."

"I'll certainly try," said Mary.

* * *

Joker plumped up the pillow, shoved it against the top of his bed and sat with his back against it, his long legs stretched out towards the television. A woman with frosted hair and glasses with red frames was hosting a studio discussion about eating disorders. She was directing questions from her audience to three young women all of whom claimed to be suffering from anorexia nervosa, though to Joker they all looked to be in good shape. The questions were almost all accusatory in nature, along the lines of "Why the hell don't you eat more?" It was the hostility from the distinctly overweight audience which surprised Joker. Generally he found Americans to be easy-going people, but there seemed to be something about food and eating which brought out the worst in them. A woman with elephantine legs and flabby arms stood up and the host stuck the microphone under one of her three chins. "I may not be thin, but I still feel good about myself," the woman bellowed. "Being large is not something to be ashamed of."

The audience whooped and clapped and the woman looked around, nodding her enormous head. Joker smiled to himself. The show abruptly changed into a commercial for a seven-day diet which promised dramatic weight loss or your money back. It was one of the ironies of the country, thought Joker, that some people consumed so much that they had to pay to lose weight, while in the inner cities children were dying because they weren't inoculated against childhood illnesses and adults were begging in the streets.

He leaned across to the bedside table and poured more Famous Grouse into his tumbler. As he raised the glass to his lips he registered movement at the periphery of his vision and his hand jerked, sloshing whisky down his hand.

It was a white cat at the window, standing with its back legs on the ledge outside and resting its paws on the glass. It was staring at Joker with emerald green eyes. The cat's left ear was mangled and torn and its fur was matted and streaked with what looked like oil. Joker raised his glass to the cat and drank. He turned to watch a commercial for fat-free, cholesterol-free blue cheese salad dressing, but the cat began to pat its paws against the window to attract his attention. Joker went over to open the window. As soon as he raised the lower section of the window, the cat jumped onto the carpet and padded over to the bed. Joker stood and watched as the cat leapt up onto the bed covers and walked stiff-legged over to the table. It sniffed delicately at the alcohol, screwed up its nose and looked disapprovingly at Joker.

"It's only whisky," he said. The cat meowed. She was female, Joker decided. "No, I haven't got any milk," he said. The cat sprang off the bed, stalked around the room, popped its head around the bathroom door, sniffed, and then jumped onto the window ledge. She looked up at Joker, gave him another plaintive meow as if telling him to have milk next time, and then ran down the fire escape.

Joker settled down to concentrate on what he was to do next. He had no problems thinking while watching television. Most of his childhood had been spent in a two-bedroomed tenement flat with two younger brothers and an unemployed father, where the television was on eighteen hours a day and privacy was a luxury he rarely experienced. At seventeen he'd joined the Army and life in the barracks wasn't much different from life at home, and before he'd left his teens he'd grown accustomed to concentrating, no matter what the distractions.

He'd now spent more than a week working behind the bar at Filbin's, usually with Shorty, though he'd met two other part-time barmen, both of them teenagers from Belfast and, like Joker, working without the proper visas. There had been no sign of Matthew Bailey, though Joker had seen several faces he recognised from photographs in files he'd read before his last undercover operation in Northern Ireland. Two were IRA hit-men who'd done time in the H-blocks of Long Kesh, not for murder but for armed robbery, and the third was a bombmaker, a small, shrewish man in his thirties with a Hitler moustache who chainsmoked Benson & Hedges cigarettes. He was calling himself Freddie Glover but Joker knew him as Gary Madden, wanted in the UK for an explosion which had killed four Army bandsmen and injured another nine.

The men were clearly at home in the bar, where they were treated almost as folk heroes – heads turned whenever they entered, smiles and nods were exchanged as they moved to their regular table and throughout the evenings free drinks would be sent over, usually the gift of one of the construction workers. Joker had asked Shorty how long the men had been in New York. Shorty had just tapped the side of his nose knowingly and winked. "Careless talk costs lives," he'd said and Joker hadn't pressed it.

Joker had yet to meet the owner of Filbin's. Though Shorty had hired him and paid his wages each evening in used dollar bills, the little man clearly wasn't the owner because Joker had seen him surreptitiously pocket money from the till on several occasions. Shorty knew everyone in the bar by name, and from conversations they'd had Joker had learned that he had been a member of the Provisional IRA since his teens, moving to the States in the early eighties. He had been one of thousands of Irish granted US citizenship in 1991 and was the only barman who was working legally in Filbin's. Joker had wanted to raise the subject of Matthew Bailey with him, but had been loath to tip his hand so soon. Shorty had a sharp mind and a quick wit, and Joker doubted that he'd give much away, especially about active IRA members. If anything, it was Shorty who was doing the probing, asking Joker about his past and testing his views as he cleaned glasses and served drinks. Joker had little trouble sticking to his cover and after the first few days Shorty's conversations had become less probing and more friendly.

The bar was a centre for the IRA's fund-raising in the city, with a small room at the back frequently used to sort and count cash, and Joker had seen several men come out of the room putting their wallets in their pockets as if they'd been collecting money. In one of few revelations, Shorty had told Joker that some IRA men on the run from the UK weren't able to work and that they drew regular wages from the organisation's funds. The bar also acted as an unofficial employment centre for the Irish community. Representatives of several construction companies would sit at tables, drinking Guinness and reading Irish newspapers, and there would be a constant stream of visitors, mainly young men, who after a few whispered words would leave with an address scrawled on a piece of paper. The construction companies always needed workers, and they paid in cash. When Joker had made it known that he'd worked as a bricklayer he'd been offered several jobs at a much higher rate of pay than he got from the bar. He'd turned down the offers, knowing that Filbin's was a far better source of information about the IRA than laying bricks would be.

Joker used the remote control to flick through the channels on the television set: *Gilligan's Island, I Love Lucy, Charlie's Angels, Mr Ed*. Nothing but repeats and game shows, all of them punctuated by the same mind-numbing commercials. He picked up the tumbler of whisky and balanced it on his stomach. He was still none the wiser about Bailey's whereabouts, and sooner or later he was going to have to intensify his search. So far he'd been ultra-careful about raising the man's name, and on the few occasions he'd mentioned it outside the bar it had got him nowhere. Joker knew that if anyone knew where Bailey was, it would be the patrons of Filbin's, but to raise the subject risked drawing attention to himself. So far he'd been accepted by the Irish community, but that could easily change. Once, late at night, he'd overheard some of the construction workers laughing about a 'Sass-man' who'd once tried to infiltrate the bar, and he guessed they were talking about Pete Manyon. By the time Joker had managed to get over to clear empty glasses from their table they'd changed the subject. It had given Joker the chills. It was easy to forget that many of the jovial patrons were active members of the IRA and had been responsible for the deaths of British soldiers and innocent civilians. Joker flicked through the television channels faster and faster, trying to think of some other way of achieving his objective which wouldn't involve him putting his life on the line. He picked up the tumbler of whisky, but as he lifted it to his lips he caught sight of himself in the mirror over the dressing table. He winced as he realised how out of condition he was. There was no concealing his thickening waistline and the unhealthy pallor of his skin.

Joker switched the television off and put the glass on the

bedside table before standing in front of the mirror. He didn't look any better vertical. He sucked in his gut and pulled his shoulders back. A bit better, but not much. With a sigh that bordered on the mournful he sat down on the threadbare carpet and linked his fingers behind his neck. With his eyes on the whisky, he began a series of hard and fast sit-ups, grunting at the unfamiliar strain on his muscles.

Frank Sullivan shared an office with four other agents in FBI headquarters at Federal Plaza in Manhattan, though it was rare for more than one of them to be there at a time. Much of their work in the Counter-Terrorism (Europe) Division involved surveillance, either sitting in the back of parked vans or in darkened rooms, watching and waiting, or meeting informers in parks or cinemas. As a result paperwork tended to pile up and Sullivan had a stack of files as long as his arm to deal with.

He poured himself a cup of black coffee from the filter machine which he and his three colleagues had bought using their own money and set it down by the pile of files in his 'in' tray. Most of the files contained answers to queries he'd sent to the Royal Ulster Constabulary in Belfast, and they were contained in pale blue FBI file covers. Information from MI5, the British counter-espionage service, was always kept in manila folders, ever since one of their files had ended up in Belfast by mistake. The file had contained an MI5 case officer's criticism of an RUC undercover operation and had caused no end of embarrassment. A flurry of memos and an FBI agent being posted to a two-man office in Fairbanks, Alaska, had been the result, along with an agreement that for ever more RUC and MI5 information would be clearly marked and kept apart. About half a dozen of the files on Sullivan's desk were from MI5.

Traffic between the FBI, MI5 and the RUC had intensified in recent years as an increasing number of IRA activists had sought sanctuary in the United States. More than a dozen top-ranking IRA officials had been killed in the UK in the previous twenty-four months, some in accidents, others shot in the course of undercover operations, several had committed suicide, a few had been murdered, their assailants unknown. Rumours were rife of a shoot-to-kill operation, questions had been asked in the House of Commons and the *Sunday Times*' Insight team had published several investigative articles suggesting that the SAS had been systematically wiping out the upper echelons of the terrorist organisation prior to the 1994 ceasefire. Nothing had been proved, however.

Up until 1992, it had been the Special Branch of the Metropolitan Police who had been responsible for keeping tabs on the IRA, as they had done since the nineteenth century when they were first formed to combat the Irish nationalists. Sullivan and his colleagues had always preferred dealing with Special Branch: unlike MI5 they were real policemen, men the FBI agents could identify with. MI5 were spies who had found themselves with a declining workload after the break-up of the Soviet Union, and most of them adopted a superior attitude when dealing with the Bureau. Sullivan had spent three months in London working in MI5's Curzon Street offices alongside the British anti-terrorist specialists as part of a now-defunct exchange programme, and it had been a disheartening experience. He found the MI5 agents cold and distant, with a public-school humour that he'd never managed to comprehend. They'd appeared to be more interested in maintaining their own sense of superiority than sharing their expertise, and he'd returned to New York feeling that the whole experience had been a waste of time. The few personal contacts he'd made during his twelve-week attachment had been no help at all once he'd crossed the Atlantic, and requests for information from Curzon Street consistently took twice as long as similar communication with the RUC.

On several occasions MI5 had sent its own agents to the United States without telling the FBI, and relations between the two agencies were, at best, strained. Sullivan pulled the manila files from the stack and began to read them first. Two of the files contained telex requests for information on IRA activists the British had apparently lost track of. Sullivan smiled and slipped them into the bottom drawer of his desk. He'd get to them eventually, but they were low on his list of priorities.

Of the remaining four files, one was MI5's reply to his request for information on Damien O'Brien, the new face working as a barman in Filbin's. Sullivan took a mouthful of hot coffee and opened the file. All it contained was a telex from Curzon Street saying that MI5 had no record of a Damien O'Brien with the date of birth supplied, though there was a seventy-two-year-old Damien J. O'Brien currently living in Dublin who was an active IRA member in the late Fifties but who was now considered to be retired. O'Brien's passport was genuine and the fingerprints which the FBI had sent did not match those of any IRA members.

The rest of the telex concerned the file held on Damien O'Brien by Criminal Records Office and detailed his two convictions for drunk and disorderly behaviour, both of which had resulted in fines, and a three-month spell in a Glasgow jail for assault. The fingerprints on the bottle of Budweiser matched those of the Damien O'Brien who had spent three months in prison. Sullivan closed the file and dropped it into his 'out' tray. O'Brien seemed to be genuine: a barman with a drink problem who was working illegally in New York. He made a note on the file cover to review the man again in three months. If he'd kept his nose clean and hadn't made contact with any of the IRA regulars, he'd inform INS and have the man deported for working illegally on a tourist visa. Meanwhile, Sullivan had bigger fish to fry.

Cole Howard had a large blackboard delivered to his office and in the middle of it he fixed the photograph of the four dummies in the desert. Around it he stuck six photographs: the BUPERS file pictures of Lou Schoelen and Rich Lovell; a shot of what he thought was probably the third sniper; the woman; the young man; and the man with the walkie-talkie. He took a stick of white chalk and linked the pictures to the centre like spokes in a wheel and then sat down in his chair. He sat unmoving for a full hour, trying to put all the facts into perspective: trained Navy SEAL snipers; two unknown men and a woman. Four targets, two thousand yards or so from one of the rifles. He took a pad of paper and began to write a list of his priorities, a habit he'd picked up in the FBI Academy.

It was dark outside when he'd finished his list and he had to switch on his desk lamp. He put down his pen and massaged his temples. His head was throbbing, a dull ache which two painkillers had failed to dispel, and he wanted a drink, badly. There were more than a dozen paragraphs scribbled on the sheets of paper and he sat back in his chair and read them through. He had to put in a requisition for phone company records for the two former Navy SEALs through Sheldon's office so that he could find out who the men had been in contact with prior to disappearing. He also wanted a tap put on the telephone belonging to Lou Schoelen's parents in case he called home, as well as access to their phone records. He would have to run the new photographs of the mystery men and the woman through the FBI's files, and he could start those wheels turning before he left for the evening. Andy Kim had to be contacted and his progress ascertained. If Bob Sanger had been as good as his word, the computer expert would already be ensconced in the White House. Howard had made a note to check that sufficient FBI programmers had been assigned to the project.

Howard had also made a note to ask Kelly about the bank accounts belonging to Schoelen and Lovell, and to see if she'd made any progress on the credit cards the men had used to hire the cars they'd driven into the desert.

Howard was now convinced he had identified two of the three snipers, but the third was a mystery. The new pictures of the snipers would also have to be run through the files in the hope that there would be a match somewhere. The third sniper seemed to have long hair, almost shoulder length, so he figured it wouldn't be too hard to identify him. He would follow Kratzer's advice and try to track down the rifles by approaching the manufacturers. He doubted that a check of their records would provide any surprises: the two rifles which had been identified were in the hands of the known snipers, but there was an outside chance that they might provide a lead.

As an afterthought, he made a note to ask the State Department for a list of overseas VIPs who would be visiting the US over the next six months. Howard sighed and massaged his temples again. The investigation seemed to be growing exponentially and he felt that it was slipping away from him. There were plenty of leads but he didn't seem to be able to get on top of any of them. He felt some satisfaction in having identified two of the snipers, but he was still no nearer knowing where they were, who their target was, and when they intended to strike. He had a sickening feeling that Jake Sheldon would regard the slow progress as failure and that he'd assign someone else to supervise the case. Howard sighed and dropped the sheets of paper into his desk drawer. The desire for a drink was almost overwhelming. He pulled a slim book from his bottom drawer and flicked through it until he found the address of a local college where a meeting was scheduled to start in twenty minutes' time. He quickly filled out the forms for the telephone records and the tap and put them into an envelope marked for Jake Sheldon. He put copies of the photographs of the snipers, the woman and the two men into another envelope and marked it up for an FBI records cross-check before putting it in his 'out' tray.

The drive to the college took less than ten minutes and there were plenty of parking spaces. It was a venue he'd visited before. The meeting room was on the first floor and a couple of dozen plastic chairs had been arranged in uneven rows facing a blackboard on which were scrawled a number of chemical equations. At the back of the room a coffee-maker bubbled contentedly, and a young man in a shabby suit was pouring milk from a carton into a row of china mugs. Howard took a seat at the back, next to a large woman in a fur coat. There were sixteen people in the room, most of them men. Howard had seen several of them before, both at the college and at other meetings. He was the third to speak. He stood up and, as he always did when addressing a group, he cleared his throat. "My name is Cole," he said, "and I'm an alcoholic. It's been three years and eight months since I had a drink."

The group applauded and Howard felt their support and love wash over him like a warm shower.

It was a hot day and the crowds streaming towards the ball park were dressed appropriately – baggy shorts, bare legs, T-shirts, and baseball caps, most of them in the orange and white team colours of the Orioles. Mary left the hotel and followed the fans. She had put on a pair of baggy white shorts which showed off her slim, tanned legs, and a blue sweat-shirt, the sleeves pulled up to her elbows. The weather in Baltimore was the most varied she'd ever experienced: three days earlier it had been so chilly that she'd needed a warm coat when she went out, the previous day it had rained, and when the sky had cleared the temperature had soared into the high eighties and the television weather forecaster had said that the humidity would be high on the day of the game. He'd been right, and Mary found herself breathing heavily so thick and moist was the air.

Street vendors had sprung up on all the roads leading to the ball park, selling hot dogs, iced drinks, and cheap souvenirs. Mary walked by a bar where the customers had spilled out onto the street, mainly good-natured young men drinking beer from cans. It wasn't the first baseball game she had been to, so she wasn't surprised at how polite and agreeable everybody appeared to be. There was none of the mindless chanting and thuggery that always seemed to accompany large sporting events in Britain, where the violence off the pitch often had a higher priority than the game itself. In contrast, American crowds were generally families out for a good time. The police directing traffic seemed friendlier than their UK counterparts, their shirts rolled up and their caps pushed back on their heads. They smiled and joked with the crowds, and appeared to be as enthusiastic about the forthcoming game as the fans. She felt totally safe as she mingled in the crowd, though she kept a wary hand on the strap of her handbag.

The ticket had been delivered to her room in a sealed envelope early that morning, but she wasn't sure which entrance to use. A large policeman saw her frowning as she studied her ticket and he asked her if she needed help. He had a badge on his chest which said his name was Murphy but his accent was a slow Maryland drawl with no trace of Irishness in it. He had a drinker's nose, though, red and bumpy like she'd seen so many times on the faces of the men in the streets of Belfast. Officer Murphy pointed to where she should go, and wished her a nice day. He actually touched his hand to the peak of his cap, a gesture she associated more with Dixon of Dock Green than an American cop. The elderly man who checked her ticket at the turnstile was just as friendly. She could never get over how polite everyone was in America. Waitresses, policemen, bank clerks, people she met in the hotel, they all smiled and seemed to take a genuine interest in her. The people in Belfast were friendly enough, but there was still a coldness between strangers which didn't seem to exist in the States.

She walked through the crowds to the stairway which led up to the level where her seat was. The stadium was buzzing expectantly, while down on the bright green playing surface players warmed up, throwing balls hard and fast and catching them with their large leather mitts. Even high up in the stand, Mary could hear the thwack of balls being hit home. Off to the side, by the dugouts, men were swinging bats, their arms extended, whirling them like propellers. Messages were being flashed onto a large electronic screen at the far end of the stadium, welcoming the fans and telling them who was on that day's team. Men rushed up and down the aisles carrying boxes of beer cans, hot pretzels, hot dogs and soft drinks, shouting their wares. Food and drink was passed from hand to hand along the rows by the fans, and money shuttled in the opposite direction to be pocketed by the vendors.

The seat on Mary's left was vacant, and to her right was a young boy, his head dwarfed by a black baseball cap with an orange Oriole logo on the front. He was eating a huge mustard-smeared hot dog and swinging his legs up and down while his father tried to attract the attention of the Budweiser-seller. Mary smiled down at the little boy and he grinned, his lips yellow with mustard. When Mary looked up, a middle-aged man wearing sunglasses was sitting next to her, a large tub of popcorn in one hand, a giant beaker of Cola in the other. He looked like a typical sports fan rather than the terrorist the world knew as Carlos the Jackal. The lenses of his sunglasses were pitch black and Mary could see her own reflection in them. "Good afternoon, Ilich," she said.

"Mary," he said quietly, turning to watch the players warming up. "It's so nice to see you again. You are as beautiful as always."

"Why thank you, Ilich. You're too kind."

He held out his tub of popcorn but Mary politely refused. The opening bars of the Star Spangled Banner began, and the stadium rumbled as the tens of thousands of fans got to their feet. Mary and Carlos followed suit, though they didn't join in the chorus of cheers when the National Anthem finished and the Orioles ran onto the field. The opposition, a team from Minnesota, sat in the dugout while their first hitter went up to bat.

"How is everything?" asked Carlos.

"Fine," said Mary. "I've rented a house overlooking the Chesapeake Bay, not far from Bay Bridge Airport." She slipped him a piece of paper on which she'd written instructions and drawn a sketch map of the location of the house, and a set of keys. "Matthew is in Florida, when he gets in touch I'll tell him to meet you in the house. How are the others?"

Carlos smiled. "A little tense," he said. "They don't like waiting. And Rashid is missing Lebanese food. Other than that, they're raring to go. At the moment they're in separate motels." He pocketed the keys and the paper. "I'll move them into the house tomorrow. How long is the lease?"

"I took it for six months, three months paid in advance. The electricity, gas and phone are connected, we won't be having any unexpected visitors."

"That is good, very good," said Carlos. He scooped up a handful of popcorn and shovelled it into his mouth. The man always ate as if it was the last food he would see for some time, thought Mary. He never left any food on his plate, and she knew that Carlos would not throw any of the popcorn away. Any remaining when it came time for him to leave the stadium would be saved and eaten later. "The weather has been variable," he said, his mouth full of popcorn.

Down below, the pitcher threw the ball and the spectators roared as it went straight into the glove of the catcher. "The changing of the seasons," said Mary. "The forecast is good. But in any event, they can compensate for the wind."

Carlos nodded. "I hope the game does not get rained out," he said. "A rain check will be of no use to us."

"You worry too much," said Mary.

"I want to succeed," said Carlos. "I cannot afford to fail."

The little boy on Mary's right was unabashedly trying to listen but she knew he was too young to follow the conversation. She smiled and the boy grinned back. His father smiled at Mary and began talking to his son about one of the players. Mary turned back to her companion. "Neither of us wants to fail," she said, keeping her voice low. "It will be all right, Ilich. Trust me."

"The luck of the Irish?" he said, grinning. He wolfed down another handful of popcorn.

"We've planned for every eventuality," said Mary. "Don't worry."

Càrlos swallowed. "You're a cool one, Mary Hennessy. Where were you during the Seventies? I could have used you then."

"The Seventies?" said Mary wistfully. "I was happily married then. I was a housewife and mother. I had a husband and I had a brother." Carlos nodded and noisily sipped his Cola through a straw. Mary looked around the ball park. Every seat was full. The Baltimore Orioles were having a good season and the city had rallied to support them. Beyond the stands were the towering office blocks of the city centre. Mary shielded her eyes from the sun with her hand as she scrutinised the tall buildings. When she turned back to Carlos, his seat was empty.

Cole Howard left it until 10 a.m. before ringing Jake Sheldon's secretary and asking if he could see the director. He wanted to be sure that Sheldon had seen the new computer-enhanced photographs and the written request for a wire tap. The secretary told him that Sheldon was at a meeting until noon but that she'd pencil him in for twenty minutes after that.

Howard picked up a set of the Clayton photographs and went along the corridor to the office Kelly shared with five other agents. She was on the phone and Howard read through the departmental notices on the wall while he waited for her to finish. "Good morning, Cole," she said brightly as she replaced the receiver. He put the pictures on her desk and watched her as she scrutinised them. She brushed her blonde hair behind her ears, her eyes wide. He saw the glint of a wedding band. She looked up at Howard and then back at the photographs. "This is amazing," she said. She was wearing a pale blue dress with short sleeves and gold buttons. It reminded him of one of his wife's expensive Chanel outfits and he wondered who Kelly's husband was and if he had money. "Are these from Clayton Electronics?" she asked.

Howard nodded. "That's right," he said. "Can you run them by the people in the car rental office? Also, I'd like you to see if you can get a match from our files. Try Interpol, too. Let's see if we can get a match now that we've improved the resolution."

"Sure," she said eagerly. "This is incredible. How on earth did you get these?"

"High-powered computers and a couple of space cadets," said Howard.

Kelly looked at the pictures of the snipers. "Pity that the snipers have got their scopes up against their faces."

"Yeah," agreed Howard. "I'll send them to Lovell and Schoelen's Navy SEAL unit and see if they can ID the third sniper. Did you have any luck chasing down their bank accounts?"

Kelly shook her head. "Both accounts were closed three months ago," she said.

"Yeah, I thought they would be," said Howard. "What about the credit cards?"

"The Justin Davies American Express card has turned up in Los Angeles," she replied. "A couple of homeboys were trying to buy a boom box with it. The local police found their apartment full of stuff they'd been buying. It was like *Wheel of Fortune*."

"How did they get the card?"

"They say they found the wallet in the street. One of the agents from our LA office is seeing them this afternoon, but they stuck to the same story all day yesterday. If they did lift it, we'll get a description eventually. The other card is still loose."

Howard nodded. "Okay. Look, I'm going up to see Sheldon at noon. I'd like you there." She nodded and went back to studying the photographs.

"There's nothing that warms my heart more than to see a good Catholic boy on his knees," laughed Shorty.

"Why don't you join me, and while you're here you can plant a big wet one on my arse," replied Joker. He was kneeling in front of the low-level shelves where the bottled beer and soft drinks were stored, restocking and making sure that all the labels were facing outwards, like soldiers on parade.

"I'd love to, but I've arranged to meet a young lady over in Queens, and if I'm not there in an hour she'll as likely start without me." The small man took off his apron and retrieved his jacket from a hook on the wall. "You'll be okay minding the shop on your own?"

"Sure, Shorty, no sweat. You enjoy yourself."

Shorty winked as he walked by the bar, heading for the door and the sunshine. "I surely intend to, Damien."

"And give her one for me!" Joker shouted after him,

standing up and stretching. He carried the empty crates into a storage room, then went back to the bar and began slicing lemons and limes. There were only three customers: two old men in tweed jackets and caps sitting at a round table playing cribbage and a long-haired young man in torn jeans who was nursing a half-pint of Guinness. He was one of the two teenagers who'd been collecting for the IRA when Joker had first visited Filbin's on St Patrick's Day, the one who'd held out the bucket. His name was Dominic Maguire, though everyone called him Beaky because of his large nose, and he was a regular visitor to the bar, both as a fund-raiser and as a customer.

"So how's it going today, Damien?" asked Beaky.

"Slow," said Joker, scraping the fruit slices into a bowl. He washed the knife in the small sink under the bar. "Where's John today? John Keenan was Beaky's friend and the two were practically inseparable.

"Over in the Bronx, seeing a lawyer. He's hoping for a shot at the next Green Card lottery."

"Good luck to him," said Joker. "You want another?"

Beaky shrugged. "I'm a bit short, to be honest, Damien."

"That's okay," said Joker, taking his almost empty glass and refilling it. "You can have this on me."

Beaky grinned. "Yer a saint, thanks a lot."

Joker poured himself a double measure of Famous Grouse and added a splash of water. He raised the glass to Beaky. "Cheers," he said. He savoured the whisky as Beaky returned the salute. "I hope John gets his Green Card," he added.

"Don't see it makes any difference," said Beaky. "There's plenty of guys can get you a counterfeit one if yez needs it. Me, I wouldn't even bother."

"Why's that?"

"Once they get their claws into you, they never let go," said Beaky. "The IRS get onto you, immigration keep checking on you, it's too much hassle. I get paid in cash, no tax, no fingerprints on file, no nothing. I've been here three years with never a problem."

"But what if you want to leave?"

"No sweat, I can get a fake I-94 and a stamp in my passport, that's all you need. When you leave, the airline looks at the I-94 and they take it off you and send it to INS. They don't know shit. They're not trying to stop people leaving, they just don't want to let you in." He took a mouthful of the dark stout and wiped the foam off his upper lip.

"It's as easy as that?" asked Joker.

"Depends who you know," said Beaky. "Why, you want something doing?"

Joker shook his head. "Nah, I'm okay so far. But I'll let you know." He finished his whisky and helped himself to another. "Say, a friend of mine was in New York some time ago, said he was trying to get a Green Card, maybe you know him. Matthew Bailey."

Beaky put his head on one side like a parrot listening to a sound it hadn't heard before. "Bailey? Yeah, a carrot top, right?"

Joker nodded. "Hair like a fox, that's him."

"Where was it I saw him? Yeah, I know, O'Ryan's Bar. Sometime last year. He was planning to go to Washington, I think."

At the mention of Washington, Joker's stomach lurched. That was where Pete Manyon's body had been found.

"Do you know where I can get hold of him?" asked Joker.

"Yeah, he was going to see a guy called Patrick Farrell, a pilot who runs some sort of aircraft leasing company between Washington and Baltimore."

"You don't know the name of it, do you?" asked Joker. "I'd really like to get in touch with Matthew if it's possible."

"No, but I'll ask around," said Beaky.

The last thing Joker wanted was for Beaky to go around asking questions about Bailey, but he knew that to refuse the man's offer would only raise suspicion. He took Beaky's glass, refilled it and then turned the subject to a robbery which had taken place just three streets away, leaving a husband and wife and their young daughter dead from knife wounds. As they talked, Joker's mind was racing. It shouldn't be too hard to track down a pilot called Patrick Farrell.

Howard looked at his watch. It was five minutes before noon. On his way to the elevator he looked into Kelly's office. She'd gone and he wasn't surprised to find her already sitting opposite Sheldon's desk. "Cole, come in, sit down," said Sheldon, waving him to the seat next to Kelly. "Kelly's just been updating me on your progress."

"That's decent of her," said Howard, unable to keep the bitterness out of his voice.

"These new photographs are really quite something," continued Sheldon, as if he hadn't heard Howard. "I'm quite hopeful that we'll strike gold with these."

"They're certainly a big improvement," agreed Howard.

"Did Kelly tell you about the bank accounts of Lovell and Schoelen?"

"She did, and I've already approved the subpoena of the telephone records, our legal boys are doing the paperwork now. Same goes for the phone tap."

Howard nodded. Sheldon toyed with a pencil thoughtfully. "The Justin Davies credit card turned up in Los Angeles, I gather. What are your feelings on that?"

"I think it's a set-up," said Howard quietly. "I think they dumped the card, hoping that it'd be picked up and be used."

"So where should we be looking for these snipers?"

Howard was about to speak, but Kelly got in first. "I've already spoken to the two rifle manufacturers – Barrett and Horstkamp. They're going through their sales records now. They sell mainly through dealers, so it'll be a question of approaching them for names and addresses."

Howard's mouth dropped. It had been his idea to track down the rifles, but she'd made it sound as if the brainwave was hers. "That's good," said Sheldon.

"That and the telephone tap are just about our only leads on the snipers," said Howard. "Unless the telephone records show up anything. Incidentally, I'd like more manpower, it's going to take some legwork."

"How many were you thinking of?" asked Sheldon, tapping his pencil on his blotter.

"Two should be enough at this stage."

Sheldon nodded. "Consider it done. Let me have a look at the rosters and I'll give you names this afternoon. Now, how are the computer experts getting on with their sniping program?"

"They should be in the White House as we speak," said

Howard. "I was planning to speak to Andy Kim today."

"Let me know how you get on," said Sheldon. He brought the meeting to a close. Howard and Kelly went down in the elevator together in silence. When the doors hissed open, Howard asked her if she'd go along to his office. He waited until the door was closed before speaking again.

"What is your problem, Kelly?" he said quietly as he went behind his desk and sat down.

He didn't ask her to sit, but she did anyway, demurely crossing her legs. She seemed totally unfazed by his question, almost as if she'd expected it. "I don't know what you mean, Cole," she said, one eyebrow arched.

"I'm heading this investigation," said Howard.

"Have I implied that you weren't?" she said.

"You appear to be taking liberties with the line of command," he said. "I report to Jake Sheldon, you report to me."

"I understand that," she said smoothly, her voice like a cat's purr.

"So can you explain why every time I leave the office, you rush up to see Sheldon?"

She folded her hands primly in her lap and studied Howard with her pale green eyes. "First, Cole, I hardly think that three visits to Sheldon's office in one month could be seen as a threat to your authority. And secondly, on two of those occasions it was Jake who called me up. His secretary had tried to contact you, but you were out of the office. The call was passed onto me, and I was asked to go up and brief him on developments. There was never any question of my trying to usurp your authority. I have the greatest respect for your abilities as an agent."

Howard took a deep breath. The supercilious look on her face left him in no doubt that she was lying on all counts, but he knew there was nothing he could do. Kelly looked at her gold Cartier watch. "If there's nothing else, I do have work to do."

Howard shook his head and waved her away. Kelly stood up, smoothed down her skirt, and left the office, her head held high.

They arrived within an hour of each other, following the instructions Carlos had given them, driving behind the house and parking on an area of tarmac which had been used as a basketball court. The view from the rear of the house was spectacular, overlooking the Chesapeake Bay, and each of the arrivals had walked down to the water and looked over the waves to the twin spans of the Bay Bridge which loomed out of the mist to the left, before heading back to the house where they were greeted by Carlos.

Mary Hennessy hadn't selected the house from the dozen or so she'd visited because of its view, breathtaking as it was, but because of the privacy it offered – the nearest neighbour was a mile away and shielded by trees. There were only two ways to reach the house – by driving down a long, winding single track road, or by water. The house was built of wood, with towering gables and sash windows, and it had been freshly painted the colour of clotted cream. It had seven bedrooms and three bathrooms, and was surrounded by three acres of well-tended lawn, green and lush despite the salt air.

Carlos had parked his car in the garage and was waiting in the kitchen, drinking a cup of black, sweet coffee, when Rich Lovell arrived. He opened the back door and stood on the porch and watched as Lovell stood at the end of the lawn, his hands on his hips, and took in the view. The former Navy SEAL went back to his red Ford Mustang, opened the trunk, and took out two cases: one a nylon bag containing his clothes, the other clearly containing a rifle. He saw Carlos as he slammed the trunk shut and he waved. Carlos raised his coffee mug in salute.

"Am I the first?" shouted Lovell as he shouldered the rifle case.

"You are, so you get the choice of bedrooms," replied Carlos. "You'll find a linen cupboard upstairs, I'm afraid there's no maid service."

"Anything'll be better than the Holiday Inn," said Lovell with a smile. He stepped onto the porch and Carlos opened the door for him. Carlos sat down at the kitchen table and opened that day's *Washington Post* as Lovell climbed the stairs and made himself comfortable in one of the bedrooms. Carlos flicked through the foreign pages but there was little to interest him. The American press was parochial in the extreme and foreign affairs were low down their list of editorial priorities. The business section contained a gloomy survey of the country's manufacturing industry, and a forecast that there was worse to come. The dollar was falling against most major currencies, and the property market was in the doldrums. Carlos smiled. The world had rejoiced when Russia and Eastern Europe had been forced to admit that Communism couldn't work. He wondered how long it would be before nations realised that pure capitalism was equally ineffective. America, which prided itself on being the richest and most successful country in the world, also had one of the highest infant mortality rates, more men in prison than any totalitarian country, and an average life expectancy worse than many Third World nations. The system was starting to break down already, and no-one would take more pleasure in the demise of the USA than Ilich Ramirez Sanchez.

Outside, he heard a car drive down the track and he went back to the porch. It was Dina Rashid. She parked her white Ford Escort next to Lovell's Mustang and, like Lovell, went to stand next to the water for a few minutes, her long, curly black hair blowing in the wind. She was so thin, thought Carlos; almost anorexic, her figure that of a teenage boy rather than the thirty-year-old woman she was. As usual, she wore black – jeans and a polo-neck sweater, with black motorcycle boots. She turned as if aware that she was being watched and she waved. "This is wonderful!" she yelled. She ran across the lawn to the porch and hugged Carlos, hard enough to drive the air from his lungs. "Everything is well?" she asked.

"Everything is perfect," he said. "Lovell is upstairs already."

"Bastard!" she said, and spat noisily to the side. "If he tries to get inside my pants again, I'll have his balls off."

Carlos grinned and slapped her on the backside. Many years ago, Carlos and Rashid had been lovers, but no longer. Their lovemaking had bonded them together, though, and they trusted each other completely. "Just so long as he can shoot, Dina, that's all that I care about."

She tightened her arms around his neck and kissed him on one cheek. "Don't worry, Ilich. I have something special in mind for Mr Lovell if he tries to touch me again." She pulled away from Carlos, and laughed throatily. Her face was tanned, the skin pulled tight across her high cheekbones, and her brown eyes flashed as she laughed. Her hair spilled over her shoulders – it was virtually the only feminine thing about her. She even walked like a man. As she went back to her car the final sniper arrived: Lou Schoelen. Rashid greeted him and they carried their suitcases and rifle bags together into the house. Carlos shook hands with Schoelen, and then showed the two of them where the bedrooms were.

Later, Carlos went out to the bottom of the garden and stood looking at the bridge in the distance. Mary Hennessy was right – the weather was improving.

Joker put the last glass up on the shelf and scratched his chin. "That's the lot, Shorty," he shouted.

"Good man," Shorty called back. He was in the basement, changing a keg which had run dry. "I'll lock up; see you tomorrow."

"Is it okay if I take that carton of milk in the fridge?" asked Joker.

Shorty laughed. "You and that cat," he said. "Sure, take it."

Joker opened the small refrigerator under the bar and took out the pint of milk. He put on his pea jacket and pulled his wool hat down over his head and let himself out, pulling the door shut behind him. It was two o'clock in the morning but the city streets were still busy. A taxi cruised by with its light on and the driver sounded his horn, letting

Joker know he was for hire. Joker shook his head, he didn't have far to walk. He decided to visit the automated teller machine on the way back to his room and he shoved the milk carton into his pocket. As he approached the bank machine he looked left and right to check that there were no suspicious characters lurking in the shadows. New York was never a safe place to be, no matter what the hour. He slid the Visa card into the machine, tapped out his PIN number, and waited while it processed his request. Two large men in raincoats, their collars up against the wind, walked on the opposite side of the road, laughing uproariously. The machine made a clunking sound and Joker reached for his cash. As he slid the notes into his back pocket he realised he wasn't alone – the two men had crossed silently and were standing either side of him. Both men were as tall as Joker but much wider, as if they spent a lot of time lifting weights.

Any hopes that they were just there to use the bank machine were dashed when one of them put a restraining hand on Joker's shoulder. "You seem to be using this machine a hell of a lot," the man said. He had a wide forehead and one thick eyebrow which went across both eyes, giving him a perpetual frown. His accent was pure Belfast.

"Aye, for a barman paid in cash, yez make a lot of withdrawals," said the other. His accent was also Irish, but softer, from Derry maybe, Joker thought. He had small, piggy eyes and fleshy jowls, but his body looked rock hard under the thin raincoat.

"So who are you guys, the bank police?" Joker asked. He turned to walk on, but the grip tightened on his shoulder.

"We'd like a wee chat, Mr O'Brien, if that's your name," said Piggy Eyes.

"Damien O'Brien it is," said Joker. "Who would you be?"

"There's no need for introductions," said The Frowner. "We've just a few questions fur yer, that's all." His hand was deep in his raincoat like a cheap hoodlum in a gangster movie, but when he pushed it forward into Joker's kidney he could feel the hard outline of an automatic, a big one. "We'll be going back to yez room with yer, okay?"

"Sure," said Joker, wishing that he'd procured himself a weapon. He'd decided against it because he hadn't wanted to attract attention to himself, but with the heavyweights either side of him he could have done with a decent gun. "Can I go on ahead and make the place presentable?"

"Very funny, O'Brien," said Piggy Eyes. "Just walk."

The three men walked through the dark streets, his two escorts laughing loudly again as if they were just friends on their way home after a night's drinking. The main entrance to the hotel was locked as it always was after midnight, but the night manager had given Joker a key because he was often getting back in the small hours. Joker unlocked the door and the three men walked up the stairs, the gun never more than a couple of feet from Joker's back. They said nothing while he unlocked the door to his room and went inside. Piggy Eyes switched on the light, then closed and bolted the door. The Frowner took the gun out of his coat pocket. It was a matt black SIG-Sauer P228, a 9mm auto-loader with a double action trigger, and the safety was off. It wasn't an especially large gun, and it seemed even smaller in the big man's hands, but without a silencer it would still make one hell of a bang. As if reading his thoughts, The Frowner took a bulbous silencer from his pocket and screwed it into the barrel.

Joker took off his hat and dropped it onto his dressing table. "Okay if I take off my coat?" he asked. Piggy Eyes nodded and Joker slipped off the jacket. He placed the carton of milk on the window sill and hung the jacket on the hook on the back of the door. The Frowner kept the gun aimed at his gut and Joker knew there was no chance of making a run for it. "Can I offer you gentlemen a dram while we talk?" he said.

"Sit down," said The Frowner, gesturing at the wing chair in the corner facing the window.

Joker did as he was told. As he walked across the room his eyes searched for something, anything, he could use as a weapon. His half-empty bottle of Famous Grouse was the nearest possibility, next to the television. He could reach it in two steps, but The Frowner would have more than enough time to plant a slug in his chest. The automatic would make a hole the size of an orange in a body. He waited for the questions to start.

Piggy Eyes went over to the window and pulled down the blinds. "Yez been asking around about Matthew Bailey," he said, his back to Joker. "We were wondering why." He turned round and stared at Joker, his eyebrows raised.

"He's an old friend, he's in the States and I just wanted to say hello."

"How long have you known him?"

Joker shrugged. "Seven, eight years maybe."

"So how come yez don't know how to get hold of him yerself?"

"I lost touch with him."

"So how did yez know he was in the States?"

"Someone told me."

"Who?"

Joker held his hands out, showing his palms. "Jesus, I don't know. Someone in Glasgow, I can't remember who."

Piggy Eyes sighed as if he was disappointed. "I don't think anyone in Scotland would know he was over here."

"What can I tell you?" said Joker.

The two heavyweights said nothing for a while. Joker knew that they were doing it to make him sweat, so he tried to relax. It was The Frowner who eventually broke the silence. "Yez told Billy O'Neill yer had a telephone number for him, but that it had been disconnected."

"Billy O'Neill?"

"Guy from Filbin's. At the Gaelic football match."

Joker rubbed his chin with his hand, feeling the stubble. "Aye, that's right, I did."

"So who gave you the number?" asked Piggy Eyes.

"I don't know," said Joker.

"Billy says yer told him that Matthew gave it to you," said The Frowner.

"I guess he must have," said Joker, a chill running down his back. They had him bang to rights.

"Well, I don't think he'd have given yer his number here, O'Brien," said Piggy Eyes. "In fact, I'm pretty bloody sure he wouldn't."

Joker didn't know what to say. He began to tense his legs, preparing to spring, either for the gun or the bottle.

"And yer told Beaky Maguire that Matthew wanted a Green Card," said The Frowner.

Piggy Eyes shook his head. "Big mistake that, O'Brien. Matthew doesn't need a Green Card."

"I must have made a mistake," said Joker.

The Frowner grinned. "That's for sure."

"So tell me, are you a Sass-man, O'Brien?" asked Piggy Eyes. He walked over to the dressing table and picked up Joker's wallet. He stood next to The Frowner as he went through it. "We had a Sass-man here a few months ago." He pulled out the Visa card and looked at it, then showed it to The Frowner, who nodded. "He had a Visa card, too. And he used the money machines a lot." They both looked at Joker. "So, O'Brien, are you a Sass-man or what?" pressed Piggy Eyes.

As the two men waited for him to answer, Joker heard a pattering on the fire escape outside. He realised it was the cat coming for its milk and that she would soon start banging on the window. It was a small chance, but in view of what his visitors already knew, it could prove to be his only chance.

"I've got friends," said Joker, "and they're not far away." He wanted them edgy so that they'd over-react when the cat made its presence felt.

"Yeah, of course you have," said The Frowner. Both men laughed. That was when the cat began hitting her paws against the glass as she had done every night for the previous week. The two heavies whirled round and faced the window. As The Frowner aimed his gun, Piggy Eyes stepped to the side and reached for the cord that controlled the blinds. Joker sprang up from his chair and lunged for the bottle. The Frowner heard him move and began to turn, but Joker already had the neck of the bottle in his grasp. He threw it as hard as he could at The Frowner's head and it caught the man on the temple. The bottle bounced off his skull and hit the bed. Before the man could react, Joker rushed forward, his hands forming fists, and he hit him twice, once in the throat, once in the sternum, and the big man went down, blood pouring from a gash on the side of his head. Joker bent down smoothly to pick up the gun which had dropped from The Frowner's nerveless fingers. Piggy Eyes kicked Joker in the side, his speed belying his bulk, sending him sprawling across the bed, but before he could continue his attack Joker had the gun up and his finger on the trigger. "Easy," said Joker, "just take it easy."

"Yez move fucking fast for a barman, O'Brien," said Piggy Eyes. On the floor, the other man groaned. Joker stepped back slowly, putting more distance between them. He rubbed his ribs gingerly. Nothing was broken but he'd be black and blue within twenty-four hours. The cat continued to pat at the window. Piggy Eyes turned to look at the window. "My friend," said Joker.

The cat meowed and Piggy Eyes shook his head. "A fucking cat," he said.

Joker chewed the inside of his lip as he ran through his options. Whatever cover he had was now blown. He had no choice but to leave New York, and Washington seemed the best bet, even though Beaky Maguire had probably told the heavyweights about Patrick Farrell, the man Bailey had been talking to. But what was he to do with the two men in his room? Killing them was out of the question, yet he needed several hours to get clear of the city. He gestured with the gun at the wounded man on the floor. "Take his clothes off," said Joker.

"You've got to be joking," said Piggy Eyes.

"I don't know how quiet this gun is with this silencer, but I'm willing to try it," he said. He levelled the gun at the man's groin.

"Okay, okay," said Piggy Eyes, hurriedly going down on one knee and stripping off The Frowner's raincoat.

"And the rest," said Joker. "Be quick about it."

The Frowner moaned and tried to resist but Piggy Eyes told him to lie still. A few minutes later and The Frowner was lying naked on the floor like a beached seal, his clothes and shoes in an untidy pile by the window. "Good, now use his tie to bind his wrists behind his back," said Joker. "And make sure it's tight because I'll be checking." Piggy Eyes did as he was told, then straightened up. "Now your clothes," said Joker. Piggy Eyes obeyed, his eyes hard. He stared meanly at Joker as he undressed and Joker knew that he was looking for an opportunity to resist. He kept the gun aimed at his groin. "Don't even think about it," Joker warned.

When the man was naked Joker had him turn round and kneel down, facing the window. Folds of fat had gathered around his waist like pink inner tubes and the flesh hung loosely around his arms. "Hold your arms out behind you, and link your fingers," said Joker. As the man followed his instructions, Joker stepped forward and clipped the gun hard against his temple, knocking him out. Piggy Eyes slumped across The Frowner's prostrate body. Joker quickly used Piggy Eyes' tie and expertly knotted it around the man's wrists. He used their belts to tie their legs together, and quickly checked that The Frowner's wrists were tightly bound. The Frowner began to cough and tried to sit up. Joker knocked him senseless with the butt of the gun. He tucked the automatic into the back of his trousers and pulled up the blinds. The cat stared at him and meowed. Joker opened the window for her and she jumped down onto Piggy Eyes and then across to the bed. Joker ripped open the carton of milk and poured some into a glass. "You, young lady, have earned yourself a drink," he said. The cat lapped happily as Joker filled his suitcase with his belongings and the clothes stripped from the heavyweights.

He found two handkerchiefs and used them as makeshift gags for his two prisoners, then picked up the bottle of Famous Grouse. He took a long pull at the whisky and then put the bottle into his suitcase. The cat finished drinking and padded back to the window and leapt smoothly onto the fire escape. She turned and meowed once as if to say goodbye and then disappeared into the night. Joker closed the window behind her, switched off the light, and carried his case downstairs.

Kelly Armstrong pounded her horn and cursed the old woman in the car ahead of her. Phoenix had one of the worst traffic accident rates, and highest insurance premiums, in the country, not because of drunk drivers or joyriding teenagers but because of all the retirees who moved to Arizona in search of a better climate. Their failing eyesight and slowing reactions meant that the city's emergency services were forever pulling them out of their wrecked cars. The woman who was holding up the traffic ahead of Kelly was a typical snowbird, a tiny, white-haired, thin-boned woman with wrinkled skin and thick-lensed glasses, hunched over the steering wheel of a car which was far too big and powerful for her. She was, thought Kelly, probably sitting on a stack of telephone books with blocks on the pedals so that she could reach them and planned her routes so that she never had to make a left turn.

"Come on you bitch, go!" Kelly fumed, pounding her horn again. Eventually the old woman realised that the traffic light had turned green and she pulled away in a series of jerks. It was a beautiful day, the sky a cloudless bright blue, the temperature in the low seventies, and to Kelly it seemed that all the snowbirds had come out to play. She savagely punched at the buttons on her car radio, hunting for a halfway decent station that would make the crawlspeed less frustrating. Eventually she found a Pet Shop Boys track and she tapped her steering wheel as she followed the snowbird at precisely five miles an hour below the speed limit.

Fergus O'Malley ran a construction company based in Litchfield Park, to the west of Phoenix and close to Luke Air Force Base. He had a reputation for quality work at reasonable prices, and he'd built up a good solid business, employing more than fifty workers. Though he'd lived in Arizona for most of his fifty-seven years he continued to play on his Irish roots, to the extent of having a shamrock logo on all his trucks and speaking with an Irish lilt. Kelly drove her Buick onto the O'Malley lot and parked next to a flatbed truck piled high with scaffolding. Two young men in overalls stopped work to watch as she climbed out of the car and walked to the office building, a white envelope under her arm. One of them whistled, but Kelly didn't react. She was used to the attention, and no longer resented being whistled at by strangers. She knew that the time to worry was when the whistles stopped.

O'Malley wasn't a man to spend money on expensive furnishings, and his offices contained only the bare essentials. There was no couch for visitors in the reception area, just a desk where his secretary laboured over an old manual typewriter. She was pulling a file from a battered filing cabinet when Kelly walked in and asked to speak to the boss. Barely had she spoken to Fergus O'Malley over the intercom than the man came rushing through the door like a whirlwind, grabbing Kelly in a flurry of arms and clasping her to his chest. He lifted her clear off the ground so that her feet swung from side to side. "Kelly my darling girl, what've you been doing with yourself?" he boomed, squeezing the breath from her body. The envelope slipped from her grasp and landed on the floor.

"Uncle Fergus, would you put me down?" she asked. "Please."

"Are you telling me I can't hug my own fair niece?" O'Malley said, tightening his grip and planting a kiss on her cheek. She could smell whisky on his breath.

Eventually he lowered her to the ground, picked up the envelope and ushered her into his office. Like the reception area, a thin film of dust coated most surfaces. He saw her look of distaste and produced a handkerchief from his trouser pocket with a flourish which he used to wipe clean a chair. "Sit, sit," he said, handing her the envelope and leaning against his paper-strewn desk. "And tell me what brings you out to my neck of the woods." Kelly opened her mouth to speak but O'Malley held up his hand. "Drink?" he said. "Coffee? Tea? A drop of the hard stuff?"

Kelly shook her head. "I'm fine, Uncle Fergus. But don't let me stop you."

"Kelly my girl, I was hoping you'd say that," he said with a smile and dashed around the desk with a speed that belied his bulk. He was a bear of a man, his work jeans stretched tight around an expanding waistline and the sleeves of his plaid shirt rolled up around thick forearms. His big hands were square and weatherbeaten and the skin on his face was roughened from years working out in the open. He pulled open the bottom drawer of his desk and took out a bottle of whisky. He found a glass hidden under a stack of receipts and poured himself a decent measure. "Here's to you; may your life be filled with laughter, may your pockets be filled with gold." He raised the glass in salute, and drank deeply. Kelly laughed. O'Malley returned to his perch and looked at her with affection. "So, what's up?"

Kelly opened the flap of the white envelope with a scarlet fingernail and took out one of the photographs it contained. "I wondered if you might know this man," she said, and handed it to O'Malley.

He scratched his chin thoughtfully as he studied the photograph. "What makes you think I'd know him?" he asked.

"He's Irish," said Kelly.

O'Malley looked at her and raised his eyebrows. "If you don't know who he is, how do you know he's from the old country?" he asked.

Kelly smiled. "Uncle Fergus, you wouldn't believe me if I told you."

"Try me," he said, and took another drink from his glass.

"He rented a car, and the woman he spoke to said he had an accent."

"Americans can't tell the difference between Irish, Australian and South African, you know that. They all sound the same to them."

Kelly shook her head. "I played her some tapes, and she recognised the accent as Irish."

O'Malley beamed and raised his glass again. "Smart girl," he said.

Kelly felt a warm glow inside. Normally she didn't feel the need for praise; she regarded it as just another technique men used to try to get through her defences. But her uncle was different and she was pleased that she'd impressed him. "So, do you know him?"

O'Malley looked at the picture and shook his head. "He looks familiar, but I can't put a name to the face." He handed it back to her.

Kelly studied his face, looking for the signs that would let her know that he was lying, but his eyes returned her scrutiny with a steadiness that reassured her. She passed him the computer-enhanced photograph of the blonde woman. "What about her?"

O'Malley's reaction was transparent. His jaw dropped and his eyes widened and he shot up off the desk. "Where did you get this?" he said.

"The desert," she said.

"Recently?"

"Uh-huh. Uncle Fergus, the suspense is killing me. Who is she? Do you know her?"

"I do, girl. That I do. But Jesus, Mary and Joseph, what the hell is she doing in Arizona?"

Rashid threw the damp towel onto the floor and pulled on an old pair of men's pyjamas. She was tying the trouser cord when the door to her bedroom slowly opened to reveal Rich Lovell standing there, leaning on the jamb with a sly grin on his face. "I sort of assumed you wouldn't be wearing a Victoria's Secret nightgown," he said, looking her up and down.

"Get out of my room," she hissed, fastening the top button of her pyjama jacket.

"Come on, Dina," said Lovell, "why are you playing so hard to get?"

Rashid picked up a hairbrush and sat down at her dressing table where she ran it through her long hair with firm, even strokes. She watched Lovell in the mirror as he closed the door behind him. "If you don't get out, I'll call Carlos," she said quietly.

"He doesn't scare me," said Lovell, walking up behind her and massaging her shoulders.

"Then you are truly a fool," she said, continuing to brush her hair.

Lovell's fingers tightened around her neck. He bent down and kissed her shoulder. She felt his beard scratch against her skin. "It's been five weeks since I've had a woman, and you really turn me on."

She stood up quickly, startling him, and she held out the hairbrush like a knife. "It's not mutual, Lovell. You repulse me."

Lovell grabbed the brush and tossed it to one side, then stepped forward and held her tightly against him. He tried to kiss her on the lips but she brought up her knee into his groin, missing his testicles but hurting him nonetheless. She pushed him hard in the chest and he staggered back, breathing heavily. He moved to grab her again but she stopped him by raising her hand. He waited to hear what she had to say, his eyes wild. "Just go," she said. She could see his erection pushing at the crotch of his jeans.

"No," he said.

She shook her head. "You couldn't handle it," she hissed.

"Handle what?" he said, confused.

"Me," she said. "You couldn't handle the way I fuck."

He smiled evilly. "Try me," he said.

Rashid licked her lips slowly. "You want it, you bastard? Well I'll give it to you. But you'll be sorry." Lovell stepped towards hcr but she held up her hands again. "No," she said. "You do it my way or you don't do it at all."

"Your way?" he said. "What do you mean?"

"Take off your clothes, and lie on the bed," she ordered. For a moment it looked as if he was going to refuse, but then he undid the buttons of his shirt, revealing a hairless chest. He smiled as he took off his shirt, dropped it onto the floor, and unzipped his jeans. He sat down on the bed as he pulled the jeans off and stripped off his socks. He lay back and took off his boxer shorts, leaving him naked on the bed. He moved to roll under the covers, but Rashid shook her head. "No, I want to watch you," she said. She picked up his shirt, sat down on the bed next to him and took his erection in her hand. She squeezed and he gasped. He reached for her but she shook him away. "My way," she insisted. Lovell smiled and she felt him grow even harder in her hand. She straddled him smoothly, then leant forward, bringing his arms above his head. He tried to kiss her but she kept her head away from him, her hair dragging across his face. With quick, deft movements she used the sleeves of his shirt to tie his hands to the headboard.

"What are you doing?" he asked, trying to pull his hands free.

"This is the way I fuck guys I don't like," she said. She

slipped off him and took the belt from his trousers, using it to tie one of his legs to the bottom of the bed.

"I don't want it like this," he said, pulling at his bonds. Rashid sat on the edge of the bed and took him in her hand again.

"It feels to me like you do," she said, gripping him. He groaned. She went over to a wardrobe and returned with one of her own belts, which she used to bind his remaining foot to the bed. "I've only ever fucked two Americans," she said. "Like you, they were pigs." She stood up and picked up her wallet. From it she took a condom in a foil packet. She opened it and sat down on the bed.

"I don't want to wear anything," Lovell protested.

Rashid slipped the condom onto him in one smooth movement. "You think I'd fuck a pig like you without a condom?" she said. She spat in his face. "You're crazy."

Lovell tried to wipe the spittle from his face onto the pillow but he couldn't reach. It dribbled down his nose and into his beard. Rashid saw his erection begin to subside and she stroked him until he grew hard once more. "Funny how you pigs lose interest when you feel threatened," she said.

"Stop it," he said. "Just untie me. I've changed my mind."

Rashid laughed throatily. "You asked for it, you bastard, and now you're going to get it." She stood up and slipped off her pyjama top. She had broad shoulders and small breasts, hardly more than slight swellings. Lovell could see that she didn't shave her armpits, and the growth there was thick and long. There was hair around her nipples. She pulled the pillow from under his head. "Lift your arse," she ordered. He obeyed and she slipped the pillow under his backside. "They were hostages, those Americans. We had

221

them in Beirut, kept them chained to radiators for months. They stank, but then Americans always stink." She slowly untied the pyjama cord and let the flannelette trousers fall around her legs, revealing thin, brown legs. The hair at her crotch was as black and thick as the tufts in her armpits. Lovell's eyes were drawn to it and she smiled. "One of them was a CIA agent, we never found out who the other one was. They were lousy fucks, Lovell. Are all Americans such lousy fucks, I wonder?"

"Untie me, Dina," said Lovell nervously.

Rashid laughed at his discomfort. She turned her back on him and went over to the wardrobe. She bent down, the movement tightening the muscles in the back of her legs and emphasising the curve of her buttocks. Despite the cold knot of fear in his stomach, Lovell felt himself grow harder. When she straightened up he moaned. She had her rifle in her hands. She caressed it lovingly, the way she'd stroked his erection, her eyes hard. Once more she sat down on the bed next to him, her skin against his. "I was ordered to kill them, but I would have done it anyway. It was a pleasure. I hate Americans, Lovell. I hate all Americans." She held a bullet inches from his face, and then chambered it.

"Let me go," he pleaded.

"You wanted to know what it was like to be fucked by me. Now shut up and enjoy it." She straddled him again and reached down with her left hand to hold him. This time she gripped him hard, digging her nails into his flesh, and he yelped. While his mouth was open wide she pushed in the barrel of her rifle, the metal clinking against his teeth. He tried to move his head to the side but she pushed the rifle forward so that the end of the barrel jammed into his cheek. "Keep your head straight, pig, or I'll push it right through

222

the flesh." Lovell did as he was told. Rashid smiled. "Now suck it, gently, as if you were sucking me." Lovell's lips closed around the metal and he made small sucking movements, like a baby at its bottle. Rashid released his erection and with her left hand she switched off the safety and slipped a finger onto the trigger. "It takes three pounds of pressure to pull this trigger," she said quietly. "I thought you'd like to know that." Her left hand went back to his erection, massaging him as she spoke. "They knew it was going to be their last fuck, but somehow I don't think they enjoyed it," she said. She used her hand to guide him inside her, just the first inch, and then she rocked her hips from side to side. Sweat was running down Lovell's face and collecting in the hollow of his throat. His eyes were wide and scared as he sucked at the barrel. She allowed him inside another inch and he felt her internal muscles grip him. "It was the timing that was difficult," she said. "Knowing exactly when they were coming." She opened her thighs and pushed down, allowing him all the way in, then she began to move up and down slowly. "I didn't want to pull the trigger until they came, you know? God, Lovell, I've never felt such power." She was moving faster now, her hair whipping around her shoulders, her skin damp with sweat. "To know that I was the last person they'd see as they died, that they died fucking me." The barrel of her rifle was driving in and out of Lovell's lips in time with the motion of her body. Suddenly she slowed, and moved her hips up so that he was only just inside her. "I'd pull the trigger and their brains would blow out over the floor and their whole body would go into sort of convulsions. Their pricks would get so big, so hard, and the convulsions would drive them deep inside me, deeper than anyone has ever gone. All women should feel what's it's like, to have a man die inside you. God, I came so hard." She smiled. "They never knew, of course. They never knew what an intense orgasm they gave me. It's like they say, Lovell, the only good Yank is a fucking dead one. I suppose I'd better thank you in advance . . ." She thrust her groin down, so hard that he gasped. "Come on, Lovell, make me come," she said, her voice deep and harsh, like a man's. Lovell tried to resist, but his limbs were bound tight and the pillow was pushing his groin against hers. He could see her trigger-finger tensing. He tried to fill his mind with images that would take his mind off what was happening, hoping that if his erection subsided she'd stop. He thought of baseball scores, old movies, decompression tables, but it was no good, he could feel himself tightening. He opened his eyes and saw that she was staring at him as she pounded against his flesh, her mouth open, her eyes glazed. Her chest was glistening with sweat like a wild horse at the gallop, and the muscles in her neck were as tight as steel wires. Her small breasts were bouncing as she moved, and his eyes travelled down her flat stomach to the triangle of hair at her crotch. As she rose and fell he could see the glistening wet condom appear and disappear like a piston. He began to shake with fear. He could feel himself building to a climax and as the woman drew back her lips in an almost canine smile, he knew that she also realised he was going to come. He wanted to scream and to beg but the barrel of the rifle was pressing down on his tongue, making him gag. His hips began to thrust into her as if they had a mind of their own. He wanted her, even though he knew it was going to be the death of him. The trigger began to move as the finger tightened. Rashid moved faster and harder. "Fuck me and die," she cursed, her internal muscles squeezing and holding, and then Lovell felt himself spurt and kick inside her and he saw the trigger pull back and the hammer begin to move. He screamed as he'd never screamed before in his life and he never heard the clicking sound the hammer made as it struck the firing-pin and drove it into the empty chamber.

Carlos heard the frantic screaming as he lay on his back in his own bedroom, and he smiled. He doubted that Lovell would try to get into Dina's bed again.

Don Clutesi poured himself a coffee and added three spoonfuls of sugar. "Do you want one?" he asked Frank Sullivan as he stirred.

Sullivan shook his head as he read the FBI file on his desk, and grunted. Clutesi walked up behind him and read over his shoulder. "Mary Hennessy," he said. "The RUC were looking for her two years ago, weren't they? Have they found her?"

"They haven't, but an agent in Phoenix might have," said Sullivan, still reading. He groped for a photograph and held it by his ear for Clutesi to take.

Clutesi took it and compared it with the photographs in the file. The hair colour was different, but other than that it was clear that they were the same person. "When was this taken?" Clutesi asked.

"Recently," said Sullivan, "that's all I know. I don't even know where he got the picture from," he said. He handed over a second photograph. "She was with a guy. Recognise him?"

Clutesi took the photograph and shrugged. "Is he IRA too?"

"He's Matthew Bailey, the IRA guy who tried to buy the missile in LA last year. There's another man, but I haven't been able to get a match from our files." Sullivan showed him the photograph of the moustached man wearing sunglasses who was holding a walkie-talkie to his mouth. "I'm going to ask Phoenix if it's okay to cross-check with the RUC and MI5."

A middle-aged man stuck his head around the door. It was Douglas Foulger who worked down the corridor in the Counter-Intelligence (Middle East) office. "Yo, Frank, you okay for softball this Saturday?"

"Sure, Doug. Who are we playing?"

"One of the Brooklyn SWAT units," said Foulger, grinning. "You'd better pack a rod." He walked into the office, nodding a greeting at Clutesi. He looked at the picture of Mary Hennessy. "Good looking woman," he said. "She looks experienced, you know?"

"She's that all right," said Clutesi. "She's an IRA terrorist who gets a kick out of torturing undercover agents." He handed Foulger the other picture, the one of the man with the walkie-talkie. "I don't suppose you know who this is?" he asked.

Foulger took one look at the picture and sneered at Clutesi. "Get outta here, Don. You're jerking me around, right?"

Sullivan's head snapped up. "You know him?"

"Come on you guys, there isn't an anti-terrorist agent in the world who wouldn't know who this is." His mouth dropped. "Jesus H. Christ, are you telling me he's in the States?"

"Who?" said Clutesi. "Who the fuck is he?"

Foulger held the photograph out in front of him. "Unless I'm very much mistaken, gentlemen, this is Ilich Ramirez Sanchez. Alias Carlos the Jackal."

Lou Schoelen switched on the small television in his bedroom and adjusted the sound level until he was satisfied that it would cover his voice. Carlos had been insistent that they were all to shun any contact with their friends and relatives until after the hit, but Schoelen thought he was being over-cautious. There was no evidence that anyone was on their trail, and besides, he had a foolproof way of ensuring that any call he made was totally untraceable. Carlos had left the house earlier, Lovell was downstairs watching television in the den, and the Lebanese woman was in her own room.

He pulled his kitbag out from under the bed and unzipped a small pocket from which he took a black plastic box about the size of a paperback book. On one side of the box were twelve grey buttons and on the reverse was a small grille covering a speaker. The electronics inside were quite simple and Schoelen had made the device for a few dollars. All the box did was to generate electric pulses which mimicked those used by the telephone companies. It was quite useless in the hands of someone who didn't understand how communication networks operated, but Schoelen was no amateur. He flicked open a small notebook and ran his eyes down the columns of figures. It had taken him ten years to gather together the information

in the book, swapping numbers with other phone hackers in
the same way that children traded baseball cards.

Schoelen dialled the telephone number of an insurance
company in Baltimore. He knew that the office would be
closed – it was after nine o'clock at night – and that the call
would not be answered. He waited until the third ring, then
pressed the grille against the mouthpiece of the telephone.
With deft movements he pressed twelve keys, one at a time,
sending tonal pulses down the line. He put the phone to his
ear and listened to a series of clicks which told him that the
call was being routed through the Baltimore exchange and
across the country to San Francisco. The clicks stopped and
he heard the dial tone again, though this tone was being
generated by an exchange thousands of miles away. So far
as the phone company records would show, he had made a
local call to the insurance company and nothing more. He
put the box back to the receiver and keyed in a second
string of pulses, which again produced a series of clicks.
This time the call was being routed down the West Coast to
an exchange in Los Angeles. Schoelen ran his finger down
to a number of a call-box which he knew was in a line of six
such boxes in Long Beach. He keyed in the pulses, and
thousands of miles away the phone began to ring.
Schoelen's fingers moved quickly because he had to get the
next pulses down the line before the phone was answered.
He keyed in another string of twelve pulses which
transferred the call to the main San Diego exchange. As the
pulses shot across the country at close to the speed of light,
the telephone stopped ringing in Long Beach.

Schoelen put the phone to his ear and once again he
heard a dial tone. This one was being generated by the San
Diego exchange, but if anyone should try to trace the call,

the trail would end at the pay phone in Long Beach. The final pulses generated by the black box set the telephone ringing on the hall table in his parents' house in Coronado. His mother answered on the fifth ring and immediately poured out a torrent of questions in her thick Germanic accent which had changed little during all her years in the United States. Schoelen waited until she'd finished. "Mom, I'm fine," he said. "No, I don't know when I'll be back. How's Willis?" Schoelen's dog was the reason for the call. Before he'd left Coronado, his Rottweiler had been off his food and had been listless at night.

"Oh, Lou, he was not so good," said his mother. "He was sick many times, so we took him to the veterinarian last week. His intestine is twisted, he said."

Schoelen's stomach lurched. "He's okay, isn't he, Mom?"

"Oh, he's fine now, he's back home, but it was expensive, Lou. Eight hundred dollars for the operation and the medicine."

Schoelen sighed with relief. He had raised the dog from a puppy and loved it with a passion. "That's okay, Mom. I'll send you the money in a couple of weeks. Is he eating okay now?"

"Like a horse. We have to take him back next week to have stitches removed, but his stomach is fixed. So, when are you coming home?"

"I don't know, Mom. This job is very important. It'll all be over in two weeks though."

"Willis misses you, Lou. And so do we. Please come home soon."

"I will, Mom. Say hello to Dad for me. I have to go now." Schoelen replaced the receiver. On the television

screen Captain Kirk and Spock beamed up to the bridge of
the Starship Enterprise.

The days of FBI agents wearing telephone company
overalls and scaling telephone poles to tap phones
disappeared with the advent of digital exchanges. Physical
wiretapping was replaced by computerised monitoring,
much to the relief of the agents who had previously been
forced to spend hours in damp basements or in the back of
vans, their ears sweating under too-tight headphones.

Once Jake Sheldon had obtained the necessary legal
approval for the monitoring of the telephone line at Lou
Schoelen's parents' house in Coronado, the details were
passed to an agent, Eric Tiefenbacher, on the fourth floor of
the FBI's East Indianola Street offices. He in turn liaised
with a fifty-year-old technician in the phone company's
headquarters, a man who had been as closely vetted as any
FBI agent. It was his job to arrange for the line to be
monitored and he did that by pressing a few keys on his
computer terminal and sending the signal along a dedicated
line to the FBI building. He did it while on a second line to
Tiefenbacher and sent a test signal down the dedicated line
to ensure that the link was good. At any one time the
technician was responsible for up to sixty telephone taps,
most of them for the FBI and the DEA, and he had enough
information to destroy a host of long-term investigations
into organised crime and corruption. He was positively
vetted every year by the Bureau, but the technician would
never in a million years consider trading the information he

had. His granddaughter had died five years earlier, knocked down by a getaway car driven by three black teenagers who had just robbed a liquor store. For him, wire-tapping was a personal crusade, a way of helping the forces of law and order against the vermin who ruled the streets.

Three walls of the office in which Tiefenbacher worked were lined with tape-recorders. The machines were voice-activated and the reels only turned when a call was made. In the centre of the room was a teak veneer desk and a chair at which Tiefenbacher chain-smoked while he monitored the tape-recorders and replaced the tapes as necessary. Each hour, on the hour, he picked up a clipboard and went from machine to machine, noting down the digits in the tape counter next to each line. The notation was a back-up check because the time of each call was electronically recorded on the tape, along with the number of the phone on the other end of the line. Call-tracing with digital exchanges had become a simple matter of computer programming.

Tiefenbacher alternated his shifts with three other agents, all of them heavy smokers, and between them they ensured that the office was occupied twenty-four hours a day, seven days a week. Some of the tape-recorders had red stickers attached, signifying that any calls had to be immediately reported to the agent involved, the rest were checked on a daily basis. Most of the agents in the building referred to the surveillance room as The Tomb and the four agents had long been nicknamed The Living Dead. All four had in one way or another offended someone high up in the Bureau. Being assigned to The Tomb was not a good career move for an ambitious agent.

Eric Tiefenbacher's transgression had been to allow his

partner to take a bullet in the chest during what was supposed to have been a straightforward arrest of a bail-jumper. He had been in The Tomb for five months and was already applying for other jobs outside the FBI. When the Schoelen tape began to turn, Tiefenbacher stubbed out his cigarette, picked up a pair of headphones, and walked over to the machine, which had a red sticker on it along with the names of two agents: Cole Howard and Kelly Armstrong. He plugged the headset into the machine and listened. The old lady made only a few calls, usually to local stores who delivered, or to the vet who had been treating her dog. The red sticker had the home telephone numbers of the two agents so that they could be contacted outside of office hours. Kelly Armstrong had visited the surveillance room soon after the phone tap was arranged, and she'd asked that she be called first if there was anything of interest. She'd told him a little about the investigation as she perched on the edge of his desk, leaning forward to give him a glimpse of cleavage. She was one hell of a hot babe, Tiefenbacher thought, with breasts that he just ached to touch. She had class, too; her clothes were stylish and he noticed that the watch she kept looking at was a gold Cartier. She was wearing a wedding ring but he was giving some thought to asking her out for a drink after work.

He listened to the conversation. The old woman was obviously talking to her son, Lou Schoelen, the man the agents were interested in. The display below the tape counter listed the number of the telephone number the old woman was talking to. The digits would be recorded on the tape at the end of the call, but Tiefenbacher scribbled them down on his clipboard so that he could tell Kelly Armstrong right away. Maybe if he impressed her, she'd be more amenable to a date.

Lisa Howard carried two mugs of coffee into the sitting room and placed them on the table, being careful not to disturb her husband's papers. "Thanks, honey," he said, looking up and smiling. "How are the kids?"

"Fast asleep," she said. "They're growing up so fast. Eddy asked me if he could start playing golf today; can you believe that?"

"I bet that'll please your father no end," said Cole. Theodore Clayton was a scratch golfer, and Lisa had been playing for years. She was good enough to turn professional, though she only played for fun.

"Daddy wants to buy him his own set of junior clubs." She sipped her coffee.

Howard put down the yellow marker he had been using to underline paragraphs of interest in the papers he was reading. "Hey, if Eddy wants golf clubs, I'll get them for him. His birthday isn't far off, they'll make a great present."

Lisa smiled thinly. "Actually, I was playing with Daddy today and he's already bought them." She saw that her husband was about to protest, so she rushed to speak first. "I know, I know, but there was nothing I could do. You know how strong-willed he is. It's just a set of golf clubs."

Howard scowled. It was more than just sports equipment, it was yet another sign of his father-in-law's interference. Howard had always strived to maintain his

233

independence, to do the best he could to support his family, but no matter how hard he worked, no matter how many hours of overtime he put in, he could never hope to compete with Theodore Clayton's immense wealth. Howard knew that it wouldn't stop with the golf clubs. Down the line there'd be offers of horses, cars, college tuition, vacations, anything the children wanted. Acceptance would become easier as time went on, and he didn't want his children to grow up thinking that everything would be handed to them on a plate. "If my son wants to take up a sport, I'd rather be the one who sets him up . . ." Howard began, but he stopped himself when he realised how petty he sounded. "Does this mean he's gone off baseball?"

Lisa smiled and shook her head, her long blonde hair spilling around her shoulders. "Of course not. He just wants to be able to play golf with me, that's all. And he'd love it if you played with us."

Howard picked up his marker again. "Yeah, right," he said. "Me on a golf course." He could feel an argument building, so it was with a sense of relief that he heard the telephone ring. "I'll get it," he said. It was Kelly Armstrong. Howard frowned and looked at his watch. She must be phoning from home, he realised.

Kelly told him about the call Lou Schoelen had made to his mother, and that the telephone company had identified a pay phone in Long Beach as the source. "Cole, I think I should go out there and co-ordinate the search," she said. "I don't think the Justin Davies credit card was a diversion, I think they really are on the West Coast. The President is due in Los Angeles in ten days, I think that's what they're planning for."

"Well . . ." said Howard.

"There's a plane leaving in forty-five minutes, I've already booked a ticket. I'll call you from our LA office."

"I'm not sure if it's . . ."

"Cole, I've already conferred with Jake Sheldon, and he says I should go."

Howard took a deep breath and closed his eyes. "In that case, Kelly, of course. Have a safe trip." He banged the receiver down and went back to the sitting room where Lisa was looking up, clearly concerned. "That bitch Kelly Armstrong," he said. "She's trying to run rings around me again."

"Well, I'm sure she won't be any match for you, honey," said Lisa.

Howard grinned. "Yeah, you might be right."

The Amtrak Metroliner rolled into Washington and the platform was soon filled with bleary-eyed commuters. Joker was one of the last to leave the train. He'd managed to grab some sleep during the four and a half hour journey, though the pain in his side was still bothering him. By the time he got out of the station, there was a line waiting for taxis and he joined it. It was a pleasant, warm day and he took off his pea jacket, wincing as he did. The woman in front of him turned, looked him up and down, and moved away, a look of disgust on her face. Joker figured he must look and smell fairly nauseating. He hadn't had a chance to wash or shave since leaving his hotel and he'd finished off the bottle of Famous Grouse on the train. The woman was elegant and wearing full make-up. Her clothes were obviously expensive and new. He could see that she was carrying her leather shoes in a Gucci bag and even the Reeboks she was wearing were pristine white. Joker wasn't surprised at her reaction.

A black man in a threadbare overcoat was moving down the line, asking for change. The woman in Reeboks turned her back on the beggar, making a clicking sound of annoyance with her tongue. "Change? Got any change?" he repeated to her back. The beggar looked at Joker, saw the condition he was in, smiled, and moved on down the line, repeating his litany to uncaring ears.

Joker wondered if the two heavyweights in his hotel room had managed to untie themselves yet, and what they would do for clothes. He smiled to himself. The Frowner's automatic was in Joker's suitcase, wrapped up in the man's trousers. It gave him a comforting feeling knowing that it was there. He doubted that they would come after him – they had no way of knowing where he'd gone. If Beaky Maguire had told them that he'd mentioned Patrick Farrell's name, he reckoned that at most they'd telephone Farrell and tell him that someone had been asking questions about him and Bailey in New York.

Joker reached the front of the line and clambered into the back of his taxi. He told the driver to take him to the nearest cheap motel and slumped back in his seat. His first priority was to get a room, a few hours sleep in a bed, and a fresh bottle of whisky. Then he'd start looking for Farrell's aircraft company.

* * *

Mary rolled over in the bed, luxuriating in the warmth of the blankets, and stretched. The clock radio on the bedside table was set to go off at nine, so she reached over lazily and switched it off. She didn't have to check out of the room until midday so she was in no rush. A shower, a leisurely breakfast, and then she'd curl up with a good book. The only agenda she had was to wait for Matthew Bailey's telephone call. She picked up the phone and ordered scrambled eggs, toast, coffee, orange juice and a copy of the *Baltimore Sun*, and then headed for the shower. In the bathroom she checked the roots of her dyed blonde hair and realised that she couldn't go much longer without having it redone.

She was just finishing off her eggs when Bailey called. "M-M-Mary," he stammered, "is everything okay?"

He sounded tense, but then he always did when talking to her. "Everything is exactly as it should be, Matthew," she said. She gave him the address and telephone number of the house on Chesapeake Bay.

"We're still going ahead?" he asked.

"Of course," she replied. "The weather's terrific here, and everybody else is already at the house. Why don't you drop by Pat Farrell and check that he doesn't have any problems before you come round to the house?"

"I will. I'll check out the plane at the same time."

"Good, that's good."

There was a pause on the line and then Bailey stammered: "M-M-Mary?"

"Yes?" she answered, tensing because she feared she was going to hear something uncomfortable.

There was another, shorter, pause. "Nothing," he said. "I'll see you." The line went dead and Mary replaced the receiver. She was beginning to get a bad feeling about Bailey. She hoped he wasn't getting cold feet.

Howard was in his office at 8 a.m. but Jake Sheldon had obviously beaten him to it. There was a message on Howard's desk asking him to call Sheldon. He picked up the phone to call Sheldon's office, but then had second thoughts and replaced the receiver. He walked down the corridor and pressed the bell at the side of the door to The Tomb. He waved at the surveillance camera above the door and the lock mechanism buzzed. He pushed open the door and stepped inside. The agent on duty was an old friend of Howard's, a twenty-year man called Gene Eldridge. Eldridge had been sentenced to The Tomb for being unable to get his weight below 300 pounds, ostensibly for medical reasons but everybody knew it was because the Bureau top brass was trying to weed out all those agents who didn't fit into its desired profile of young, healthy go-getters. He was a good-natured man, grey-haired with a florid expression, who had to have his suits tailor-made. He always wore a large handkerchief in his top pocket which he would produce with a flourish to mop his forehead at frequent intervals.

"Cole, how's it going?" asked Eldridge. He was standing at the far end of the room wearing headphones. He waved Howard over. "Come and listen to this." He slipped off the headphones and passed them to Howard. A man and a woman were talking on the line, though the man's input consisted mainly of heavy-breathing and grunts. The woman, whose voice was husky and deep, was describing what she wanted to do with the man in graphic terms. "He's a drug dealer the DEA are on to," said Eldridge. "He makes one of these calls every morning." The man on the line was building to a climax and Howard handed the headphones back to Eldridge, who unplugged them from the tape machine. "So what brings you back to The Tomb?" he asked.

"Tap on a house in Coronado, name of Schoelen. A call was made last night. Who was on then?"

"Eric Tiefenbacher," replied Eldridge, wiping his forehead with his red cotton handkerchief. He sat down at the desk, his massive thighs squashing together like plump cushions. "Is there a problem?"

"No, it's not a problem. He called Kelly Armstrong last night about a call made to the Schoelen home."

"Yeah, the ice maiden. Eric's had the hots for her for some time. Watch that one, Cole, she's on the fast track. Her husband's a big wheel in the Justice Department, isn't he?"

"No idea. Can I hear the call?"

"Sure." Eldridge pointed. "That's the machine over there. Take the tape off and play it on the machine next to it. Just in case a call comes in while you're playing it. You haven't forgotten how to do it?"

Howard gave the overweight agent a withering look. "No, Gene, I haven't forgotten." Howard had spent seven months in The Tomb after the Bureau had first discovered his drinking problem. It wasn't a time he liked to think about. He replaced the tape, and put the original on the machine Eldridge had indicated. He switched it on and the two agents listened to the conversation.

"Nice guy to be so worried about his dog," said Eldridge. He handed the clipboard to Howard. "You wanna fill this in for me, too?"

Howard took the clipboard and wrote down the time the tape had been changed, followed by the tape counter number. "Like riding a bicycle," he said, passing it back to Eldridge. "How long have you been here now, Gene?"

The big man shrugged. "Four years, I guess."

"How come you don't try to get out?"

"You mean why don't I lose the weight? Hell, Cole, I've tried. I don't even eat that much."

Howard walked over to a wastepaper bin and looked down. There were several Burger King wrappings lying there, along with two empty packs of cookies. "Yeah, right," he said.

"Besides, this isn't too bad, you know? It's regular hours, it's clean, it's safe, and it all goes towards my pension just the same. You were different, Cole. Your time in The Tomb was just a slap on the wrist, for me it's an exile." He wiped his forehead with the handkerchief. "So what's with the tape?"

"I'm trying to track down the guy, I'm hoping that the conversation will tell me where he is."

Eldridge looked at the clipboard. "According to the notes Tiefenbacher made, the call was placed from a public phone in Long Beach."

"Yeah, that's what it said, all right. Kelly's out there."

"But you think different?" asked Eldridge. Howard winked. "I suppose that means the ice maiden has rushed off on a wild goose chase?" Howard grinned. "What a fucking shame," said Eldridge. "I guess she'll be mighty pissed at young Tiefenbacher?"

"Okay if I borrow this tape for a while?" asked Howard.

"Hey, hold on a minute, Cole, you know as well as I do that the tape has to stay within the building. You can taint it as evidence if it leaves our jurisdiction."

"It's not evidence; we're just trying to track down the guy, that's all. I've a couple of experts I want to listen to the tape, and then I'll bring it right back."

"Today? You'll bring it back today? On my shift?"

Howard nodded. "By lunchtime, Gene, I promise." Back in his office, Howard dialled through to the Image Processing and Research Labs at Clayton Electronics. It was answered by McDowall, who sounded as if he was drawing on a cigarette. "This is Cole Howard, of the FBI," said Howard. McDowall coughed and Howard smiled. "Is that a joint?" he asked.

"Jeez, you guys know everything," said McDowall. "So what can we do for you, Special Agent Howard?"

Howard explained what he wanted and arranged to go round to the lab immediately. There was another message from Jake Sheldon on his desk, but Howard ignored it. Thirty minutes later he was in the laboratory with McDowall and Wyman. The sweet smell of marijuana still lingered in the air and McDowall had a slightly spaced-out look about him.

"That the tape?" asked Wyman.

Howard nodded and gave it to him. "The quality is good, but it's the background I'm interested in."

Wyman went over to a tape deck and motioned for the FBI agent to join him. "You'd better show me which bit you want," he said.

They played the tape through to the point where Schoelen had called his mother. "This is it, from here on,"

241

said Howard. "There's some noise in the background as if he had the radio or TV on. Can you bring that up for me?"

"No problem," said Wyman. "Compared with what we do with video, this is Stone Age stuff." He looked over at McDowall, who was biting a thumbnail. "Bill, can you digitise this for me?"

"Sure thing," said McDowall, who sat down at a computer. He pecked at a few keys. "Okay, run it," he said.

Wyman pressed the play button and the conversation was replayed over a loudspeaker. When it had finished, McDowall gave Wyman a thumbs-up. "Got it," he said. He hit more keys and the conversation played over the speaker again. "This is in the computer, not on tape," Wyman said to Howard.

Wyman pulled a chair over next to McDowall and sat down. The two men talked together in rapid jargon, leaving Howard in the dark as to what they were doing. For all he knew, they could be speaking another language. McDowall's fingers played across the keyboard, with Wyman offering advice, and lines of numbers scrolled across the screen. After ten minutes, Wyman nodded and sat back, a big grin splitting his face. "Try it," he said. McDowall pressed a key and the speaker crackled into life. This time there were no voices. There were some musical notes, then a burst of what could have been static, then muffled voices.

"Sounds like TV, for sure," said Wyman.

"Can you enhance the voices?" Howard asked.

"We can take out the higher frequencies, that should take the edge off it," said McDowall. He bent over the keyboard, his hair swinging forward, and his head moved in time with the pecking of his fingers like a small boy during a piano lesson. When he replayed it, there was a noticeable improvement, though Howard still couldn't work out what was being said.

"Keep playing it," he said.

"Put it in a loop," suggested Wyman.

McDowall pressed more keys and the section was repeated over and over as the three men listened.

"That sound, the electronic noise, it's sort of familiar," mused Wyman.

"I'll try to enhance it," said McDowall. "I'll mute the lower frequencies first, see if that helps."

The three men listened as McDowall played on the computer keyboard. It came to Howard in a burst of inspiration, and he laughed out loud. "It's a phaser!" he cried.

"Man, you're right," said McDowall.

"Beam me up, Scottie!" cheered Wyman.

"Guys, I can't thank you enough," said Howard. He took the tape and headed back to the office. On the way out, Wyman pointed out that phasers were used both in *Star Trek* and its successor, *Star Trek: The Next Generation*.

When he arrived back at FBI headquarters, there was a third message from Sheldon on the desk, a note saying that Bill McDowall had called, and a series of faxes from the State Department listing overseas VIPs who were due to visit the United States in the coming months. As he called McDowall, he screwed up both notes and lobbed them through the air and into his wastepaper basket. McDowall answered, and gleefully told Howard that he had done some further work on the end of the phone call, which was still stored in their computer, and that they were reasonably sure that they could pick out Spock's voice – it was *Star Trek* and not its successor. Howard thanked him. Knowing that *Star Trek* had been on television when Schoelen made his phone call was a major step forward. At first he'd planned to ring around all the television stations but on the drive back to his office he'd had a brainwave and instead he rang the publishers of *TV Guide*, the weekly magazine which published television programme listings throughout the country. He found a co-operative editor there who took only a few minutes to identify those stations which had been playing the science fiction show. There were six in all. The phone company gave him the numbers of the stations, and he called them one at a time, identifying himself as an FBI agent and asking for the programme controller. In each case he asked if they would run the tape of the show broadcast the previous evening and see if a phaser had been fired at about twenty past the hour, the time of the call. Most thought at first he was joking, but Howard gave them the number of FBI headquarters in Phoenix so that they could call back and check that his request was genuine.

Eventually he had arranged with all six stations to check their shows and call him back. The first two calls reported no phasers at the time Howard was interested in, but he struck gold with the third. Captain Kirk had indeed fired his weapon, and seconds later he'd had a conversation with Spock before beaming up to their starship. The station was WDCA-TV which served the Baltimore-Washington area. Howard smiled as he hung up. He had a good feeling about the way things were going. The remaining three stations rang back within ten minutes of the WDCA-TV call and all were negative. Howard was elated. He finished his coffee and then called up to Jake Sheldon's office. Sheldon's secretary told him to go right up.

Sheldon raised one eyebrow when Howard entered his office. "Been out of the office, Cole?" he asked softly.

"Yeah, sorry about that, but I was chasing up the Lou Schoelen telephone tap," he said, dropping into the chair opposite Sheldon's desk. "I didn't get your message until a few minutes ago."

Sheldon adjusted the cuffs of his immaculate blue suit. "I understood that Kelly was chasing up that lead," he said.

"I'm not convinced that the call came from Long Beach," said Howard. He noticed that there were three files on Sheldon's desk. He tried to read the names on them but they were obscured by the man's arms.

"According to Kelly, the call was made from a public phone there. Several of the Barrett rifles which were sold through West Coast dealers are still unaccounted for, and the President is going to be in LA for the anniversary of the 1992 riots. The evidence seems pretty strong to me." He linked his fingers on the desk and waited for Howard to reply.

Howard smiled thinly. Kelly hadn't mentioned that she'd heard back from the gun dealers. Yet another secret she'd kept from him. "Lou Schoelen was a telephone hacker," said Howard. "He was almost busted by AT & T while he was a SEAL for using and selling black boxes, the gizmos that get you long-distance and international calls for free. He's perfectly capable of rerouting his calls and sending us on a wild goose chase."

Sheldon frowned. "Did you tell Kelly this?"

"I didn't get the chance," Howard replied. He told the director about the analysis of the tape and how he'd identified the television station on the East Coast.

"So you're saying that Schoelen made the call from

the Baltimore-Washington area?"

"Seems that way," agreed Howard. "And from what he said to his mother, whatever it is they have planned is going to take place within the next two weeks. I think I should go to Washington."

Sheldon nodded. "It's worth a try. You should speak to Bob Sanger while you're there." He ran a hand through his pure white hair. "There's something else you should know," he said. "I had a call from the director of the Counter-Terrorism office in New York while you were out. His name's Ed Mulholland. Seems they've identified three of the photographs you sent to them. One is Mary Hennessy, an IRA activist who is on the run from the British. One of the men is Matthew Bailey, another member of the Provisional Irish Republican Army. He's been responsible for the deaths of four policemen in Northern Ireland." Sheldon passed over two of the three files. Howard opened the top one. It contained a handful of faxes, including a file photograph of Bailey which was a close match of the ones generated by Theodore Clayton's computer experts.

"He's a sniper?" asked Howard as he flicked through the faxes.

"He's used a Kalashnikov in Belfast, but more as an assault weapon than sniping," said Sheldon. "He uses explosives, mainly."

Howard opened the second file and looked down at a photograph of the blonde woman. It was the same woman who had been pictured in the desert. "This doesn't make sense," he said. "Why would the IRA be involved with SEAL snipers?"

"Expertise," said Sheldon. "Before the 1994 ceasefire

they were using a former Green Beret to shoot British soldiers across the border between the north and south. We know who the guy is, we know he's based in Cork on the west coast of Ireland and we know he uses a Barrett."

"So why didn't the IRA use him in the States?"

"Because as soon as he sets foot here, he'll be arrested. Sheldon passed a third file across the desk. "The second man is Ilich Ramirez Sanchez." The FBI agent opened it and saw several surveillance photographs of the moustached man with the receding hairline. "You probably know him as Carlos the Jackal, the Venezuelan terrorist responsible for kidnapping OPEC ministers in Vienna in 1975 and a machine-gun attack at Tel Aviv Airport which left twenty-five dead in 1972, and a whole host of other atrocities. We're still trying to find out how he got away from the French. It would never have happened if *we'd* caught him, I can tell you. All sorts of alarm bells are ringing over in New York, Cole. It was assumed he was in hiding somewhere in the Middle East. If he's now in this country . . ." He left the sentence unfinished.

Howard scanned the file. Like every law-enforcement officer in the world, he was all too well aware of who Carlos was. There was a list of the terrorist groups he'd been connected with, and it read like a list of Who's Who in International Terrorism: the Popular Front for the Liberation of Palestine, the Turkish Popular Liberation Front, the Quebec Liberation Front, the Baader-Meinhof Gang, the Japanese Red Army, the Organisation for the Armed Arab Struggle. There was, however, no mention of the IRA. He looked at the photographs again. There was no doubt that it was the same man that had been filmed in the Arizona desert.

"Have you told Sanger yet?" Howard asked.

Sheldon shook his head. "I wanted to talk to you first. I think it would be helpful if you saw Ed Mulholland in New York for a briefing from Counter-Terrorism. I'll call the White House while you're en route. Cole, now that we know who is involved, this has the Bureau's absolute top priority. In view of the way the investigation has progressed, Ed Mulholland will be taking command."

The news hit Howard like a punch in the stomach. "I have everything under control," he protested. "I don't see that . . ."

Sheldon held up a hand to silence him. "I understand your feelings, Cole, but it has now become an anti-terrorism matter. We need specialist input, and Ed has seniority. It has to be that way."

Howard wanted to argue, but he knew that it would be pointless. If a terrorist such as Carlos was involved, then it was only natural that Counter-Terrorism would become involved. And if the section's director wanted to handle the investigation, he would obviously be the ranking agent.

"I've already agreed with Ed that you continue working on the investigation, and that you report to us both, in tandem. The background you already have will be invaluable, and Ed is keen to have you on his team for this one. Is that okay with you?"

Howard sighed. At least he wasn't being taken off the case. "Based here or in New York?" he asked.

"Wherever Ed wants you," said Sheldon, "though from what you've told me it looks as if your focus is going to be the East Coast. Do you want to call Kelly back and have her go to New York with you?"

Howard fought back the urge to smile and looked

steadily at Sheldon. "She seemed very enthusiastic about following up on the Barrett rifles," he said, "so maybe we should let her carry on with that. Manpower isn't going to be a problem, I suppose?"

"Ed will assign you all the men you need on the East Coast and the Secret Service will give you all the help they can."

"We're definitely assuming that Carlos and the IRA are after the President?" Howard asked. He thought of the State Department list on his desk. "He's always been pro-Irish, right? Isn't it more likely that the IRA would go for a British target?"

Sheldon settled back in his chair. "According to Mulholland, the world's top terrorists were in Baghdad in the summer of 1991, summoned by Saddam Hussein. Carlos was there, so were the IRA. There were people from the Abu Nidal organisation, the Japanese Red Army, and anyone else who was prepared to do Saddam's dirty work. He's long been a supporter of terrorist organisations and after Desert Storm he decided to call in favours owed. We don't know for sure what Saddam had planned, but it's clear he was planning revenge against the countries who forced him out of Kuwait."

"And that's what our anti-terrorist people think this is about? Revenge for Desert Storm?"

Sheldon nodded. "Remember the attempt to kill George Bush in Kuwait in April '93? The car bomb? That was Saddam's work."

"And we retaliated with a cruise missile attack on Baghdad. Didn't that teach him a lesson?"

Sheldon smiled. "The man won't rest until he's had his revenge, Cole. It's an Arab thing. And each time he loses face he becomes even more determined."

Howard shrugged. "I can't think why the IRA would want to be involved in a Presidential assassination, but if they were acting for Iraq, then it makes more sense, I guess."

"They could also be doing it for the oldest reason of all – money," said Sheldon. "Do you know much about the Irish situation?"

"I know that the IRA are fighting for independence for Ireland. They want the British troops out, and self-determination."

Sheldon nodded. "That's fine as far as it goes, but there's more to it than that. It's more a struggle for power and money. And if this Jackal character is paying enough, I'm sure Bailey and Hennessy will do exactly what he wants."

"Even if he wanted to assassinate the President? You think they'd do that?"

"They've committed unthinkable atrocities in Britain," said Sheldon. "Some years ago they blew up Lord Mountbatten while he was in a small boat with a group of children. The boat was reduced to splinters . . . there was nothing left of the people. They buried empty coffins."

Howard shuddered, but he still wasn't convinced. He could feel a growing sense of panic in his stomach and he tried to quell it. "Now that we know of the IRA involvement, perhaps we should be looking at the possibility of alternative targets," he suggested.

"British, you mean," said Sheldon. Howard nodded. "Agreed, but I think we have to assume that the President is at risk, until we know the full extent of the IRA involvement," he said.

"What about former Presidents?" asked Howard. "If Saddam went for Bush in '93, maybe he'll try again."

"Bush's people have been informed and he'll be keeping out of the public eye for a while. The same goes for high-ranking military officers. But the President can't do that. He can't hide."

Howard felt a sudden wave of apprehension. He sensed the assignment getting out of control; there were so many angles, so many things he had to do, and he was beginning to fear that the job was too much for him. He picked up the files and went back to his office. In the old days he would have reached for a bottle to kill the butterflies, but he hadn't touched a drop for almost four years and had no intention of starting now. He sat down heavily at his desk, looked at his watch and pulled open his bottom drawer. In a slim black book he found mention of an Alcoholics Anonymous meeting which was due to start in an hour's time. When he'd first stopped drinking, he'd attended an AA meeting pretty much every day. The clinic which Theodore Clayton had sent him to made giving up easy, it was as secure as most Federal prisons and Howard had been under twenty-four hour a day supervision while he underwent detoxification. Later, while he was in group and individual therapy, there was so much to do that he didn't have the time to miss drinking. The clinic, hidden away on an exclusive estate to the south of Phoenix, prohibited visitors or any contact with outsiders for the first month, and it forced him to address his alcohol problem and to accept that it was an illness, not a weakness.

When he left the clinic, thirty pounds heavier and feeling better than he'd felt in more than five years, his counsellor's last words were a reminder to attend daily AA meetings for at least a month. Howard remembered how he'd smiled and shook the man's hand, thinking that he had his alcoholism licked. Within three hours the craving for a drink had reduced him to a cold sweat and shaking hands and he'd reached for the slim black book.

Now, he attended AA meetings at least once a week, more if he was gripped by the craving for a drink. An hour. He had time to call New York first. He picked up his copy of the FBI's internal phone directory and looked up the Bureau's Counter-Terrorism unit with responsibility for the IRA. He found it under Counter-Terrorism (Europe) and saw that their office was based in Federal Plaza in Manhattan. The director in charge was listed as O'Donnell Jr, H. C. All the FBI's offices were linked through a secure internal communications system so he could phone internally and not have to use an outside line. He dialled through to O'Donnell's extension but after six rings it was answered by a secretary who informed Howard that he was out of the office. Howard ran his finger down to the list of agents in the Irish section and asked for the first name there: Clutesi, D. The secretary transferred his call and this time a bored-sounding man answered. Howard identified himself and explained that Ed Mulholland had sent over files on Bailey, Hennessy and the Jackal. He asked the New York agent if he'd check two more names for IRA connections: Rich Lovell and Lou Schoelen. Neither was known to Clutesi. "You want me to try the RUC or MI5?" he offered.

"RUC?"

"Royal Ulster Constabulary," explained Clutesi. "The Northern Ireland police. They've got a hell of a good intelligence network. And MI5 is the British Intelligence

Service, they keep their own files on Irish terrorists. We've set up a system for information-sharing. I can run all the names through their files."

"Pictures, too?" asked Howard, pulling his own computer terminal closer and switching on the VDU.

"Sure," said Clutesi. "It'll take time, though. Our computers aren't linked yet, we have to do it through messengers. The MI5 files might take a bit longer than the RUC. They seem to be dragging their feet lately. Politics, you know?"

"I understand," said Howard, who wasn't sure that he did.

"Do you know much about the IRA?" Clutesi asked.

"Not much," admitted Howard. "Just what I read in the newspapers."

Clutesi laughed. "Yeah, well we both know how reliable they are, right? I'll send you a couple of recent background papers the CIA put together. I think you'll find them useful. And I've a briefing paper our director, Hank O'Donnell, wrote for internal consumption last year."

Howard thanked Clutesi and told him he'd be in New York the following day. He spent the time before his AA meeting reading the files on Matthew Bailey and Mary Hennessy. Bailey was twenty-six years old and had been what the IRA call 'an active volunteer' since he was nineteen. The RUC had three warrants out for his arrest for a series of murders in Northern Ireland. He was involved in the ambush of two police officers who were gunned down with a Kalashnikov assault rifle, though there was some doubt as to exactly who pulled the trigger. He was also seen in an East Belfast police station shortly before a bomb exploded in the reception area, killing an RUC officer and injuring six members of the public. Another RUC officer was killed in a car-bombing and equipment similar to that used in the device was found at an apartment where Bailey was known to have visited. The evidence against Bailey seemed to Howard to be conclusive, but even more damning was the testimony of a highly placed IRA activist who turned police informer in 1993 and who had already been responsible for the trial and imprisonment of more than a dozen terrorists.

The file included a note from the RUC that Bailey had left Northern Ireland for the South, followed by reports that he had flown to the United States. An FBI anti-terrorist unit working on the West Coast had almost trapped Bailey in a sting operation to sell him a ground-to-air missile, but he had disappeared only hours before he was due to take delivery. The Counter-Terrorism (Europe) unit had reported seeing Bailey in New York at the end of the previous year, mainly entering several Manhattan bars known to be centres of IRA fund-raising. The last sighting had been in November. Since then, nothing.

Mary Hennessy was forty-nine years old and a widow, according to her file. Her husband had been killed in a shoot-out three years previously when his car was ambushed by what was believed to have been a Protestant hit squad. Liam Hennessy had been a leading Belfast lawyer but had also acted as a senior adviser to Sinn Fein, the political wing of the Provisional Irish Republican Army. The men responsible for the attack were never caught, and the file detailed a speech Mary Hennessy had made at the funeral in which she accused the British Government of conducting a political assassination. She believed that it was the SAS who murdered her husband as part of a British plan to obliterate the IRA as a viable terrorist organisation.

In the file was a separate FBI research paper which went into the alleged shoot-to-kill operation in some detail, though its resolution was inconclusive. What was known for sure was that some two dozen top IRA activists had died within a four-week period which followed the downing of a 737 airliner en route from London to Rome. The IRA had never officially claimed responsibility for the bombing of the jet, but the device was known to have been planted by a female bomb-maker who was killed when the SAS stormed the London flat which she and other IRA members were using as a base. Following the death of the woman, Maggie MacDermott, and her colleagues, a six-month bombing campaign came to a sudden halt, leaving the British authorities in no doubt that the IRA cell had been responsible. Several days after the downing of the jet, in which more than one hundred people died, two IRA terrorists were shot dead in a pub in Dublin by masked gunmen who were believed to be members of the Ulster Defence Volunteers, a Protestant para-military group. More assassinations followed and it seemed as if there was a tricolour-draped coffin being lowered into the ground every day. Several top-ranking IRA chiefs died in suspicious road accidents, running off cliffs at high speed or smashing in to trees on perfectly clear roads, and there were half a dozen supposed suicides, varying from a bathroom electrocution to self-inflicted shotgun wounds. Within four weeks the IRA was totally demoralised. Many of its members fled from Northern Ireland to the South or to the United States.

British newspapers ran screaming headlines about a

shoot-to-kill operation being sponsored or encouraged by the government, but generally the press and the public seemed to think that whatever was happening was a just retribution for the terror the IRA had wreaked in the United Kingdom. That there was indeed a shoot-to-kill policy was vehemently denied by the Prime Minister and the Army, and no evidence was ever produced to prove beyond a doubt that the killings were government-sanctioned. However, one of the FBI's analysts had run several statistical tests on the sudden deaths and determined that the odds of the twenty-four assassinations, suicides and road accidents occurring within a four-week period were of the order of six billion to one. There was no doubt that the killings were premeditated and the work of one group, but whether it was the SAS, MI5, the Army, or Protestant extremists, was still a mystery and one that was never likely to be solved. Whoever was responsible, the end result was the temporary destruction of the IRA as a terrorist threat. Most of those killed were the leaders and the planners, and without them the IRA was a headless snake, thrashing around waiting to die.

For a time it was Mary Hennessy who had tried to pull the organisation together, beginning with her anti-British speech at her husband's funeral. She called in vain for a public inquiry into the IRA deaths but her appeals were ignored and a year after burying Liam Hennessy she went underground, becoming a fully-fledged terrorist for the first time in her life. She organised a bombing campaign in Belfast which resulted in the destruction of an RUC station and an Army barracks. When Northern Ireland became too dangerous for her she moved over the border. From the South she made frequent forays back into Northern Ireland, her attacks always aimed at the British forces or the Royal Ulster Constabulary. Her fight was not religious in any way, it was political and aimed at those she blamed for the death of her husband. According to the FBI file she was responsible for the death of three undercover SAS officers who had been caught operating in the border country. Her torture of the men had been especially brutal and she'd been branded by the tabloid press as 'The Black Widow'. It appeared as if she had become mentally unbalanced after the death of her husband, and she was described in one RUC report as borderline psychotic. Mary Hennessy had never come close to being captured, and the last report in the file said that she was living close to Dublin, staying with various IRA sympathisers and still trying to rebuild the terrorist organisation.

Appended to the file was a comprehensive list of all the IRA's terrorist attacks over the previous twenty years. Howard was familiar with many of the atrocities: car bombs, sniper attacks, fire bombs, torture. No-one seemed to be beyond the range of the terrorists. They'd come close to killing Margaret Thatcher at a Conservative Party Conference by blowing up the hotel she was staying at, and during the run-up to the Gulf War they'd managed to launch home-made mortars against Number Ten Downing Street while Prime Minister John Major was meeting with his War Cabinet. Judges, Army officers, politicians, all had been assassinated by IRA hit squads, and for every terrorist captured and imprisoned, another dozen were waiting to take their place.

Howard looked at his watch and realised it was time to leave. He drove quickly through the afternoon traffic and reached the office where the meeting was to be held shortly before two o'clock. The office belonged to a leading lawyer whom Howard had met on several occasions. There were more than a dozen people there, most of them men and most, like Howard, wearing business suits. A taxi driver served coffee as they took their places in the chairs which had been brought into the plush office. The lawyer allowed the large office to be used for AA meetings once a month, but Howard had seen him at other venues: basketball courts, scruffy basements in run-down buildings, back rooms in public libraries.

The group sat and listened to one of the members, an out-of-town fertiliser salesman called Gordon, tell his life story. It was depressingly familiar: a good job, steady income, a wife and child, more stress than he could cope with, and a descent into the bottle. Gordon told the group he hadn't had a drink for six months, and he was warmly applauded.

Howard was next to speak and he took his place in front of the two ranks of chairs. The first time he'd attended an AA meeting he'd been more than a little cynical, he'd considered the public breast-beating to be little more than mental masturbation, that the speakers were just taking pleasure from publicly reopening old wounds. He had trouble too in dealing with the religious aspects of the meetings and the reliance on God, until a long-term AA member had suggested that he think of God as a Group of Drunks, and from that point on he'd become a convert. Now, after almost four years of regular attendance, Howard knew how valuable the meetings were in the battle against the bottle, and that telling others about his setbacks and successes strengthened his own resolve.

He put his coffee cup on the desk and clasped his hands

behind his back. "My name's Cole, and I'm an alcoholic," he said. "Hi, Cole," the group chanted. "It's been almost four years since I had a drink," he continued. The group applauded and there were several cries of "Well done". Howard waited until the clapping died down. "I didn't know I had a drinking problem, I guess no-one in the office had the courage to tell me. But I was making mistakes, both at work and at home. There were arguments with my co-workers and fights with my wife. Everything came to a head when I crashed our car. Well, it was my wife's car, really, but I was driving. We both had our seat belts on, or I'm sure we'd have died. I hit a truck, we went off the road, and the next thing I knew, I was in hospital. My father-in-law found out, and he personally booked me into a clinic to dry out."

The group nodded encouragingly. He knew that some of those present, including the lawyer, had heard his story several times, but they still expressed support. "I'm grateful to my father-in-law, but recently I've found myself resenting the influence he has on my life. On all aspects of my life. At the time I had a drinking problem he went to my employer and made sure that I kept my job, and I'm grateful to him for that, but now he interferes at home, he tries to influence my children, he seems to be coming between me and my wife. That puts me under a lot of stress, and that makes me want to drink again. I know that I have to learn to stop resenting him, but it's difficult. I know that he cares about his daughter very much, and that he wants what's best for her. God, there are times when I want a drink so bad. It's worse now than it's ever been. I know that it would be easy to give in, to pick up the bottle and start drinking again, but I know that would be the biggest mistake I could make. Alcoholism is a disease, and it's a disease for which there's no cure. I'll be an alcoholic for the rest of my life, but that doesn't mean I have to drink. I can fight it, but it's one day at a time. I just have to accept that some days will be harder than others." The group applauded again, and Howard returned to his seat, feeling revitalised and with the urge for alcohol in a temporary retreat.

Todd Otterman sat in reception, tapping the file against his knee. The hotel foyer was busy, with several members of a dental convention queuing up to check out. Bellboys scurried back and forth, running suitcases outside, while girls in black and white uniforms processed the guests as quickly as possible, their smiles starting to wear thin.

Otterman had never met Gilbert Feinstein but he recognised the type as soon as he stepped out of the lift. Hair too long and untidy to be fashionable, a slight stoop, and eyes that continually sought the floor. According to the file Feinstein was twenty-four years old and had been working in the hotel kitchens for the past year. He had dropped out of high school and had a succession of minimum wage jobs, interspersed with short prison sentences for drug possession. It was after his second spell in prison that he'd written the letter to the President, spelling out in no uncertain terms what he wanted to do to him and his family. The letter had been one of the more graphic received at the White House, and the details of what Feinstein had planned for the First Lady's cat had raised a few smiles among the Secret Service agents.

Feinstein went over to the reception desk and spoke to one of the girls. She pointed to where Otterman was sitting and Feinstein's shoulders slumped as if he knew what was coming. He walked over and stood before the Secret Service agent. "You wanted to see me?" he said, his voice unsteady.

Otterman flicked open his ID and showed it to Feinstein. "You know what it's about, Mr Feinstein?"

Feinstein nodded. "Did you have to come here, to my work?" he said, his voice a monotone. "You could lose me my job."

Otterman motioned to the seat next to his. "Sit down, Mr Feinstein. You've been through this before so let's make it as painless as possible, shall we?" Feinstein sat down and began to bite his nails. "So, how do you feel about the President these days?" Otterman's tone was conversational, almost friendly.

"He's doing a wonderful job," sneered Feinstein. "Economy's looking good, foreign policy's never been better, everything's just hunky-dory."

"Had any more thoughts about what you'd like to do to his family?"

Feinstein sighed. "Look, I wrote that letter two years ago. I'd taken a couple of tablets, I was as high as a kite, I don't even remember mailing it."

"I understand that, but unfortunately it stays on file."

"But I didn't mean it! I was just a kid, a crazy kid."

One of the girls at reception looked over. "Try not to raise your voice, Mr Feinstein," said Otterman quietly.

"You're persecuting me!" Feinstein hissed.

"Mr Feinstein, we've never met before today."

"Not you personally. I mean the White House, the Secret Service. You won't leave me alone."

"Once you threaten the President of the United States, your name goes on file and it stays there. What do you think? You think we should just ignore someone when they threaten the President? Have you forgotten what you wrote? I've got a copy here if you want to refresh your memory."

"No, I remember," said Feinstein. "What is it you want?"

"You probably know that the President is coming to Baltimore next week."

"Yeah, I read that in the *Sun*."

"So we think it would be a good idea if you left the city for a while. Your parents live in Chicago, right?" Feinstein nodded and continued to chew his fingernails. "We'd like you to visit Chicago for a few days. From Monday to Thursday."

"Not again," said Feinstein, "you're not running me out of town again?"

"It's not just you, it's everybody on the watch list, so don't take it personally. You leave town on Monday, and you check in with our office in Chicago." He handed Feinstein a card. "This agent is expecting to see you on Monday evening, and you'll check with him twice a day until Thursday morning. Then you can come back."

Feinstein looked as if he was about to burst into tears. "I don't believe this, I don't believe you can screw with my life like this. This is America."

"It's precisely because it's America that we can screw with your life," said Otterman.

"I made one mistake, and I have to pay for it forever."

"No, you've made lots of mistakes, but you made one big one, and that's what you're paying for," said Otterman. "You know the procedure; if we don't hear from you in Chicago we'll come looking for you here. And you don't want that, do you?"

"I'll lose my job, I don't have any vacation days coming," Feinstein whined.

"Tell them you're sick, tell them anything. Just get out of the city."

Tears welled up in Feinstein's eyes. "When will it be over? When will you leave me alone?"

Otterman shrugged. "You're only on our watch list, it's not as if you're one of our quarterlies. If you behave and don't write any more silly letters, you could be off the watch list in three years or so."

Feinstein shook his head and wiped his eyes. "It's not fair," he sobbed.

"Son," said Otterman, standing up and straightening the creases of his black suit pants, "life isn't fair." He walked out of the hotel, leaving Feinstein alone with his tears. Otterman had two more visits to make before midday.

The chambermaid knocked nervously on the door. "Mr O'Brien?" she called. There was no answer so she knocked louder. She knew that Damien O'Brien tended to arrive back at the hotel in the early hours of the morning and stayed in bed late, and she knew better than to barge in unannounced. On one occasion she'd used her pass key and walked in to find him sprawled naked on the bed, an empty bottle of whisky in his hand, fast asleep and snoring like a freight train. It wasn't an experience she cared to repeat.

"Mr O'Brien!" she shouted, and used her key to rap on the door. "Housekeeping!" She looked at her watch. It was well past the time when he normally left for work, so perhaps he had left the Do Not Disturb sign on his door-handle by mistake. She slid her key in the lock and turned it gingerly, placing her ear against the wood and listening for any sound. "Housekeeping, Mr O'Brien," she repeated. The curtains were drawn but they were old and threadbare and enough light seeped in for her to see without switching the lights on.

She stepped into the room, a clean sheet and towel draped over one arm, and called out again, just in case he was in the bathroom. She gasped when she saw the feet sticking out from behind the bed, thinking that he was drunk again and that he'd fallen onto the floor. For the first time she noticed a buzzing noise, the sound an alarm clock might make if it was on a low setting. She walked further into the room and peered nervously around the bed. "Mr O'Brien?" she said, her voice trembling. She realised with a jolt that there were two pairs of legs, white and hairy, tied at the ankles. She dropped the sheet and towel as her hands flew to her mouth and she backed away, her breath coming in small, forced, gasps.

She ran down the stairs to reception and got the day manager, who picked up a baseball bat which he kept behind his desk. He held it in both hands as he went into the room, switching the light on and calling out the guest's name. The manager had been in the hotel business a long time, and he knew that people did strange things in hotel rooms: they tied each other up, they took drugs, they did things to each other they wouldn't, or couldn't, do in their own homes. He'd once found a woman swathed in polythene and tied spreadeagled to a bed after her boyfriend had collapsed in the bathroom with a heart attack. It would take a lot to surprise the manager. The buzzing noise got louder as he got closer to the end of the bed. He used his bat to gingerly prod one of the feet. There was no reaction so he stepped up to the window where he could look down on both bodies. They were men – big, heavy men – bound and gagged. There was blood, a lot of blood, and the manager could see several bullet wounds, gaping holes in the chests and heads. Flies buzzed around the wounds, feeding on the still-wet blood.

Howard drove home from the AA meeting to pack. If the snipers were indeed based on the East Coast it would be some time before he would be back in Phoenix. Lisa was in the kitchen, chopping herbs with a large knife and reading from a cookbook. "Home for lunch?" she said.

"I wish," he said. He explained that he was flying to New York and that for the foreseeable future he would be working with the Counter-Terrorism section.

"Oh God," she sighed, "what about dinner tonight?"

"I'm sorry, Lisa, you'll have to handle it without me."

"But Cole, this has been planned for weeks!" She threw the knife down on the chopping block and stood with her hands on her hips, her eyes blazing. "You'll just have to tell them you can't go!" Howard laughed, amused at her defiance. Only the daughter of Theodore Clayton would think of standing up to the FBI. His reaction only made her all the more angry. "You can fly out tomorrow," she said, "A few hours won't make a difference."

"It's an important case, honey, and a few hours might make all the difference. It's the case your father has been helping me with." Howard knew that invoking her father's name was his best chance of defusing her anger.

Lisa shook her head, took off her apron and threw it down on top of the knife. "Cole, I don't know why I put up with this," she said.

"It's my job," he said, lamely.

"Well, it needn't be," she said. "You could accept the job Daddy keeps offering. Head of Security at Clayton Electronics would be a great career move. It would pay much more than the Bureau gives you. And you wouldn't be sent off to the other side of the country at a minute's notice." Howard held his hands up in surrender. It was an argument they'd had many times, and it was one he'd never managed to win. "And it would mean the children would get to see more of their father," she pressed.

"I have to pack," said Howard, and he beat a hasty retreat. Lisa followed him up the stairs and stood behind him as he grabbed clean shirts from his wardrobe and dropped them into an overnight bag.

"How long will you be away?" she asked, folding her arms across her chest.

"I've no idea," he said over his shoulder. He had the uneasy feeling that if he looked her in the eye he'd be turned to stone on the spot.

"I don't know what you think you're achieving by selling your soul to the FBI," she said.

"Better the devil I know . . ." muttered Howard.

"What's that supposed to mean?" she said, her voice hard and accusing. "Are you saying that Daddy's the devil, is that what you're implying?"

Howard zipped his bag closed. "It's an expression, Lisa, that's all. I mean that FBI work is what I do, it's what I do well. I don't want to be a lapdog for the great Theodore Clayton. I don't want him to own me."

"Own you?" she said, her voice rising in pitch. "Who paid for this house? The car? You think we could live like this if it wasn't for my father's money? If it wasn't for my father you'd still be buried in the Surveillance Department. It's my father you owe, not the Bureau. Sometimes I think you forget where your loyalties should lie."

Howard froze and for several seconds he stared at her, unable to believe the cruelty in her voice. "Thank you, Lisa," he said softly. "Thank you for that."

He walked by her, down the stairs and out of the front door. Part of him hoped that she'd run after him or call him back, but he wasn't surprised when she let him go without a word. As he drove away, he could feel her sullen anger, sitting over the house like a storm cloud waiting to break.

It was a hot day and Joker turned up the air-conditioning in the rented Chevrolet Lumina. It was a big, comfortable American car and Joker enjoyed the way it handled. It had been a long time since he'd been at the wheel of a car and he'd forgotten the sheer pleasure it gave him to drive down an open road at speed. His eyes flicked to the speedometer and he braked to keep within the 55 mph speed limit. From his jacket pocket he took a green pack of Wrigley's chewing-gum and unwrapped it with his left hand before popping the gum into his mouth. He'd picked up a bottle of whisky from a liquor store and had a couple of slugs for breakfast, and if he was unlucky enough to be pulled in by a cop it would be better to smell of spearmint than whisky.

His side still ached where he'd been kicked and when he'd woken up that morning it was to find the flesh a vibrant shade of green. Luckily, it seemed there was nothing broken, but it was going to be painful for some time. The dashboard clock read 13:30. Joker had been up since 8 a.m. and an hour later he'd visited the cuttings library of the *Washington Post*. He'd asked to see the papers for the week when Pete Manyon had been killed and had drunk a styrofoam cup of black coffee as he'd read the articles detailing the discovery of the body, its identification, and its eventual export back to the United Kingdom. In none of the papers did the story merit more than a dozen paragraphs. Joker had been surprised to find out how violent a city Washington was. He'd assumed that because it was the political heart of the country, it would be one of the safer places to be, but in fact it was the murder capital of the United States with drive-by killings and torture regular occurrences and usually drug-related. When Manyon's body was first discovered, the police had assumed that he had been involved in the drugs trade because of the way he had been tortured. Practically skinned alive, the paper said, and suggested it had been the work of one of the city's vicious Jamaican gangs. His fingers had been systematically cut off with a pair of bolt cutters or a very sharp knife and he had been castrated. There were rope burns on his wrists and ankles. According to the paper, Manyon had died from loss of blood.

In the UK such a killing would have been front page news but in the Washington paper it was tucked inside and was one of five murders reported that day. There had been a suggestion from one of the Homicide detectives investigating the case that the fingers had been removed to hinder identification, but Joker knew that wasn't why Manyon had been mutilated. The first article had carried a photograph of Manyon's face, no doubt cosmetically tidied up by some helpful undertaker, and several days later a motel manager had come forward saying that one of his guests had disappeared leaving his clothes, and passport, behind. The passport photograph matched the face of the man in the morgue, and Pete Manyon was identified as John Ballantine, a life insurance salesman from Bristol, England, who was on an extended vacation.

The last article appeared ten days after the body had been discovered and detailed the arrival in Washington of Ballantine's sister and how she had flown back to England with the body. There were no further stories, and Joker assumed that the murder had remained on the Washington police's unsolved list. It hadn't been hard for Joker to imagine what Manyon had gone through during the hours he'd been tortured. He'd been in the farmhouse in Northern Ireland when Mary Hennessy had gone to work on Mick Newmarch. Joker rubbed his left wrist as he drove. It still bore the scars he'd made trying to wrench himself free from the handcuffs Hennessy had used to secure him to the radiator. Newmarch had told them everything, of course, no amount of training or spirit could withstand the sort of things Hennessy did with her knife. Joker would never forget Newmarch's screams, nor the look of pleasure, almost rapture, on Mary Hennessy's face as she'd used the blade.

A horn sounded behind him like the warning cry of some prehistoric monster and Joker realised he'd been drifting across the lanes of the highway. A huge truck roared by, the name of a meat packer on the side, its massive wheels only inches from his door. His knuckles were almost white, so hard had he been gripping the steering wheel, and he could feel sweat dribbling down his back despite the cold air streaming from the air-conditioning.

The newspaper library also had copies of every telephone directory in the United States, and Joker had gone through the ones for the Washington area, writing down the numbers of all the aircraft leasing companies, flying schools and local airlines. There was no home listing for a Patrick Farrell in the Washington City directory so he widened his search to the surrounding areas: Maryland, Laurel, Anne Arundel, Montgomery and the Greater Baltimore area to the north, and Arlington, Fairfax and Prince Georges to the south. He found only one P. Farrell and that was in a town called Laurel, about midway between Washington and Baltimore. In the Montgomery County Yellow Pages he found a Farrell Aviation listed and he'd smiled to himself, unable to believe his luck. If the surname hadn't been used in the company name he'd have had to call round about three dozen aviation firms. There was a pay phone in the lobby of the *Washington Post* and he'd used it to call the company. A bored-sounding secretary had told him that there were two Patrick Farrells, father and son, the father owned the company, the son ran it. She'd given Joker directions to a small airfield some twenty miles north-east of Washington.

As he drove to the airfield, Joker wondered if it was the father or the son that Matthew Bailey had contacted. There was no way of knowing. The son would be nearer Bailey's age, but the father was more likely to have emigrated to the States from Ireland, giving him stronger connections with the IRA. He was going to have to play it by ear.

In the trunk of the rental car was Joker's suitcase. He'd checked out of the Washington motel that morning and was planning to find a new place closer to Laurel. He had no definite plan as he drove along the Interstate 95, other than to check out the company and maybe sit outside for a while, on the off-chance that Bailey visited. He'd used the Visa card to buy a pair of powerful binoculars and they were in a plastic carrier-bag on the back seat.

The airfield was difficult to find – there were no signposts and eventually Joker had to ask for directions at a filling station. It was surrounded by trees so Joker didn't see it until he was virtually on top of it. It turned out to be little more than a grass strip with a few hangars and a single-storey brick building on which there was a sign which said Farrell Aviation and a logo of a green propeller with a hawk above it. A line of small planes faced the grass landing strip, many of them with covers over their cowlings as if they didn't get flown much. The asphalt road Joker was on wound through the trees and curved behind the hangars before widening out into a large area in front of the Farrell Aviation building where several cars were parked. Joker slowed his car down and pulled up in front of a hangar which had a large 'For Rent' sign on the door with the telephone number of a Baltimore real estate company. A bearded man in blue overalls appeared from the neighbouring hangar, wiping his hands on a rag. He stood looking at Joker for a second or two and then walked over. Joker got out of his car and stood looking up at the hangar.

"You interested?" the man said. His voice was laconic, almost sleepy, but his eyes were sharp and alert.

"Could be," answered Joker, "but not for me, my brother-in-law services small planes, he's looking for a base near Baltimore."

"You're English, right?" said the man.

Joker nodded. "Yeah, my sister married a guy from Boston. You get much business here?"

The man shrugged. "Not really, not what you'd call passing trade. There's no Flight Service Station here, and no fuel. You have to pull your own business in, pretty much. What sort of work does your brother-in-law do?"

"Small planes, Cessnas mostly. He buys up wrecks, does them up and sells them. There's always a market for 152s and 172s."

"Oh sure," the man agreed.

"You run your own business?" Joker asked.

"Yeah, routine servicing mainly. I have my regulars and there's a small flying club based here. We used to have a flying school but they closed."

"What about Farrell? They do okay?"

The man nodded. "Leasing, mainly. They own most of the hangars here. They do an eye-in-the-sky service for a few radio stations – you know, watching the traffic jams, stuff like that. And they do some film and television work. They do okay."

"Farrell? That's an Irish name, right?"

"Pat's Irish all right," said the man. "He's even painted green stripes on most of his planes."

Joker took a pen from his jacket pocket and wrote down

the name of the company handling the leasing of the empty hangar. "I'll pass this on to my brother-in-law," he said. "Thanks for your time."

"Sure, hope you decide to move in. It'd be good to have fresh faces around."

The man walked back to his hangar while Joker climbed back into his car. He drove slowly down the road and through the trees. There were many other things he wanted to ask the man, but he knew that he would be pushing his luck if he'd prolonged the conversation – it wouldn't take much to set alarm bells ringing over at the Farrell building.

A few hundred yards before the asphalt road joined the main highway, Joker saw a track which wound into the trees and he stopped for a closer look. It appeared to be overgrown and hadn't been used in a while. There was no-one around so he turned off the road and drove cautiously down the track. When he was sure he was far enough away from the road so that he couldn't be seen, he stopped the car. He took his binoculars from the back seat and his bottle of whisky from the trunk, and walked through the trees. He walked for half a mile or so until he reached a spot where he could see the front of the Farrell building in the distance, but remain well hidden from the airfield. He dropped down next to a wide chestnut tree and sat with his back propped up against it. His view was restricted by the trees between him and the airfield but he could see the cars parked in front of the building, and the main entrance. He focused the binoculars on the car number plates and found that he could read them easily, so he knew he'd have no problem seeing the face of anyone who went into or came out of the building. He uncapped the whisky bottle and drank deeply. He might be in for a long wait, but he had nowhere else to go.

Cole Howard read through the FBI file on Ilich Ramirez Sanchez on the direct flight from Phoenix to New York. Coach Class was almost empty and he had a whole row to himself, so he stretched out and put his briefcase on the seat next to his. A stewardess asked him if he wanted a drink and Howard caught himself about to ask for a whisky and Coke. He ordered an orange juice instead.

The file on Sanchez was about five times as thick as those of Matthew Bailey and Mary Hennessy, and included reports from virtually every intelligence agency in the world. The first page contained a list of the aliases the terrorist had used: Carlos Andres Martinez-Torres, Ahmed Adil Fawaz, Carlos Martinez, Hector Lugo Dupont, Nagi Abubaker Ahmed, Flick Ramirez, Glenn Gebhard, Cenon Marie Clarke, Adolf José Muller Bernal, and his real name – Ilich Ramirez Sanchez. He was born on October 12, 1949, in Caracas, Venezuela, the son of a millionaire lawyer, Dr José Altagracia Ramirez. The lawyer, whose politics tended towards the extreme Left, named his three sons after Lenin: Ilich, Lenin and Vladimir. The boys spent most of their childhood travelling around Latin America and the Caribbean with their mother, Elba Maria, who was separated from their father. When he was seventeen, Ilich Ramirez Sanchez was sent by his father to a Cuban guerrilla training camp near Havana, and in 1969 he enrolled in the Patrice Lumumba Friendship University in

Moscow, regarded by many as a terrorists' finishing school, and the following year he joined one of the world's most notorious terrorist organisations: the Popular Front for the Liberation of Palestine.

The stewardess returned with his orange juice and Howard thanked her. He rubbed his eyes. Reading under the artificial lights was a strain, but there was still a huge amount to get through. He sipped his juice and began to read again. In 1971 Carlos was invited by Dr Wadi Haddad, the operational chief of the PFLP, to a guerrilla seminar at a PFLP camp in the south of Lebanon along with young terrorists from the Japanese Red Army and the Baader-Meinhof Gang, and shortly afterwards he was assigned to the PFLP's foreign operations bureau, assisting in the machine-gun attack at Tel Aviv Airport which killed twenty-five and injured seventy-seven.

In July 1973 he took over the organisation's European terrorist cell, the Commando Boudia. In December of that year Carlos tried to assassinate Edward Sieff, the president of British retail stores chain, Marks and Spencer, because of his close links with Israel. He talked his way into Sieff's London home and shot his target in the face at point blank range – his favourite method of assassination. Incredibly, Sieff's teeth absorbed most of the bullet's impact and he survived. In 1974 Carlos threw a bomb into the London branch of the Israeli Bank of Hapoalim. A typist was injured. He moved to France and with Commando Boudia planted car bombs in front of the offices of various Jewish magazines, and threw an M26 fragmentation grenade into a newspaper kiosk on St. Germain-des-Près, killing two and injuring thirty-four. The following year Carlos and his team managed to get hold of Russian anti-tank bazookas and a three-man team flew out from the Middle East to help operate them. In January 1975 they fired one of the RPG-7s at an El Al plane at Orly Airport. They missed, and instead hit a Yugoslav plane. Later that year Carlos masterminded the kidnapping of the OPEC ministers in Vienna, taking them at gunpoint on a hijacked plane to North Africa where he was paid an $800,000 ransom before setting them free. Carlos was also linked to a whole series of terrorist attacks, kidnapping and murders, including the massacre of eleven Israeli athletes at the 1972 Munich Olympics, the bombing of a French nuclear plant, and helping the Japanese Red Army attack the French Embassy in The Hague where they took the ambassador and his staff hostage.

The French counter-espionage service, the Direction de la Surveillance du Territoire, came close to arresting him in Paris two years later, but Carlos killed two unarmed DST agents and a Lebanese informer. A French judge sentenced him to life imprisonment in his absence in 1992, and there were murder warrants for his arrest issued by the authorities in Austria and Germany and still on file.

By the late Seventies, Carlos had by all accounts retreated from the terrorist scene, and the world's intelligence services were having a hard time keeping track of him. He was seen in London in May 1978 but there was no trace of him leaving or entering the United Kingdom at that time. Howard wondered if the IRA had helped him.

Satellite surveillance photographs taken in 1983 suggested he was at a Libyan training camp instructing terrorists for Colonel Gaddafi, though the same year he claimed to have killed five people in bomb attacks in France. He forged links with the Hezbollah in Lebanon in their fight to end the French military presence in the country, and, in October 1983, fifty-eight French soldiers died when their barracks were bombed. There were reports that he was in India in 1985, and in 1986 stories circulated in Middle Eastern newspapers that he had been killed and buried in the Libyan desert.

The opening up of the Communist bloc provided evidence that Carlos had spent time in the early Eighties in Hungary, East Germany, Czechoslovakia, and other Communist regimes, but after the break-up of the Soviet Union, Carlos found himself with few friends. In 1991, after relations between Syria and the United States improved following their co-operation during Operation Desert Storm, Carlos was asked to leave Damascus by the Syrians, who sent him to Libya. The Libyans refused to allow him into the country, fearing US and British reprisals. Relations between the US and Libya were already fraught in the wake of the Lockerbie bombing.

Eventually the Yemen offered him sanctuary, but Carlos later moved to the Sudan. Home was a ground floor apartment in the capital, Khartoum, and it was from outside the three-storey apartment block in August 1994 that he was kidnapped by France's anti-terrorist service, the DST. The DST had drugged Carlos and flown him to Paris where he was placed in solitary confinement in the basement of La Santé prison. The events that followed had been so well publicised that Howard didn't need to read the end of the file. Carlos' escape from French custody was still under investigation, with the French blaming the Iraqis, Iraq pointing the finger at Iran, the Iranians accusing Libya, and the Libyans saying it had been the Palestinians. Even the IRA had been mentioned, along with the suggestion that they had masterminded his escape in return for favours he had done the Irish terrorists in the past.

The report was incredibly detailed, but it also contained contradictions. Carlos was said to despise Arabs, yet often countries in the Middle East were his paymasters. Dr Wadi Haddad was a mentor in the early Seventies, yet Carlos was later implicated in the Palestinian guerrilla leader's assassination. He was not a Communist yet there were suggestions that the KGB were behind several of his operations and he spent long periods hiding in Communist countries. He was the world's most successful terrorist, yet he also had a reputation for taking chances and for being unreliable. As Sheldon had said, Carlos was one of a number of terrorists who visited Baghdad between August 1990 and January 1991 prior to an Iraqi-sponsored terrorist campaign against Britain and the United States. Yet just ten years earlier he was paid by the Syrians to come up with a plan to overthrow Saddam Hussein. He was prepared to work for the highest bidder, but had been born with the proverbial silver spoon in his mouth and had never been short of money.

Howard dropped the file on top of his briefcase and rested his head against the back of the seat. He felt almost light-headed as he realised that he was on the trail of the world's most wanted man. If he could capture Carlos there would be nothing he couldn't achieve, inside or outside the FBI. His hands began to shake and he gripped the seat rests. The excitement was almost painful, and so was the apprehension. He wanted a drink. A real drink.

* * *

Darkness crept up on Joker as he sat under the chestnut tree watching the brick building which housed Farrell Aviation. There was no point at which he was aware that day had given way to night, it was a process so gradual that it came almost as a shock when he realised that stars were twinkling in the sky and that the moon was hanging overhead, so clear that he could see the individual craters on its surface. A succession of people had entered and left the brick-built building during the afternoon, but there had been no sign of Matthew Bailey. He'd come to recognise two young men in blue overalls bearing the green propeller logo; they'd made several visits to the building and Joker assumed they were mechanics working in the Farrell hangars. Throughout the day several small planes had taken off and landed on the grass strip, including an old biplane which had been towing an advertising banner.

Lights were still on in one of the offices and a blue Lincoln Continental stood alone in front of the main entrance. Joker was waiting for the last person to leave before calling it a night. Stake-outs were nothing new to him. He'd lain in the hills of the Irish border country for days at a time with nothing more than a camouflage sheet to protect him from the bone-chilling winter rain, soaked through to the skin and shivering with the cold. Catching IRA terrorists as they crisscrossed the border between North and South was a matter of infinite patience and concentration, days of inactivity followed by frantic seconds of gunfire. Sitting under a tree on a pleasant evening was a breeze by comparison.

The light in the office went off and Joker put the binoculars to his eyes and trained them on the entrance. After thirty seconds or so the glass door opened and a large man stepped out, a briefcase in his hand. A lone light was on above the door and Joker could see that the man was in his early sixties, grey-haired with ruddy cheeks as if he spent a lot of time outdoors. He was wearing a red polo shirt and white shorts, with knee length socks, and he had a beer drinker's stomach which hung over his shorts like a late pregnancy. Joker assumed that he was Patrick Farrell Senior, but as he had no way of identifying the man he kept an open mind. He could just be a hired hand. The man locked the door and climbed into his car. A few seconds later he drove off and Joker heard the engine fade away into the distance. He listened to the sounds of the forest: the clicking of insects, the hoot of an owl, the faraway howl of a wild cat, and tentative rustlings in the undergrowth. Joker waited a full thirty minutes until he was sure that the man wasn't returning. He moved quietly through the trees and out onto the airfield, heading first for the hangars to satisfy himself that all the mechanics had left.

The sliding doors to the hangars were locked and Joker couldn't see any lights inside. He slipped silently through the shadows to the Farrell building, careful to keep away from the light above the main door. There was an alarm bell high up on the wall and he could see that the windows were wired, but it was a simple system and one which he could by-pass with little trouble. Around the back of the building there was a drainpipe which ran by a small frosted window, probably a bathroom. It looked climbable and when he pulled at it he could feel that it was strong enough to bear his weight. He hoped to get what he wanted without resorting to breaking and entering, but if it proved necessary he wouldn't have any problems gaining entry to the offices. He headed back to his car. He'd already earmarked a motel a couple of miles away from the airfield where he could catch a few hours' sleep.

Kelly put up the collar of her long green cashmere coat and kept a wary hand on her bag. She walked quickly, her heels tapping on the sidewalk like a blind man's cane. She looked over her shoulder, left and right, more to check that there were no potential muggers nearby than because she feared she was being followed. She found Filbin's and stood for a while looking through its murky leaded windows. Behind the polished wood bar stood a diminutive barman, polishing a glass like he expected a genie to appear and grant him three wishes. Kelly pushed open the door and walked into the warm and smoky atmosphere of the bar. Several customers looked up to see who the intruder was and their gazes lingered. Even wrapped up in her coat she was still something special to look at, especially in a downmarket bar like Filbin's. She ignored the avaricious stares and walked to the end of the bar closest to the door, her hand still on the clasp of her bag. The elf-like barman walked over to her, still polishing his glass. "What can I get you, my dear?" he asked.

She leaned forward. "Are you Shorty?" she asked, keeping her voice low.

The barman laughed. "What do you think?" he replied, and put the clean glass on a shelf. He grinned at two young men who were huddled over pints of Guinness. "She wants to know if I'm Shorty!" The three men laughed together and Kelly felt her cheeks redden.

Kelly waited for the laughter to die down, then leaned her elbows on the bar. She motioned with her finger and Shorty moved closer. "My name's Kelly Armstrong," she whispered. "Fergus O'Malley said I should speak to you."

Shorty's mouth dropped. "You're O'Malley's niece?" he said. "Jesus, I wouldn't believe an ugly old sod like him could be related to a looker like you."

"Why, thank you, I think," smiled Kelly.

Shorty frowned. "But Armstrong is a Prod name? What's a good Catholic girl doing with a name like Armstrong?"

"I married an American," she explained. "And he's neither Catholic nor Protestant." Shorty nodded thoughtfully. "So, can you help me or not?" Kelly asked.

Shorty looked around the bar, saw that there were no customers waiting to be served, and motioned to a table in the corner. "Sit over there," he said. "What can I get you?"

Kelly said she'd have a Coke and went over to the table to wait for the barman. Shorty joined her, gave her a glass of Coke and sipped a malt whisky from a balloon glass. He smacked his lips appreciatively, all the time his eyes never leaving Kelly's face. He shook his head in wonder. "Fergus O'Malley's niece," he mused. "Who'd have thought it?"

Kelly was beginning to tire of the man's attitude. "My uncle told you I'd be coming?"

"Aye, that he did."

"And what I wanted?"

"Aye." He took another sip of whisky, the creases deepening in his brow. "You wouldn't be offended if I asked you for identification, would you?" he said.

Kelly wondered how Shorty would react if she produced her FBI credentials, but instead she showed him her driving licence. Shorty studied it and then handed it back to her. "Well?" she said.

Shorty placed his glass on the table and folded his arms. "The person you're looking for doesn't want to be found," he said quietly. Kelly said nothing. "By anyone," he added. Kelly raised an eyebrow. "Your uncle said it was important, but he wouldn't tell me what it was about."

"He doesn't know," Kelly said. They were both speaking in low voices, their heads bent forward.

"Would you like to tell me?" asked Shorty.

"I can't do that," she said. "Do you know what she's involved in?"

"No," admitted Shorty.

"But you know how to reach her?"

Shorty didn't reply. A customer stood up at a nearby table, put on his coat and left.

"You trust my uncle, don't you?" Kelly pressed. Shorty nodded. "And he told you to help me, didn't he?" Shorty nodded again. He reached into his back pocket and pulled out his wallet. He tapped it on the table, then opened it and took out a card. He looked at the handwritten telephone number on the card and handed it to her. "I can reach her at this number?" asked Kelly.

Shorty shook his head. "No, but it's the number of a man who might be able to help you – if you can persuade him that you're to be trusted." He drained his glass, stood up and went back to the bar. Kelly slipped the card into the pocket of her coat and left. The two young men drinking Guinness watched her go. So did FBI agent Don Clutesi, his eye pressed to the camcorder on its tripod at the window overlooking Filbin's. Clutesi didn't recognise the woman, but she was clearly a cut above the normal type of customer who frequented the bar. Clutesi wondered if she was a hooker on the make. Young, blonde and pretty, what other reason could she have had for visiting a bar alone? She'd spoken to Shorty but Clutesi hadn't picked up anything from the listening devices. Either they'd been out of range or they'd been whispering. Clutesi made a note in his incident book and stretched his arms above his head. He was tired, but there was another two hours to go before he was due to be relieved. Then he had to go back to Federal Plaza to meet the agent from Phoenix.

An FBI driver was waiting outside JFK holding a sign with Cole Howard's name on it, and he carried Howard's bag to the car. They made polite conversation on the drive into Manhattan, about the Mets, the weather, and the murder of three DEA agents in the Bronx that afternoon.

The driver took Howard into Federal Plaza and helped him obtain a visitor's pass which Howard clipped to the breast pocket of his suit. The receptionist rang the Counter-Terrorism Division to tell them that Howard was on the way up, then she told him which floor to go to. The driver nodded goodbye and Howard headed to the elevator.

When the doors hissed open a small, shrewish woman with grey hair and a reluctance to look him in the eye took him along to Mulholland's office. Ed Mulholland was in his fifties, with a craggy, lined face and a grey, military crewcut. He had a bone-crushing handshake and looked as if he worked out a lot.

"Cole, good to see you. Jake Sheldon speaks very

highly of you. You want coffee? Tea?"

Howard shook his head. "No, I'm fine."

Mulholland looked over Howard's shoulder. "Katie, can you get Hank along for this, please? And ask Frank Sullivan and Don Clutesi to sit in, too. Thanks."

As the secretary scurried away, Mulholland motioned to two grey sofas which were set at right angles to each other in the far corner of his office. The sofas faced a low, square brass and glass table on which were scattered half a dozen law-enforcement magazines. "Let's sit over there, shall we, Cole, it'll give us a bit more elbow room." As the two men walked across the office, Mulholland slapped Howard on the back, a friendly pile-driving blow which almost rattled his teeth. "I'm really glad to have you on the team, Cole, you've done some great work on this. Great work."

Mulholland reminded Howard of a crusading general who'd happily lead his men into battle, rushing towards a hail of bullets in the sure and certain knowledge that he couldn't be touched, while all around him his adoring troops fell dying and wounded. He inspired confidence, but Howard felt that he was a bit too gung-ho, and too lavish with his praise. Howard put his briefcase by the side of one of the sofas and sat down, smoothing the creases of his trousers. Mulholland pulled over a high-backed swivel chair and placed it facing the sofas. A balding man of medium height in a cheap brown suit came into the office. Mulholland introduced him as Hank O'Donnell, Jr, director of the Counter-Terrorism section. O'Donnell looked more like a career bureaucrat than an anti-terrorism agent, and when Howard shook hands with him he noticed that his fingers were stained with ink as if he'd been writing with a leaky pen. He had a file under his arm. As O'Donnell moved to sit down on one of the sofas, Howard saw that the seat of the man's pants were shiny as if he spent a lot of time sitting down.

Another man entered the office and Mulholland introduced him as an agent from the Counter-Terrorism (Europe) Division. Frank Sullivan was tall with sandy hair, a sallow complexion and a sprinkling of freckles across his snub nose. He explained that Don Clutesi was out on a surveillance operation and that he would be back in the office within the hour. Sullivan sprawled on the sofa while Mulholland eased himself into the chair like some omnipotent monarch taking his throne.

"This is by way of a pre-briefing prior to a meeting which we'll be having with the Secret Service in Washington later tonight," said Mulholland, his massive forearms folded across his barrel chest. "I want to get a feel for exactly what we're up against here. Cole, you've done the lion's share of the work on this, why don't you bring us up to speed?"

Howard nodded and picked up his briefcase. He unlocked it and took out the files it contained, and dropped two of them onto the glass table. "Mary Hennessy and Matthew Bailey, both members of the Provisional Irish Republican Army, both wanted for murder by the British," he said, "and both of them were filmed taking part in an assassination rehearsal in the Arizona desert." He put a third file on the table. "Ilich Ramirez Sanchez, AKA Carlos the Jackal, the world's most notorious terrorist responsible for a string of murders, hijackings and kidnappings. He was with Hennessy and Bailey in Arizona as they put three snipers through their paces." He put the two Navy personnel files on the desk. "Rich Lovell and Lou

Schoelen," he said, "former Navy SEALs and expert snipers. Capable of hitting targets at a range of two thousand yards. The third sniper we haven't managed to identify yet."

Hank O'Donnell coughed quietly. "I think we might be able to cast some light on the third sniper," he said, and handed his file to Howard. "Dina Rashid, Lebanese, one of the Christian militia's best snipers."

Howard opened the file. A colour photograph of a thin-faced girl with long brown hair, dark skin and black eyes was clipped to the inside cover. Howard remembered that the third sniper in the video had long hair.

"According to our Middle East Division, Rashid has been missing from Beirut for the past five months, and there's a general request out for information on her whereabouts," O'Donnell continued. "We've no record of her entering the US, but then we had no record of Hennessy, Bailey or Carlos passing through Immigration, either. You'll see from the file that she and Carlos are not exactly strangers." He coughed, almost apologetically. "In fact, for a time they were lovers."

Howard nodded, and put the file on top of the rest. "We all know that Carlos was one of a number of terrorists summoned to Iraq by Saddam Hussein, and it's generally assumed that they were briefed on a terrorist campaign aimed at the States and the United Kingdom."

Mulholland leant forward, linking his fingers. "It's more than an assumption, Cole. The IRA were among those who attended the meetings in Baghdad and only weeks afterwards they launched a mortar attack on Downing Street."

Sullivan nodded. "There were several known IRA

terrorists reported in Iraq over Christmas 1990, and the mortar attack was on February 7, 1991. The British Prime Minister, John Major, was in the Cabinet Room with his War Cabinet, and they were damn lucky not to have been killed. One of the mortars landed in the garden of Number 10 Downing Street and cracked the windows. Margaret Thatcher had installed blast-proof net curtains some years previously – that's what saved them."

"There's no suggestion that Hennessy or Bailey were involved, is there?" Howard asked.

Sullivan shook his head. "Special Branch have their theories, but neither Hennessy nor Bailey was mentioned. Bailey was in the States at the time, anyway."

"I remember the bombing, but I didn't realise that Iraq was behind it," said Howard.

"That's the way Saddam wants it," said O'Donnell, quietly. "It's revenge he wants, not publicity."

"Which brings us to the target," said Mulholland. "Bob Sanger has already put the Secret Service's Intelligence Division on full alert. But are we sure that the President is the target?"

Howard sat back, his hands on his knees. "I don't know, Ed. I just don't know. I haven't had time to put together a comprehensive list, but the British Prime Minister is over here in a few days, the Prince of Wales is here on a Royal visit next month. A number of British politicians and business leaders are coming, and many of them could be a target. Most of the visiting politicians are from the Conservative Party, and several of the businessmen are in defence industries."

Mulholland nodded. "Tell me about these computer experts you have over at the White House," he said.

Howard explained about Andy Kim's work on the computer model of the assassination.

"Have you thought about inputting different targets into the program?" asked Mulholland. "Could we do all the British VIPs?"

"We've thought about it, but there are time constraints, and who do we put forward as targets if it isn't the President? We don't have the resources to run the model for every visiting dignitary, even if we restrict ourselves to the Brits. And what about other American possibilities? We could consider every member of Congress as a potential target. There are just too many names. And who says it's a politician? There are plenty of likely targets in the military who Saddam would like to see blown away."

Mulholland nodded. "What are the time constraints you mentioned?"

Howard explained about the telephone tap and that Lou Schoelen had told his mother everything would be over within two weeks. When he told the group about identifying the television station from the *Star Trek* episode, they laughed.

"Outstanding," said Mulholland.

"Inspired," added O'Donnell, slapping his own leg.

"So, we know the hit is going down on the East Coast, and that it's going to go ahead within the next two weeks. What are our options?" asked Mulholland.

"We could cancel all the President's public appearances for the next two weeks," said Howard.

"He'd never agree to that," said Mulholland.

"In view of the circumstances . . ."

Mulholland shook his head. "I've already run the idea by Bob Sanger – his view is that Presidential security is already one hundred per cent, there is nothing more that can be done short of putting him in a nuclear shelter."

"We could put out a press release saying he had a medical problem," suggested Howard.

"That's certainly been done before, but the view from the White House is that the President can't run for cover every time we uncover a conspiracy," said Mulholland. "If we did that, he'd never leave the White House. I gather there's an element of pride, too. If Saddam Hussein is behind this, the President doesn't want to give him the satisfaction of showing that he's afraid."

"What about putting them on the Ten Most Wanted List?" asked O'Donnell, his voice low as if frightened of intruding.

"Who? The snipers or the terrorists?" asked Mulholland.

"I thought the snipers," said O'Donnell. "If they know we're on to them, they might get cold feet."

"In which case they might try again some other time," said Howard.

"Cole's right," said Mulholland. "Plus, it's Carlos who's planning this, I'm sure, and if the snipers back out he'll get others. This Rashid woman sounds like she's got personal reasons for being involved, so she's unlikely to be scared off. But we could put Bailey and Hennessy on the list. Carlos, too. They're wanted terrorists."

"And what would we put on the wanted poster?" asked Howard. "We don't have fingerprints, and they haven't committed a crime in the US."

"There was Bailey's attempt to buy the missile in LA," said Sullivan. "There are legitimate reasons for the FBI being interested in Bailey and Hennessy."

"Hardly justifies putting them on the Ten Most Wanted,

though, does it?" asked Howard. "You're going to get a lot of questions from the media, too, especially if we let it be known we're searching for Carlos. I assume we're not going public on why we want these people."

"That's for sure," said Mulholland. "But we could just push the terrorist angle. Cracking down on the IRA as part of a joint operation with the British."

"It'd be a first," said Howard. "The media would be sure to start asking questions. And I doubt if it would get results quickly enough. You have to remember the two-week deadline."

"What about the British?" asked O'Donnell. "Are we bringing them in on this?"

"What are your feelings, Hank?" said Mulholland.

O'Donnell shrugged. "Relations aren't exactly cordial between the Bureau and MI5 at the moment," he said. "Too many cooks, you know?"

"But we're keeping them informed, right?"

"There are information memos in the system, but not red-tagged," said O'Donnell. "We've told them that Bailey and Hennessy have been seen, but we haven't told them about Carlos yet. I hadn't thought it necessary at this stage."

"Do you have any thoughts as to why the IRA have teamed up with Carlos?" asked Mulholland. O'Donnell chewed the inside of his lip thoughtfully and Mulholland smiled. "Just shooting the breeze, Hank. Nothing written in stone."

O'Donnell nodded. "At this stage of the investigation, anything has to be conjecture," he said slowly. "If you were to press me, I'd say that the IRA is smoothing the way for Carlos, that he's in charge and they're arranging passports, driving licences, hotels, the infrastructure that would be required by an operation of this nature. Carlos hasn't operated in the United States before. As far as we're aware, this is his first time in the country. The IRA, however, has a long tradition of involvement in the US. Much of their fund-raising is done here, and the US is often used as a safe haven when things get too hot for them in Ireland. The Irish community also networks better than almost any other minority group. There are legal networks offering jobs, advice and support, but there are underground networks too, supplying weapons and counterfeit papers. Carlos wouldn't be able to plug into those networks, but Hennessy and Bailey would."

O'Donnell's views were greeted by a succession of nodding heads. Mulholland cracked his knuckles, the small explosions echoing around the office. "It goes without saying that the capture of Carlos would be a major coup for the Bureau. However, I agree with Cole that we can't launch a manhunt for Carlos without facing some pretty awkward questions from the media. And as he pointed out, going after the snipers won't get us anywhere. Lovell and Schoelen appear to be nothing more than hired guns. Bearing in mind the time constraints, I think we should go all out to find Bailey and Hennessy, on the assumption that they are with Carlos. But Carlos is our prime target. And I mean target, gentlemen. Whether we apprehend him dead or alive isn't the issue."

Mulholland looked over at Sullivan. "Frank, you're going to have to put pressure on your informers – find out where Hennessy and Bailey are, what ID they're using, who they spoke to, the works. Put the squeeze on anyone who's overstayed their visa or who's working here illegally. Anyone who doesn't co-operate gets put on the next Aer Lingus flight back to Ireland. And I want you to contact all our offices in those cities with large Irish communities and get them to put feelers out. Don is going to be coming with us to Washington, but I'll assign you all the manpower you need." Mulholland saw that Howard wanted to speak. "You have something in mind, Cole?" he asked.

"Just a thought," said Howard. "I don't think putting Hennessy and Bailey on the Most Wanted List will produce results in time. Why don't we go public instead? Run their photographs on one of the TV shows – America's Most Wanted or Unsolved Mysteries – the shows that get viewers to solve crimes."

"I don't think going public on an assassination conspiracy is the way to go," said Mulholland, frowning.

Howard shook his head. "We fake it," he said. "We run their photographs and descriptions, but we say we're hunting them for armed robbery or drug smuggling. Get the viewers to call in if they've seen them. Some of those shows have really high success rates."

"That's an idea," said Mulholland. "They do owe us favours, that's for sure. It'd be a rush job, though. Let me speak to a producer I know; if it can be done in time we'll go for it." He slapped his knees with his big hands. "Okay, let's get to it. Hank, grab Don when he gets here, we'll meet downstairs in forty-five minutes. Make sure that everyone knows that for the next few days we'll be based at the White House. Katie will have the numbers. Frank, thanks for sitting in on this. We'll be depending on you to get some sort of handle on Carlos."

O'Donnell and Sullivan left the office, but when

293

Howard made a move to follow them, Mulholland grabbed his shoulder and pulled him back. "Wait a moment, will you, Cole, I'd like a word?" He closed the door behind the departing agents and then stood leaning against his desk, his legs crossed at the ankles and his huge forearms folded across his chest. "First, I just want to repeat that I think you've done a first-class job on this investigation so far. I'm not the sort of director who takes credit for his operatives' hard work, I want you to know that. When this is all over, credit will go where it's due, I promise you." He smiled, showing chunky white teeth that were so close together they seemed to be a seamless strip across his mouth. "Nail your colours to my mast, and I'll back you all the way."

Howard nodded, unsure whether or not the director was being totally honest. He'd been in the FBI long enough to know that it was action that counted, not words. "I sure appreciate that," he said.

"Secondly, I wanted to talk to you now about our meeting with Bob Sanger. I gather you two have met?"

"Once, to brief him on Andy Kim's computer model."

"What did you think?"

Howard watched Mulholland's eyes, sensing a trap. For all he knew, Mulholland and Sanger could be bosom brothers. He shrugged casually. "He seemed very professional. He was keen to move the Kims into the White House to give them access to Secret Service data. But as you said, he seems to think that Presidential security is above reproach. I think he was humouring me."

"Yeah, that's Bob's way," said Mulholland, grinning. "You've got to remember that Bob Sanger has only one function in life – to protect the President. He's not interested in arrests, in solving crimes, in tracking down fugitives. All he cares about is getting the man through his term of office in one piece. Bob is like most of the top echelons of the service, he came up through the ranks. They start with the quarterlies and the watch lists, clearing the way in advance of a presidential visit, then they move up to actual bodyguarding, running interference in crowds, standing around the motorcade, escorting him wherever he goes. They spend their entire time waiting for some maniac to take a pot-shot at the President, and they know that when that happens, they have to throw themselves in the path of the bullet. That's what the Service is there for – to take the bullet meant for the President. Something happens to the men who take on that job. You get to see it in their eyes, it's the same thousand-yard stare you see with Vietnam veterans. But something changes behind the eyes, too. Their perspective alters, after a while they start to think of themselves as above the rest of the law enforcement agencies. They think they're an élite, and that there's nothing they can learn from anyone else. They forget that we have a quarter of a billion people to protect, with millions of offenders. I'm not saying Bob Sanger's gone that way, but I'm not surprised that you thought he was humouring you. When we meet with him I want you to remember that his interest, his only interest, is to protect the President. It's the Bureau that wants to capture Carlos, Hennessy and Bailey. We'll be working with the Secret Service, but their objectives are different. They'll be just as happy for Carlos to leave the country as they would be if we captured him. Bob is more likely to prefer to put Carlos on the Ten Most Wanted list than to try a softly-softly approach. If he tries to suggest that, let me handle it, okay?"

"That's fine by me," agreed Howard.

"Good man," said Mulholland. He pushed himself up off the desk and slapped Howard on the back. "Okay, Cole, let me phone my producer friend and then we'll get that chopper to Washington."

The ringing phone jolted Patrick Farrell awake, but it took several seconds for him to clear his head. He was a deep sleeper and it took a lot to rouse him. He reached over for the receiver and grunted.

"You asleep, Pat?" an Irish voice asked. Farrell recognised Matthew Bailey's Gaelic tones.

"Shit, Matthew, what time is it?" Farrell sat up and scratched his chest. The digits on his clock radio glowed redly. It was one-thirty.

"You alone?" asked Bailey.

Farrell looked down at the sleeping body next to him. "Sort of," he said. "Where are you?"

"Not too far away, Pat, old son. Everything on schedule?"

"No problems here," replied Farrell.

"I'll be dropping by tomorrow morning, I want to put the Centurion through its paces, okay?"

"Fine, I'll have a few bottles of Guinness ready," laughed Farrell.

"Eight hours between bottle and throttle, remember," said Bailey.

"Yeah," said Farrell, "right." The sleeping figure next to him began to stir. Farrell reached down and ruffled the mane of black hair on the pillow. He lowered his voice. "Matthew, everything's cosy here, but you might have a problem in New York. Do you know a guy by the name of O'Brien? Damien O'Brien?"

There was silence at the other end of the line for a while. "I know a Seamus O'Brien, but I can't think of a Damien," said Bailey. "There is a Damien J. O'Brien, lives in Dublin, one of the old school, but he must be in his seventies now and I never met him. What's up?"

"There was a Damien O'Brien asking questions about you in New York a few days ago. Said he was a friend of yours." An arm snaked through the sheets and Farrell felt a hand crawl across his thighs. He opened his legs and smiled.

"Seamus is getting on eighty years old and he's in an old folks' home in Derry, far as I know," said Bailey.

"Thing of it is, Matthew, is that a couple of the boys went round to have a word with this O'Brien, to see what his game was. Police found them tied up in O'Brien's room, both of them shot dead."

"Bloody hell," whispered Bailey, his voice so faint that Farrell could barely hear him. The inquisitive hand found its target and began to squeeze. Farrell stifled a groan. "What about this O'Brien?" asked Bailey. "Where is he now?"

"Your guess is as good as mine, Matthew. He did a runner."

"Sass-man, you think?"

"Dunno, he seemed okay from what I was told. Shorty gave him a job in Filbin's, and you know that Shorty can smell SAS a mile off. O'Brien was a boozer, damn near an alcoholic."

"So what do you think? Was he on to us? Was he trying to find out who did Manyon in?"

"Manyon?"

"The SAS officer that Mary got hold of. He was using the name Ballantine, but his real name was Pete Manyon."

"O'Brien didn't mention Manyon, it was you he was asking for."

Bailey snorted. "Jesus, Pat, he'd hardly waltz around Filbin's asking about an SAS officer, would he?"

"Yeah, sorry," said Farrell. The hand in his groin was a distraction he could well do without, but it felt so good he didn't want to push it away. He slid down the bed.

"You okay, Pat? You're breathing heavy," said Bailey.

"Just tired, that's all. Maybe this guy O'Brien was working for the Feds, and they pulled him out when our guys got suspicious."

"Feds wouldn't kill our men, surely?" said Bailey. "MI5 would, and so would the SAS, but not the Feds. Not unless there was a shoot-out."

"No shoot-out, the guys were tied up and naked, shot in the face and chest. Police reckon it was a gang killing, maybe drug-related."

"Fuck!" exclaimed Bailey. "What in God's name is going on? You think O'Brien knows where I am?"

"Matthew, nobody knows where you are."

"Yeah, that's right enough. You haven't seen anyone strange around the airfield?"

"Come on, you're getting paranoid," said Farrell.

"Yeah, maybe, but I'd feel happier if you kept your eyes open."

"Okay, I will do," said Farrell. The hand between his thighs was becoming more insistent. "Look, I'll see you tomorrow, I've gotta get back to sleep. I'm knackered."

"Okay, Pat, old son, get a good night's kip. I'll be at the airfield at six. Cheers."

The line went dead before Farrell could complain about the early start and he shook his head as he replaced the receiver. He rolled over and looked down at the young man next to him. "Right, you sod, I'll make you suffer for that."

"Oh good," sighed the man, pulling Farrell down on top of him.

Cole Howard looked down on the lights of the Capitol as the helicopter descended out of the clouds. Washington was breathtaking at night, the national monuments illuminated in all their splendour while the drug dealers and hookers carried out their trades in the dark places in between. Crack cocaine, AIDS, murders, Washington had more of them than almost any other city in the world, but from the air none of that was visible and Howard looked down as entranced as a sight-seeing schoolboy.

It wasn't his first trip in a helicopter but he was still a little uneasy. He could never forget that the whole contraption depended on a whirling rotor which was held in place by a single steel nut. Even with the headphones on he could hear the roar of the massive turbine of the JetRanger helicopter and his buttocks tingled from the vibration. It was difficult to imagine that the machine could hold itself together, even though he knew that flying in a helicopter was a hundred times safer than driving on the roads below.

The pilot's voice came over the intercom, and even it

was vibrating. "Folks, you should be able to see the White House down there on the right. I'll make one pass over the grounds and then we'll go in for a landing. The winds are gusting up to twenty knots so it might be a bit bumpy, but nothing to worry about." Sitting next to Howard was Don Clutesi, a cheerful, portly man with slicked back hair that glistened with oil whom he'd liked the moment they'd been introduced. His handshake had been damp as if he sweated a lot, but the grip was firm, and he spoke with a nasally Brooklyn accent, like a gangster from a B-movie.

Howard looked down to the right and saw the home of the President, impossibly white amid the bright green lawns. Clutesi had seen it, too, and he gave Howard a thumbs-up and nodded. Behind the building Howard saw the white H in a circle, denoting the helicopter landing-pad, and some distance away a fluorescent orange wind-sock, swinging in the wind. As the pilot swung the JetRanger around Howard thought suddenly of his wife, and how upset she'd been when he left. He'd tried calling her from New York but the line was continually busy. Either she was punishing him, or she was on the phone to her father, pouring her heart out. Now it was almost two o'clock in the morning. He wondered if it was too late to call her.

The helicopter levelled off and before Howard realised they'd touched down the skids were rested on the landing-pad and the rotor blades were slowing. When the rotors had stopped turning the co-pilot slid open the door for the passengers and Howard, Mulholland, Clutesi and O'Donnell filed out, ducking their heads even though there was no danger. Howard supposed it came from seeing too many war movies where the grunts jumped out of their Hueys with the rotors still turning, bent almost double with their M16s at the ready. Mulholland went out of his way to shake the hands of the pilot and co-pilot and congratulate them for a good flight.

A Secret Service agent was waiting for them, and Howard was amused to see that, even though it was the middle of the night, the man was wearing sunglasses. He either knew Mulholland or had been well briefed because he went straight up to him and welcomed him to the White House before introducing himself to the rest of the FBI agents. His name was Josh Rawlins and he looked as if he'd only recently left college. He told the agents that their luggage would be taken care of and took them through a back entrance where they had to show their FBI credentials to an armed guard, and along a corridor to a staircase. Small watercolours in gilt frames were hanging on the wall to the right of the staircase and the carpet was a deep blue. It was, Howard realised, a far cry from the offices he worked out of in Phoenix. "We've come through the West Wing into the Mansion," Rawlins explained. "The President's private apartments are here, and our offices." At the top of the staircase was another corridor off which led several polished oak doors. Bob Sanger's was the third along. Rawlins knocked on the door and opened it. A young secretary, brunette with piercing blue eyes which were enhanced by the blue wool suit she wore, smiled and told them to go straight in. Rawlins said goodbye and went back down the stairs.

Sanger was sitting at his desk, his shirt-sleeves rolled up and his pince-nez eyeglasses perched on the end of his nose as he perused a stack of papers. Through the window behind Sanger, Howard could see the floodlit lawns stretching out towards Pennsylvania Avenue.

Sanger looked up as if surprised by their entrance, but Howard was sure the head of the Secret Service's Intelligence Division would have been informed that their helicopter had arrived. Sanger stood up and walked around his desk to shake hands with Mulholland. He greeted Hank O'Donnell next, and then Howard, leaving Howard in no doubt as to the pecking order of the investigation. Don Clutesi was the last to have his hand shaken. Sanger's office was three times the size of Jake Sheldon's in FBI headquarters in Phoenix, with oil paintings on the wall, a thick pile carpet the same dark blue as that covering the stairs, and solid antique furniture, all highly polished dark wood and gleaming leather. Sanger's secretary came into his office and helped to arrange four chairs in a rough semi-circle facing the desk and the FBI agents took their places.

"Isabel, can you call down to Rick Palmer, tell him and Andy Kim to come up?"

Sanger waved his hand over the papers on his desk. "This Carlos is one mean son-of-a-bitch," he said quietly. "What the hell are we going to do about him?"

Mulholland folded his arms across his chest. He quickly explained their plan to pursue the two IRA terrorists, Bailey and Hennessy. Sanger nodded as he listened, scrutinising Mulholland over the top of his spectacles. Mulholland went on to describe how the FBI planned to run a fake story on a TV crime programme about the two Irish terrorists being wanted for a drug-smuggling operation in Florida. Mulholland had managed to get hold of his producer friend before they'd caught the helicopter and he'd received a guarantee that the item would be broadcast in two days' time.

"Why don't we just put Carlos on the Ten Most Wanted?" Sanger asked.

Howard realised that Mulholland had been right, that Sanger would rather frighten Carlos off than try to apprehend him. Mulholland stood up, walked around his chair and rested his forearms on it. "Bob, at this stage we think we have a real opportunity to capture the entire cell: Carlos, Hennessy, Bailey and the three snipers. It's unlikely that they know that we have identified them, or that we know they are on the East Coast. If we play this just right, we could bag them all."

"But from what you told me about the Lou Schoelen telephone call we only have two weeks. By the way, Cole, the *Star Trek* lead was good work."

Howard smiled at the recognition. He looked over at Mulholland and nodded almost imperceptibly, acknowledging that the FBI chief had kept his word – he had obviously told Sanger that it was Howard who had broken the case open.

"Schoelen said that it should all be over within the next two weeks," agreed Mulholland.

Sanger sniffed as if he had the beginnings of a cold. He took off his spectacles and began to slowly polish them with a red handkerchief. "So put Carlos and the snipers on the Most Wanted list and get all your agents looking for them," he said.

"We don't have the time, and if we mobilise the FBI in total, we'll have to go public," said Mulholland. "It means posters up on Post Office walls, police precincts, the whole bit. If we do it through television, we can be economical with the truth."

Sanger nodded. "So we let the great American public do

the FBI's job, is that it, Ed?" He smiled, looking over the top of his spectacles.

Mulholland smiled back. Howard had the feeling that the two men had a history together and that they took a perverse pleasure in winding each other up.

"We know it's going to happen within the next two weeks, and we know it's going to be on the East Coast," said Mulholland. "Your men must be doing the rounds, checking the President's itinerary and running down the watch list and the quarterlies. Why not give your men photographs of Carlos and the rest, and get them to show them around as part of your security sweep? Your agents are going to be checking all the hotels anyway, they can kill two birds with one stone. We can use FBI manpower to try car-rental companies, stores, filling stations, and the rest. But we confine the search to only those places on the President's itinerary."

There was a knock on the door and Sanger's secretary showed in Andy Kim and a young man with a military haircut and pock-marked skin. Kim saw Howard and went over to shake his hand while Sanger introduced the other man as Rick Palmer, a Secret Service programmer.

"Rick, could you give us a briefing on the progress you've made so far in identifying possible venues for the assassination?"

Howard saw Kim visibly stiffen and he knew that the news was not good. He gave the Oriental an encouraging smile. Palmer scratched his right cheek as if the scars there were itching. "We're up to the end of August, and so far nothing has matched, not in the ninety percentile which is the level we agreed on," he said. "About half a dozen have come close, one was as close as the eighty-six percentile."

Sanger didn't appear surprised by the news and Howard had the feeling that he had asked for the situation report for Mulholland's benefit rather than his own. "Are any of the half-dozen on the East Coast?" Sanger asked.

Palmer looked across at Kim, who pushed his horn-rimmed glasses higher up his nose and cleared his throat nervously. "One is in Boston, and another, I believe, is in Philadelphia," he said, his voice shaking.

Sanger nodded. "Cole has two pieces of information which may help you," he said. "First, we now have reason to believe that the assassination is being planned for sometime in the next two weeks." Andy Kim's face fell as he realised that if that was the case, his model must have missed the venue already, or there was a fault in his programming. Deep creases formed in his forehead and he looked as if he was in pain. "Secondly, the snipers appear to be in the Baltimore-Washington area, at least for the moment. In view of the time-frame, I don't think it likely they will be moving too far. I think we should go back to the start and recheck all the venues in the east of the country for the upcoming fourteen days."

Palmer was also frowning, and he looked at Kim, who shrugged. "We'll start right away," said Palmer.

"I wonder if maybe we should be looking at the possibility of other targets," said Howard.

"For instance?" said Sanger.

"The Senate, and the Pentagon. I can think of several high-ranking military officers who would be high up on an Iraqi hit list. I also have a list of visiting VIPs from overseas."

Palmer and Kim both expressed surprise at the mention of an Iraqi hit list and Howard realised that neither of the computer experts was aware of how far the investigation had gone. They were still treating it as a mathematical problem rather than a criminal investigation.

Mulholland and O'Donnell were nodding in agreement and Sanger looked from one to the other as if gauging their reaction. "Widening the search will take more time, more people," he said. "I suggest we concentrate on the Presidential venues for the next two days, if they still come up negative, we run the program through venues where the President isn't expected but where we know other possible targets will be. Ed, when do you expect the pictures of Bailey and Hennessy to go public?"

"Two days," said Mulholland. "Tuesday evening. If my producer comes through."

"He'd better," said Sanger. "The following week could be too late." He pushed his handkerchief back into his trouser pocket and looked at his watch. "Gentlemen, it's now almost three o'clock. I've had rooms arranged for you at a hotel nearby. There are cars waiting to take you, and they'll collect you first thing so we can make an early start." The door opened and his secretary appeared. Howard wondered if Sanger had pressed a concealed button because he hadn't touched his desk intercom or telephone. A young man stood behind the secretary, carrying a Polaroid camera. Sanger explained that their photographs would have to be taken for their White House passes, so one by one they stood with backs to the wall as the camera flashed and whirred.

When they'd finished, Sanger asked his secretary to show them to the cars. "And make sure their luggage hasn't gone astray," he added. He looked at Mulholland and shrugged. "Sometimes it happens," he explained.

* * *

Joker's internal alarm clock woke him at five o'clock in the morning. His mouth tasted sour and there was a thick coating of something unsavoury on his tongue. He swallowed, but his throat was so dry he almost gagged, so he lurched to the tiny bathroom and drank from the tap. He showered and wrapped a thin towel around his waist, then went back into the bedroom and bent down by the side of the bed. From under the mattress he pulled out the gun and silencer. The SIG-Sauer P228 appeared to be brand new; there was scarcely a mark on it and the silencer had never been used. There were thirteen cartridges in the clip, which Joker recognised as 147 gram Hornady Custom XTP full metal jacketed hollow point loads. Joker was no stranger to the gun or the ammunition. He knew that XTP stood for 'extreme terminal performance'. The bullets had no exposed lead at the nose and the hollow points meant the bullets would mushroom out on impact, increasing their penetration and the amount of damage they did. They were real man-stoppers and because they were big bullets they came out of the gun at a relatively slow 978 feet per second. Joker had smiled at the number of bullets the clip held. He knew that another SIG-Sauer model, the P226, actually held even more bullets – sixteen – but even thirteen was too many. If he ever got himself into a situation where that number of bullets were necessary, he'd be dead. The 'spray and pray' method beloved of the paintball amateur warriors didn't work in real life. It was drilled into the SAS recruits from their first day in the Killing House – two shots per target, both to the chest. If you had time then maybe a third in the head to make one hundred per cent sure, but in a hostage situation with handguns it was two – bang-bang and then onto the next target. And if you were up against more than two targets you'd made a big mistake because no matter how many bullets you had in the clip you were outgunned. Only an amateur firing almost at random would need thirteen rounds. And when it came to killing, Joker was not an amateur.

He dried himself and put on a pair of blue Levi jeans and a black polo shirt and wrapped the gun in his pea jacket. He carried it out to his car and shoved it behind the driver's seat, then went to reception and paid his motel bill, using his Visa card. The roads were clear and Joker drove quickly to the address in Laurel where Patrick Farrell lived. The house was a two-storey detached Colonial standing in several acres of lawn with a Stars and Stripes flapping from a pristine white flagpole. The number of the house was on the mailbox which stood at the end of the gravelled drive. Joker slowed but didn't stop. Standing in front of a basketball hoop was the Lincoln Continental which Joker had seen outside Farrell Aviation. Satisfied that the man he had seen closing up the office was Patrick Farrell, he drove back to the airfield.

Matthew Bailey was already waiting outside the Farrell Aviation building when Patrick Farrell arrived. Bailey looked at his watch and sneered. Fifteen minutes late. He climbed out of his car and stood by the main entrance to the building.

Farrell waved. "Hi, Matthew; sorry, my alarm didn't go off."

Bailey sneered again. More likely the old sod had been

pulled back into the bed for a quick one by whichever rump-rustler he was hanging around with these days. Farrell had never been especially choosy about the company he kept, in bed or out of it, but he was a first-class pilot and essential to Mary Hennessy's plan, so Bailey just smiled and waited for him to open the double-glass doors.

"You want a coffee first?" Farrell asked.

Bailey declined, saying that he wanted to take the plane up right away. Farrell got the message and opened a metal cabinet behind the reception desk. Inside were more than a dozen sets of keys hanging on hooks, each with a metal tag denoting the call sign of the plane. He took out a set of keys, closed the cabinet and picked up a sectional chart from a table.

"Headsets?" asked Bailey.

"In the plane," said Farrell. The two men walked together towards the line of small planes which faced the grass strip. "You had no problem getting the licence?" Farrell asked.

"Nah, the school you recommended were ace. They arranged the written for me, gave me about half a dozen lessons and then fixed me up with an FAA examiner. Piece of cake." Bailey had been taught to fly by pilots from the Libyan Army, and could pilot a variety of single- and multi-engined planes. During a six-month stay, courtesy of Colonel Gaddafi, the Libyans had given him a full grounding in instrument flight, and taught him how to fly the French-made Alouette 111 helicopter. Flying in the States on a Libyan licence was obviously out of the question, so Farrell had faked up a logbook showing some fifty hours of flying lessons and Bailey had gone out to New Mexico to get a new FAA licence under an assumed name. The licence was only good for single-engine fixed-wing aircraft, but that was all Bailey intended to fly.

"You've flown a Centurion before?" Farrell asked.

"Sure," said Bailey. "What year is it?"

"It's an '86, one of the last that Cessna built. But it's not a straightforward 210, it's an Atlantic Aero 550 Centurion upgrade, done by a company down in North Carolina. They upgraded the power plant and the propeller, now she's got a top speed of 180 knots, range of 850 miles, takeoff ground roll of twelve-fifty feet. Here she is."

The plane was white with green stripes down the side and the company's green propeller and hawk logo on the two doors. Farrell pulled out the cowling covers and untied the ropes which kept the wings and tail tethered to the ground while Bailey walked around, checking the flaps, tail assembly and landing gear. He stood and watched as Farrell took fuel samples from the drain valves to check that there was no condensation or contaminants in the tanks. It was a beautiful day for flying, blue skies as far as he could see with the merest hint of clouds at twenty thousand feet or so. The wind-sock pointed to the south-west but it was hanging almost vertically.

Farrell threw his last fuel sample on the ground, checked the oil level and nodded to Bailey. "Okay. Let's go," he said. The two men climbed into the cockpit and strapped themselves in. "Controls handle pretty much the same as the 210," said Farrell. "Stall speed with the flaps down is 56 knots, with flaps up it's 65 knots. After take-off bring the flaps up at 80 knots, best rate of climb is 97 knots which should give you about thirteen-hundred feet per minute." He unfolded the sectional chart in his lap and pointed to the airstrip. "We're within the Baltimore-Washington

International Terminal Control Area once we get above twenty-five hundred feet and on up to ten thousand feet. If you keep below twenty-five hundred you've no problem, but if you go through that ceiling you have to have the transponder on and be in radio contact with Baltimore Approach. We're going to stay below two thousand until we're out over Chesapeake Bay, but when we go up I'll call them anyway, just so they know who we are. The airspace is real busy around here because you've got BWI, Andrews Air Force Base and Washington Dulles International, and their air space overlaps. Which way are you going to be heading on the day?"

Bailey smiled. "Best you don't know, Pat, old son," he said.

"Sure, whatever," said Farrell. "Just keep an eye on the sectional and keep below the TCA and you won't have any problems."

Bailey nodded. The two men put on their headsets and tested them. Farrell asked him to pick up the plastic laminated checklist and together they ran through it before starting the engine. Bailey ran his eyes across the four by three array of flight gauges and the stack of avionics and radios. The plane was impressively equipped with a Bendix/King KMA 24 audio panel and beacon, dual KX 155 nav-coms and KR 87 ADF and a Cessna 400-series DME. There was also a Phoenix F4 loran receiver which would pinpoint the plane's position, a WX-10 Stormscope to spot thunderstorm cells and an autopilot.

"You wanna take her up?" Farrell asked, his voice sounding tinny through the headset.

"Sure," said Bailey.

"Okay, just bear in mind you'll need every inch of the

STEPHEN LEATHER

runway to get airborne. Treat it as a short-field take-off and
you won't go far wrong."

Bailey ran through the Centurion's checklist: cowl flaps
open, wing flaps set to ten per cent, elevator and rudder
trimmed for take-off, autopilot disconnected and controls
free. He increased the throttle to 1700 rpm, feeling the
plane judder as the engine growled, then checked the
gauges, the magneto and the propeller, before taxiing to the
end of the grass runway. He kept his feet on the brakes until
the engine was running at full power, then released them,
allowing the plane to lurch forward. It accelerated
smoothly and Bailey soon had the plane in the air, his hands
light on the controls. He retracted the gear as they passed
over the edge of the field and he levelled off at two
thousand feet. "Sweet," he said. He trimmed the plane for
level flight, reset his heading indicator, and then headed
east, towards the Chesapeake Bay, while Farrell called up
Baltimore Approach.

Joker stopped at a filling station and filled the tank of his
rental car. He paid for his fuel and bought a couple of packs
of chocolate cookies and a six-pack of Coke. They didn't
sell liquor but he had a half-bottle of Famous Grouse in his
glove compartment, so he wasn't too distressed.

He hid the car in the same spot he'd used the previous
afternoon and made his way to the chestnut tree, carrying
his whisky and provisions. The gun he left under the
passenger seat, wrapped in a newspaper. The grass was
damp from the early morning dew so he dropped his pea

jacket down and sat on top of it. He checked out the Farrell Aviation building with his binoculars. There were two cars parked outside, but neither was Farrell's Lincoln Continental. He settled down with his back to the tree and opened the whisky bottle, toasted the building, and drank deeply.

There was a clock radio by the bed and Cole Howard set it for 8 a.m. so that he could telephone his wife first thing in the morning. Bob Sanger had arranged for cars to pick up the FBI agents at eight-thirty prompt. When the alarm went off Howard rolled over, switched it off and groped for the phone. He misdialled the first time and woke up an old man who by the sound of it didn't have his teeth in. Howard redialled and Lisa answered on the fourth or fifth ring.

"Hiya, honey," he said.

"Cole?"

Yeah, right, thought Howard. How many early morning phone calls did she get from guys calling her 'honey'? She was obviously still unhappy. "Yeah, it's me. How are the kids?"

"They're fine."

That was all. No questions, no concern, just the children are fine, why the hell are you bothering me so early in the morning? "You up already?"

"Golf," she said.

The monosyllabic treatment. Always a bad sign. "Yeah? Who are you playing?"

"Daddy."

A two-syllable word, but not one that Howard wanted to hear. "Honey, I'm sorry," he said, the words spilling out before he could stop them. He didn't feel in the least bit responsible for the argument but he wanted it to end, and if the only way of achieving that was by apologising, then so be it.

"There's nothing to be sorry about," she said, which meant that there was.

"Okay, well, I just wanted to let you know that I got here safely, that's all."

"Okay," she said, as if his safety was the very last thing on her mind. "Well, look, I'm supposed to be teeing off at eight and I've a lot to do. Do you know when you'll be back?"

"Two weeks at the most," he said. She didn't complain, she didn't gasp in horror, she just said okay and ended the call. Ouch, thought Howard, was he in trouble.

He shaved and showered and went down to the reception area, where O'Donnell and Clutesi were already waiting. "Ed says we should go on ahead and he'll take the second car," said O'Donnell.

The three men made small-talk during the drive to the White House, not knowing how secure the driver was. They had to show their FBI credentials to gain admittance and the guard checked their names off against a list on his clipboard.

Bob Sanger was already at his desk, working his way through a stack of computer printouts. He greeted them but didn't ask about Mulholland, so Howard guessed the FBI chief had already called in. Sanger took them along to an office which he'd had made ready for the FBI team, and introduced them to an overweight, middle-aged secretary by the name of Helen who was to be assigned to them for the extent of their stay. She was cheerful and eager to please and had already arranged for their White House passes, which they clipped to the breast pockets of their jackets.

Howard looked around the office, and realised immediately that there wouldn't be anywhere near enough telephone extensions or desks. He turned back to Helen but before he could speak she told him that she'd already been onto the relevant White House departments and that equipment and supplies would be arriving later in the morning. Howard asked her to show him where Andy Kim and Rick Palmer were working and she smiled brightly and took him down to the ground floor and along a corridor to a mahogany door. "It used to be a secretarial pool," she said. "I once spent eighteen months behind that door. We called it The Tomb."

Howard smiled. "I know exactly what you mean," he said. "I spent a few months in a place called The Tomb, myself."

She left him at the door and Howard watched her large thighs rub together as she waddled rather than walked down the corridor. He could hear the sound of nylon hissing against nylon long after she'd turned the corner.

Howard knocked on the door and went in. Andy Kim was there, sitting in front of a large colour VDU, with Bonnie standing behind him, her hair tied back in a long ponytail. They both looked dog-tired and Howard realised that neither of them had slept the previous night. There were a dozen desks crammed into the office, a large white board on which computer language and several complex equations had been written in red and black ink. To the left

STEPHEN LEATHER

were two small camp beds. The Kims were engrossed in the computer terminal and it was only when Howard went to stand behind them that they realised he was in the room.

"Cole!" said Bonnie. "Hi! Andy said you'd be here for a while." There were dark bags under her eyes and her hair was less shiny than he remembered. Her husband was clearly tired, too, more so than when he'd seen him the previous night.

Andy Kim stood up and shook hands with Howard, but avoided his eyes. Howard sensed that he was embarrassed and that things weren't going well. "You two look like you could do with a good night's sleep," said Howard.

Bonnie squeezed her husband's shoulders. "He hasn't slept for three days," she said.

"I must be doing something wrong," Andy hissed, his eyes on the screen. "I must be missing something."

Howard wasn't sure what to say. The news that the snipers were planning to make their move within the next two weeks had clearly shaken Andy, but Howard didn't want to appear condescending by telling him not to worry.

"We're going back to square one," Bonnie explained. "We're checking all the angles and distances in the model first, then we're going to check all the venues from today onwards."

"But I'm sure we did it right the first time," said Andy.

"Andy, you've got to remember that it might not be the President who's the target. You could be doing everything right and still not get a match. Have you tried any of the other possibilities? The Prince of Wales, for instance, or the British Prime Minister?"

Andy looked up. "They didn't match either, but I'm sure it's the President they're after," he said. "I can feel it. And

316

if they succeed, it'll be my fault. I couldn't live with that, Cole. I really couldn't."

Bonnie smiled nervously at Howard as if apologising for his touchiness. "What will you be doing, Cole?" she asked.

"We've a lead on the snipers and the people who are helping them," he said. "The Bureau and the Secret Service are working together to try to find them."

"What are your chances?" asked Andy sharply.

Howard shrugged. "I'm hopeful," he said.

"What sort of odds?" Andy pressed.

Howard smiled tightly. "I dunno, Andy. You can't treat an investigation like an equation. There're so many influences, not the least being luck. We could literally stumble over them, they could get pulled in for speeding or one of our men could walk right by them. I can't give you odds."

A computer printout was lying by the side of the visual display unit and Howard picked it up. "It's a list of the President's appointments for the next two weeks," Bonnie explained.

Howard flicked through it. Most were on the East Coast, though there was a two-day trip to Los Angeles and visits to Dallas and Chicago. "Dallas," he mused, loud enough for the Kims to hear.

"I thought we were concentrating on the East Coast?" said Bonnie.

"Sorry, I was just thinking out loud," said Howard. "It's hard not to think of Dallas when you think of a presidential assassination. But the evidence we have points to it being on the East Coast." He continued to read through the printout. The President was a busy man, no doubt about it, with up to twenty visits a day: breakfast meetings, lunchtime speeches, opening ceremonies, tours of factories, fund-raising activities, sports events. Howard wondered when the man actually found time to run the country. "I hadn't realised he moved around so much," he said. "I guess we always think of the President as sitting in the Oval Office."

"Yeah, I wish that was true," said Andy Kim. "But it's worse than that printout suggests." He ran his hand through his mop of black hair. "It's not just one program per visit. Say he's being shown around a factory. He could visit a dozen different sites, plus travelling to and from it, and we have to rerun the program for each of them. Say he walks a hundred feet from a car to the entrance of a hotel. We have to pick points every ten feet and run them through the program. That's ten operations for one walk. Every time he gets into or out of a limo we have to put that through the model. You wouldn't believe how complex it is."

"But it's going to be okay," said Bonnie, sympathetically.

"I hope so," said Andy Kim.

The office door opened and a man in running gear stepped inside. He was wearing grey shorts, scuffed training shoes and a white sweatshirt which was damp with sweat, and he was breathing heavily. Andy Kim looked around at the visitor, then turned back to his computer. The jogging gear was so unexpected that it took Howard several seconds to recognise the face of the President of the United States.

"Hi, you guys, I thought I'd just stop by and see how you're getting on with this computer model thing," he said. The mid-Western drawl was instantly recognisable from thousands of sound-bites on television news, and Andy's head whirled around in an astonished double-take. His mouth dropped and his hands slid off the computer keyboard. Bonnie was equally stunned.

The President closed the door and walked over to the Kims. A small towel was hanging around his neck and he used it to wipe his forehead. "Bob Sanger expects great things from this," he said. He stuck out his hand and Andy Kim stared at it as if it was a loaded gun. It was only when Bonnie pushed his shoulders that he stood up and shook the President's hand. "I'm Andy Kim," he said, his voice trembling. Bonnie nudged his shoulder again. "Oh, and this is my wife, Bonnie."

Bonnie shook his hand. "Agent Bonnie Kim, of the FBI," she said, lest the President assumed she was just there for moral support.

"Pleased to meetchya, Bonnie," said the President. He turned to Howard. "You're Cole Howard, from Phoenix?" he said. Howard nodded and received the same warm handshake, a firm grip which went beyond the normal presidential hand-holding where hundreds of the faithful had to have the flesh pressed in as short a time as possible. The President's handshake suggested that the man was truly glad to have made Howard's acquaintance. "Bob told me about that *Star Trek* thing. Awesome detective work, Cole. Awesome." He bent down and stared intently at the computer screen. The President looked leaner than he did on television, and his hair seemed darker. Howard recalled the rumours that he'd dyed his hair grey during the presidential campaign to give himself a more mature image, and he caught himself looking for dark roots. "So, Andy, why don't you show me what this machine can do?" the President asked.

319

Nervously at first, but with increasing confidence, Andy Kim showed the President how his computer model worked, calling up several upcoming venues and superimposing the three sniping positions on top of them. The President asked pertinent questions demonstrating considerable familiarity with computer systems and Andy was soon talking to him as an equal.

Eventually the President straightened up and arched his back as if it was troubling him. "I tell you, Andy, I'm really impressed with this. It's really important that we show these terrorists that they can't push us around. We can't allow them to dictate to us in any way. Saddam tried it in Kuwait, and we showed him the error of his ways. We're going to show them that they can't scare the President of the United States."

"You don't plan to change your schedule at all, sir?" Howard asked.

The President looked Howard straight in the eye. "Not one iota," he said. "If I give any sign of being afraid, they'll have won. You cannot show weakness to people like Saddam Hussein. If I hid inside the White House every time I was threatened . . . well . . . I'd never leave, would I?"

"I guess not, sir," agreed Howard, though he doubted that the President had ever faced a threat like the one posed by Carlos the Jackal and the Irish Republican Army.

The President smiled. "Well, guys, I've got to go, but I want you to know that I think you're doing one hell of a job. One hell of a job." He wiped his face with the towel as he left the office.

Andy Kim looked at his wife as if unable to believe what he'd seen. She nodded silently. Howard rubbed the back of his neck. The President seemed totally unfazed by the fact that some of the world's deadliest terrorists were trying to get him in the sights of their rifles.

Carlos and Mary Hennessy walked together down the sloping lawn, towards the grey-blue waters of the Chesapeake Bay. The sky above was clear and blue and a fresh breeze blew from the east, ruffling their hair and carrying with it the tang of salt.

"You chose the house well, Mary," said Carlos. "It is perfect for our needs."

"I had a lot to choose from," said Mary. "The housing market all through Maryland is depressed, so many home-owners decide to rent rather than sell and take a loss."

Carlos nodded and reached up to stroke his thick, black moustache. "The great American capitalist system is grinding to a halt," he said.

"Why Ilich!" said Mary, in mock surprise, "I didn't realise you were so political."

Carlos narrowed his eyes and studied the woman by his side. He found Mary Hennessy a shrewd, intelligent woman with many admirable qualities, but he was frequently confused by her sense of humour and her use of irony and sarcasm. It was a very British trait even if it was delivered in her lilting Irish accent. She was joking, he decided, and he smiled. Despite his vocation, Carlos was not in the least bit political. He had served many masters during his career, from all points of the political spectrum, and had never considered himself aligned to one or the other. Carlos was a businessman, pure and simple, and he served only one political colour: green – the colour of money.

"What about you, Mary Hennessy, how political are you?"

Mary's brow creased as if the question had caught her by surprise. Seagulls screeched and dived over the white-topped waves and high overhead a small plane banked and headed down towards Bay Bridge airfield. "Political?" she said, almost to herself. "I used to be, I suppose. Now, I'm not sure."

They came to the end of the lawn and looked down onto a thin strip of stony beach which bordered the water. To their left a wooden pier stuck out into the bay like an accusing finger.

"You have family?" Carlos asked. He had known Mary Hennessy for almost six months, but this was the first time he'd ever spoken to her about something other than the operation they were planning. There had always been a hard shell around her that he'd never been able to penetrate, but he had the feeling that something about the water was evoking old memories and opening her up.

"I have a son and a daughter, in their twenties," she said, almost wistfully. "I haven't seen them for a long time."

Carlos nodded. "I understand how you feel. I haven't seen my wife or children for a long time."

She turned to look at him. "But you'll be going back to your children, Ilich. I'll never see my family again. Ever. There's a difference."

She walked away, stepping off the grass and on to the beach. She was wearing a white linen shirt and pale green shorts and as she walked away Carlos admired her figure. It was hard to believe that she was the mother of two children, let alone two adults in their twenties. He'd already noticed that she wasn't wearing a bra under the shirt, nor did she appear to need one. Carlos smiled as he realised he was ogling Mary in the same way that Lovell had been leering at Dina Rashid. Not that Carlos would ever make a move on the IRA activist. She was a beautiful, sexy woman, but she was almost one of the most professional operators he had ever come across and she commanded respect from everyone she came into contact with. Besides, thought Carlos, Magdalena would kill him if she ever found out. Kill him, or worse.

He followed Mary down the beach and soon caught up with her. She knelt down to pick up a stone. Her breasts pushed against the material of her shirt and Carlos admired her cleavage. She looked up, her eyes twinkling with amusement, and Carlos knew that he'd been trapped. He shook his head and walked on as she straightened up and skipped the stone over the waves.

"My husband was always the political one," she said behind him. "He was a lawyer and an adviser to the IRA. He said that politics was the only way to succeed, that violence would provoke only intransigence. He was all talk, Ilich, and it got him killed."

Carlos continued to walk down the beach and Mary followed him. "I was just a wife and mother then, but that changed when the UDA killed my brother. They gunned him down in front of his wife and children, at Christmas. I was there, I was covered in his blood."

"Your brother was in the IRA?" asked Carlos.

"All the men in our family were," she said. "It wasn't something you thought about. You know how the Palestinians feel about Jewish settlements on the West

Bank? Well that's how the Catholics feel about the Protestants in Northern Ireland. They've no right to be there, it's our country. The Protestants control everything in the north of Ireland: jobs, police, education, social services. Catholics are second-class citizens."

"And you and your husband tried to change that?"

Mary drew level with Carlos. "He tried to persuade the IRA High Council to negotiate with the British Government. He believed that Thatcher and then Major would be prepared to make concessions and that they wanted to pull their troops out of Northern Ireland."

"You sound as if you didn't agree."

She looked at him sharply. "I didn't," she said. "And I wasn't alone. When Liam tried to stop the campaign of violence, we sent our own people to the mainland."

Carlos said nothing. There was an intensity burning in her eyes that he had seen in zealots around the world. A conviction that they, and only they, knew what was best for the world. The sort of conviction that would lead her to betray her husband.

"It went wrong, badly wrong," said Mary quietly. "A civilian airliner was bombed. In retaliation the British Government ordered the killing of the top two dozen or so of the movement's leaders. Including my husband."

Carlos stopped, stunned. "What are you saying?"

"They sent the SAS against us, with orders to make hard arrests."

"Hard arrests?"

"Another name for assassination. Some were straightforward ambushes, others were made to look like suicides or accidents. They're good at killing, the SAS. They're the real professionals. My husband was gunned down as he sat in his car. The RUC said it was Protestant extremists, the same group that had killed my brother." She reached up and wiped her eyes with the back of her hand. "They killed the men I loved, Ilich. This is my way of getting back at them."

Revenge, thought Carlos. The strongest motivation of all, stronger even than money. She had said men, not man, Carlos noticed. Plural. He doubted that it was a slip, and he doubted too that she had meant her brother, but he knew better than to pry, despite the silent tears.

"We will succeed, Ilich, we have to."

Carlos nodded. "I know. Though I'll be honest, Mary, I do worry about this. There's so much that could go wrong."

"It's been planned to perfection," she said quickly. "But even if something goes wrong, we can wait and try again. The basic idea is sound, it's just the opportunity we need. Everything is set to go, but it's not written in stone. We have the team, we have the equipment."

"Another time will mean another rehearsal."

"So?" she said quickly. "So we rehearse again. Remember when the IRA almost killed Thatcher at the Conservative Party convention in Brighton. My husband then said that they have to always be lucky, but we only have to be lucky once."

"He was right, of course. But after so much planning, I wouldn't want to go through it all again."

Mary looked at him slyly. "You miss your wife and children?" she said.

Carlos knew she was right. "It has been a long time," he said. "That's why I'm so keen that we succeed the first time. Then my family can have a home together."

Mary sniffed. "That's the difference between us," she

said. "If we do succeed, you get a safe haven for your family. But I will never be able to see mine again. I have been on the run for a long time, but it will be nothing compared with what lies ahead."

"I know, I know," said Carlos.

They walked together in silence for a while. The small plane which had been practising landing and taking off at the Bay Bridge airstrip climbed into the sky and headed back west, its single engine buzzing like an angry wasp.

"Has something happened between Lovell and Rashid?" Mary asked eventually.

"Happened? In what way?" replied Carlos.

Mary smiled and gave the man a knowing look like a mother silently admonishing a child she knew was being less than honest. Her eyes were dry but there was a redness about them. "You know exactly what I mean," she said.

Carlos chuckled softly. "The American was making unwanted advances, and Dina took care of it."

"Took care of it? What did she do? He's like a scalded cat whenever she's around."

"She had sex with him."

Mary looked at him, astonished. "She had sex with him, and now he's scared witless?"

Carlos kept his face straight. "The way she tells it, her encounter wasn't exactly what you'd call safe sex, not for him anyway." Carlos could contain himself no longer and he laughed loud and hard, throwing his head back and showing uneven, yellowing teeth. His laughter echoed across the bay until it was lost among the screaming of the seagulls.

* * *

Patrick Farrell Senior arrived in his blue Lincoln Continental shortly before eight o'clock, scratching his pendulous beer gut as he scanned the skies around the airfield. Not long afterwards his mechanics began arriving and Joker heard the rumble of the hangar doors being rolled back. Small insects buzzed around Joker's head, and he waved them away halfheartedly. They made a sound like miniature chainsaws as they zipped by his ear and for each one he swatted away, there were two more waiting to torment him.

He put the binoculars to his eyes and surveyed the Farrell Aviation building. In one of the ground-floor offices he could see Farrell talking on the telephone as he stood at his desk. A buzzing sound, louder than the annoying insects, filled the air above his head. He looked up and through the tree canopy overhead he saw a single-engine plane coming into land. It flashed overhead and then turned to the left, aligning itself up with the grass strip, and then passed from Joker's field of vision. He heard the engine note change as the pilot throttled back prior to landing. Joker put the binoculars back to his eyes. Through them he saw Farrell, still on the phone, peer through his window at the arriving plane.

The plane came into view as it reached the end of the grass strip and taxied back towards the hangars. Joker saw that it was in Farrell Aviation's colours and bore its green propeller and hawk logo. The pilot and co-pilot were wearing headsets and sunglasses and it was impossible to tell if they were men or women. The plane came to a halt and the occupants took off their headsets and climbed out. They were men, one tall and thin with dark hair, the other short with a mop of unruly red hair. As they walked towards the Farrell Aviation offices, Joker trained his glasses on the shorter of the two men. He caught his breath as he recognised the face of Matthew Bailey, grinning and twirling his headset as if he didn't have a care in the world.

As Mary Hennessy and Carlos stepped into the kitchen, the telephone began to ring. Mary picked it up while Carlos opened the refrigerator in search of breakfast. Carlos took out a slice of cold pizza and chewed on a huge chunk as he watched Mary's frown deepen. She agreed to whatever it was the caller was saying, and motioned with her hand for Carlos to pass her a pen. He picked a blue ballpoint and handed it to her. She scribbled an address on the margin of the front page of the *Baltimore Sun* and replaced the receiver.

"Trouble?" asked Carlos, his mouth full of dough and tomato sauce.

"I'm not sure," she replied, tearing off the corner of the paper. "Someone wants to meet me. Now."

"I'll come with you," said Carlos.

"No," said Mary. "I have to go alone."

Ronald Hartman's secretary buzzed through on his intercom and told him that there was a Secret Service agent in the outer office asking to see him. The secretary was new to the job and was clearly in awe of the visitor, but Hartman was well used to dealing with the men responsible for the President's safety. He had worked in hotels in Los Angeles, Chicago, Detroit and Boston before moving to Baltimore and the routine was always the same. He'd read in the *Baltimore Sun* about the President's forthcoming visit to the city, and he knew that beforehand the Secret Service would be around for the list of guests and employees. He told his secretary to send the visitor in.

The man was in his early twenties with the regulation athletic build, close-cropped hair and dark suit. He smiled, showing perfect white teeth and pink gums, and flashed his Secret Service credentials. His name was Todd Otterman and when he sat down he carefully aligned the creases on his trouser legs. He began to explain about the President's trip to Baltimore but Hartman held up his hand to silence him.

"I've been through the routine before, Agent Otterman," he said. "You want the guest list to compare with your watch list, correct?"

Otterman nodded, grateful that the hotel manager knew the ropes.

"Three days before the visit, one day after?" asked Hartman.

"Perfect," said Otterman. As Hartman leant forward and spoke to his secretary through the intercom, Otterman took an envelope from the inside jacket of his pocket.

Hartman finished briefing his secretary. "You can pick up the records at the reception desk, there'll be a printout and a floppy disc waiting for you."

"I wish every hotel was as efficient as yours, Mr Hartman," said the agent. He slid six colour photographs out of the envelope and handed them to the manager. "One more thing, could you tell me if you recognise any of these people?"

Hartman flipped through the photographs. He had a good memory for names and faces, an essential attribute for anyone wanting to do well in the hotel industry. The top picture was of a pretty blonde woman and another of the same woman but with dark hair, followed by three younger men, a middle-aged man with a receding hairline and a moustache, and a sharp-faced young woman with long, dark curly hair. Hartman needed only a few seconds for each photograph to be sure. He'd never seen any of them before. He shook his head and gave them back to the agent. "I'm sorry, no," he said.

"You're sure?" said Otterman.

"Quite sure," said Hartman, frostily. Much as he wanted to help, he didn't take kindly to his professional abilities being questioned.

Otterman stood up and shook hands with the manager, thanked him for his help, then went back out to reception where a teenage girl with gleaming braces on her teeth and a black name badge with 'Sheena' on it smiled and gave him a manila envelope. Otterman looked inside and saw a computer disc and a roll of computer printout. He thanked her and showed her the photographs. "So, Sheena, have you seen any of these people?" he said.

"Guests, you mean?" Her braces glinted under the fluorescent strip lights overhead.

"Guests, in the restaurants, walking outside, anything," he said.

She screwed up her eyes as she went through the pictures and Otterman wondered if the girl needed glasses. She held up the picture of the woman, Mary Hennessy. The picture of her as a blonde. "I sort of remember her," she said, her voice uncertain. "Let me ask Art."

She went to a tubby young man in a black suit and they both stood looking at the two photographs of the woman. The man came over and introduced himself as Art Linder, an assistant manager. "I think this is Mrs Simmons. From London. She stayed with us last week for a couple of days." He held up the photograph in which she was a blonde. "She was a blonde, but you could see the roots growing through. She was a looker . . . for her age."

Otterman couldn't believe his luck. "Can you give me her details," he asked. "Registration card, credit card details, list of phone calls she made, the works?"

"No problem," said Linder. "What has she done?"

"That's classified, I'm afraid," said Otterman, who was loath to admit that he didn't know. Like the rest of the agents scouring the city gathering guest lists to compare with the watch list stored in the Secret Service computer, he had been told only that identifying the men and woman was to be accorded the highest priority.

Matthew Bailey and Patrick Farrell stood in front of the Farrell Aviation building for almost half an hour, talking animatedly as Joker watched through the binoculars. At one point Farrell gave something to Bailey but Joker couldn't make out what it was. Eventually Bailey handed his headset to Farrell and the two men said goodbye.

Joker got to his feet and rushed back to his car. He climbed in and wound down the windows so that he could hear when Bailey drove down away from the airport. He heard Bailey drive away and he followed him. The Irishman was driving a dark blue sedan which was totally inconspicuous in the mid-morning traffic so Joker had to stay closer then he'd have preferred. Bailey drove up towards Baltimore and then headed east, towards Chesapeake Bay. Joker kept him in sight all the way, constantly changing lanes and the distance from his quarry in the hope that he'd be harder to spot. His heart was racing and his hands were sweating on the wheel. He wanted a slug of whisky but knew that it wouldn't be a good idea to drink from the bottle while driving along at 55 mph. You never knew when the next vehicle might be an unmarked police car.

Mary parked her rental car next to a red Jeep and switched off the engine. As it cooled she massaged her temples and studied the motel. It was a Best Western, close to Highway 40: quiet, anonymous, and the perfect place for a trap. She trusted the man who'd telephoned her, trusted him with her life, but she was still apprehensive. She studied the cars in the parking lot, looking for anything that might be driven by an undercover agent, and checking for any signs of surveillance. She knew she was whistling in the dark. If this was a trap they would be well hidden and the first she'd know of it would be the thud of a bullet followed by the crack of the shot. Her heart began to race and her hands were damp on the steering wheel. She steadied herself. "It's okay," she whispered. "It's okay."

She wanted to restart the car and drive away, but if there was any chance that her operation had been compromised, she had to know. Her contact in New York had said that the meeting was vital to the success of her operation, and that was enough for Mary. Her handbag was lying on the passenger seat and she opened it just enough to reassure herself that the gun was there and that the safety was off. She felt like a mouse sniffing at a cheese-baited trap, knowing the risks but wanting the cheese nevertheless. Her mouth was dry and she swallowed. She looked around the car park again, hoping that she'd see something that would give her a reason to leave. There was nothing. She picked up the bag. If they were going to kill her they'd wait until she was out of the car so that there would be no doubt that they had the right person. If it was the Americans, they'd be using a SWAT team with telescopic sights, if it was the SAS they'd have handguns and they'd get in close. Either way the end result would be the same – blood on the concrete. Her blood. She shivered and reached for the door handle. The door swung open and she stepped out. A noise to the right made her flinch, but it was a child bouncing a ball against a red truck. The child's mother called him from the door to a room and he picked up the ball and ran to her, giggling.

Mary sighed and slammed the door shut. The sound echoed around the car park like a scaffold's trapdoor. The mother smacked the back of the child's legs and pulled him into the motel room. Mary took a deep breath and began to walk across the concrete to the two-storey block of bedrooms. Room number 27, her contact had said. It was on the ground floor, and the curtains were drawn. A maid was pushing a trolley full of towels and cleaning equipment along the upper level, its wheels squealing as if in pain. Mary stood in front of the door. She looked left and right, then opened her bag and slipped her hand inside. The cold metal was comforting. She knocked on the door, and realised that it was open. She pushed it with the flat of her hand. "Hello?" she said. There was no reply but she could hear the sound of running water. She reached her hand inside, feeling for a light switch. She found it, but when she flicked it up nothing happened. Either the bulb was broken or it had been removed.

She peered into the gloom. Her hand tightened around the gun and she stepped inside. The bathroom door was closed but she could see a strip of light at the bottom and the shower was on full blast. Mary moved into the room and carefully closed the door behind her.

"Take your hand out of the bag," said a woman's voice. "And if it comes out with a gun, I'll shoot."

The voice was calm and assured, and Mary slowly obeyed, raising her hands above her head.

"Turn around and put your hands against the wall," said the voice. Mary did as she was told, mentally cursing herself for her stupidity. She shouldn't have come alone, she shouldn't have entered the darkened room, she shouldn't have fallen for the oldest trick in the book. She closed her eyes and took a deep breath as a hand patted her down expertly, running down her sides and the small of her back. She felt the hand slide into her bag and pull out the gun and then heard it being thrown onto the bed. The hand went back into the bag and Mary shifted her weight off her arms. Before she could move, the barrel of a gun pressed into the small of her back.

"Don't even think about it," said the voice calmly.

Mary opened her eyes and looked down. She saw a hand with red-painted fingernails take her wallet out of the bag and then the barrel was removed from her back. The woman stepped away and Mary realised she was going through the credit cards and identification.

"These are good," said the woman. "Very good."

Mary felt her mouth go dry and she swallowed. "You're Kelly Armstrong?" she said.

"Uh-huh," said Kelly. "And despite what these say, you're Mary Hennessy. I've been looking for you for some time."

Mary frowned. If she'd been caught in some sort of FBI sting the room should have been full of armed agents by now, and if it was an SAS trap then she'd be dead on the floor. It didn't make any sense. She heard the woman walk away to the other side of the room. Mary turned her head quickly and saw Kelly peering through a gap in the curtains. She had the striking looks of a television anchorwoman, with backswept hair and a sharp profile. She was wearing a black jacket and a skirt which showed off her long, tanned legs and she held a large automatic in her right hand. In her left she held Mary's wallet. Mary's frown deepened. Kelly turned to look at her and Mary faced the wall again.

"You came alone?" Kelly asked.

"That's what you wanted," replied Mary, her eyes on the wall.

"You can turn around now," said Kelly. She put Mary's wallet on a bedside table and clicked on a small lamp.

Mary pushed herself away from the wall and turned to face the younger woman. "What's this all about?" she asked. "I was told you wanted to see me, that you had information for me. Why all this cloak and dagger charade?"

Kelly smiled. "You're a very dangerous woman, Mary. I had to make sure that you didn't come in with guns blazing."

"What is it you want? Have you come to take me in, is that it?"

Kelly laughed softly. She reached into her jacket pocket and took out a small leather wallet. She threw it onto the bed, close to the gun. Mary reached out her hand, and for a brief second considered grabbing the gun. She looked up and saw that Kelly was watching her closely. Mary picked up the wallet and opened it. Her heart sank as she saw the FBI credentials. "I know about the assassination," said Kelly quietly.

Mary's mouth dropped. She looked at the door, expecting it to burst open to admit a dozen gun-toting FBI agents, but it remained firmly closed. "I don't know what game it is you're playing, but let's cut to the chase, shall we? I thought you wanted to talk."

Kelly placed her gun on the bedside table. "Oh I do, Mary," she said softly. "And I want to help." She walked over to an easy-chair and sat down, crossing her long legs like a secretary preparing to take dictation.

Mary looked at the gun on the bed, and then back at Kelly. "Who are you?" she asked.

Kelly raised an eyebrow archly. "Kelly Armstrong, special agent with the Federal Bureau of Investigation."

"And?" said Mary, sensing that there was more to come.

"And Colm O'Malley was my father."

The revelation hit Mary like a blow to the stomach. "Colm O'Malley?" she repeated.

"Didn't they tell you? Didn't they tell you that Fergus is my uncle?"

Mary shook her head. "No, they didn't." She sat down on the edge of the bed. "But you're American," she said.

"I am now," she said. "My parents divorced when I was a kid." Mary looked up sharply. "I know, I know, Catholics don't get divorced," she said. "My mother was American, she went back to the States and divorced him there. I hardly saw him when I was growing up, but later, when I was in my teens, I used to go to stay with him. Things were never right between him and my mother, she wouldn't even let him come to my wedding." She grimaced as if in pain. "She couldn't stop me going to his funeral, though." She reached up as if to casually slip a strand of her blonde hair behind her ear but she brushed her cheek with the back of her hand and Mary could see that she was close to tears.

"My husband died, too," said Mary quietly.

Kelly looked at her fiercely. "I know," she said. "You think if I didn't know I'd be sitting here talking to you like this?" Her anger subsided as quickly as it had flared. "I'm sorry," she said.

Mary said nothing and the two women sat in silence for a while, united by unspoken memories.

"How could they do it?" Kelly asked eventually. "How could they murder them like that?"

"The SAS have a saying," said Mary. " 'Big Boys' Games, Big Boys' Rules'."

"That doesn't excuse what they did," said Kelly. "It doesn't even explain it. They gunned my father down like an animal."

"I know," said Mary.

"Like an animal," Kelly repeated. She looked up

337

sharply. "I want to help, Mary." There was a new brittle-ness in her voice, like splintered glass.

"You don't know what you're saying," said Mary. "You don't know what we're planning."

Kelly snorted softly. "You'd be surprised," she said. "I know you're planning an assassination using three snipers, and that one of the snipers will be more than a mile from the target. I know that two of the snipers are former Navy SEALs, Rich Lovell and Lou Schoelen, and that you organised a full rehearsal in Arizona to calibrate your weapons. And I know that the assassination is set for sometime within the next two weeks." Mary sat in stunned silence as Kelly ticked off the points on her fingers. Kelly smiled smugly. "The only thing I don't know is who you're planning to kill."

"My God," whispered Mary.

"So?" asked Kelly.

"My God," repeated Mary. "Does the FBI know all this, too?"

Kelly shrugged. "Some of it. They know that Lovell and Schoelen are the snipers, but so far they're not aware that there's an IRA connection."

"Do they know who else is involved?"

Kelly shook her head. "Just the SEALs."

"How did you find out that I was part of it?" asked Mary.

"Someone with an Irish accent hired one of the cars you used in the desert. That set bells ringing in my mind and I took the photographs to my uncle. He recognised you."

"But the FBI doesn't know I'm involved?"

"Not yet, no. But they're using computers to enhance the photographs so I would guess it's only a matter of time. So who's the target?"

Mary shook her head as if trying to clear it. "Photographs?" she said. Realisation dawned. "The plane," she mumbled. "It must have been the plane."

"There was a video-recorder on board," said Kelly, "the whole thing was filmed."

Mary looked at her watch, and then at the FBI agent. "And you want to help?" she said. "Knowing what that entails, you want to help?"

"If the target is who I think it is, yes, I'll help. I want to hurt the British the way they hurt me." She stared at Mary with an intensity that bordered on fanaticism.

Mary nodded slowly. "The Prime Minister," she said.

Kelly let out a deep breath with the sound of a deflating tyre. "I knew it," she said. She stood up and walked to stand in front of Mary. "I'm with you," she said. "I've been waiting for a chance like this for a long time."

Rich Lovell sat on the side of his bed, a sheet of polythene spread over the quilt so that it wouldn't be stained by his disassembled Barrett rifle. The former Navy SEAL stripped, cleaned and lubricated his weapon every day, whether or not it had been fired. Slowly and methodically, he checked that the chamber was empty and broke the rifle down into its three major components: the upper receiver group, containing the barrel and telescopic sight; the bolt carrier group; and the lower carrier group, including the trigger components. He picked up the upper receiver group and checked that the barrel springs weren't overstretched and that the impact bumper was in good condition. The muzzle brake was tight, as were the scope mountings which had been set during the Arizona rehearsal. He carefully put the upper receiver group back on the polythene and picked up the bolt carrier group. He looked to see that the ejector and extractor were under spring pressure and weren't chipped or worn. As his hands performed the functions they'd done thousands of times before, his mind emptied. Cleaning his rifle was a form of mantra for Lovell, bringing an inner peace that he rarely felt at other times. He de-cocked the firing mechanism, then depressed the bolt latch and worked the bolt in and out, feeling for any signs of roughness. There were none. There had been none the previous day, there would be none the following day, but every day he checked. He held the bolt down and peered at the firing-pin, confirmed that it wasn't broken or chipped, and then examined the firing-pin hole for signs of erosion. There were none.

He inspected the bolt latch and the cocking lever, then replaced the components on the polythene sheet.

The last group to be checked was the lower receiver. He pulled the bolt carrier back and checked that the mainspring moved freely and that the trigger mechanism was in good condition.

When he was satisfied that everything was as it should be, he inserted his bronze-bristle bore brush through the chamber end of the barrel and made six passes with rifle-bore cleaner. He unwrapped a pack of small cloth patches and he pushed them through the bore one at a time with the brush until they came out completely clean. The dirty ones he screwed up and threw into his wastepaper bin. He used another piece of cloth to dry off any parts of the upper receiver group which had come into contact with the cleaner. He took a small bottle of CLP – cleaner, lubricant and preservative – and soaked a square of material with it before passing it through the barrel. He held the end of the barrel to his eye and squinted down it to check that it had a thin coating of CLP. Satisfied, he poured CLP on another cloth and generously lubricated the bolt, the bolt carrier and the receiver, and then lightly rubbed it over all the metal surfaces.

When all the individual components were glistening with the CLP he assembled the rifle with crisp, economic movements. He stood up and went over to the window where he put the rifle to his right shoulder and put his eye close up to the telescopic sight. The reticle graduations came into focus, superimposed on the green lawn. He aimed the rifle at the base of a small bush and tightened his finger on the trigger. The image in the scope was rock steady despite the weight of the rifle. Lovell knew better than to pull the trigger without a bullet in the chamber: to do so could damage the firing-pin. He swung the rifle slowly across the lawn, breathing softly and slowly. Marksmanship was to a large extent a function of breathing and it was something he practised almost as much as actually firing the weapon. The road filled the scope and he followed it back towards the highway. The view turned blue and then Lovell was looking at the face of Matthew Bailey. Lovell smiled and smoothly followed Bailey with the rifle, keeping the man's forehead dead in the centre of the scope. Instinctively his finger pressed harder on the trigger, shallow breathing to keep his chest movement to a minimum. He became totally focused on Bailey, then when he was sure he had the shot made he held his breath and mentally the trigger was pressed and the bullet leapt from the barrel at more than three thousand feet per second. "Bang," he said, softly.

He took the rifle from his shoulder. Through the window he saw Bailey drive up and park at the side of the house. A flash of colour at the periphery of his vision caught his attention and he narrowed his eyes. It was a car, moving slowly at the far end of the driveway. Lovell put the rifle to his shoulder once more and closed his left eye. Through the open eye he saw the windshield of the car centred on the reticle and he edged the rifle over to the right, centring it on the face of the driver. He was looking at a pair of deep set, watery eyes above cheeks which were threaded with broken veins as if the man had a drinking problem. His thin lips were moving together as if he was chewing and he had a deep frown. The man was clearly watching Bailey as he walked to the front door.

Lovell placed the rifle on the plastic sheeting and went downstairs. Carlos and Dina were sitting at a long pine table in the kitchen. Dina was pouring tea from a brown earthenware teapot and she looked up as Lovell opened the door.

"Would you like a cup of tea?" she asked. She smiled evilly at Lovell and licked her lips, her eyes boring into his. She took great pleasure in making him nervous.

"Bailey's just arrived, and there's someone following him," he said.

"Who?" asked Carlos.

"One guy, looks like a rental car. He's not the cops, that's for sure. And he doesn't look like any FBI agent I've ever seen."

Carlos stood up. Dina's hand froze, the teapot suspended in mid-air. "Where's Schoelen?" Carlos asked.

"The den," said Dina.

Carlos looked at Lovell. "Get him. Where is this guy?"

"End of the drive."

"The two of you work your way behind him." He opened a drawer in a tall pine dresser and took out a heavy automatic which he handed to Lovell.

The kitchen door opened and Bailey walked in, a blue nylon duffel bag over his shoulder. He immediately saw the looks of surprise on their faces. "What?" he said. "What's happened?"

"You were followed," said Dina, contemptuously.

"I was what?" he said, shocked.

Lovell clattered down the stairs to the den. Carlos turned to Bailey. "Go back outside, walk up and down as if you're waiting for something."

Bailey dropped the duffel bag on the floor. "Where's Mary?" he asked.

"She's out," snapped Carlos. "Now get outside." Lovell and Schoelen came upstairs from the den and rushed out of the rear door, towards the water. "Dina, you should go out with Matthew. Give whoever it is something else to look at."

Dina nodded and went out. "What's happening, Carlos?" Schoelen asked.

"We'll soon find out," he said, his voice flat and hard.

Joker tapped the steering wheel and chewed his gum. He had watched Matthew Bailey take his bag out of the car and go inside the house and he'd checked out as much of the building as he could see with the binoculars. Now he wasn't sure what to do. One thing was certain, he couldn't stay in the road for too long, not during broad daylight. He put the binoculars to his eyes again. Bailey walked out of the front door and onto the lawn. He looked at his wristwatch and walked slowly back to where he'd parked his car.

"Now, my boy, what are you up to?" Joker murmured to himself. A woman, dark haired and thin, came out of the house and Bailey turned round to look at her. Through the binoculars he saw Bailey frown and his lips move. Joker trained the binoculars on the woman, moving up from her waist, past boyish breasts to her tanned face, framed by long, dark hair. He took the binoculars away from his eyes and wiped his forehead with the back of his hand. It came away wet. He had switched off the car engine while he watched the house and with the air-conditioner off the temperature had soon mounted. The car windows were closed and he opened them. In the distance he saw the woman and Bailey standing together, her hand on his shoulder, and he put the binoculars back to his eyes. The woman was saying something but he couldn't read her lips. Joker wished he had one of the microphone amplifiers he'd used on surveillance assignments with the SAS. They could amplify a whisper from more than two hundred yards away.

Bailey answered her, and his concern was evident. Something was worrying him. He tried to read the man's lips but it was beyond him. He was so busy concentrating on Bailey's lips that the first he knew of the gun by his neck was when the cold metal pressed up against his flesh. "Don't even think about moving," said a soft American voice.

Joker kept the binoculars pressed to his eyes, his mind

racing. A second man appeared at the passenger window. He reached through and pulled out the ignition key. "Drop the binoculars," said the first man, "and put both hands on the steering wheel."

Joker did as he was told. "What's up?" he asked.

"You're British?" asked the man with his key.

Joker seized the opening. "I'm a tourist, I'm lost," he said.

The gun was rammed hard against his throat. "With binoculars?" said the man to his right. "Don't screw us around."

From what Joker could see there was only one weapon, and that was pressed against his neck. If he was outside that would have been a major mistake, he could have twisted away from the gun and the man would have been close enough to hurt, with a slash to the throat or a backfist to the nose, but there was no room to move in the car so he had to sit where he was and wait. If the man kept as close when Joker climbed out of the car he'd be reasonably sure of overpowering him.

"Okay," said the man to his right. "Keep your hands on the wheel while I open the door. You move your hands, you're dead."

"Hey, I'm not doing anything, I'm just sitting here," said Joker. He chewed his gum and tried to look unconcerned.

The car door clicked and swung open. The gun was still against his neck and Joker weighed up the odds of pushing the door, slamming it into the man and grabbing for the gun. He decided against it. He felt the gun move away as the man stood to the side to open the door all the way. Joker's gun was under the passenger seat but he knew he hadn't the slightest chance of reaching it. He would make his move as soon as he got out of the vehicle. Two men but only one gun. He'd been up against worse odds before and triumphed.

The man on the right side of the car opened the passenger door. He bent down and Joker turned to see what he was doing. As he moved he realised his mistake, but he was too late, the butt of the gun smashed into Joker's temple and everything went red and then black.

Cole Howard became progressively more impressed with Helen as the day wore on. Brand new desks and filing cabinets were delivered before ten o'clock and late in the morning white-overalled technicians arrived to install enough telephones for a small army, and a digital switchboard which they put on her desk. Calls could be put through the board or go direct to the extensions. Half a dozen FBI agents had arrived from Washington headquarters and they had been briefed by Hank O'Donnell before hitting the phones, contacting FBI offices throughout the country and wiring over photographs of the assassination team.

A light lit up on Helen's switchboard and she took the call, while Howard and Ed Mulholland stood in front of a white board, drawing up the President's schedule as a series of boxes, using different colours according to the level of risk: black for inside meetings where no sniper could reach him, green for places where he was moving and an unlikely target, and red for those venues where he was exposed and potentially vulnerable.

"Ed, there's a call for you," Helen called over.

"I'll take it here, Helen," he called, gesturing at the nearest extension. It warbled once and Mulholland picked it up. He listened, grinned, said a few words and then hung up. He beamed at Howard, wide creases forming in his craggy face. "Report from our Baltimore office. Mary Hennessy stayed at a hotel there two days ago. Positive ID, and we're getting credit card details now."

Howard made a fist and shook it. "Yes!" he hissed.

"We're on the right track, Cole, no doubt about it," said Mulholland, eagerly. "And we're getting closer."

Consciousness returned to Joker like waves breaking over a beach, but each time his mind cleared an undertow of blackness would pull him back and he'd return to nightmares where guns fired, knives slashed and men died screaming. The pain was there whether he was conscious or not, a dull ache behind his right ear and a burning soreness in his wrists as if his hands were being sawn off with a blunt hacksaw.

During periods of consciousness his eyes would flicker open and he could see the tips of his shoes resting on the floor, limp as if they belonged to a dead man. He was somewhere dark and hot with metal pipes above his head and wooden panels on the wall. The pain in his wrists became sharper as if hot needles were being forced between the bones. His shoulders were aching and he could feel his arms being pulled from their sockets, then he surrendered to the dark undercurrent again and he dreamed of a dark woman, a long, sharp knife in her hand and evil in her eyes, laughing as she cut and sliced. Some time later his eyes flickered open and she was there, her face only inches from his, a cruel smile on her face, saying something, but he couldn't hear her because of the ringing in his ears. He fainted again and when his eyes opened next she was gone and he was alone with the pain.

His arms had become tubes of meat, numb in the middle with intense, searing pain at either end. He lifted his head, a movement which sent waves of nausea rippling through his stomach, and fought to focus on his arms which were stretched out above him. His wrists were shackled by a shiny steel chain flecked with blood, and the chain was looped over a metal pipe which ran across the ceiling. The chain was supporting all his weight, and it was biting deeply into his wrists. He tried to push himself up with his feet but he could barely reach and he teetered on his toes. He was still groggy and the effort of balancing was too much – he slumped forward and the pain made him grunt.

Time dragged interminably. His head throbbed with the rhythm of his thudding heart, the chain around his wrists felt as if it had worn through to his bones, and he could feel the sockets of his shoulders about to pop. His mouth was bone dry and his throat had swollen up so much that he had to force each breath into his lungs. He squinted up at his wrists and he saw the chain was fastened with a small brass padlock. Another, bigger, padlock kept the chain secured to the pipe. He knew how to pick locks, but his hands were in such bad shape he also knew that it would be beyond him, even if he could reach them.

He tried to balance on his toes again, to give his arms some measure of relief, but when his toes failed him and he had to drop down, the pain in his wrists was a hundred times worse. He had no way of measuring time, but daylight was seeping into the room from somewhere behind him so he knew it wasn't yet dark.

Over to his right was a flight of steps leading up to a door. At the base of the stairs was a workshop table and various tools were lying there: a file, a set of screwdrivers, a saw, pruning-shears, a pair of bolt-cutters. There was a box of table salt and a wooden block from which protruded the black plastic handles of a set of kitchen knives. Joker had a bad feeling about the knives and the salt.

His shirt was soaked through with perspiration and he felt beads of sweat dribble down the back of his legs. The door at the top of the stairs opened and a figure was framed in the light behind it. The figure reached for a light switch and fluorescent lights blinked into life, flooding the basement with stark, white light. Joker screwed up his eyes and tried to focus on the figure on the top of the stairs. Shoes clicked on the stairs and two other figures appeared at the doorway. Joker heard masculine voices and a harsh laugh and then she was standing in front of him. Mary Hennessy. Her hair was dyed blonde and lightly permed, but other than that she had changed little from the last time he'd seen her, face to face. "I know you," she said quietly.

Joker tried to speak but his throat was too sore and dry to form words. He coughed and tasted blood at the back of his mouth.

She turned to the two men behind her. "Gentlemen, meet Sergeant Mike Cramer of the Special Air Service. A hired assassin for the British Government."

Joker shook his head but the movement made him dizzy and his vision rippled like a mirage. He groaned and tried to lick his dry lips. One of the men, with a receding hairline and a thick, black moustache, spoke. "Are you sure?" he asked Hennessy. His accent seemed vaguely Middle Eastern.

"Oh yes," said Hennessy. "I'm quite sure." She turned back to Joker and grabbed his shirt. She twisted and ripped it open so that his chest and stomach were bared, gleaming wetly under the fluorescent lights. She stepped to the side so that the men could see the thick, raised scar which ran from his sternum and across his stomach, down to his groin. Slowly, almost sensuously, she ran her index finger along the length of the scar, down to where it disappeared into his jeans. Joker felt his scrotum contract defensively. "I can see Sergeant Cramer remembers, too," she said softly.

The Colonel was clearing his desk before going home, loading all confidential papers into the sturdy wall-mounted safe behind his desk and signing a stack of memos and requisition forms with his fountain-pen. The administrative work was the least attractive part of his job, but he knew that more careers died on the bureaucratic battlefields than ever were lost in combat. He treated paperwork exactly the way he faced a military operation: scouting ahead for ambushes, looking for terrain that would give him an advantage, and always keeping an eye over his shoulder for sneak attacks.

His telephone rang and he answered it as he read a report on a recent training exercise in the Brecon Beacons. The voice on the other end of the line was a typical upper-class

British accent, polite but slightly bored, and the caller apologised for bothering the Colonel even though what he had to say was of the highest priority. "We have contact," said the voice.

The Colonel put his pen down on the desk. "Where?" he asked.

"A house near Chesapeake Bay, not far from Baltimore," said the voice. "Cramer followed a man there and was apprehended outside the house. We believe the man he was following was Matthew Bailey."

The Colonel smiled. "Excellent," he said.

"There was also a woman with Bailey. We don't have a positive identification yet, but it could be Hennessy."

"Even better," said the Colonel. The operation was proving to be every bit as successful as he'd hoped. "How many men do you have on the ground there?"

"Two at the moment, but more on the way. I don't want to move before we have sufficient manpower on site."

"That is understood," answered the Colonel.

"You realise there could well be some delay, and that Cramer has been compromised? I wouldn't want any misunderstanding on this point."

"That is also understood," said the Colonel. That had been the position from the start. Mike Cramer was on his own. And he was expendable.

Joker coughed and spluttered awake, as water dripped down his face and splattered onto the concrete floor of the basement. He shook his head but immediately regretted it

351

as the pain was acute, as if his brain was being squeezed by giant pincers. His eyelids were heavy and it required an effort of will to force them open. Mary Hennessy was standing in front of him, a red plastic tumbler in her hand. Satisfied that he had regained consciousness, she dropped the tumbler into a bucket of water which stood on the floor next to the workshop table. "Don't fall asleep on me, Cramer," she said. "I'd hate you to miss any of this."

The bright fluorescent lights burned into Joker's eyes and he screwed up his face as he tried to focus. His hands felt as if they'd swollen up like blood-filled balloons and that the slightest tear would cause them to burst. He tried moving his fingers. He could flex them, but the movement brought with it an agonising pain. He licked his cracked lips, trying to get some of the moisture from his face.

"Can't talk, huh?" said Hennessy. "Perhaps you'd like a drink?" She bent down and refilled the tumbler. She held it to his lips but as his mouth opened gratefully she took it away. "Maybe later," she said softly. "When you've told me what I want to know." She let the tumbler fall back into the water.

He and Hennessy were alone in the basement. He didn't remember the men going back up the stairs and closing the door, and he didn't remember passing out. He was sure that the bucket of water wasn't there the last time he was conscious. He looked down at it longingly. The surface rippled and Joker licked his lips again. This time, he tasted blood.

"Normally I give a little speech at this point," said Hennessy, standing in front of him with her hands on her hips. She took an elastic band and used it to tie back her hair in a ponytail. "I explain that you'll tell me everything eventually and that you might as well save yourself the pain. I usually lie, too. I explain that once you've told me everything, I'll let you go." She smiled. A few strands of hair were loose across her forehead and she brushed them away. "But you've been through this before, so we don't have to bother with the preliminaries." Slowly, her eyes never leaving his, she started to roll up the sleeves of her white linen shirt. It was hot in the basement and she was sweating, the moisture glistening on her tanned skin as she moved. "Do you have anything to tell me, Sergeant Cramer?"

Joker shook his head, the movement making him wince. The tendons in his legs felt as if they were on fire and his toes ached from the effort of maintaining his balance. His shirt was ripped open at the front and she'd unzipped his jeans so that his stomach was hanging out, the white scar lying against the flesh like a snake burrowing down into his groin. "Not Sergeant Cramer," he said, the words coming out slowly. "Not any more."

"That's right," she said, smiling brightly. "You left the SAS, didn't you?"

She finished rolling up her shirt-sleeves and wiped her hands on her cotton shorts. She breathed deeply, her chest rising and falling, droplets of sweat dripping down her cleavage. She undid the top button of her shirt and waved the material to and fro, trying to create a breeze that would cool her skin.

"So what was the problem, Mr Cramer?" She put the emphasis on the civilian title. "Couldn't hack it any more?" She picked up a large pair of scissors and tested the point with her fingertips. Satisfied with their sharpness, she stood by Joker's side, so close that he could smell her sweat. She grabbed the sleeve of his shirt and pushed the blades of the scissors up his arm, catching the material. "Was that it? Couldn't take the pressure?" She began to cut the shirt, along the top of the sleeve to the neck, taking care not to catch his flesh. The scissors made small tearing sounds like an animal feeding.

The tips of the scissors grazed Joker's neck and he tried to twist his head away. The movement caused him to lose his balance and his full weight pulled down on the chains which bit into his swollen wrists. Hennessy waited until he'd hauled himself back on to the balls of his feet before continuing to cut away the shirt, this time from the sleeve down to the shirt tail. She reached the bottom of the shirt and it fell loose around Joker's waist. She walked behind him, stroking his back with the handle of the scissors. Joker's skin crawled. He wondered if he could kick her hard enough to do damage, but he dismissed the thought. Even if he killed her, the men were still upstairs and he could see no way of freeing himself from the chain around his wrists. "You're not so fit any more, are you, Mr Cramer?" She cut the opposite side of his shirt away and threw the scraps of material onto the floor. She walked slowly back to the workbench and put down the scissors before turning back and scrutinising the man hanging before her. "I remember last time what a hard body you had, Mr Cramer. Flat stomach, strong thighs, muscular arms. There wasn't an ounce of fat on you then. Have you taken a look at yourself recently?" She slowly walked up to stand in front of him and placed a soft hand on his stomach.

"Do you have a girlfriend? What does she think about the mark I left on you?" She drew one red-painted nail along the thick scar. "Or are you too embarrassed to show it to anyone?"

She forced down the zipper of his jeans and pulled them down around his knees. She left them there, killing any idea he had of trying to kick her. In one swift movement she yanked down his boxer shorts, leaving him totally exposed. Joker felt his manhood shrink and his scrotum contract, sensing danger and trying to beat a retreat. Hennessy smiled at his reaction. "Can't talk? Is that it?" She bent down and refilled the tumbler. "Perhaps a drink might help." She threw the water into his face, hard. This time Joker managed to open his mouth and drink some of the water. He swallowed gratefully.

"So, why were you following Bailey?" she asked.

Joker dragged up what saliva he could and spat at her. He missed, and Hennessy smiled and shook her head sorrowfully. She refilled the tumbler with fresh water and put it on the workbench. "I thought you'd say that," she said as she ripped open the box of salt. She poured a handful into the tumbler and stirred it with the blades of the scissors. "You know the routine, Mr Cramer. Any time you want me to stop, just start talking." She picked up one of the kitchen knives and held it up to the light as she scrutinised the stainless-steel blade. She seemed unhappy with her selection and chose another. She walked over to Joker and held the tip of the blade under his nose, close to his left nostril. It was a short-handled knife with a sharp point, the type used to cut vegetables. She flicked the nostril with the blade, but not hard enough to draw blood. Joker stared at the knife. Hennessy rested the point against his left nipple and gently circled it with the blade, the way a lover might tease with her finger. She walked around Joker slowly, her eyes on his, drawing the knife along his skin but not cutting the flesh.

"I'm not alone," said Joker.

Hennessy licked her lips. "If the cavalry was waiting outside, I rather think they'd be in here by now, don't you? Face it, Mr Cramer. It's just you and me. Oh, I forgot to tell you – our nearest neighbours are a mile away and we're in the basement. The previous owner used it as a playroom for his three young children, so it's well soundproofed. Feel free to scream your heart out." She paused to allow her words to sink in. When she spoke again her voice sounded almost friendly. "Why were you following Matthew Bailey?" she asked.

"You," hissed Joker.

"You were after me?" she said, testing the point of the knife with her thumb. "And when you found me? What then?"

Joker remained silent.

"There was a gun in your car," she said.

"Not mine," he croaked.

He bit down on his lip in anticipation of the pain to come. He heard her take a breath, then she pushed the point of her knife against his shoulder and twisted it so that it screwed into his flesh like a drill, gouging into the muscle so deeply that he was sure she'd go through to the bone. Joker screamed and twisted away, trying to escape the blade but his momentum swung him back, driving it even deeper. His scream became a roar, the pain so intense that it swamped the agony of his wrists.

Hennessy took the tumbler of salt water and, with a

smile that was almost canine, threw it onto the new wound. Joker screamed and passed out.

Cole Howard was reading through the file on Carlos the Jackal when his phone rang. It was Kelly Armstrong.

"Hiya, Kelly, how's LA?" he asked.

"Actually, Cole, I'm calling from Dulles Airport. The credit card was a dead end, so Jake Sheldon said I should give you a hand in Washington. That seems to be the focus of the investigation, right?" Howard closed his eyes and leaned back in his chair. He'd hoped that he'd seen the last of Kelly Armstrong for a while. At least until he'd wrapped up the investigation. "Hasn't he spoken to you yet?" she asked.

"No, he hasn't," said Howard, unable to keep the bitterness out of his voice.

"Well, never mind," said Kelly. "He filled me in on the investigation so far and agrees that I'd be of more use working with you. Could you arrange clearance for me at the White House? I should be there within the hour."

"Okay," said Howard. "You know that we've identified the people in the desert?"

"Sheldon's already briefed me," she said, with maddening cheerfulness. "Ilich Ramirez Sanchez and the IRA. It's a strange combination. How's the computer simulation going?"

"Slowly," admitted Howard. "And now we know of the IRA involvement, we're going to have to widen our search. I'll explain when you get here."

"I'm on my way," she said brightly and hung up, leaving Howard with a dead phone pressed against his ear. Helen came up to his desk and handed him a handwritten note. While he was on the line, Jake Sheldon had phoned and he wanted Howard to return his call. Howard went over to the office coffee machine and poured himself a black coffee. What he wanted more than anything was a real drink.

Joker knew it was a dream, he knew that Mick Newmarch was dead and buried in the graveyard in Hereford, but that didn't stop the horror of what he saw. He was handcuffed to a radiator, his wrists sore from pulling against them, his arms aching from the wrenching. He was throwing himself from side to side, trying to slip out his bleeding wrists, trying to pull the hot pipe away from the wall, trying anything so that he could help Newmarch and stop the gut-wrenching screams. He kept trying to avert his eyes from what was happening in the centre of the room but the cries and the screams kept pulling him back.

His head slowly turned as if it was being forced around against his will. The lights were on in the farmhouse kitchen, the drapes drawn and shutters closed. Mick Newmarch was sprawled naked on a heavy oak table, his wrists shackled to the table legs at one end, his feet bound with hemp ropes at the other. His white skin was flecked with blood. Newmarch's head was thrashing from side to side and he kept trying to raise his shoulders off the table like a wrestler resisting being held down for the count. Standing over him, wearing a bloodstained apron like some demented butcher, was Mary Hennessy, her blonde hair tied back with a piece of black ribbon. That was wrong, Joker knew, her hair back then wasn't blonde, she was a brunette.

Hennessy had a pitcher in her hands and she poured water over Newmarch's face as he struggled. The water slopped off the table, carrying with it the blood from his wounds, and they pooled together on the tiled floor in pink rivers. The procedure had been the same for more than four hours. The verbal threats, the torture, the wounding, and then, once her victim had slid into unconsciousness, the water. "Come on Sass-man, look at your friend," she said to Joker. "Look at him. You're next."

She carried the empty jug back to the sink and refilled it from the cold tap. On the table, Newmarch sobbed like a baby, the cries wracking his whole body like spasms. Joker wanted to help with all his heart, but there was nothing he could do. After the first three hours she hadn't been interrogating Newmarch: there had been no need for that because he'd told her everything. The two SAS men had been undercover, working as labourers on a farm close to the border during the day and hanging around the local pubs at night, trying to pick up any intelligence which would help the Army in its fight against the IRA. Newmarch had slipped up, his room had been searched and he'd been caught with a Smith & Wesson automatic under his mattress. They'd come for them at night, put black hoods over their heads and thrown them in the back of a Land-Rover. When the hoods had been removed they'd found themselves handcuffed in the farmhouse with Mary Hennessy.

She'd started on Newmarch first, for no other reason

than that he'd sworn at her when she asked them for their names and rank. She'd told him in minute detail what she planned to do, and her words had chilled Joker. Not what she'd said, but the way she'd said it, as if she was relishing the experience. She'd used the bolt-cutters first, removing Newmarch's fingers one at a time, waiting between amputations for him to regain consciousness and using a poker heated on the farmhouse range to cauterise the wounds so that he wouldn't die from loss of blood. Newmarch had told her everything as he begged her to stop. He told her what he and Joker were doing, where they were based, previous operations they'd worked on, and the names of six other SAS men who were working undercover in the border country.

Hennessy took a large, shiny knife and held it up so that Joker could see it. "Watch, Sass-man," she said. She held his gaze almost hypnotically, and try as he might he couldn't look away. She reached down to Newmarch's groin and with her left hand she cupped the man's scrotum like a greengrocer weighing plums. She edged the blade under the testicles, keeping it horizontal. Newmarch screamed, a blood-chilling yell that echoed around the white-walled kitchen, and then slowly, almost sensually, Hennessy sliced the knife upwards, severing the scrotum. Newmarch passed out, but the silence was worse than the screaming. Joker had never seen so much blood, it poured like a waterfall over the table and splashed onto the tiles. Hennessy walked over to Joker, the ruptured tissue in her hand, and slapped him across his face, left then right. That was wrong, thought Joker, she hadn't slapped him until later, until he was shackled to the table. He knew that he was dreaming, but the slaps kept coming, burning his cheeks. It was only a nightmare, one he'd had many times before, but the pain in his wrists was excruciating.

Slap, slap, slap. Joker opened his eyes. It was no dream, he was still hanging from the pipe and Mary Hennessy, blonde and three years older than when she'd tortured and killed Mick Newmarch, stood before him. "Wake up, Cramer," she said. She drew back her hand and slapped him again. He blinked and felt tears sting his eyes. "Are you crying, Sass-man?" she asked.

Joker shook his head. "No," he said. The inside of his mouth felt red raw as if the lining had been stripped away.

"How did you know Bailey was here?" she asked.

"Followed him," said Joker. He had to keep her talking, he knew, because when he stopped talking she'd hurt him again. It was almost a game. If he kept silent, she'd hurt him. If he told her everything, she'd kill him. His only chance of survival was to extend the middle period as long as possible.

Hennessy smiled and ran her finger down the scar on his stomach. "From where?" she asked.

Joker coughed and tasted blood. Her nails scratched the thatch of hair around his stomach and slowly travelled down to his groin. "From where?" she repeated.

"The airfield," he said.

Her hand burrowed between his legs and he felt her nails tighten around his scrotum. The movement would have been almost sexual if Joker hadn't been so terrified and if Hennessy hadn't had such a murderous gleam in her eyes. "How did you know he'd be there?" she said. The fingers tightened.

Joker's mind whirled. He had to work out what she knew and what she didn't, give her only the information she already had and spin the rest out until he could find some way of escaping. She knew he was in the SAS, she knew his real name, there was a reasonable chance that the men in New York had told her that he'd been asking questions about Bailey in Filbin's. All of this she probably knew, so what secrets was she after? What did she want to know? The fingers squeezed, suddenly and viciously, and he screamed. His testicles felt like eggs being clamped in a vice and he was sure that one more turn and the shells would crack and splinter. Hennessy's hands relaxed but the pain didn't decrease, it seemed to spread up his spine and into his stomach. He drew one of his legs up as far as he could and that seemed to ease it somewhat, but it was still excruciating. Hennessy's hand slid back to his groin and hovered inches from his aching reproductive organs. "Don't play dumb with me, Cramer. I haven't even started with you yet. Remember Newmarch? That's nothing compared with what I have in store for you if you don't talk."

"New York," said Joker slowly. "I heard Bailey was in New York."

"Heard?" she repeated. "How did you hear that?"

"Pete Manyon," replied Joker.

"Ah, yes," said Hennessy, removing her hand. She picked up something from the workbench and held it in front of his face. It was his wallet. "Damien O'Brien," she said. "Good Irish name, that, Cramer." She took out the UK driving licence. "Looks genuine," she said, and dropped it on the floor. She held the Visa card. "This is definitely the real thing," she said, throwing it down. "In fact, all your paperwork seems first class, Cramer. I suppose that makes it an official operation, right?"

"Yeah," he said. He closed his eyes. Hennessy threw the wallet at his face.

"So how come you look like shit, Cramer? How come the SAS sends a wreck like you after Bailey?"

Joker said nothing, because it wasn't a question he could answer. Hennessy went back to the workbench and picked up the pruning shears. Joker's hands clenched as he recalled what she'd done to Newmarch's fingers. His wrists rubbed against the chain and he felt blood run down his arms.

"It doesn't make sense, Cramer. There are plenty of Sass-men they could have sent, guys like Pete Manyon. Young, fit, smart. Why would they send you?"

Joker swallowed and felt the metallic taste of blood at the back of his throat. He tried to talk but no words came. He swallowed again. "Water," he managed to croak.

Hennessy smiled. "You want water?" she said. She picked up the beaker and held it to his lips. He felt the liquid against his cracked and bleeding lips and he swallowed greedily, realising too late that it was salty. He coughed and choked and spat it out, his throat on fire.

Hennessy laughed and dropped the tumbler back into the bucket. "Let me give you the questions first," she said. "I want to know what you were told Bailey was doing here. And I want to know why they sent you." She held up the pruning shears. Joker moaned and raised his head, the movement sending stabs of pain through his neck and shoulders, and focused on his wrists. The chains had rubbed deep into the flesh and there was fresh wet blood on the shiny metal.

Hennessy grabbed his hair and wrenched his head back.

"So, are you ready to tell me why you were following Bailey?" she hissed.

Joker swallowed. What could he tell her? That he was tracking Bailey to find her. And why was he looking for her? To kill her. Joker didn't want to think what she'd do to him if he told her that. "Orders," he said.

Hennessy let go of his hair and tapped the blades of the shears against her cheek. "When did you leave the SAS, Cramer?" she asked.

"Three years ago," he said.

Hennessy nodded. "Why?"

Joker closed his eyes. "Medical discharge," he said.

Hennessy waited until he opened his eyes again. "Because of that?" She nodded at the scar on his stomach and groin.

"Yes," said Joker.

"So now whose orders are you acting on?" she asked.

"They brought me back," he said, each word grating on his tongue.

"Why you?" she said.

Joker closed his eyes again. It didn't hurt quite as much in the dark, as if the fluorescent lights were keeping the nerves to his brain on constant overload. In the darkness he could concentrate on the pain in his wrists and chest and try to will it away.

"Don't pass out on me again," said Hennessy softly. Joker felt the tip of the shears press against his left breast, circling. He opened his eyes. She held a paper cup of water to his lips. He tested it with the tip of his tongue and to his surprise it wasn't salty. He drank, deeply, but after the third swallow she took it away. Joker licked his lips, not wanting to waste a drop.

"Why did they bring you back?" she asked.

Joker shook his head. "I don't know," he said.

Hennessy narrowed her eyes as realisation dawned. "It was me, wasn't it? You were after me?" She threw the paper cup away, her eyes blazing. She placed her left hand against his breast and stroked the nipple with her thumb. It stiffened involuntarily as she circled it, rubbing it slowly. Joker tried to back away, his feet shuffling along the floor, tangled in his jeans and boxer shorts, but she gripped his nipple between her thumb and first finger, a look of contempt in her eyes. "Don't," he said, hating himself for begging and knowing that it wouldn't do any good. She slipped the blades of the shears either side of the nipple and grunted as she forced the handles together. Joker felt the blades bite through his flesh and click together somewhere deep inside the muscle behind the breast and then the pain lanced through his chest as if he'd been impaled on a metal spike. Joker screamed and he felt himself start to black out. He grabbed for the oblivion, welcoming it because it would put an end to the pain, but it was elusive, and the more he tried to pass out the clearer his thoughts became. Hennessy knew exactly what she was doing and she stood by his side, waiting for his breathing to steady so that she could continue.

Mary walked into the kitchen and closed the door to the basement behind her. Carlos and Bailey were sitting at the table, drinking tea and talking in low voices. They both looked up as she walked over to the fridge and took out a can of Diet Coke.

"Did he say anything?" asked Carlos. His hand was buried in a bag of chocolate chip cookies and he put one in his mouth, whole.

Mary smiled thinly. "He's talking," she said, popping the tab on the can. She sipped it. Bailey was looking at her with horror in his eyes and she realised there was blood on the front of her shirt, a thin dribble of red that ran down her left breast. "He's unconscious now. I'll leave him for a while. It's always more effective if they have a chance to think about their options."

She pulled out a chair and sat down at the pine table. "He says he followed you from the airfield, Matthew. And he says he heard about the airfield in New York."

Bailey nodded, his hands tight around a white mug. "That's what Pat Farrell said," agreed Bailey. "Did he admit to killing the two guys?"

"We haven't got to that yet," said Mary.

"Who sent him here?" asked Carlos, tossing another cookie into his mouth. He chewed noisily and with relish.

"He says the SAS, and I believe him," answered Mary. "His ID looks genuine, which means that it's Government sanctioned."

The two men nodded. "Where's everyone else?" asked Mary.

Carlos gestured upwards. "Stripping their rifles," he said.

"Do you think we should stay here?" Bailey said.

Mary shrugged. "I don't see why not. He seems to be acting alone."

Carlos frowned. "You think the British Government would send one man?"

"It's possible," replied Mary. "And this man is unusual. He left the SAS some time ago, and I think a large part of that is because of what I did to him in Ireland three years ago. I killed a friend of his, and I nearly killed him."

Carlos nodded. "So you think it's a personal vendetta?"

"I think there's a strong possibility," she answered.

"I think we should m-m-move," stammered Bailey. "Now."

"I think you're over-reacting," said Mary. "Let me have another few hours with him. I should know everything when I've finished."

"But if he's not alone, we c-c-could have the SAS swarming all over the house by then," said Bailey. His stutter had returned, Mary noticed.

"Matthew, if the SAS were here, we wouldn't be having this conversation," she said. He nodded, but Mary could see that he wasn't convinced. "Look, first things first. He saw you out at the airfield, so I think we should move the plane. Could you fly it over to Bay Bridge airfield?"

"Now? Sure, no p-p-problem," replied Bailey. He was clearly still worried.

"It's going to be all right," Mary said reassuringly. "It'll all be over soon. We'll be in Florida and then Cuba and we'll have done something they'll talk about in Ireland for ever more. We'll be heroes, you and I."

Bailey sighed and ran a hand through his red hair. "I'm f-f-frightened that it's all going to f-f-fall apart," he admitted.

Mary narrowed her eyes. It wasn't the operation that was in danger of falling apart, she realised. It was him.

"He's just one man," she said. "And soon he won't

even be much of a man." She reached up behind her hair and set it loose, shaking it from side to side. She'd undone the top three buttons of her shirt because of the stifling heat down in the basement and she could feel Bailey's eyes on her breasts. "I'm going to take a shower," she said. "Then I'll get back to work on Cramer."

She went out of the kitchen, and was halfway up the stairs when she realised that Carlos had followed her into the hall. He obviously had something on his mind. "What is it?" she asked.

"This Armstrong woman. Are you sure we can trust her?"

Mary sat down on the stairs and looked down at Carlos. "Her father was Irish," she said.

"But she's an FBI agent," said Carlos. "How do we know she's not setting you up?"

Mary smiled. "In the first place, there's no need. It's not as if the FBI need to gather evidence against either of us, is it?" She brushed a strand of blonde hair from her face and eased it behind her ear.

"But why are you so willing to trust her?" pressed Carlos.

"Her father was in the IRA," she said quietly.

Carlos was stunned. "Oh come on," he said. "Are you telling me that the FBI recruited a woman whose father was a terrorist? Even the Americans aren't that stupid."

"Colm O'Malley was her natural father. Her mother was American and they divorced when Kelly was only a few years old. The woman moved back to the States and remarried. As far as the FBI are concerned, Kelly Armstrong is the original all-American girl."

"And this O'Malley, this Colm O'Malley, what happened to him?"

Mary studied Carlos thoughtfully. "He was killed," she said quietly. Carlos said nothing, waiting for her to continue. Mary took a deep breath, as if preparing herself. "Colm was a good friend of my husband's and a member of the IRA High Command. His brother, Fergus, still lives in Phoenix. He has a business there and he's a fund-raiser for NORAID. The O'Malleys were good people, and committed to the Cause." She fell silent as her mind was flooded with images from the past. "Colm was a victim of the British Government's shoot-to-kill policy," she continued. "The police blamed Protestant extremists, but it was an SAS operation."

"The same operation that ended in the death of your husband?"

Mary nodded. Her eyes were damp. "And others," she said.

"How much does she know about what we plan to do?"

"Most of it. She's going to talk to her office in Phoenix and then get herself transferred to the main investigation in Washington."

"And you're sure she doesn't know of my involvement?"

"I didn't tell her, and she didn't mention it."

"But you said the FBI know that Lovell and Schoelen are involved?"

Mary nodded. "They've identified them from computer-enhanced photographs."

"Then it's only a matter of time before they identify me."

"That's probably true, Ilich," Mary admitted.

STEPHEN LEATHER

"Does the FBI know that you're involved?"

"According to Kelly, the last time she spoke to her boss they'd identified only the Americans. That could have changed by now, of course. If the photographs are as good as she says and if they run them through Interpol . . ." She left the sentence unfinished.

"And despite that, despite the fact they're on to us, and despite the nature of the target, she still wants to help?"

"She hates the British, Carlos. Hates them with a vengeance." Her eyes blazed. "She hates them as much as I do." She turned her back on him and went upstairs. The door to Schoelen's room was closed. She knocked and pushed it open. The sniper was sitting on the edge of his bed, polishing the barrel of his rifle.

"Hiya, Mary. What's up?" he said.

Mary closed the door behind her and leant against it. Schoelen saw from the look on her face that something was wrong. He put down the weapon, frowning. "You phoned home," she said flatly. "You put the whole operation at risk because of a bloody dog."

Schoelen was stunned. "How . . ."

"It doesn't matter how I know, I just know," she said quietly. "You're a lucky man, Schoelen. If we had more time I'd kill you now, myself. But we don't, so I need you. But you put one foot wrong again and it's all over. I'll put a bullet in your skull myself. Do I make myself clear?"

Schoelen closed his mouth and nodded slowly. His eyes were on the trickle of blood on her shirt.

Mary smiled. "Good."

"Does Carlos . . ."

"No," interrupted Mary. "He doesn't. And if I were you I'd pray that he doesn't find out."

She left the room, leaving Schoelen holding his head in his hands.

Ed Mulholland's television producer friend had agreed to run the story on Mary Hennessy and Matthew Bailey at the end of the regular programme. He had also agreed to issue a separate 1-800 number so that calls would be routed directly to the FBI's temporary office in the White House. Mulholland called a meeting of the FBI agents after lunch, and they sat and listened as the anti-terrorist chief briefed them on how they were to handle the calls. He leant against his desk, his legs crossed at the ankles and his large forearms folded as if he was hugging his barrel chest. Helen sat to one side, taking notes and occasionally looking at him like an adoring wife.

"The programme starts at eight o'clock, and our segment will be broadcast at eight-fifty," he said. "Their photographs will be on screen, and the announcer will say that we're looking for them in connection with a drug-smuggling ring in Florida. The reason we're saying Florida is because we have no evidence that they've actually been there, which means any calls from that part of the country can be ignored, at least at this stage. Millions of people will be watching, and most of them are really keen to get involved, some of them too keen. We'll get malicious hoax calls, we'll get well-meaning citizens who have just made a mistake, and we'll have the crazies who'll say they've seen Elvis if they think it'll get them on prime-time television. For every genuine sighting we'll have a hundred red herrings."

Cole Howard looked around the room, which was crammed with desks and filing cabinets. Two dozen FBI agents had been assigned from the main Washington office to work with the New York team, and the air-conditioning was finding it difficult to cope. Helen had arranged for several free-standing fans to be brought in and most of the agents tried to stand where they could feel some sort of breeze. Don Clutesi was standing next to Howard, sweat trickling down his face. He grinned at Howard and made a wafting motion with his hand. "Hot," he mouthed, and Howard nodded in sympathy. The one person missing was Kelly Armstrong. Howard had suggested that she compile a list of alternative targets; the IRA involvement opened up the possibility of British targets and Howard had shown her the list of visiting VIPs which he'd obtained from the State Department, including British Members of Parliament and chief executives of leading UK companies. Two names which had immediately set alarm bells ringing were the British Prime Minister, who was visiting the East Coast, and the Prince of Wales, who was due in New York in the summer. Howard had asked Kelly to speak to the Secret Service and the State Department to come up with a more comprehensive list of potential targets and venues which could then be cross-checked with Andy Kim's computer simulation. Kelly had been surprisingly enthusiastic about the task and had been out of the office all afternoon. Howard was pleased at her absence. He had high hopes for the television broadcast, and wanted Kelly as far away as possible. He hadn't even told her what Mulholland had planned, and took a sly pleasure in having manoeuvred her away from the action.

"Calls will initially be routed through Helen,"

Mulholland continued. Helen beamed and raised her pencil in acknowledgment. "Calls from the Baltimore-Washington area will be put through to either me, Cole, Don or Hank. If we're lucky enough to get a flood of calls, we'll switch some of you guys over. We'll have a separate desk to handle calls from the Arizona area, because we know that they were there originally. But all other calls will be put through to you on a rotating basis, depending who's free. Helen will be issuing you with questionnaires to fill in for each call." He held one up to show them. "Basically, all we want is the name and number of the caller, who they saw and where, and any information they have which might be pertinent: description of their vehicle, names they were using, and so on." He held up another sheet. "You'll have this information in front of you, detailing the aliases we know they have used, car registration plates and details of credit cards. If you get a match, inform us on the Baltimore-Washington desk, otherwise file them according to the state they were seen in. Helen has a filing system rigged up over there." He pointed to a set of filing cabinets. "Any questions?" He was faced with a wall of shaking heads. He clapped his hands. "Okay, let's do it," he said. The agents went back to their desks. Cole Howard decided to visit Andy Kim and the programmers. He found Andy crouched over his computer, a worried frown on his face. "What's up, Andy?" Howard asked, putting his hand on the man's shoulder. On the screen was a complex line-drawing of what appeared to be a baseball stadium surrounded by urban sprawl.

Andy shook his head, then flicked his hair out of his eyes. "Nothing fits, Cole," he said despondently. "Take a look at this." Howard looked over his shoulder. "This is

Oriole Park in Baltimore – the President's due to be there tomorrow evening with the Prime Minister. This is one of the most obvious possibilities. He was going to be driven to the ball park but Sanger has cut out ground transportation wherever he can and now he'll be arriving by Marine One, the helicopter. He's vulnerable leaving the helicopter, but only for a few seconds, and he's safe walking to his box because then he's inside. Obviously he presents the best target while in the box watching the game. But I can only fit two of the snipers into office blocks or hotels which overlook the ball park. There's nowhere for the third sniper, the one who is furthest away."

"So you know it's not going to be at the ball park?" said Howard.

"But Cole, it's like that for every venue we try. We can find space for one sniper, occasionally two, but often it's the third one that screws us up." He tapped the screen. "It's so high up, there aren't many buildings that tall. In the desert, he was on the butte, remember?"

"I remember," said Howard. "So he could be on a hill maybe?"

Andy nodded. "I ran the topography through the computer as well as the buildings. If he was on a hill we'd spot it. Camp David, for instance, where he is today with the Prime Minister. We ran the surrounding woods through the program, but no match." He turned to look at the FBI agent, his eyes reddened from not enough sleep. "That third sniper is a real problem," he said.

"Could it be something other than a building?" Howard asked. "A plane, maybe?"

Andy shook his head. "Planes move too fast for a sniper, and they're too unstable."

Howard frowned. "A helicopter?"

"Too much vibration."

Howard shrugged. "Let me give it some thought, Andy," he said. "In the meantime, why don't you try ignoring the long shot? – concentrate on the two closest. That would give the Secret Service boys something to work on. I mean, better safe than sorry. They can check out all the venues where two out of three match, couldn't they?"

Andy nodded. "That's a good idea."

"There's something else that's been worrying me," said Howard. "The two men and the woman, the ones on the ground close to the target."

Andy frowned. "What's wrong?" He ran his hand through his hair, brushing it away from his eyes.

"We've been assuming that they're organising the hit, right?"

"Right," agreed Andy.

"Well, what if they're not? What if they're actually part of the hit? What if they're carrying guns?"

"And if the snipers fail, they'll finish the job?" said Andy, his eyes sparkling.

Howard nodded. They had all been assuming that Carlos, Hennessy and Bailey were helping the snipers calibrate their sights. But it was perfectly possible that they could actually be part of the assassination. "I'm going to speak to Bob Sanger about it," he said.

"So even if we find the snipers, the President might still be at risk?"

"That's what I'm frightened of," said Howard. He saw that Andy had a direct line on his desk and he noted down the number. He looked around the office and saw a dozen programmers, including Rick Palmer, hard at work, but no sign of Bonnie.

"Bonnie's at home, I told her to get some sleep," said Andy, as if reading his mind.

Howard squeezed his shoulder. "That's where you should be," he said.

"There'll be plenty of time for sleep when all this is over," said Andy, turning back to the screen.

Howard patted Andy on the back and returned to his office. His desk faced the one being used by Don Clutesi, who was lounging back in his chair, his phone lodged between his chin and his shoulder. He winked at Howard as he sat down. Howard picked up his own phone and called home. He'd been ringing all day but no-one had answered and he'd assumed that Lisa had been out playing golf. This time she answered and she appeared no less lukewarm than the last time they'd spoken.

"Do you have any idea yet when you'll be coming back?" she asked.

"Hopefully we'll make some progress tonight. I'll call you tomorrow, I should have a better idea then. How are the children?"

"Asleep," she said. Howard wondered if she'd played golf with her father that day. The seconds ticked off with neither of them speaking. Lisa broke the silence. "Cole, why do you have Trivial Pursuit cards in your suit pockets?" she asked.

"Excuse me?" said Howard, bewildered by the change of subject.

"I was taking out some of your suits for cleaning and I found them in an inside pocket."

"Ah," said Howard.

"So what gives?"

"I was practising," he said.

"You mean you were cheating," she said.

Howard groaned inwardly. "Honey, I wasn't cheating. I was just going over a few cards before we had dinner with your father, that's all."

"Cole, to me that sounds like cheating. I think it's despicable. Are you so insecure that you have to resort to cheating to beat my father at a board game?"

Howard sighed. Sometimes there was no arguing with her. "Maybe we could talk about this when I get back," he said.

He could picture her shaking her head, a look of contempt on her face. "The subject is closed," she said. "But I just want you to know I think you've behaved really badly. Beating my father shouldn't mean that much to you."

"Can I say goodnight to the kids?" Howard asked.

"I already told you, they're asleep," she replied. Howard had the impression that she wasn't telling the truth and that she was depriving him of the children as a punishment.

"Well, tell them I called, will you? Please."

"Sure," she said curtly and Howard knew that the message wouldn't be passed on. "Goodbye."

Howard was left with the buzzing of a disconnected line in his ear. As he replaced the receiver, Don Clutesi did the same. "Any luck?" Clutesi asked.

Howard smiled thinly. "Very little," he said. "You?"

"According to Frank, the credit card Hennessy was using was applied for in New York two years ago. The driving licence is a valid New York State one and was taken out eighteen months ago."

"That suggests that this has been a long time in the planning," said Howard.

Clutesi shook his head. "Not necessarily. The Irish are always setting up fake identities and paperwork so that they have a steady supply. They probably wouldn't know that Hennessy was going to use it."

"What about the photograph on the driving licence?"

"Probably just a close match. Blonde woman in her late forties; who's going to look any closer than that? No-one looks at the photograph anyway. Passports are a different matter, but the IRA have plenty of contacts within INS; they can get a genuine one within a few days."

"What about getting records of her credit card?" Howard asked. "That way we can find out where she's been."

Clutesi mopped his brow with the back of his sleeve. "Already in hand," he said. He looked at his wristwatch and nodded over at a large-screen television which Helen had positioned at the far end of the office. "Not long before the show starts," he said.

Mary Hennessy wiped her hands with a white towel, leaving crimson streaks on the material. She threw it onto the workbench and studied the man hanging from the overhead pipe. Two rivers of dried blood ran down his chest like stigmata – one from the hole where his right nipple used to be, the other from a strip of flesh some six inches long which hung down over his stomach like some demonic tongue, red and glistening under the fluorescent lights.

Joker was unconscious, breathing heavily through his nose like a sleeping dog. Thick, clotting saliva bubbled from his lips and greenish yellow slime oozed from his nostrils. He was a disgusting mess, but most of the damage was superficial, Hennessy knew. Painful, excruciatingly so, but a long way from death. Over the coming hours she would take the SAS man closer and closer to extinction, narrowing the gap with exquisite skill and enjoying every moment of the journey. It wasn't pain that people died from when under torture, or shock, it was loss of blood. The human body contained about five litres, and Hennessy knew from experience that a man could lose almost half of that before the body failed. The skill was to prolong the torture, allowing the body to manufacture more blood to replace that which was lost, and to give wounds a chance to stop bleeding. By stopping and starting, the procedure could be prolonged almost indefinitely. It was almost like sex, she thought, gradually taking a man to orgasm, holding him to almost the point of coming, and then stopping, letting him subside until he was ready to start again. As she could build the pleasure until it was almost unbearable, so it was with pain. When he'd suffered enough she'd push him over the edge, into the eternal abyss, and she'd be standing in front of him, watching him as he took the final plunge.

He'd pretty much told her everything she needed to know. He was working alone, recruited by his former masters because they knew he had a personal grudge against her, and because he was in such a bad state health-wise no-one would ever believe that the SAS would use him. He had the perfect cover.

He'd seen the plane but had no idea what part it, or Patrick Farrell, played in their plan. He hadn't known about

Carlos or the snipers, and he knew nothing of what had happened in Arizona. She'd taken him to such levels of pain that she was certain he wasn't lying or holding anything back. In agony there was only truth.

She picked up the pruning shears, the blades crusted with dried blood. Joker's chin was jammed against his chest, which rose and fell in time with his breathing. Hennessy went behind him and looked up at his bound wrists. The hands were clenched into tight fists, the wrists red raw and the fingers white as if drained of blood. He was a tall man, a little over six feet, and with his arms stretched up above his head his fingers were out of reach. She tapped the shears against her hand, her lower lip jutting forward as she frowned like a little girl. After a few seconds she knelt down in front of her victim like a nun praying for penance before a life-size crucifix. She looked up at him but he was still unconscious, his deep-set eyes like black circles in his ashen face. Slowly, almost sensually, she undid the laces of his training shoes and slipped them, and his socks, off his feet. Joker groaned and coughed, and Hennessy sat back on her heels, watching him. The coughing spasm opened up the wounds on his chest and fresh blood began to flow. Hennessy kept her eyes on his face as she removed his jeans and shorts. She threw them into a dark corner and then squatted down, pushing the blades of the shears around the little toe on his left foot. She pressed the handles together and felt the shears bite into the skin. They met resistance, and she knew she'd reached the bone, but there was no reaction from the man. She released the pressure and took the shears away, watching the blood blossom from the two deep cuts on the toe. She wanted him conscious and able to appreciate the full horror of what she was about to do. She stood in front of him and slapped him, the blows echoing around the basement like pistol shots. His eyelids fluttered open and she saw his eyes focus on her face. She grabbed his hair and yanked back his head. "Wake up, Sass-man," she hissed. "It'll soon be over."

Joker snorted as if he was trying to laugh. Hennessy walked away. She leant against the workbench and studied the injured man. Joker lifted his head and squinted at her. "What do you want from me now?" he asked, his voice faltering.

Hennessy smiled and shook her head. "You've told me everything I need, Cramer. You know nothing. Nothing that can prevent me from succeeding, anyway."

Joker swallowed. "So now you're going to kill me, right? Why don't you just get on with it, you bitch?"

Hennessy threw back her head and laughed as if someone had told a joke at a cocktail party. "Oh no, Cramer, we're not going to rush this. But I wanted to talk to you first. You and Newmarch were both part of the Government's shoot-to-kill operation, weren't you?"

Joker licked his lips. "Water," he said.

Hennessy could see that talking was an effort because his throat was so dry and she wanted him to speak, so she filled the tumbler from the bucket of water. As she walked towards him she saw his left leg tense as if preparing to try to kick her. She stopped and wagged a warning finger at him.

Joker grimaced. Hennessy kept her distance as she walked around behind him and as she held the beaker to his lips she kept a wary eye on his legs. She let him drink all of the water before taking it away. "After the airliner went down, the British Government initiated a shoot-to-kill operation, Cramer, and you were part of it," she said, putting the tumbler back in the bucket. It gurgled as if filled with water and sank to the bottom. "Newmarch told me how he was involved, but I never got round to asking you," she said. "Who did you assassinate, Cramer?" Joker said nothing. "Newmarch told me who he'd killed. But you know that, don't you, because you were there? He murdered three members of the IRA High Command, remember? My husband was murdered in that shoot-to-kill operation, Cramer. Three men wearing ski-masks surrounded his car as it arrived home one night. They shot his driver first, then they pumped a total of twelve bullets into his body. Two of them were into his head at close range. I heard the shots, and I knew before I even opened the front door what had happened. I held him in my arms, even though he was already dead. There was so much blood, Cramer. So much blood."

Her cheeks were reddening and she put up a hand to her face as if testing the temperature of her face. "It took the ambulance half an hour to get there, as if they knew that he was dead and they didn't care. The police didn't want to know, either. The RUC didn't even send a forensic team around to survey the area. They just towed away the car and took a statement from me. Case closed. Like they didn't care, either. Like they expected it. So, Cramer, were you one of the men in ski-masks?"

"I didn't kill your husband," said Joker, his voice little more than a whisper. "And I didn't kill Sean Morrison, either."

At the mention of Morrison's name, Hennessy's head jerked up. Her eyes narrowed. "How do you . . .?"

"I read your file," he said before she could finish.

"Do you know how they killed him?" she asked quietly. Joker shook his head.

"He died here, in the States. In New York. Sean was found in his bath, with his throat cut. There was a razor blade in his hand and blood everywhere. The New York City Police Department said it was suicide." She raised her eyebrows. "Sean always used an electric razor. I never saw him with a razor blade. Ever. They killed my husband. And they killed the man I loved. You and your cronies did that, Cramer." She walked up closer to him, but kept her distance from his legs. "You want to know something, Cramer? Liam and Sean had nothing to do with the bombing of the airliner. They were trying to stop the bombings on the mainland, they were doing all they could to get the IRA to negotiate with the British Government. There was no need to kill them, no need at all." Her eyes were blazing with anger and her small hands formed tight fists by her side. "You bastards killed them, and if it takes me forever I'll have my revenge. On you and the rest of your kind." She picked up the pruning shears and waved them under Joker's nose. "I'll make you bleed like they bled, until there's not a drop left in your body."

She knelt by his feet and grabbed at his left ankle, forcing the blades down towards his toe. As the metal touched his skin the door to the basement was flung open and Bailey came down the first few steps, shouting. "Mary! Mary!"

Hennessy's head jerked up and the blades of the shears sliced together, narrowly missing Joker's toe. He pulled his foot back and it slipped from Hennessy's grasp. She stood up, alarmed. "What's wrong?" she asked.

"The television," he shouted. "We're on the bloody box."

Hennessy frowned, totally confused. "What do you mean?"

Bailey leant against the rail and gripped it with both hands. His face was pale and his eyes were wide and manic. "Just come and look. They're bloody well on to us." He scrambled back up the stairs and Hennessy followed him.

Carlos was in the sitting room, sitting the wrong way on a wooden chair, his arms clasped around the back as if he was giving it a bear hug. Rashid was curled up on a green sofa, her legs tucked up under her chin. Both were facing the television screen on which were two colour photographs: Hennessy and Bailey. Underneath their pictures was a 1-800 number.

Carlos looked up as she came into the room. "We have a problem, Mary."

"What did they say?" she asked. "Do they know what we're planning?"

Carlos shook his head. "They said the FBI wants you in connection with a drug-smuggling operation in Florida."

"What?" Hennessy was stunned. She looked at Bailey, who was equally astonished.

"Why didn't that woman Armstrong tell you about this?" Carlos spat.

Hennessy ran a hand through her hair. "I don't know. She's only just made contact with the agents in Washington. Maybe they didn't tell her."

"Or maybe they don't trust her. Maybe she's blown?"

"I arranged to meet her tomorrow, I'll be sure to ask her then," said Hennessy, her voice loaded with sarcasm.

Carlos looked as if he was going to argue, but he calmed himself down. He stood up and swung the chair back so that it was against the wall. "Okay, okay, let's sort out what we do next," he said. "The FBI obviously don't want to give the real reason that they're looking for you. The drugs story doesn't mean anything. What matters is that they know that you're in the country and that they're looking for you."

"We have to call it off," said Bailey, his voice trembling.

"No," said Carlos.

"Definitely not," said Hennessy.

"But they're onto us . . . they know we're here, they . . ."

"Matthew, they think we're in Florida. Not Baltimore." Hennessy could see that the younger man was starting to fall apart. He was physically shaking and his eyes were darting between her and Carlos.

"Maybe they followed me there, maybe they know where I am now . . ."

Hennessy went over and put her hands on his shoulders. "Listen to me, Matthew, if they knew where we were they wouldn't be putting our photographs on national television. They don't know where we are, and they don't know what we're doing. There's nothing they can do to stop us, not now." She held his gaze, smiling reassuringly and squeezing his shoulders.

"B-b-but what about the Sass-man?" he said.

"He knows nothing either," she said reassuringly. She turned to look over her shoulder at Carlos. "We're going to have to leave the house," she said quietly. "The woman who leased it to me might have been watching. And they're sure to get a line on the credit cards we've been using."

"I agree," said Carlos. "We can book into a motel for tonight, there shouldn't be a problem so long as you stay out of sight."

Hennessy turned back to Bailey. "It's going to be all

right," she said. She could feel him shaking and she stroked the back of his neck.

"What about Cramer?" asked Carlos.

Hennessy kept her eyes on Bailey. She didn't want to leave him alone, he seemed ready to run off in a blind panic. She had to calm him down. "Can you handle it, Ilich?" she asked quietly.

Carlos understood immediately. "Of course," he said.

Rashid unwound herself from the sofa and put a hand on Carlos' shoulder. "Let me, Ilich," she said softly. Carlos was about to refuse when he felt her press the full length of her lithe body against his back. "Please," she whispered into his ear, her breath warm against his neck.

Ed Mulholland stood with his hands on his hips as he watched the short item on the FBI hunt for Hennessy and Bailey. Within seconds of the 1-800 number appearing at the bottom of the screen, all the lights on Helen's console began to blink. Mulholland's producer friend had warned him that he would be overwhelmed by the response. The programme had more than two dozen people answering its own phones, and there were just as many police officers on hand to follow up serious leads. The show had an admirable record: during the five years it had been running they had helped capture more than three hundred perpetrators, including sixty-seven murderers. It had also consistently increased its viewing figures and was now one of the network's top money-spinners. The jaded American viewer, fed up with a diet of unfunny comedy shows and under-budgeted made-for-TV movies, couldn't get enough of reality television and its real-life heroes and villains.

Helen began to work her way efficiently across the console, passing the calls on to the agents with a minimum of fuss. As soon as she dealt with a call and switched it across to one of the desks, its light would begin to flash immediately as another call came through. She was wearing a pair of lightweight headphones with a microphone suspended an inch from her lips. She smiled across at Mulholland, happy at her work. She was an absolute treasure, Mulholland had realised, and he decided that when the operation was over he'd try to persuade her to leave the White House staff and join the FBI in New York.

He went over to the Baltimore-Washington desk where Hank O'Donnell and Don Clutesi were already taking calls, phones pressed against their ears as they made notes on large pads. Cole Howard looked up. "It's working, Ed," he said.

"There was never any doubt, Cole," answered Mulholland. "We'll have them, don't you worry."

The phone in front of Howard rang and he picked it up.

Joker clenched and unclenched his hands, trying to get the circulation flowing. His arms felt as if they would pop out of their sockets at any moment and he stood up on the tips of his toes in an attempt to ease the pain. The movement reopened the wounds on his chest and back and he felt warm blood ooze from under the fresh scabs. He knew that his time was limited, that Mary Hennessy was preparing to end it. He had watched her toy with Mick Newmarch for several agonising hours before ending his life with a savage castration. Joker was determined that he wouldn't go the same way. If she came close enough he was prepared to lash out with his feet, and even if he wasn't lucky enough to land a killing blow he might be able to disable her for a while. He flexed his legs one at a time as he looked around the basement. The pipe he was chained to was as thick as his thigh, and sturdy. There were brackets holding it to the concrete ceiling every six feet or so. Just beyond one of the brackets was a bend in the pipe, and just before the bend was a joint, where a straight section had been connected to a piece which curved through ninety degrees, off to the left. Joker wondered if the joint might be a weak point. If he could get up to the pipe and crawl along it, maybe his weight would be enough to pull the sections apart. He leant his head back and looked up. His hands were about twelve inches away from the pipe and he wouldn't be able to get enough leverage to jump up. If he could swing himself up, he might be able to grasp the pipe with his feet, but he'd been hanging for so long he doubted that he'd have enough strength in his stomach muscles. He began lifting his legs one at a time, drawing his knees up to his stomach. He could do it, just, but the pain was almost more than he could bear. And he could only imagine what effect it would have on his injured wrists when it came to lifting both legs off the ground.

He had no way of knowing how long Hennessy would be away. Something had clearly spooked Bailey. Perhaps he'd be better trying to break the pipe before she came back. He breathed slowly and deeply, bracing himself for the pain he knew would come. His preparations were interrupted when the door to the basement opened and he heard footsteps on the stairs. He looked up like a schoolboy with a naughty secret, expecting to see Mary Hennessy. He was surprised to see a young woman, skinny with long, dark hair. She stopped halfway down the steps and he heard the click-clack of a round being chambered in a handgun. As she got closer he saw her eyes were narrow, almost Oriental, and her face was thin and pointed. She wasn't conventionally pretty but she had an animal presence which was both attractive and disturbing. She was wearing tight black leather jeans and a purple T-shirt, cut low at the arms so he could see that she didn't shave her armpits. In her right hand was a matt black handgun. At first glance it looked like the P228 which he'd taken from the men in New York, but without the silencer. As she got closer he saw that it was a Smith & Wesson model 411. It was a lightweight handgun with a four-inch barrel but it was more than capable of blowing a sizeable hole in his body.

"Hello, Mr Cramer," she said, her voice heavily accented. "We haven't been introduced. My name's Dina." Joker said nothing as she looked him up and down, her gaze concentrating on his groin. She smiled coyly. "You don't seem very pleased to see me." She transferred the gun to her left hand, then reached out to touch his stomach with her free hand. She ran her hand down to his groin and stroked his pubic hair, a sly grin on her face. "I bet I could make you glad to see me," she said. Her fingers tightened around him and she squeezed. Joker brought his knee up, hard, powering it into her groin. All the breath went from her lungs and she pitched forward, her legs buckling. Bolts of pain shot through his wrists and Joker yelped involuntarily. The woman staggered forward, her head banging into his chest, his blood smearing against her face. The gun clattered to the floor at his feet and her hands went to her groin as her breath came back in small, puppy-like, gasps. Joker leant back, taking more of his weight on the chain, and slammed his knee up into her chin, snapping her head back with an audible crack. Her eyes rolled up and she made a wheezing sound, then she slumped to the ground, stunned rather than unconscious. She fell face down and she tried to pull herself away from Joker, her fingernails scrabbling along the concrete floor. Joker looked down. His right ankle was next to her neck and he lifted it and placed his foot against the back of her head, trying to hold her still. She pushed up against him and tried to get to her knees and he thrust down harder. Her breathing was steadier and he knew she was getting her strength back – he wouldn't be able to hold her down for much longer. He raised his leg and before she could react he drove down with all his might, slamming his heel into her temple so hard that he heard bone and cartilage splinter. He felt something warm and sticky gush over his foot. He lifted his knee and brought his heel down again, smashing into the same place and feeling the skull break. Her feet beat a rapid tattoo on the floor and he knew she was dead, it was just that her body hadn't realised it yet.

He looked around for the gun and couldn't see it. He realised she must be lying on it. He levered his foot under her arm and with a grunt he forced her over. As her head lifted from the floor her left eye plopped out of its socket and hung grotesquely on her cheek, gelatinous fluid dripping from it. Her hair was matted with brain tissue and blood and as he flipped her onto her back it spread out in a pool around her head like a scarlet halo.

The gun was by his feet, its safety off.

She'd closed the door when she'd come down into the basement and she'd made very little noise as she died, so Joker reckoned no-one upstairs would have heard. He used the tip of his right foot to slide the gun so that it was between his feet, careful not to touch the trigger. He was finding it difficult to focus, and sweat was pouring off his forehead and dripping into his eyes. He shuffled his feet together and manoeuvred the firearm so that its butt was angled up, its barrel away from him. It was going to hurt, he knew, and he tried to prepare himself. He doubted that he'd have the energy for more than one attempt, and he prayed that he wouldn't pass out. He took a deep breath, then brought both feet off the ground, swinging them up and taking all his weight on his bound wrists. It felt as if his hands were being ripped from his wrists and he screamed before he bit down on his lip. He contracted the aching muscles in his stomach and pushed up with his legs, trying to maintain his momentum. His legs were dead and his abdomen felt as if it was going to collapse. He screamed, partly in agony and partly out of frustration. He tried to blank out the pain and imagined that he was back in basic training, hanging from wall bars and doing repetitions of leg-lifts, building strength and stamina. He grunted and sweated and held on to the image, remembering the old sergeant-major who'd cursed out any of the recruits who couldn't manage at least fifty of the torturous leg-lifts. He screamed again and realised that his knee was banging against his chin. He opened his eyes and saw his legs were up, the gun almost slipping from between his feet. Two more inches and it would be in his hands. He held his fingers wide like a child trying to catch a ball and brought his knees closer to his face, the pain in his wrists like red-hot manacles searing down to the bone. He felt something warm and hard against his fingers and he grabbed the butt of the pistol – just in time because his legs fell back to the floor, his stomach and leg muscles cramped and strained.

He stood up on tiptoe to relieve the strain on his wrists. His body was bathed in sweat and all his wounds were open and streaming blood. He shook his head, trying to clear his vision. Under normal circumstances he was a crack shot with a pistol, but his present predicament was far from normal. He could barely focus on the chain where it wrapped around the pipe, and the sights on the gun kept splitting apart as his vision blurred. He blinked and screwed up his eyes, bringing the sights into line with the chain. He took a breath, let half of it out, and squeezed the trigger, twice. The shots echoed around the basement, the sound deafening him. The chain was still in one piece. There were two metallic streaks on the pipe, the closest to the chain was some three inches away. It might as well have been a mile. He concentrated and fired again, two shots. The second bullet slammed into the chain, breaking one of the links before ricocheting into a wall, and Joker felt the chain unravel from around the pipe, dropping all his weight onto his legs. They couldn't take the strain and they buckled underneath him, leaving him sprawled across the woman's body.

His hands were still chained together, the broken link had been on the section passed around the pipe. He didn't have time to try to free his wrists because Hennessy and Bailey and whoever else was upstairs would have been certain to have heard the shots, despite the sound-proofing. He could see two light switches, one at the top of the stairs and one close to the bottom. He felt himself begin to lose consciousness and he fought against it, shaking his head in an attempt to clear it. He staggered over to the lower light switch and flicked it off, plunging the basement into darkness.

Cole Howard made notes in his tiny, cramped handwriting, filling in the gaps on the photocopied report sheet. The caller was a housewife who had been buying a set of saucepans at a Glen Burnie shopping mall when she'd seen a woman she thought might be the one in the photograph. She'd bought a large pepper mill and the caller remembered that her hair looked as if it had been dyed blonde. She'd used a credit card because the woman recalled having to wait while it was swiped and approved.

Howard thanked her and hung up. He doubted that Mary Hennessy would be out shopping for pepper mills prior to an assassination, but every call had to be verified. It wouldn't be difficult – an agent would be assigned to visit the store to find out if the salesperson could identify Hennessy's picture and obtain details of the blonde's credit card. It was a simple enough call to check, but it would take several hours. And within the space of ten minutes following the telephone number flashing onto the television screen there had been at least eighty calls and still all the lights were flashing on Helen's console. The workload was building quickly, and Howard wondered how many men Mulholland would be willing to assign to the case. So far his commitment had been open-ended, but the calls were racking up at a frightening rate.

Don Clutesi had his own receiver pressed to his ear and was frantically taking notes, nodding his head animatedly. He kept saying "yes, yes, yes" as he scribbled. Howard couldn't hear what else he was whispering into the phone but he was clearly excited about something. He wasn't just filling out the report form, he was taking additional notes and Howard peered over, trying to read them upside down. Clutesi saw him and he wrote in large capital letters at the top of his notepad – "Got them!"

Howard frowned. The phone on his desk rang but he ignored it as he scrutinised Clutesi's notes. Helen looked across at him, realised he was otherwise engaged, and took back the call. Clutesi replaced his receiver. "A woman in Baltimore leased a house overlooking the Chesapeake Bay to a woman answering Hennessy's description," he said, clearly elated. "Seven bedrooms and three bathrooms. And the woman used a cheque and ID with the same name that Hennessy used on the credit card she paid for the hotel room with. It's her, all right." He punched the air and grinned.

"How long did she take the house for?" asked Howard.

"Six months; she paid three months in advance."

Clutesi waved Ed Mulholland over and quickly briefed the anti-terrorism chief on what he'd learned. Mulholland beamed. "That sounds like it," he agreed. "Okay, you and Cole take the chopper out there now. I'll have a SWAT team from Baltimore secure a perimeter around the house. They should be in place by the time you get there."

Clutesi scribbled down the address of the house and the phone number and address of the woman who'd made the call. "Her name's Martha Laing; I told her someone would be in touch," he said. "It'd help if someone could take her out to the house and liaise with the SWAT team commander – supply him with floor plans and the like, in case we have to storm the place."

Mulholland nodded and took the piece of paper. "I'll have it taken care of, Don." He handed a cellular telephone to Clutesi and another to Howard. "Now you and Cole get to it. The chopper'll be waiting for you at the pad."

Carlos had smiled when he heard Cramer scream. He knew Dina Rashid's ways and that a simple straightforward killing wasn't her way. She had to have her amusement first. In some respects she was similar to Mary Hennessy, but whereas Dina got some twisted, perverse sexual thrill out of seeing her men squirm, Hennessy seemed to do it simply to be cruel. Carlos couldn't imagine Mary Hennessy having sex with a man before killing him, whereas that was Dina's favourite method.

Mary had gone upstairs with Bailey to pack and to warn the two Americans. Carlos had grabbed a kitchen cloth and was quickly working around the kitchen, removing fingerprints as quickly as possible from those surfaces most likely to have been touched. He loaded all the dishes and cutlery into the dishwasher and switched it on, and then headed for the sitting room. As he began to rub down the television set he heard two shots, and then silence. He nodded to himself as he worked the cloth around the set's controls. Dina Rashid was a true professional, despite her sexual quirks, and he much preferred working with her than the two Americans. He moved across to the coffee table and ran the cloth over it. There were several magazines on the table and he gathered them up and took them to the kitchen. As he threw them into a black garbage bag he heard two more pistol shots from the basement, and he frowned. Dina would never need more than two shots at close range. He dropped the bag on the floor and rushed over to the door which led to the basement stairs. He stood to the side and eased it open. The basement was in darkness. "Dina?" he called. There was no answer. "Dina?" he repeated. There was only silence. Carlos slammed the door shut with his foot and turned the key in the lock. He pushed the kitchen table over and jammed it up against the door before walking quickly to the hall. He called the others down and quickly explained what had happened.

"Aren't we going to see if she's all right?" asked Schoelen. He looked at Hennessy as if fearful that he was going to get the blame for the operation falling apart.

Carlos shook his head. "If she was all right, she'd have answered," he said. "There were four shots. We can assume she's dead." Lovell smiled and Carlos glared at him. "Unless you want to go down, Lovell?" he said, staring menacingly at the sniper. Lovell averted his eyes.

"So what do we do, Ilich?" asked Mary. She knew how close Dina and Carlos were. It would have to be his decision.

"We leave, now," said Carlos, his voice level. He looked at Schoelen. "You and Lovell go to the motel you stayed at before you moved here. Take both cars and take Mary and Bailey with you, but keep them under cover in the back of the car. I'll see you there within an hour. Okay?"

"Okay," agreed Schoelen.

"What will you be doing?" asked Bailey, nervously.

"I'll get rid of the evidence," he said. "First put all your things in the cars." He pulled a pistol from the waistband of his trousers and gave it to Schoelen. "While they're loading the cars, you stay in the kitchen. If you hear anything, shoot through the door."

"What about Dina's stuff?" asked Mary.

"I'll take care of that," said Carlos. "Now I suggest we move quickly. I don't think we have much time."

As Mary, Bailey and the snipers carried out their bags, Carlos went up to Dina's room. Her rifle was in its case on top of her wardrobe and he took it down, opening it to check that everything was there. He found a small leather bag containing tools and cleaning equipment in the top drawer of her dressing table and he took that, too. Her pyjamas were hanging on the back of the door and Carlos held the jacket against his face, breathing in her fragrance. He would miss Dina Rashid, but he had no time to grieve for her. Not just then.

He took the case and the bag, along with his own suitcase, and went outside. He put them in the trunk of the car and slammed the lid shut and then went into the garage where he picked up a red can of gasoline. As he walked back to the house, Hennessy and Bailey came out, each carrying a suitcase. Bailey seemed even more apprehensive than usual and he was continually looking at Mary as if asking for approval. Carlos knew that Mary would be able to calm him down once they were away from the house. Behind them, Lovell left the house, carrying his gun case over his shoulder. Lovell got into his red Mustang and drove off first, while Bailey and Hennessy climbed into Schoelen's rental car. Carlos headed back into the house.

He started upstairs, in Dina's room, sprinkling gasoline on the bed and across the carpet to the door, leading a trail which went down the stairs, through the sitting room, and into the kitchen. Schoelen was leaning against the sink, the pistol in both hands. He raised one eyebrow as he watched Carlos pour the gasoline over the floor. "Planning a barbecue?" he asked sardonically.

Carlos sloshed gasoline over the kitchen table and against the door leading to the basement. "You'd better get your things and get to the car," he said.

"Sure thing," said Schoelen, handing the gun back to Carlos.

"Any sound from our friend?" Carlos asked.

Schoelen shook his head and went upstairs to gather his belongings and rifle. Carlos heard him walk back down the stairs, the car door open and close, and a few seconds later the car start up and crunch down the driveway.

Something inside Carlos refused to let him leave without trying to reach Dina one last time, even though he knew it was futile. He stood by the door and rested his head against the jamb. "Dina!" he called. "Dina, can you hear me?"

There was no answer and Carlos slapped the wood in frustration. "Damn you, Cramer," he cursed under his breath. "May you burn in hell."

The air was thick with gasoline fumes and Carlos was beginning to feel a little light-headed. He picked up the cloth he'd used to wipe down the furniture and slopped it around the sodden floor. There was a box of matches by the stove and he carried them out through the back door, keeping the sodden cloth away from his trousers. He struck a match and lit one end of the cloth. It burned fiercely and he tossed it into the kitchen where it made a whooshing sound as the fumes ignited. He turned away and climbed into his car.

Down in the basement, Joker heard a man's voice shouting for Dina and a few seconds later a car started up and drove off. He listened and heard a crackling sound like paper rustling. The basement was completely dark except for a rectangle of light at the top of the stairs, outlining the door. Joker recalled that at some point he had seen light coming into the room from somewhere behind him, but now there was only blackness. He steadied his breathing and listened. There was only the crackling noise. No voices. No footsteps. He'd heard three cars drive away, so that meant at least three people had left the house, but he didn't know how many there had been originally. He'd seen Bailey, and Hennessy, and the man with the moustache, and the two Americans who'd hauled him out of the car. That meant at least five, plus the dead girl. There could be two waiting for him upstairs.

His wrists were still chained together so he switched the light back on with his mouth while keeping his gun targeted at the door. When there was no reaction he went over to the workbench where Mary Hennessy had kept her tools and knives. He found a keyring with several keys on it and one of them fitted the padlock which fastened the chain around his wrist. He winced as he unlocked the padlock and unhooked it from the chain. The scab which had formed over the hole in his right breast split open and fresh blood dribbled down his chest. Every movement of his right arm sent bolts of pain deep inside his chest. Joker gritted his teeth and rubbed the circulation back into his battered hands. He found his shorts and jeans and pulled them on, followed by his training shoes. It wasn't that he was cold, it was more that he didn't want to fight naked. He winced as he pushed his right foot into his shoe. Hennessy had damn near severed his toe.

He crept over to the far wall, looking for the source of the light he'd seen earlier. There was a shutter high up, and he opened it to find a locked window with three thick bars blocking any exit. There was only one way out of the basement, and that was through the door. He went back to the stairs and tiptoed up, his back close to the wall, the gun at the ready. The higher he got up the steps, the louder the crackling became. Tendrils of smoke drifted up from the bottom of the door and when he put his left hand flat against the wood he could feel the heat burning through. He turned the handle and pushed, but the door was locked.

He went down the stairs and picked up the pieces of his shirt. He soaked them in the bucket and draped them over his head and shoulders, then upturned the bucket and poured the rest of the water over his body. It stung when it ran over his cuts and abrasions but he ignored the pain, knowing that it would be a matter of minutes before the wooden structure began to collapse. He ran back up the steps and fired two shots at the lock. He kicked the door hard and the wood splintered. He kicked it again and it opened, but only a few inches. Something was blocking it. Thick, cloying smoke billowed in, making him cough. He wrapped one of the pieces of wet cloth over his mouth and kicked harder but the door wouldn't budge. Through the gap he could see flames flaring up from the floor and a wave of heat singed his eyebrows. He put his shoulder to the warm wood but could make no impact on it. He pulled the door shut and wiped his face with one of the wet cloths. The door was held in place with two hinges, each with six screws. He took a step back down the stairs and fired two shots at the top hinge and it buckled. The lower hinge disintegrated the first time Joker fired at it, his ears ringing with the sounds of the shots. He did a quick tally of the bullets he'd fired. Four at the chain, two at the lock, three at the hinges. Nine shots. The 411 held eleven cartridges in the clip, so that left two shots, assuming the clip had been full originally.

He seized the door handle and pulled it towards him. The wood around the hinges fractured and the door fell towards him, banging him on his head. He dragged it down and it fell against the stairs. The heat leapt at him like a wild animal, pushing him and threatening to steal the breath from his lungs. As the door clattered by his side he saw the table which had been blocking his escape. It was lodged between the door frame and the sink unit. He'd never have moved it by pushing. He clambered over it and leapt through a sheet of flame that sprang from the floor. He could feel the hairs on his arms crisp and burn and he held the wet cloth over his mouth so that he wouldn't singe his lungs. He narrowed his eyes, looking for a way out. A figure appeared to his left, a man in sweatshirt and jeans carrying a gun. It wasn't any of the men Joker had seen earlier. The man raised his gun but Joker fired first. The stranger got off one shot which ripped a chunk out of Joker's shoulder, but Joker fired as he'd been trained to, two shots to the chest. Bang bang. The man's arms slumped to the side and the gun fell to the floor, his mouth open in surprise. Two red splotches grew on his chest, so close that they formed a figure eight. Joker saw a door which seemed to lead to the outside. He aimed his gun at the lock but realised the gun was empty. He twisted the door handle and to his amazement it opened and he staggered outside, gulping in the cold night air. He fell to his knees, coughing and spluttering. He heard movement behind him and the man he'd shot fell out of the door, taking several unsteady steps and crashing face forward onto the grass. He smelled of burnt meat and his hair was smouldering. Joker rolled him over onto his back. He was still alive, but only just, and Joker knew there was nothing he or anyone could do to prolong his life. Both shots were smack in the centre of his chest.

The man's eyes fluttered open. He had no eyebrows left and there were large blisters on his cheeks. His eyes fought to focus on Joker's face. "You Cramer?" he croaked.

Joker was stunned. The man had an English accent. He nodded.

"You bloody fool," the man said, forming the words slowly and painfully. "I'm with Five."

Joker's mind swam. Five meant MI5, the British Security Service.

"I was . . . coming . . . to help you," the man said.

Joker held him, not knowing what to say. "Are you alone?" he asked, looking back at the house.

The man shook his head and closed his eyes. "Partner . . . following . . . Hennessy . . ." he gasped.

"How did you know they were here?" Joker asked.

The man was wracked by a series of coughs, and blood dribbled from between his lips. "Followed you," he said. Joker looked over his shoulder. He had to get further away from the burning house, which crackled and spat behind him, but he knew that to move the dying man would hasten his demise. "How bad?" the man asked, his voice cracking.

"It's bad," said Joker. There was no point in lying. If their positions were reversed, Joker would want the truth. Joker took one of the man's hands and squeezed. There was more he wanted to know. "Who told you to follow me?" he asked.

The man shuddered. "London," he said.

"You followed me from New York?"

"Yeah," said the man, the word coming out in a long-drawn-out gasp.

"Why?" Joker asked. Blood was pouring from his shoulder wound but he ignored it.

There was a pause. Back in the house, something exploded. "Bait," the man said.

"Yeah," said Joker, "that's what I thought. Thanks."

The man squeezed Joker's hand, then he sighed once and the fingers went limp. Joker staggered to his feet and walked away from the burning house. He was still carrying the gun in his right hand, even though the weapon was now useless. He managed only two dozen steps before his legs collapsed underneath him and he fell to the grass, unconscious.

Carlos drove quickly, wanting to put as much distance between himself and the house before the neighbours saw the flames. The motel was midway between Baltimore and Washington, a good forty-five minute drive from the house.

There was little traffic on the road and Carlos was soon on the main three-lane highway which led to the Capitol. He kept his speed up in the high eighties and made good use of his rear mirror – the last thing he wanted was a State Trooper on his tail. He caught up with Schoelen after ten minutes of hard driving, and he braked and tucked in three cars behind him. Schoelen appeared to be alone in the car and Carlos nodded to himself, pleased that Hennessy and Bailey had followed his advice and were keeping out of sight. He assumed they were in the back, lying down.

Schoelen was driving in the centre lane, sticking religiously to the speed limit. Under the circumstances, with his two passengers just recently featured on a television programme with millions of viewers, he was being prudent. As they drove along at 55 mph, Carlos continued to check his rear-view mirror.

He didn't see the tail at first because the guy was hanging back and switching lanes every few minutes. Once he actually overtook them and at first Carlos thought that perhaps he'd made a mistake, but then he realised it was when they were between intersections with nowhere for them to turn off. The driver was alone, and as the interior of his car was illuminated by passing headlights, Carlos could see he was in his late thirties to early forties, clean-shaven and wearing spectacles. That was all Carlos could see without making it obvious he was looking. Carlos was certain that the tail wasn't after him but, to be sure, he slowed down, allowing Schoelen to get almost a mile ahead. He was right, the tail stuck with the sniper, usually keeping half a dozen cars back. Carlos couldn't see any other cars, which surprised him because he knew that successful tailing depended on using several vehicles and rotating them frequently. Using one man and one car was asking for trouble. It couldn't be the FBI or the Secret Service because they'd call in back-up immediately. He thought of the SAS man locked in the basement of the burning house. It couldn't possibly be him, but what if he had a partner? That didn't make sense either, Carlos realised. If Cramer had a partner, he'd have told Hennessy about him under torture. And what sort of man would allow his partner to be captured and held by a woman with Mary Hennessy's reputation? Surely he'd have called in the police? None of the possibilities made sense, but there was no denying that the man was following Schoelen.

Carlos had the advantage in that he knew where Schoelen was going, so he waited until just before the exit ramp before getting any closer. He caught up with Schoelen and his tail on an unlit road which wound between leafy woodland dotted with impressive houses with private driveways and three-car garages. Most had flagpoles and basketball hoops, Carlos noticed. And probably a couple of .44 Magnums under the mattress and a shotgun in the den, he thought wryly. White, upper-middle-class America. Clean, wholesome and armed to the teeth.

Ahead he could see the tail, who was having a harder time staying inconspicuous. There was no sign of Lovell. Carlos wondered whether Schoelen would spot that he was being followed. He doubted it, Schoelen was a military sniper, not an intelligence operative. He was sure Mary Hennessy would not have been so careless. There was little traffic on the road so Carlos hung back and whenever possible drove with his headlights off. Carlos ran through the possibilities. He could wait until Schoelen arrived at the motel before confronting the tail, but if there were other motorists around he might not be able to act. He could drive ahead and find some way of warning Schoelen, but what then? As soon as he communicated with Schoelen he'd be spotted. No, that wouldn't do. He could force the tail off the road, but he might sustain damage himself. There was only one solution. Keeping a firm hand on the steering wheel, Carlos leant over and opened the glove compartment. He took out the gun which Lovell had found in Cramer's car, a SIG P228 with a bulbous silencer. A nice weapon, well balanced and compact. He placed it on the empty seat next to him and opened the passenger window. He accelerated smoothly, the wind noise roaring by the open window. Schoelen was still sticking to the speed limit and Carlos quickly gained on the tail. He reached over to pick up the gun and flicked the safety off with his thumb. The grip settled easily in Carlos's hand and he rested the barrel on the passenger seat as he drove up behind the tail.

He waited until the road was clear in front and behind, then indicated that he wanted to overtake. Carlos pulled out to the left, the power steering making one-handed control effortless. He drew level with the tail, his indicator lights still blinking, and looked across at the driver. The driver appeared relaxed, he looked over at Carlos, who smiled and nodded. The driver smiled automatically; his eyes flicked back to the road, and then across at Carlos again. This time he frowned, but before he could react Carlos raised the gun. There was just a slight coughing noise from the P228 as the tail's window exploded with the first shot and the bullet buried itself in the man's shoulder. Carlos fired twice more, both shots hitting the man in the side of the head. A fountain of blood sprayed from the man's skull and the car lurched to the right as his nerveless fingers lost control. Carlos accelerated and in the mirror he watched the tail veer off the road and smash into a tree. A few seconds later the car burst into flames. Carlos smiled and put the gun back into the glove compartment before closing the window. Ahead, Schoelen drove on, oblivious to what had happened.

Don Clutesi saw it first and he tapped Cole Howard on the shoulder. They were wearing headsets which cut out the thudding roar of the rotors and allowed them to speak to each other and to the pilot and co-pilot. He pointed to the burning house some six miles away by the side of the Chesapeake Bay. There were no streetlights or other houses close to it and the inferno seemed to be suspended in the darkness. "See that?" Clutesi asked.

"You think that's it?" said Howard, squinting into the distance.

The pilot's voice came over the headsets. "That's where we're headed," he said. The co-pilot began calling up Baltimore air-traffic control to request that they inform the Fire Department. His call was acknowledged.

Howard slapped his knee. There was no sign of a SWAT team in the vicinity of the house, no lights on the road. He was hardly surprised, they'd probably be driving out from the city, whereas the FBI JetRanger helicopter was zipping through the air at more than one hundred knots.

The pilot took the helicopter down to about five hundred feet above the ground and banked around the house. "Jesus, look at that," said Clutesi.

For a moment Howard imagined that he could feel the

heat from the blaze but he knew that they were too high. The pilot switched on a searchlight below the helicopter and an oval patch of light appeared on the grass below. Over the headset, Howard heard the co-pilot tell air-traffic control that he was landing.

Clutesi pounded Howard on the shoulder again and pointed. "Here comes the cavalry," he said. In the distance, about a mile from the house, they saw a convoy of vehicles speeding along the main road in the direction of the house. "That'll be the Ninjas. Better late than never."

"There's no rush – I don't imagine there'll be anyone hanging around," said Howard. A blue car at the rear of the house exploded in a sheet of flame as its fuel tank detonated. The pilot yanked the helicopter up and away and chose a landing spot further away from the house. The oval light grew smaller and brighter as they descended and then the skids gently bumped the ground. The co-pilot turned around in his seat and handed flashlights to Howard and Clutesi and indicated that they could disembark. The two FBI agents climbed out, the still-turning rotors making their jackets flap around their waists. Both agents were armed and they took their handguns from their holsters as they jogged across the lawn to the house. The convoy of cars and vans turned down the drive to the house and Clutesi headed in their direction, holding his badge and gun aloft.

Howard saw a figure lying on the grass about fifty yards from the house, stretched out and unmoving. He went over and knelt down beside the body. It was a middle-aged man, bare-chested with wicked cuts across his back as if he'd been whipped. There was also a nasty gunshot wound on one shoulder but it didn't look fatal. The man's right hand was holding a compact black handgun, his finger still on the trigger. Howard took a pen from his inside jacket pocket and used it to pry the gun from his fingers. He rolled the man over and winced as he saw more wounds on the man's chest. His right nipple was missing, a red, crusty scab in its place, and it looked as if a strip of flesh had been ripped out, exposing the muscle underneath. "Hell, what happened to you?" Howard said under his breath. The man's eyebrows and chest hair were singed from the flames and his cheeks and nose were red as if he'd been under a sunlamp for too long. Howard bent down and put his ear close to the man's mouth. He couldn't hear anything above the crash of falling timbers and crackling wood, but he felt the man's breath on his cheek.

Clutesi ran over, followed by two men in blue overalls and body armour. Clutesi knelt down beside Howard. "He dead?" asked Clutesi.

Howard shook his head. "Not yet," he said.

One of the men in overalls introduced himself as the commander of the SWAT team, Scott Dunning. Howard asked him to arrange an ambulance.

"You'd be better off using the chopper, airlift him to Shock-trauma in the city," said Dunning. "It'll take the bird ten minutes but it's almost an hour by road."

"Good idea," said Howard. He patted Clutesi on the back. "Don, you go with him. I'll check here. When you get to the hospital, call Ed, let him know what's happening."

The commander called over two of his men and had them pull out a stretcher to carry the injured man to the JetRanger. As the helicopter turbine roared and it lifted into the air, Dunning and Howard surveyed the burning building. "Not really much need for a SWAT team, is there?" observed Dunning tersely. His men were standing beside their vehicles, the flames throwing long flickering shadows behind them.

"Not unless you've got a fire engine with you," said Howard.

"Afraid not, not today," said the SWAT commander.

"Fire Department's on their way," said Howard. "We called them from the chopper."

One of the members of the SWAT team, a young man with a rifle and telescopic sight, wandered over the lawn towards the house. "Tom, stay by the vans until the lab tech boys get here," Dunning shouted. The man waved and went back to the van. "He's new," explained Dunning. "He's a crack shot but a menace around a crime scene."

Howard nodded. He walked slowly around the area where the body had been lying, looking at the grass. He was trying to work out where the man had been shot. The shoulder wound was from the front, so his first thought was that he'd been shot as he'd left the house, by someone outside. He shone the flashlight on the grass, looking for footprints. He saw a few drops of blood where the man's feet had been and he began working his way back to the house, sweeping the flashlight beam from side to side. He found several more spots of blood and revised his first impression. The man had been shot in the house and had been running away before he'd passed out, either from loss of blood or the effects of the smoke.

Someone was shouting and he looked to his left. The young SWAT sniper was pointing towards the house and yelling. Howard shaded his eyes with his hand and squinted in the direction he was pointing. There was something lying on the ground, close to the door. Howard went closer but the heat drove him back. It looked like another body. He

went over to the sniper and borrowed his rifle. He
shouldered the weapon and looked through the telescopic
sight. It took him a while to centre the cross-hairs. Through
the scope he saw the man's sweatshirt burst into flame and
his skin bubble and crack. There was nothing they could do
– the SWAT team had protection against bullets, not fire,
and until the fire engines arrived they could only stand and
watch.

The motel could be seen from the road; a red neon sign over
the main entrance indicated that there were vacancies. The
building was U-shaped, with the two wings pointing away
from the road, either side of a car park and swimming pool.
Lou Schoelen parked his car outside the entrance and went
inside to arrange his room. Carlos stopped his car some
distance from the motel and watched, checking that no-one
else had tailed the sniper. After a few minutes, Schoelen
appeared, swinging a key. He got back into his car and
drove slowly around to the parking area. Carlos followed
him and pulled in next to him.

Hennessy and Bailey climbed out of the back of the car,
and walked quickly with Schoelen to the ground-floor
room, carrying their bags. Carlos took his cases from the
trunk and went after them. As he reached the door, which
Schoelen was holding open for him, Lovell walked up. "Hi,
guys. What's up?"

"Inside," said Carlos.

When they were all gathered in the room, Schoelen hung
the 'Do Not Disturb' sign on the handle and closed it. "You

were followed, Lou," Carlos said quietly. "You were followed all the way from the house."

Schoelen's mouth dropped in disbelief. "Are you sure?" he asked.

Carlos sneered but didn't reply.

"What happened?" asked Mary.

"I took care of it," said Carlos. Bailey went into the bathroom, ripped the protective plastic covering off a glass and poured himself a drink. His hands were shaking.

"Do you know who it was?" Lovell asked.

Carlos shook his head. "I said I took care of it, I didn't say I stopped for a chat," he said.

"A friend of Cramer's?" asked Bailey.

"A friend wouldn't have left him in our care for so long," said Carlos. "Whoever it was, he was alone."

"Maybe he was waiting for back-up," said Lovell, and Carlos nodded.

"Possible," agreed Carlos.

"That's it then," said Bailey. "It's over. It's f-f-finished."

Carlos's eyes hardened as he looked at Bailey. "It's not finished," he said coldly. "I said I took care of it." He looked at Mary and she nodded, acknowledging that Bailey was her problem and that she'd handle him.

"You're missing something," said Lovell. "Without Rashid . . ."

"Without Rashid we can still go ahead," interrupted Carlos. "I will take her place."

Lovell and Schoelen looked at each other, astonished. "How?" said Schoelen. "We don't have time to rehearse again."

"I have used Dina's gun before, in the Lebanon. I have a

tendency to aim a little high, but other than that I will have no problem using the scope as she has set it. I can compensate for the very slight difference in our eyes."

"You've been a sniper?" asked Lovell.

"I have killed with a rifle," said Carlos.

Lovell shrugged. "Okay, okay," he said. "So what do we do now?"

"You and Lou take your room, Mary and Matthew can have this one. I'll arrange a room for myself. We all meet here tomorrow morning at ten for a final run through."

If Schoelen and Lovell were surprised at the suggestion that Bailey and Hennessy should share a room, they didn't show it. They took their bags outside and Carlos closed the door behind them. There were two double beds in the room and Bailey had slumped down onto one, his head in his hands. "I'll go and fix up a room," Carlos said to Mary. "Will you be okay?" She nodded. "I'll leave the rifle here," he said, picking up his bag. As he left the room he saw Hennessy put a hand on Bailey's head and ruffle his hair.

Lovell was waiting for him outside. "I don't like the way Bailey is shaping up," he said.

"Neither do I," said Carlos. "But we need him."

"He's cracking up already," said Lovell. "I've seen guys like him before, in combat. They talk a good war, but when the bullets fly they shit themselves and hide under the bed. I don't think he's going to cut it tomorrow."

"He's tougher than he looks," said Carlos. "They don't tolerate wimps in the IRA. He's just on edge because we've been waiting so long, that's all. Mary will straighten him out."

"And if she doesn't?"

Carlos smiled. "Then I will."

Cole Howard stood watching the fire fighters coil up their hoses and restack their equipment on the engines. What remained of the wooden house hissed and smoked in the moonlight. There was a surprising amount of the building still standing, but it was clear that what remained would have to be demolished. Much of the rear of the house had fallen in and the roof had collapsed. A stone chimney at the side of the house was still in one piece and smoke was feathering from the top as if a fire was burning in the grate below.

One of the fire engines drove off, the faces of fire fighters inside streaked with soot and sweat. The SWAT team had already departed and Howard was waiting to hear from one of the Fire Department's investigators who was walking through the wreckage. They'd recovered the second body, a badly burnt man, when they had the fire under control. The corpse was charred and smouldering and Howard would never forget the smell. He'd covered his mouth with his hand as he'd put his head close to the blistered and blackened flesh. He found what he was looking for. Two bullet holes in the chest. Dunning had called Baltimore County Police and arranged for the medical examiner and a crime lab tech team before he'd taken his men and gone back to the city. He seemed to resent the fact that there had been no-one for his SWAT team to take down.

Howard heard shouts of warning and a large blackened beam fell to the ground, not far from where the investigator was standing. He turned and waved, signalling that he was okay. Two of the fire fighters walked over to him, axes in their hands. The investigator, a black guy in his late fifties called George Whitmore, knelt down and touched something on the ground before lifting his gloved fingers to his nose. Whitmore stood up and spoke to the fire fighters with axes. They nodded and began to chop away at something while Whitmore watched. The thwacks of the axes were replaced by the sound of tearing wood and then the three men disappeared. Howard frowned. One minute the fire fighters were standing together, the next they'd vanished as if the ground had swallowed them up. Behind him, another fire engine drove off, its work done.

Howard walked towards the smoking ruins, running his hand across his stubbled chin. The walls around the kitchen, and the floor above it, had been totally destroyed, and all that remained of that side of the house were smoking timbers and blackened appliances. As he got closer he saw that the fire fighters had opened up a stairway leading to a basement. A white helmet appeared, followed by the bulky shoulders of George Whitmore. He pulled a face at the FBI agent. "Another one down there for the ME," he said. He took off his helmet and tucked it under his arm, reaching inside his waterproofs and coming out with a pack of cigarettes and a Zippo lighter. "Want one?" he asked Howard, who shook his head. Howard looked around the remains of the kitchen as the investigator lit up. Everything above the kitchen area had been gutted and what remained of the ground floor was covered in a thick layer of ash. Despite the devastation, there were still signs of domesticity – the dishwasher door had popped open and inside were plates and cups, a floor mop stood by the refrigerator, its head melted but its handle surprisingly untouched, and a kettle stood on the stove.

"Can I look?" Howard asked.

"Better if you don't," said Whitmore. "There's still a lot of smoke down there, and the stairs are in a bad way. Wait till the guys have made it safe." He took a long pull at his cigarette and exhaled deeply, blowing the smoke into the air with a look of contentment on his face.

"Okay," said Howard. "What can you tell me about the body?"

"Woman, late twenties maybe. Hard to tell 'cos her face is all mashed up."

"Shot? Smoke?"

"Not shot, that's for sure. Smoke? I don't think so, I think she was dead before the fire, but you'll have to wait for the ME to take her apart in the chop-shop before we know for sure." He drew deeply on the cigarette again. "Sure is some weird shit down there, though."

"What do you mean?"

"Knives, a pair of shears, all of them covered in blood. Bits of chain on the floor."

"You think she was tortured?"

The big man shrugged. "Maybe. There's a man's wallet down there. I didn't touch it, thought the crime lab technicians might want to take a look first." A timber crashed somewhere at the other side of the house and he put his helmet back on. "You'd better move back, Agent Howard, this isn't exactly safe right now."

Howard nodded and walked away from the smouldering wreckage. In the distance he heard an ambulance siren, heading towards the house. He wondered why they were bothering with the siren.

Mary picked Bailey's glass off the floor and went over to her suitcase. She opened it and took out a bottle of malt whisky, keeping an eye on him as she unscrewed the cap and poured out a double measure. "Here, drink this," she said, holding out the glass.

Bailey took it and swallowed it in three gulps. "I'm sorry," he said.

"That's all right," she said. "We're all a little apprehensive."

"This isn't Ireland, Mary," he said. "They electrocute k-k-killers here." He looked up at her and she saw that his left eyelid was flickering. "I've got a bad feeling about this."

Mary held the bottle of whisky between her hands, gripping it tightly. "No-one is going to catch us. A couple of Sass-men have got close, that's all. And they've been taken care of. You've dealt with the SAS before. You've gone up against them and you've always come out on top. And you know why that is? It's because you're fighting for something you believe in and they're doing it for money. They don't believe that the British Government is right, they do it because they pay their wages. They're hired guns, and we're freedom fighters. That's why we'll win in the end." She put the whisky bottle on the dressing table next to a Gideon's Bible and sat down on the bed opposite Bailey. "A few more hours and it'll all be over."

"Let's just go home, Mary," he said. "We c-c-can try again some other time."

"We'll never have another opportunity like this. Everything's in place; we can't fail. All we have to do is stay calm and do our jobs and they'll talk about this for years to come."

Bailey began to shiver like a wet dog and Mary shook her head sadly. "Matthew, you're better than this," she said soothingly. "Pull yourself together. It's going to be all right." She stood up and stroked his cheek and he tried to kiss her palm. She let him, trying not to show the distaste she felt. He licked her thumb and then sucked it like a baby feeding. With her other hand she stroked the back of his head as she watched herself in the mirror over the dressing table. Bailey had a vital part to play in the following day's operation, and he had to be kept under control, for twelve hours at least. After that, it no longer mattered. "Stand up," she said.

He did as he was told, his head bowed. She took off his spectacles, dropped them on the bed behind her, and put her arms around his neck. "You're one of the IRA's best, you know that," she said. She waited for him to kiss her, knowing that he would, knowing that it was necessary, but dreading it nonetheless. She could smell his breath, a bitter, fishy odour, and his lips were dry and crusty. She closed her eyes and waited. His lips pressed against hers and his tongue forced itself between her teeth. She gagged but forced herself to respond. His hands went clumsily to her breasts, groping rather than caressing, and his erection stabbed against her groin. His kisses became harder, more aggressive, and his hands moved behind her, grabbing her backside as if he was scooping up handfuls of sand. He buried his face in her neck and began murmuring her name over and over again.

His hands went down to her shorts and he pushed them down roughly around her knees, then did the same with her underwear. Before she could move, his hand was between her legs, fumbling and probing, and he kissed her again. He was slobbering like a wild animal. He shoved her back onto the bed, almost on top of his spectacles, and then he began grunting as he ripped off her shorts, throwing them into a corner and unzipping his trousers.

"Mary, I've always wanted you," he panted, falling on top of her. Mary opened her legs, closed her eyes, and filled her mind with images of Sean Morrison.

Joker awoke in confusion, unsure where he was or if he was still in danger. Before his eyes opened, his hands flew up in front of his face as if fighting off invisible demons. His first thought was that he was back in the basement but then he realised that the ceiling was a series of square polystyrene tiles and that the walls were white. His wrists had been bandaged, and professionally by the look of it, and his body felt numb as if he was floating on a cloud. Painkillers, he realised. He was in a hospital. There were smears of black ink on his fingertips. Someone had taken his fingerprints while he was unconscious. He tried to lift his head up but a bolt of pain ripped through his back. A low dose of painkiller, he realised. He lay back and gathered his thoughts. The last thing he remembered was the fire, and clambering out of the burning building. And the stranger, the man from MI5. The man he'd killed.

Something moved at the foot of his bed and Joker realised he wasn't alone. He raised his head again, more slowly this time, and saw a uniformed policeman getting out of a chair. "Water," Joker gasped.

The cop scowled. "What do I look like, a fucking nurse?" he said.

Joker lay back and closed his eyes. Something was digging into his hips and he felt around with his hands. There was a chain around his waist, and when he pulled it something rattled under the bed. "The doctors said not to handcuff you because of the damage to your wrists," said the cop. Joker opened his eyes to see the man looking down at him. "But if you try any tricks with the chain, the cuffs go straight on. Understand?"

"Understand," croaked Joker. "Where am I?"

"Shock-trauma, University of Maryland," the cop answered. The cop walked back to his chair and sat down. Joker realised he wasn't there to question him, which meant that the heavyweights were on their way. He was surprised that homicide detectives weren't waiting at his bedside. Joker ran through his options, and they were few and far between. There were two corpses at the house, one with a crushed skull, the other with two bullets in its chest. A search of the house would show up his wallet and ID and a forensic test would show that he'd fired the gun which had killed the MI5 agent. His cover story as an itinerant barman would last about thirty seconds under any half-competent interrogation, and that was before he was asked to explain his wounds. He turned his head and saw that his shoulder was bandaged and he felt two dressings on his chest.

He remembered what the dying MI5 agent had said. The

Colonel had sent him to America as bait, to lure Hennessy and Bailey out into the open so that the Five agents could capture or kill them. Hard arrests. The Colonel had never intended that Joker should succeed, and probably didn't even expect him to come out of it alive. The Five agents had seen him taken prisoner, and they must have known what was happening to him inside the house. They did nothing, and Joker ground his teeth as he realised that they had probably been sitting in their car, swapping jokes and stories, as Hennessy ripped the flesh from his body. It was the betrayal that hurt Joker most, more than the cuts in his back, the bruised and battered wrists and the wounds in his chest. He'd been set up, right from the start, by a man he'd trusted. Trusted and damn near worshipped. And that meant that Joker couldn't rely on the Colonel standing up for him now that he was blown.

The door to his room opened and a nurse walked in. She was a pretty black girl with short hair and eyes that were so green Joker assumed she must have been wearing coloured contact lenses. She was wearing blue-green scrubs and had a stethoscope hanging around her neck. She picked up a clipboard from the bottom of the bed and she read through his charts. "So you're awake, Mr O'Brien?" she said.

"Water," he gasped.

She went over to a small sink in the corner of the room and filled a glass. Joker tried to sit up but he was still weak. The nurse held the back of his head while he drank. "Okay?" she said when he'd finished.

"Thanks," said Joker.

"How do you feel?" she asked.

"Sore. And weak."

"You've lost some blood, but we haven't given you a

transfusion," she said. "It was the smoke that did most of the damage. A few days' rest and you'll be okay." She grinned. "Your injuries look worse than they are. Honest."

Joker smiled thinly. "That's good news," he said.

"Except for that old wound across your stomach. The doctors were wondering how you got that one." When Joker didn't enlighten her, she clipped the board to the foot of his bed again.

The cop winked at her. "Any chance of getting a TV in here? For the Bird's game?"

"Sure, hon," said the nurse.

"Bird's game?" repeated Joker.

The nurse nodded. "The Orioles, our baseball team. They've won their last eight games. Your Prime Minister is throwing out the first pitch."

"Maybe I'll make the game," he said.

"Don't bank on it, Mr O'Brien," she said, "you'll need some bed rest for a while. The TV is the nearest you'll get."

"Yeah," agreed the cop. "He ain't going nowhere, hon."

The nurse left. Joker tested himself to see how hurt he actually was. His shoulder was his only real problem, but that only hurt when he moved it. His arms and legs were sore and his wrists felt as if they were still cut to the bone. The wounds in his chest would take some time to heal, and he was still a little weak, but he could tell that he was quite capable of walking out of the hospital. The only thing stopping him was the chain around his waist and the six feet tall black guy in the cop's uniform.

* * *

Mary Hennessy watched the minute hand of her wrist watch crawl around as she lay with her back to Matthew Bailey. He was snoring noisily, his backside thrust out so that he slept in a V shape which deprived her of most of the bed. His love-making had been rushed and nervous and, Mary thought as she slipped her hand between her thighs, it had been painful. She hadn't let Bailey know how much he was hurting her. In fact, she'd made all the right noises, encouraging, urging him on, calling out his name. It had been an act, the same sort of performance she'd given for her husband during the last years of her marriage, and she didn't feel any less ashamed with Bailey. It had been almost five years since Mary Hennessy had been with a man, and she'd tried to make Bailey slow down, to arouse her before penetrating her, but he was too eager and he'd mistaken her gasp of pain for a moan of pleasure. She shuddered under the bedclothes as she recalled his bitter-smelling breath and bad teeth and the way he continually pushed his probing tongue into her mouth. She'd waited until he was asleep before slipping into the bathroom and showering. She had a bottle of Listerine mouthwash in her washing kit and she'd gargled with it for more than a minute, trying to rid herself of his taste. Later she'd climbed into the other bed but Bailey had woken up and asked why she wasn't sleeping with him. Reluctantly she'd crawled back into his bed, hoping that he wouldn't try to touch her again, and she'd thanked her lucky stars that he fell asleep almost immediately.

Mary drifted in and out of sleep, but she was never really relaxed. It was partly because she was apprehensive about what was due to happen later that day, but she was also worried that Bailey would wake up and want to make love to her again. It seemed an eternity before the sky lightened outside and birds began to sing. The hour hand of her watch reached seven o'clock and she rolled slowly out of bed so as not to disturb Bailey and dressed quietly. Only when she'd brushed her hair and put on lipstick and mascara did she draw the drapes and wake up Bailey.

He rubbed his eyes sleepily. "What time is it?" he asked.

"Just after seven," she said. "You'll have to move the plane to Bay Bridge."

"God, yes," he said. "I'd forgotten." He threw back the bedclothes and Mary turned away, not wanting to see him naked. He came up behind her and grabbed her, and she could feel him getting aroused. She twisted around and put her hands on his shoulders. "We don't have time," she said.

He pouted. "Later?"

Mary nodded. "Later," she promised.

He nodded and began to dress, pulling on the same shirt and jeans he'd worn the previous day. Mary noticed that Bailey no longer stammered in her presence. He seemed more confident, and she hoped that her sacrifice had paid off. "Which car shall I take?" he asked.

"Schoelen's," she said, tossing him a set of keys. "Have you got a baseball cap or something you can wear?"

He ran his hand through his red curls. "Hide the hair, you mean? Yeah, good idea." He sorted through his bag and came out with an Orioles cap and waved it. "Pretty apt, yeah?"

As he dashed out of the room he tried to kiss Mary on the lips, but she moved her head at the last minute so it landed on her cheek. "Later," she said, fighting the revulsion in her stomach.

* * *

The black nurse brought Joker a breakfast tray at eight o'clock in the morning: a clear plastic cup of orange juice, scrambled eggs, toast with a smear of margarine, and a pot of cherry yoghurt. And a white plastic spoon to eat it with. Joker didn't know whether it was to ensure that he couldn't hurt himself or to make sure that he wouldn't be a danger to anyone else, but he felt like a baby as he ate. The cop watched him. "You want some?" Joker asked, holding out the spoon, dripping with eggs. The cop scowled. A large revolver was holstered on his right side and on his left was hanging a large black nightstick.

After breakfast, a doctor in a white coat came in and took his blood pressure and withdrew a small blood sample from his left arm. The doctor, who didn't introduce himself, asked Joker how he felt. Joker shrugged. "Sore, and tired. I'll mend."

"I'm sure you will," said the doctor. "We haven't given you any blood, we try not to these days unless absolutely necessary. All you need is time." He pointed to Joker's stomach. "Who did that for you?"

Joker smiled. "You mean who stabbed me, or who fixed it?"

"The surgery," said the doctor.

"Northern Ireland," said Joker. The man's interest seemed professional and he saw no reason not to enlighten him.

The doctor sat on the edge of Joker's bed, careful not to touch his legs. He was a small man with a neatly clipped moustache and crooked teeth and a pair of spectacles with circular lenses. He had four pens lined up in the pocket of his white coat, and everything about the man was trim and tidy. Joker could imagine that any surgery the man

425

performed would be meticulous and that his stitches would be as neat as those of a seamstress. "I have done some stomach and intestinal surgery – do you mind?" he said, nodding at Joker's midriff.

"Go ahead," he said. Joker wasn't the sort of man who enjoyed showing off his war wounds, but he liked the doctor's openness and he figured he owed him something for his treatment.

The doctor opened up the gown and frowned at the scar. "The knife went in here?" he asked, and pointed to the top of the scar. Joker nodded. "And the knife went down, then across?" Joker nodded again. The doctor shook his head in bewilderment. "It's the sort of scar you'd expect to see in ritual suicide," he said. "It's the way the Japanese used to do it. Down and then across, to do the maximum damage to the gut. It's not an easy thing to do. It takes a long time, and it's incredibly painful."

"You're right on both counts," said Joker.

"It wasn't self-inflicted? Someone did this to you?"

"They sure did."

"I don't understand," said the doctor, running a finger lightly down the scar. "Didn't you fight back? Didn't you run?"

Joker grinned. "I was chained to a table, Doc. I wasn't going anywhere."

"Why? Why did they do it?"

"It was a woman. She wanted me to die, and she wanted me to die slowly," said Joker.

The doctor's eyes widened. "It's a wonder you didn't."

"I came close," said Joker. "I was lucky, I was helicoptered to a hospital in Belfast. They're used to dealing with catastrophic bomb injuries; they saved my life."

"There must have been major damage to the small and large intestines?"

Joker nodded. "I lost about two feet of tubing, and I had to wear a colostomy bag for a year. But it's fine now. No problems at all."

The doctor closed up the gown. "It's good work," he said admiringly. "You know, of course, that you shouldn't be drinking?"

"How did you know I was?" asked Joker.

"The first blood sample we took from you would have lost you your driving licence if you'd been at the wheel of a car."

Joker laughed. "Hell's bells, Doc, I haven't touched the hard stuff for at least twenty-four hours!"

The doctor looked serious. "You shouldn't put your digestive system under that sort of pressure."

Joker held up his bandaged wrists. "Doc, the booze is the least of my problems."

The doctor smiled and stood up, brushing the creases out of his white coat. "I suppose you're right," he said. "Do you feel well enough to answer some questions? From the FBI?"

"They're here?"

"There are two FBI agents outside. I wanted to check on your progress first."

"And?"

"You seem to be strong enough."

Joker smiled. "Send them in then, Doc. Let's see what they want."

The doctor left the room and a few minutes later two men entered. One was small and overweight, with dark, slicked-back hair, and a shiny suit. The other was taller and fair-haired and carrying a large envelope and a portable cellular phone. They both flashed badges so quickly that all he could see was a blur of metal. "FBI," said the taller of the two.

"Do you have names?" Joker asked.

"Don Clutesi," said the smaller man. Joker spotted the antenna of a cellular phone sticking out of his right jacket pocket.

"Howard. Cole Howard," said the man with the envelope.

"From?" said Joker.

"I work out of the Bureau's Phoenix office, Special Agent Clutesi is with the Counter-Terrorism Division in New York."

Joker nodded. The fact that the FBI and not the city's Homicide Division were handling his interrogations suggested that they knew that this was more than a murder case. And Clutesi's presence meant that they knew the IRA was involved.

"We'd like to ask you a few questions," said Howard. He turned to the uniformed cop and suggested that he go out and get a cup of coffee. The cop accepted the offer, eagerly. Clutesi went and stood with his back to the door, a small notepad in his hand.

"Am I under arrest?" asked Joker, pointing to the chain around his waist.

"Not at this point, no," said Howard. He held up his right hand, the finger and thumb an inch apart. "But you're about this far away from being arrested for murder, and then you become part of the process and there's nothing we can do to help you," he said.

"Ah. So you're the Samaritans now," said Joker. He

wasn't in the least intimidated by the men or the badges. He knew that a large part of interrogation was game-playing and that if it suited the FBI he'd be in a cell somewhere awaiting trial. They clearly wanted something from him, and he had a good idea what it was.

"Not exactly," said Howard, coldly. He pulled over the chair in which the cop had been sitting and sat down, crossing his legs and looking at Joker with cold blue eyes. "Would you like to tell me what happened?"

Joker was still lying on his back, and he felt at a disadvantage to the two FBI agents. He had to squint down his chest to see Howard, and Clutesi was over to his left. It was as if the two men had moved so that he couldn't see them both at the same time. He slowly raised himself into a sitting position, trying to conceal the pain. "I was being held by two members of the Provisional Irish Republican Army," he said simply. Howard and Clutesi were stunned by his lack of guile.

"You know who they are?" asked Howard. He tapped the envelope against his leg and in a flash of intuition Joker knew that it contained photographs of Bailey and Hennessy. The FBI agents were clearly on their trail and must have known that they were at the house on Chesapeake Bay. They had probably assumed that Joker had seen Bailey and Hennessy, but it had obviously come as a shock to discover that he knew who they were.

"Mary Hennessy and Matthew Bailey," Joker said.

"They tortured you?"

"Yes," said Joker.

"The girl in the cellar, did you kill her?"

Joker didn't answer. They hadn't cautioned him but without the protection of the Colonel it wouldn't take much

429

for them to put him in a windowless cell and throw away the key.

"The man outside the house," continued Howard. "He'd been shot twice in the chest. Do you know who he is?"

"I think he's an MI5 agent. The British security service. I don't know his name."

Howard and Clutesi looked at each other in astonishment. "Who the hell are you, Mr O'Brien?" asked Howard. "For a start, is O'Brien your real name?"

Joker looked levelly at Howard, who was obviously the more senior of the two agents. "I think we're going to have to talk some sort of deal before I go any further," he said softly.

Howard's eyes hardened. "We're not talking any deals, Mr O'Brien. This is a criminal investigation, nothing else."

Joker smiled. "Oh dear," he said. "I think I just wet myself."

"This isn't funny, O'Brien," said Howard.

Joker looked at Howard, his face hard. "I know it's not funny, Agent Howard," he said, raising his bandaged wrists. "I was the one they took down into the basement, don't forget that. She tortured me, she pulled me apart with knives and shears, then they tried to burn me alive."

"She?" queried Howard. "Mary Hennessy did that to you?"

Joker nodded. "Everything but the bullet in the shoulder," he said.

"Why? Why was she torturing you?"

Joker smiled. "I suppose it was because I didn't tell her what she wanted to know when she asked me nicely."

Howard ignored Joker's baiting. "What did she want to know?"

"What are you after, Agent Howard?" said Joker.

"What do you mean?"

"You're obviously not here because of what happened to me. You're after Hennessy and Bailey, right?" Howard nodded, almost imperceptibly. "So we're on the same side here."

Howard shook his head. "I'm not the one who's been leaving a trail of corpses," he said.

Joker sneered. "One was a girl who was going to kill me while I was strung up by the arms, the other was a guy who came at me with a gun. There isn't a court in the country who wouldn't see either as self-defence."

Howard raised one eyebrow. "And what about the two men you killed in New York. They were bound and gagged when you shot them in the back of the head."

"What?" said Joker, confused. "What the hell are you talking about? They were alive when I left them."

"So what are you saying, that someone else slipped in and finished them off for you?"

Joker frowned and rubbed his temples with the ends of his fingers like a mind-reader trying to guess a playing card. It could have only been the men from MI5. They wanted him free and clear on Hennessy's trail, but Joker had no idea that they'd gone as far as to commit murder. He looked up. "I took their gun, the P228. If they were shot, it wasn't from that gun."

"But who's to say you didn't have two guns?" asked Howard. "You shot them with your own weapon and then dumped it, keeping theirs. That's what I'd do. What about you, Don?"

The agent by the door nodded. "Makes sense," he said. "Thing of it is, though, is that the gun they found on him wasn't a P228. It was a Smith & Wesson model 411."

"That was her gun," said Joker. "I don't know what they did with the P228. I never saw it again once they took it off me." A thought suddenly struck him. "The gun that the MI5 agent had. Compare that with the bullets in New York. You might get a match there."

"We might," agreed Howard. "So, what did Mary Hennessy want from you?"

"She wanted to know how I'd managed to find her."

"And you told her what?"

"That I'd traced Bailey from New York. Found him in Maryland and he led me to their house."

"Anything else?"

The FBI agent was persistent, and Joker knew that his first instinct had been right, it was the IRA activists that they were interested in, not him. If he played his cards right, he might be able to extract himself from his present predicament. But handling the FBI men would be every bit as dangerous and demanding as dealing with Mary Hennessy. The chain was digging into the small of his back. "She wanted to know if I knew what she was doing."

"And do you?"

"No, I don't."

"Did she believe you?"

"Eventually."

"So why didn't she kill you?"

"She tried. Or rather, she sent down that other girl to finish me off. Do you know who she is?"

Howard shook his head. "And identification is going to be difficult after what you did to her face," said the FBI agent.

Joker had the feeling that Howard wasn't being totally

honest, and that he did know who the girl was.

"Why were you following Hennessy and Bailey?" Howard asked.

Joker had expected the question, but it wasn't until Howard asked it that he decided how to reply. He'd realised that there was no way he could expect any help from the Colonel or from his old Regiment, they would presumably deny all knowledge of his involvement in any official operation. Joker opened his gown and indicated the old scar on his stomach. "She did this to me in Ireland three years ago." At the door, Clutesi whistled softly through clenched teeth. Howard stood up for a closer look. "I was a sergeant in the SAS." When Howard didn't react, Joker added: "The equivalent of your Special Forces."

Howard raised an eyebrow. "I've heard of the SAS," he said. "I'm waiting for you to get to the point."

"I was part of an undercover operation in the Border Country. Our cover was blown, she killed the guy I was with, and she started on me. An Army patrol found us and she escaped, but before she left she ripped open my guts. She said she wanted me to die slowly, so that I could think about her as I bled to death. Her timing was lousy and the Army got me to a hospital in time."

Howard nodded and Clutesi took notes. "Three years ago, you say?" said Howard. "Why now? Why did you come after her now?"

"Another SAS officer was killed near Washington some weeks ago," said Joker. "He'd been tortured. And it was Hennessy's signature."

Howard was tapping the envelope against his legs again and Joker knew it wouldn't be long before the FBI agent showed him the contents. "You said you traced Bailey to

Maryland. You followed him here from New York?"

Joker shook his head. "I was told that he was down here."

"So you were told about the house while you were in New York?"

"No. I heard that Bailey had been meeting with a guy who owns an aviation company here."

"What was his name?"

"Patrick Farrell. His company is Farrell Aviation."

"So what happened? You staked out the airfield?"

"That's right."

"And you saw Bailey there? And followed him to the house?"

Joker nodded. "You've got it."

Howard frowned and rubbed his chin. "So, this MI5 agent, where does he come into the picture? He was working with you?"

Joker snorted. "Hardly. The first time I saw him was when he came at me in the house with a gun."

"So he was following you? Without you knowing?" There was a look of surprise on his face.

"I guess so."

Howard rubbed his chin again, giving Joker the impression that he didn't believe him. "Did you see anyone else at the house?"

"Two Americans. They caught me in the car. And another guy, looked like he was from the Middle East."

Howard and Clutesi looked at each other, the amazement evident in their faces. Howard stood up and opened the envelope. He took out a stack of glossy colour photographs and began handing them to Joker one at a time. "Do you recognise these people?" he asked.

The first photograph was of Hennessy, an old one, before she'd dyed her hair. Joker held it up. "Mary Hennessy. You know she's blonde now?" Howard nodded. "She looks as if she's lost weight, too," Joker added. The next photograph was of the Middle Eastern type with the receding hairline and thick moustache. Joker took a quick look at the back, hoping that there would be some sort of caption there. There wasn't. "Yeah, this guy was there."

"Did it look as if he was in charge?"

Joker shrugged. "Maybe," he said, noncommittally. He went through the rest of the photographs. Bailey was there, and so were the two Americans. There was also a picture of the girl Joker had killed in the basement. "Yeah," he said. "They were all in the house."

Howard took the photographs back and put them into the envelope. "Do you have any idea where they might have gone?" Howard asked.

"I was the one being tortured," said Joker, "they weren't exactly letting me in on their plans, you know?"

Howard and Clutesi looked at each other and Joker had the feeling that it was because they weren't sure what to do next, not because they were playing some sort of psychological game. "Do you want to tell me what's going on?" Joker asked eventually.

Howard looked across at Clutesi and slipped the manila envelope into his jacket pocket. "I've a phone call to make. We'll talk again later." The two FBI agents left the room, and a minute or so later the uniformed cop returned, carrying a styrofoam cup of coffee.

* * *

435

Matthew Bailey kept his left hand on the control wheel as he set his radio transmitter to the Bay Bridge Unicom frequency, 123.0 MHz. He called the airfield up as he levelled the Centurion off at two thousand feet over the Chesapeake Bay and asked them for a runway advisory. Through his headset he heard a young woman tell him that runway 29 was in use and that the winds were coming from the west at about six knots. There was no other traffic in the pattern and he took the plane down to one thousand feet, flew parallel to the runway and then made two gentle left turns before touching down.

The airfield was slightly larger than the one where Farrell Aviation was based, and it had a hard runway which was at right angles to the water. Bailey taxied over to two petrol pumps by the side of a white-painted wooden hut where a teenager in blue overalls topped off his wing tanks. "Can I tie down over there?" Bailey asked.

"How long are you staying?" said the teenager, hanging up the fuel hose.

"Should be leaving tomorrow," said Bailey. "Maybe tonight." He was wearing dark glasses and his Orioles baseball cap hid his red hair.

The teenager pointed to a group of small planes. "Over there'll be just fine," he said.

"Great, thanks," said Bailey. He went over to the hut and paid a girl for his fuel and for the tie-down fee, then started up the Centurion and taxied it over to the parking area. After he'd secured the plane he used a public phone to call for a taxi. He wanted to get back to the motel as quickly as possible. He'd always known that Mary felt the same about him as he did about her. The previous night had been fantastic, the best sex he'd ever had. She had a terrific body, and he'd loved the way she'd gasped and moaned as he mounted her. God, there was so much he wanted to do with her. He wanted to make love to her in every possible way, to do things with her that he'd only read about before. Once the hit was over and done with, he'd ask Mary to go away with him. She was older than him, sure, but that wasn't a problem. She was everything he'd ever wanted in a woman, and more. And he'd prove to her how good he was, in bed and out of it. They'd be a great team. The best. He found himself growing hard and he paced up and down impatiently.

Cole Howard stood in the corridor outside Joker's room in the Shock-trauma unit, tapping the antenna of his mobile phone against his cheek. "You liaise with the anti-terrorist people in the UK, what do you make of him, Don?" asked Howard. A nurse pushed open the door behind them and wheeled a television set inside.

Clutesi shrugged. "He looks like shit, doesn't he? Not what you'd expect an SAS soldier to look like. But he sounds as if he knows what he's talking about. I think he's on the up and up. What do you plan to do with him?"

"I'm not sure," replied Howard. "The forensic guys are doing a comparison on the bullets at the moment, but he admits killing the MI5 agent and the girl."

Clutesi frowned. "We're not going to charge him with the killings, surely?"

Howard shook his head. "No, it looks like self-defence. But it's going to be harder to explain away the two bodies in his hotel room in New York, isn't it?"

"Not if he's right and the gun the MI5 man had on him was used to kill the men in New York. But that's going to take time, and you know as well as I do that more often than not the bullets are so knocked about that the forensic boys never get a match." Clutesi looked at his watch. "You hungry?"

"Sure," Howard replied. He hadn't eaten breakfast. He'd spent most of the night with the lab techs going over the scene of the fire, and had caught a few hours' sleep on a cot in the bureau's Baltimore office. Food had been the last thing on his mind.

"We can spare half an hour, right?" asked Clutesi.

"What have you got in mind?"

"Maryland crab cakes," said Clutesi. "You've never eaten anything like it. The best place is just down the road." He saw Howard's frown and grinned. "I spent two years in the Baltimore office before I moved to the Counter-Terrorism Division. How about it?"

Howard agreed and the two men caught the elevator down to the ground floor. "It'll do O'Brien good to sweat it out for a while," said Howard as they stepped out into the street.

"I dunno about that," said Clutesi, "he doesn't seem like the type who'd sweat easily."

Clutesi headed confidently down the street and Howard matched his stride. Several nurses were standing in a group, smoking and talking in the hot sun. Howard guessed that the hospital had a no-smoking policy. It was a bright, sunny day, with barely a cloud in the sky, and the sidewalks were shimmering in the heat. It was humid, too, and most of the people out on the streets were casually dressed in loose shirts and shorts. Most of the passers-by were black, and clearly poor. Their surroundings were also down-at-heel, ranks of row-houses with peeling paint and rotting window frames. Some of the houses had been converted into offices but many had 'For Rent' signs in their windows. The shops were also showing signs of wear and tear, with lacklustre window displays and apparently few customers. There were plenty of cars on the roads but most were old and in need of repair. Clutesi took Howard towards a large multilevel building with a sign saying 'Lexington Market' on the side. There were groups of blacks standing in groups around public telephones, mainly young men in hundred dollar Reeboks, Malcolm X baseball caps and heavy gold chains around their necks and wrists. They glared at the two FBI agents with hostile eyes.

"Drug dealers," said Clutesi. A tall, thin black man, the front of his blue jeans stained around the groin, was waving a fist in the air and screaming at no-one in particular, his eyes vacant.

"Why don't they clean this place up?" asked Howard, who was finding it difficult to imagine why Clutesi had taken him there to eat.

"Hey, this isn't so bad," said Clutesi. "There are areas in the city that are a hundred times worse than this, places where two FBI agents couldn't walk without a full SWAT team in attendance. There's a drive-by killing somewhere in the city pretty much every day, usually innocent bystanders getting shot in the process, and most of it is drug-related. The middle classes have all moved out to the suburbs. There are no jobs for those left, and with the economy in the state it is there's not much chance of things changing.

"The government never really got to grips with the city's problems," continued Clutesi. "They've made big investments, like the new stadium, the shopping malls at the Inner Harbour and the National Aquarium, and this development, Lexington Market, but they haven't done anything about the quality of the life for the people here. It's not tourist attractions they need, it's jobs."

"Did you enjoy your two years here?" asked Howard.

Clutesi pulled a face. "For an FBI agent, it's an okay posting. I mean, you wouldn't want to be a homicide detective here. It's mainly blacks killing blacks, with crimes investigated by white detectives answerable to a black commissioner of police. You're caught between a rock and a hard place. At least as an FBI agent you know you're not here forever, and when I was here they were a good bunch of guys. But it's not New York, that's for sure."

He pushed open a glass door and ushered Howard inside. "Welcome to Faidley's," he said.

Howard was standing at one end of a large room with high ceilings around which reverberated animated conversation and the sound of eating and drinking. The smell of fish and crabs was almost overpowering. Around the edge of the room were a number of stands selling a variety of seafood. There were tanks containing large, mournful fish and lobsters with their claws bound with elastic bands, fresh fish lying on beds of crushed ice while behind them black men in bloody aprons chopped off heads and removed guts. In the far corner Clutesi saw a stall selling shrimps and thick salmon steaks, and in the centre of the room was a raw bar where customers stood and ate oysters on the shell and drank beer. In the centre of the bar section women were wielding sharp knifes, opening oysters and clams with professional flicks of their wrists.

Over on Howard's right was a counter section with a queue of people, black and white, waiting to be served. The place was packed, with most of the diners standing by chest-high tables and eating with their hands. Howard peered curiously at the counter. "These are the best crab cakes in Baltimore," said Clutesi, "probably in Maryland."

They reached the front of the queue and Clutesi ordered two crab-cake platters. A few seconds later two plastic trays were slammed down in front of them. Howard picked up his and looked at it. The crab cake was about the size of a baseball and looked as if it had been formed by being squashed between two hands. He lifted the tray to his nose and smelled, a warm blend of crab and spices. The meal came with bread and a salad, and Howard's mouth was watering.

"You want a beer?" Clutesi asked.

Howard shook his head. "No, thanks. Maybe a Coke."

Clutesi paid the bill. "It's on me," he said, "just in case you don't like it."

They carried the trays over to a vacant table. There were no seats. "Makes for a faster turnover," said Clutesi, seeing Howard look around for a chair. "Besides, they taste better standing up."

Howard took a bite of his crab-cake sandwich and raised his eyebrows as he chewed.

"Good, huh?" asked Clutesi.

"Fantastic," agreed Howard. "Oh shit," he added, recognising the figure walking towards him. "What the hell is she doing here?"

"Huh?" said Clutesi, his mouth full of crab cake.

"Kelly Armstrong, young, thrusting would-be superstar

and a real pain in the butt." Kelly walked up to the table, smiling. "Kelly, this is a pleasant surprise," he said through gritted teeth. "How did you know where to find me?"

"The FBI office said that you were with a Don Clutesi and that if you weren't at the hospital with the suspect he'd probably be eating at Faidley's."

"They know me so well," said Clutesi sheepishly.

"So you'd be Don Clutesi?" said Kelly, offering her hand. Clutesi shook it warmly.

"And you'll be Kelly Armstrong," he said. "Cole has told me lots of good things about you."

"Oh really?" said Kelly, raising an eyebrow and leaving him in no doubt that she didn't believe him. Howard offered Kelly lunch, but she shook her head, saying that she'd already eaten. "Cole, why didn't you tell me about the television broadcast yesterday?"

Howard shrugged. "You were chasing up the alternative targets," he said.

"It would have been nice if you'd kept me fully briefed."

"I thought Jake Sheldon had already done that."

Kelly's eyes flashed and she looked as if she was going to snap at him, but with a visible effort she regained her composure. From her handbag she took several sheets of paper, neatly folded, which she handed to him. "These are what I've come up with after talking to the State Department and the Secret Service. I've put all the East Coast possibilities on a separate sheet and there's a full itinerary for the VIPs at the ballpark. Did you get anything from the suspect in Shock-trauma?"

"Damien O'Brien? He's not a suspect," said Howard.

Kelly's forehead creased into a frown. "I don't follow you."

Howard took a large bite of his sandwich, so Clutesi filled her in on what O'Brien had told them.

"Does he know what they're planning?" she asked.

"If he does, he's not telling us," said Clutesi.

"But we're assuming it's an East Coast hit?" she said. Howard nodded. "What about the snipers? Do we know where they are?"

"Not yet," admitted Clutesi. "We got an address but it was on fire and they were long gone by the time we got there. All we found was O'Brien and a couple of corpses." Two black teenagers in leather jackets and jeans looked round with their mouths open and Clutesi realised he'd been shouting above the noise. He lowered his voice. "We were close, though. Damn close."

"What's your plan now?" Kelly asked Howard.

He shrugged. "We're going to have another talk with Mr O'Brien. You?"

"I thought I'd talk to the local police, check over their security arrangements. Will you be going back to Washington?"

"I'm not sure," said Howard. "Depends on what else we get from O'Brien."

"Do you need my help here?"

"No, we can handle it," said Howard. He smiled. "Keep up the good work."

She looked as if she was going to say something else, but instead she just nodded, said goodbye to Clutesi, and walked away. Both men watched her go, as did several other diners. "She's hot," said Clutesi.

"She's a bitch," said Howard. "A poisonous, ambitious, nasty bitch."

"Turned you down, huh?"

Howard glared at Clutesi. "Don't even joke about it," he said.

Clutesi grinned and looked at the door which was closing behind her. "Thing of it is, she looks familiar. Like I've seen her somewhere before."

"Yeah? In Phoenix, maybe?"

"Never been to Phoenix," said Clutesi thoughtfully. "But I'm sure I've seen her somewhere." He shrugged. "It'll come to me eventually."

The two men ate, chatting about Clutesi's days in the Baltimore office, keeping the conversation general because the tables were crowded. Later, as they walked back to the Shock-trauma Unit, Clutesi raised the subject of O'Brien again. "You want me to check with the British?" he asked.

"About O'Brien? Or the MI5 agents?"

"Both. The shit is really going to hit the fan, that's for sure. They're not supposed to be here without clearing their operation with us first."

"Is it possible they did clear it?"

"Doubtful. Hank O'Donnell could confirm that for sure. But it wouldn't be the first time that they've operated here without our okay. You know how it works, both the Bureau and the CIA send people to the UK without letting the British know what we're up to. It depends on how much we trust our opposite numbers, and how sensitive the operation is."

Howard nodded thoughtfully. "Can you call up Frank and see if he's gotten anywhere with O'Brien's fingerprints – the girl's too? And then call up our Baltimore field office and get them to pull in Patrick Farrell."

"Sure," said Clutesi. They reached the hospital and Clutesi took his cellular telephone from his pocket. Howard did the same and the two men found a quiet corridor before dialling.

As Clutesi called up the New York Counter-Terrorism Division, Howard rang through to the White House office where Ed Mulholland was directing operations. Helen answered on the third ring, her voice pleasant and professional, though Howard knew she couldn't have had much sleep. He'd called from the burning house on Chesapeake Bay at ten o'clock the previous night and she'd been on duty then. She put him through to Mulholland, who also seemed to be firing on all cylinders. Howard quickly explained about O'Brien, and the information he'd given him. Mulholland listened without interruption. "Sound kosher?" he asked when Howard had finished his briefing.

"I think so," said Howard. "We've faxed his prints to New York, Frank Sullivan's running a check."

"So what do you think, Cole? Do you think they'll call it off now?"

Howard hesitated. "I'm not sure," he said. "If it was me, I'd lie low for a few months and then try again. But these are terrorists, they're used to taking risks. In fact, the more I think about it, the more convinced I am that they're going to go ahead regardless. From what O'Brien has told me, Hennessy seems to be on some sort of personal crusade."

"Do we have a fix on where the hit is going to be?"

"No, and we're no nearer finding out when, either. Though I get the feeling it's going to be soon. According to the President's itinerary, he's going to be in the Baltimore-Washington area for the next three days."

"Yeah," agreed Mulholland. "I spoke to Bob Sanger last night and he agrees with you. He's swamping the area with

445

Secret Service agents and tightening up the presidential guard."

Howard snorted. "I thought security was already as tight as it could be," he said.

"Yeah, well I think he's more worried about covering his arse than anything else," said Mulholland.

"Ed, wouldn't it be much easier to withdraw The Man from view until this has been resolved?"

"Bob's already been to see the President, and his views haven't changed. The President insists that he can't be held hostage in the White House by an assassin. He's allowing the extra security, but he's not prepared to cancel a single appearance. That goes for the Prime Minister. We've been in touch with his security people, and the PM has made it clear that he is not willing to cancel any engagements either. He says they don't bow to IRA threats in the UK and they're not prepared to do so here."

Howard had expected that to be the position, but was disappointed nonetheless. "How many calls have you had?" he asked.

"About two hundred so far, but they're still coming in," said Mulholland. "It's like every man and his dog has seen Bailey or Hennessy; we've had sightings from San Francisco to Key West and all points between. About a dozen are from the Baltimore-Washington area and we're working on them now."

Howard told Mulholland how O'Brien had tracked Bailey from an airfield, and that he was pulling Patrick Farrell in for questioning.

"What do you think that's about?" asked Mulholland.

"Could be their escape route," said Howard. "If they do succeed, they'll need a way out. Look, I've an idea that I want to run by you. This guy O'Brien is the only one who's actually seen Hennessy, Carlos and Bailey close up. I was wondering if we could use him in some way."

"What do you have in mind?" asked Mulholland.

"I want to have him around the President, not as part of the guard, obviously, but close by, in case they try anything at close range."

"Yes, but I thought we were assuming they were snipers, right?"

Howard explained Andy Kim's theory that Hennessy, Bailey and Carlos might be intending to be close to the target, as shown in the Mitchell video, either to guide the snipers or as a fall-back position if the sniping went wrong.

"So you want O'Brien on the ground looking for them?" asked Mulholland.

"He's seen them in person, whereas we're only working from photographs. If they do try to get close to the President they're as sure as hell going to be disguised. He might be able to spot them by the way they walk, the way they hold themselves. You know as well as I do that you can often identify a person from a distance by the way they move. O'Brien's the only one who can do that."

"Yes, but you don't even know this O'Brien's background, Cole."

"Like I said, we're running a check on him now. He claims to be a former SAS soldier who worked against the IRA in Northern Ireland. He's as well trained as our Special Forces guys, and he's worked undercover."

"But you said he'd been tortured, and shot," said Mulholland.

"He's hurt, but not too badly," replied Howard. "I've already spoken to his doctor. He says most of his injuries are superficial, and though he'll be a bit weak for a few days, he's in no danger."

"I'm not sure how close Bob Sanger will want him getting to the President." It sounded to Howard as if Mulholland was looking around for reasons to say no.

"I know it's a long shot, but if it was explained to him in the right light . . ."

Mulholland laughed. "Okay, Cole, I'll run it by him. You let me know what Sullivan says. He's going to check with London, right?"

"Right. And we're running the prints of the dead girl through the computer, too."

"You think she's the third sniper, Dina Rashid?"

"There's a strong possibility, yes. And if one of the snipers is dead, that increases the possibility of them changing their plans and going for a close-in hit." Clutesi stood in front of Howard, his cellular phone at his side, making a small waving motion with his free hand. "Wait one second, Ed," said Howard. "What's up?" he asked Clutesi.

"Frank says the dead girl is Dina Rashid for sure," Clutesi answered.

"What about O'Brien?"

"Nothing on our files, or Interpol's. We're checking with MI5 but, bearing in mind what happened to their man, they might not be especially helpful."

Howard nodded and spoke into his phone. "Ed, Frank says the girl in the basement is definitely Dina Rashid. He's still checking out O'Brien's story."

"Okay. Let me speak to Bob Sanger and then I'll get back to you. Oh, I almost forgot, Jake Sheldon was on the phone from Phoenix. He wanted to know how Kelly

Armstrong was getting on with our team here in Washington. He seems to think very highly of her."

"Yeah, she's doing a great job," said Howard, bitterly.

"That's what I told him," said Mulholland. "Okay, Cole, talk to you soon." The line went dead.

"Everything okay?" asked Clutesi.

"Peachy keen," said Howard.

Matthew Bailey took a cab from Bay Bridge airfield to the Marriott Hotel in Baltimore, and there he waited a full thirty minutes before catching another cab to the airfield where Farrell Aviation was based. He kept his baseball cap pulled down and had his dark glasses on, but he needn't have bothered: neither driver even bothered to look at him. He had the taxi drop him at the airfield car park and he waited until he was sure that he hadn't been followed before getting into his rental car. He drove back to the motel, eager to be with Mary Hennessy again, but knowing that he had to stick to the speed limit. He couldn't understand why the Americans had chosen 55 mph; it was a snail's pace compared with what he was used to in the United Kingdom. He tapped the wheel impatiently, then flicked through the channels on his car radio. There were advertisements on every one: for restaurants, repair shops, store sales, beer, supermarkets. It was as if the stations had banded together and co-ordinated their advertisement breaks so that there was no escape. He'd noticed the same phenomenon on American television. He switched the radio off and concentrated on the road ahead. He was no longer nervous about the forthcoming operation – he was looking forward to it, keen to show Mary what he could do. The anticipation was a hard knot in his stomach, and it made him feel more alive than he'd felt in a long time. Mary had been right, they'd talk about this day for a long, long time in the bars of Belfast. Songs would be sung and glasses would be raised and Matthew Bailey and Mary Hennessy would be remembered forever.

He parked the car at the rear of the motel and rushed to the room, his heart pounding. He realised that he hadn't taken the key with him and he knocked impatiently. His face fell when Mary opened the door and he saw that Carlos, Schoelen and Lovell were already there. Lovell was wearing a short-sleeved white shirt with the Farrell Aviation hawk and propeller logo on the back and on the breast pocket. Mary ushered Bailey inside and closed the door behind him. "Everything's okay?" she asked.

Bailey nodded. "The plane's at Bay Bridge, fully fuelled. It'll take half an hour to get there from the city; by the time we get to the field it'll be deserted. There's no tower there, and so long as we head south immediately, we won't cut through the Baltimore TCA."

Carlos nodded and held out his hand, palm upward. "I'll look after the keys, Matthew," he said.

Bailey looked over at Mary and she nodded agreement. Reluctantly, he handed them over.

"I've been on the phone to Farrell, and everything's fine at his end," said Mary. "He hadn't seen the television last night, and I didn't enlighten him. Don't bring it up when you see him, I don't want him spooked."

"Sure," said Bailey. He desperately wanted to get Mary on her own but there didn't seem to be any way he could manage that: Lovell was lying on one of the beds, his arms behind his head, staring up at the ceiling, and Carlos had seated himself on the dressing table, swinging the keys to the Centurion around his index finger. Mary looked stunning. Bailey remembered how smooth and firm she'd been in bed, how her legs had gripped him like she was riding a stallion, squeezing and holding him, and how good she'd smelled – musky, like an animal in heat. He felt himself growing hard and he shook his head.

"Matthew, are you all right?" Mary asked.

Bailey blushed. "I'm fine," he said.

"We're going to do a final run through," she said. "You give a wind reading, as if you were reading it off the computer. Okay?"

"Sure."

Schoelen was already taking his rifle out of its case. Carlos looked at Lovell. "Let's get to it, Rich."

Lovell rolled off the bed and opened the case containing his Barrett rifle. Carlos took Dina's rifle and checked it while Mary opened her suitcase and picked up five transceivers in black leather holsters, with earpieces and body microphones. She gave one to Bailey and he clipped it to his belt and inserted the earpiece. The microphone he attached to the neck of his shirt.

The rest of the men set up their transceivers and Mary spoke to them one at a time, checking that they could receive and transmit. When she was satisfied that the equipment was working, the three snipers moved to different parts of the room, all facing the same direction, towards the door. Bailey stood by the bathroom door and Mary leant against the dressing table, her arms folded across her stomach. The snipers had their rifles to their shoulders, but their fingers were outside their trigger guards.

Mary let them make themselves comfortable and waited until she could see that their breathing had steadied.

"Check One," she said.

"Check One," repeated Lovell.

"Check Two," said Mary.

"Check Two," said Schoelen.

"Check Three," said Mary.

"Check Three," said Carlos.

"Check Wind," she said.

"Two One Five at Nine," said Bailey. The imaginary wind was blowing from two hundred and fifteen degrees at nine knots. The snipers mentally calculated how they would adjust their aim.

"Two One Five at Nine," repeated Lovell.

"Two One Five at Nine," said Schoelen.

"Two One Five at Nine," said Carlos.

"With you, One," said Mary.

Lovell pressed the scope to his eye. "Target sighted," he said. "Countdown starting. Five, four, three, two, one." He made a firing motion with the index finger of his right hand, and then continued to count in a steady, even voice. "One thousand and one, one thousand and two." As he said 'two', Schoelen made a similar firing motion. Lovell's count continued. "One thousand and three." Carlos pretended to fire his rifle. "One thousand and four," said Lovell. All three snipers lowered their rifles.

Mary nodded enthusiastically. "Excellent," she said. "If we can do that for real, all three bullets will arrive within half a second of each other. Any problems?"

Everyone shook their heads. They'd practised the

manoeuvre hundreds of times and it was now second nature to them all.

Mary looked at her wristwatch. "Matthew, you and Rich had better go and meet Farrell." Bailey frowned and began to protest, but Mary raised a warning eyebrow and he shut up. "I'll see you at the airfield at eight o'clock," she said. Lovell packed his rifle away and shouldered the case as Bailey changed into a short-sleeved white shirt like the one Lovell was wearing.

Bailey desperately wanted some sort of physical contact with Mary, a hug or a kiss, but he realised that it was out of the question while the others were there. He'd have to wait. "Okay, Mary," he said. He raised a fist in silent salute. "See you later." He left the motel room, the knot in his stomach growing like a cancer. Rich Lovell followed him, winking at Schoelen on his way out. Mary picked up her handbag.

"Are you going to see the Armstrong girl?" Carlos asked.

"That's right," she replied. "She's going to tell me how much the FBI know and she's got details of the stadium security for me."

"I want to come with you."

"No," said Mary, sharply.

"I want to talk to her."

Mary caught Schoelen's eye and with a shake of her head indicated that he should leave the room. Mary waited for him to close the door before rounding on Carlos. "Are you crazy?" she shouted. "Kelly might be prepared to help me, but what the hell do you think she'll say if she knows you're involved? Jesus, you're Carlos the Jackal! I'm Irish, she has a reason for helping me. You, you're a . . . a terrorist!"

Carlos looked at her, astonished by her outburst. Then he smiled, and gradually the smile turned into a laugh. Mary realised what she'd said, and she laughed with him, her anger forgotten. "I'm sorry, Ilich," she said.

Carlos laughed all the louder, and wiped a tear from his eye with the back of his hand. "You're right, of course. If she sees me, she might have a change of heart. You must go alone." He regained his composure, but he was still clearly amused. "But be careful."

She leant forward and kissed him gently on the cheek. "I will," she promised. "I'll be back within the hour."

Carlos watched her go before picking up the telephone at the side of the bed. He tapped out a number and within seconds a man's voice answered. "I'm calling in for the final time," said Carlos.

"You have problems, I understand," said the voice.

"You saw the television broadcast?"

"I would think that most of America saw it," said the voice. "You are still going ahead?"

"The problems are not insurmountable," said Carlos. "Security will be tighter but we now have a contact who is in a position to make it easier for us. Everything will continue as planned."

"I understand that Rashid is no longer a part of the team."

Carlos took a deep breath. "That is true." The man on the other end of the line said nothing and Carlos knew that he was waiting for an explanation. "I will be taking her place."

"You can do that?" said the voice.

"I can," said Carlos.

"I must see you first," said the man.

"Now?" said Carlos, surprised.

"Now," repeated the man.

Carlos did not argue. He picked up a pen and scribbled down an address on a sheet of motel notepaper.

Joker lay back in his hospital bed, his arms at his sides. The painkillers were wearing off and he was becoming aware of the injuries to his body: the bullet wound in his shoulder was a small point of pain surrounded by a dull ache, like a toothache; his wrists were sore and it felt as if his hands were barely connected to his arms, that the bones and cartilage had been stressed to their limit and that they would never heal; and his legs ached as if he'd run a marathon. Worse by far, though, was the wound on his chest, the deep hole where his right nipple had been hacked off. The hole felt as if it went right to his spine and was liquid inside, though the dressing was clean and dry.

On balance, though, Joker considered that he'd been lucky. After his last encounter with Mary Hennessy he'd been in a hospital bed for three weeks and restricted to a liquid diet for months. As he tested and checked his various body parts, he realised that his bladder was full and that a visit to the bathroom was a pressing need.

The uniformed cop was slouched in his chair, his cap tilted on the back of his head, reading the *Baltimore Sun*. "Can I go to the bathroom?" Joker asked.

The cop looked at him with bleary eyes and put down the newspaper. "No," he said. He returned his attention to the paper.

"Ah, come on," said Joker. "What do you expect me to do? Wet myself?"

The cop shrugged. He kept his eyes on the paper and pointed to a glass bottle on the cupboard next to the bed. "Use that," he said laconically.

"What, from here?" said Joker, indicating the chain that bound him to the bed.

The cop sighed mournfully, folded his newspaper and stood up. He kept his distance from the bed just in case Joker decided to lunge for his gun. He picked up the bottle by its neck, handed it to Joker, and went back to his seat.

Joker looked at the bottle in his hand, and back to the cop. "Is it too much to expect a little privacy?" he asked.

"Yes," said the cop, reading.

"Terrific," said Joker. He slipped the bottle under the covers and prepared to urinate into it. Just as he started, the door to his room opened and the two FBI agents stepped inside. Joker looked up. "Hell, if I'd known that my taking a piss was going to be this popular, I'd have sold tickets," he said.

"Don't let us interrupt you," said Howard. He turned to the uniformed cop and asked him if he wanted to get himself another cup of coffee. The cop cheerfully accepted and slipped out of the room. Clutesi closed the door behind him and stood next to it, his arms folded across his chest. The FBI agents waited while Joker finished filling the glass bottle. He slipped it out from under the bedcovers and made a half-hearted attempt to put it back on the bedside table. It was clear he couldn't reach, and he looked expectantly at Howard. Howard looked at Clutesi.

"Oh, come on," protested Clutesi.

"Someone's got to do it, Don," said Howard.

"He can put it on the floor," said Clutesi.

"Can't reach the floor," said Joker. "Unless I drop it. But if I drop it, it's going to splash everywhere."

"Shit," said Clutesi. He held out his hand disdainfully and took the bottle over to the washbasin. He poured the contents down the sink and washed his hands.

"Our Counter-Terrorism Division has never heard of a Damien O'Brien," said Howard. "We're checking your prints out with MI5 in London." Joker's grin abruptly vanished. Howard continued to look at him, gauging his reaction. "What do you think they're going to tell us?" Howard asked. Clutesi dried his hands on a paper towel.

Joker looked at the ink stains on his fingers, as if verifying that his prints had been taken. He looked up at Howard. There was more to this than a murder investigation. The FBI agents were obviously after Hennessy and Bailey, and the deaths of the girl and the MI5 agent seemed to be secondary to that. If Joker played his cards right, he might be able to find a way out of this mess that didn't involve him spending a lifetime in a Federal penitentiary. If the FBI had sent his fingerprints to MI5, an identification would be forthcoming fairly soon. "My name's Cramer," he said slowly. "Mike Cramer."

Howard raised an eyebrow. "So you were lying before?"

"Only about my name," said Joker. "Everything else is the truth."

Howard nodded thoughtfully. "You came into this country with a false passport?"

"Yeah. Sort of."

"Must have been a good one," said Howard.

"Yeah, it was."

"So where did you get it from? And why didn't you use your own?"

"A friend got it for me. He works for the Department of Immigration and he owes me a favour. It's a genuine passport, it's just the name which is different. I didn't think it made sense to try to tail Hennessy using my own name."

"You still say you're working alone?" said Clutesi, his voice loaded with disbelief.

"You think if I had any back-up at all, they'd have allowed this to happen to me?" asked Joker. "Why don't you guys tell me what's going on here? What do you think the IRA are up to?"

Howard took the envelope out of his jacket pocket and flicked through the photographs inside. He handed the picture of the man with the receding hairline and moustache to Joker. "You saw this guy, right?"

"In the basement," said Joker.

"His name is Ilich Ramirez Sanchez. Most of the world knows him as Carlos the Jackal."

Joker's jaw dropped. "The IRA's working with Carlos? What the fuck are they up to?"

"To be honest, Cramer, we were kind of hoping you'd be able to tell us."

Joker shook his head. "I didn't even know he was Carlos," he said. "That explains why Hennessy kept on asking me how much I knew. She wanted to find out if I knew what they'd planned. Whatever it is, it must be bloody important."

Howard nodded and took back the photograph. "We know they were working with three world-class snipers, one of whom you killed in the basement."

"The girl?"

"The girl. Dina Rashid, a Lebanese. The other two are former Navy SEALs."

"And who do you think they're trying to kill?"

Howard smiled enigmatically. "Cramer, we're the FBI agents, we're the ones who're supposed to be asking the questions here."

"It must be someone important, right?"

"We think they're planning to kill the President. And soon."

Joker frowned. "Why would the IRA want to help assassinate the President of the United States? It doesn't make any sense."

"It does if you know that Carlos and representatives of the IRA were guests of Saddam Hussein in Iraq not so long ago."

"What? You think Saddam Hussein is behind it? What would he have to gain by killing the President?"

Howard shrugged. "Revenge for Desert Storm, we think. He's never forgiven the States or Britain for forcing him out of Kuwait. But it doesn't end there. There was the cruise missile attack on Baghdad after the Iraqis tried to kill George Bush in Kuwait. And the Iraqi fighter we brought down recently in the no-fly zone was a real slap in the face for him. He hates the US with a vengeance. As a result we've seen a growing number of terrorist attacks here. We had a big one in New York in '93, remember? The World Trade Center. They killed six people, and they were planning to blow up the Holland and Lincoln tunnels under the Hudson River and the United Nations headquarters. We caught the guys, but next time we might not be so lucky."

"The IRA weren't involved, were they?"

"Not that we can prove, but the bomb was similar to ones

that have been used in Northern Ireland and London. We believe that the IRA have been helping Muslim fundamentalists in several locations around the world."

"But you said this time they're planning to use snipers?"

"We know they were practising a sniper hit in the Arizona desert several weeks ago. And we're talking real long-distance stuff. We think one of the snipers is going to be firing from two thousand yards away."

"Two thousand yards?" said Joker, with the emphasis on thousand. "You mean two hundred, surely?"

"No, two thousand yards. Six thousand feet. Our sniping experts tell us that the bullet will take four full seconds to reach its target."

Joker looked stunned. "That's incredible," he said. "You don't think they're still going ahead, do you? Now that you know what they're up to?"

Howard shrugged. "We don't know. There's another problem. We think there's a chance that Hennessy, Carlos and Bailey might be planning to be nearer the target."

Intuitively, Joker realised what the FBI agent wanted from him. He was the only person who'd seen the three terrorists close up. "In case the snipers fail?" he said.

"Or helping with the co-ordination," said Howard.

"When do you think they'll do it?" asked Joker.

"We don't know. But soon. Assuming they don't cancel."

"Carlos isn't a man who's likely to be scared off," said Joker. "I remember what he did in Vienna with the OPEC ministers. If anything, I think he'd relish a challenge. So, Agent Howard, what is it you want from me?"

Howard looked at Clutesi and then back at Joker. "We want to put you close to the presidential guard. Not as part of the President's protective screen, but as an observer. You know what Carlos looks like, in the flesh. If he's in disguise, you might spot him."

Joker scratched his chin and winced as he moved his injured shoulder. He indicated the chain with his left hand.

"You'll be released into the FBI's custody," said Howard. "I'll be taking a chance on you, Cramer, but I don't think you'll let me down."

Joker looked at him with hard eyes. "Yeah, and if Hennessy or Carlos sees me around the President, maybe they'll take a shot at me first."

"That's possible," agreed Howard.

"Do I get a gun?"

Howard smiled and shook his head. "It's going to be hard enough to persuade the Secret Service to let you within a mile of the President, I don't think there's much chance of you carrying a gun."

"Bullet-proof vest?"

"That I think we can arrange," said Howard. "Does that mean you'll do it?"

Joker nodded. "I'd do anything to get another crack at that bitch."

"I thought you'd say that," said Howard.

Marty Edberg pointed at the television monitor showing a close-up of the Orioles scoreboard. "Go to two," he said. His assistant pressed a button on the console and the picture flashed up on the large screen in the centre of the wall of monitors. The picture wavered crazily and Edberg slammed his hand down on the console. "Wendy, would you ask that shithead Lonnie to stop fucking jerking himself off when we're with him, please."

Wendy spoke into her microphone, translating Edberg's outburst into constructive criticism which wouldn't upset the cameraman too much. The picture steadied.

"Better," said Edberg. "Thank you. Now, let's go to four."

Wendy depressed the button for camera four and a close-up of the pitcher's mound filled the main screen. Several men in suits and sunglasses were checking the ground, bent double as if they were looking for dropped change.

"Good, now to six." The picture on the main screen flicked to a long shot of the baseball diamond taken from a camera high up in the stands. Edberg looked across to the small monitor showing camera two's output. It was wobbling again. "I'll have Lonnie's balls if he doesn't shape up," hissed Edberg. There was a knock on the door to the television control room and Edberg looked up, annoyed at the disturbance. "Go away!" he yelled. "Let's go to three, with a slow panning shot of the crowds behind the batter," he said.

Wendy spoke quickly to the cameraman on three and pressed another button. On the main screen the picture showed rows and rows of empty seats. A man in a grey suit and sunglasses was walking slowly down an aisle, checking underneath the seats. Several uniformed police officers were leading sniffer dogs along the rows. The knock on the door was repeated, and it opened. Two men with short hair and square jaws stood in the doorway wearing dark suits and sunglasses. Edberg sighed mournfully, recognising the suits and the demeanour. Only Secret Service agents and rock stars insisted on wearing their sunglasses indoors. "Yes, guys? What can I do for you?"

"Mr Edberg?" said the agent on the left.

"That's right."

"Did Bob Sanger of our Washington office speak to you yesterday about the live feeds?"

Edberg nodded. "He did, but it's damn irregular."

"Actually it's not," said the agent. "We've done it many times, just not at this ballpark, that's all." He flipped open a black leather wallet and showed Edberg his credentials. The other agent, who still hadn't spoken, did the same. "We're with the Technical Security Division. Our truck is downstairs." The agents stepped to the side and Edberg saw that there were two men wearing white overalls and carrying tool boxes standing outside the door. "These technicians will run the feeds to our truck and establish a communication link with you."

"You realise that you won't be able to direct the cameramen, you'll just be getting the feeds that come through to our console?" said Edberg. "I already explained that to Sanger – you can have the feeds but I call the shots."

"That's understood," said the agent. "We're just looking for a way to increase our surveillance of the crowds, that's all. But if we see something and we'd like a closer look, and the camera wasn't going out live, I'm sure you wouldn't mind giving us a close-up – if we asked you, of course. It is the President's safety we're talking about, after all."

"Yes, yes, I know," said Edberg testily.

The two men in overalls entered the control room and

scanned the monitors and racks of electronics equipment. One of them pointed to a blank monitor which was labelled 'ten'.

"Is there something wrong with that one?" he asked.

Edberg shook his head. "That'll be the overhead shots taken from the blimp," he said. "That won't be on line until it's in the air, about half an hour before the game is due to start."

"We can take a feed from it?" asked the technician.

"Sure, you just won't pick anything up for a while. We can put a test signal through it if you want to check your connections."

"That'll be great," said the technician, kneeling down and opening up his tool box. The two agents stood at the rear of the control room and watched the technicians work. Edberg could see the butt of what looked like a machine pistol sticking out of the back of one of the men's jackets. He jerked his head away as if he'd been caught looking at something he shouldn't have. Wendy was looking at him anxiously.

"Okay, Wendy, let's go to seven. And tell Lonnie he's got the fucking shakes again."

This time there were no games: no open doors, no missing light bulbs, no running showers. Mary knocked gently on the door and Kelly opened it. Kelly looked tired and agitated. She paced up and down as Mary closed the door. A television set was on in the corner, but the sound was muted.

"I didn't know, they didn't tell me," said Kelly, before Mary could speak.

Mary put her bag on the bed. "I know," she said.

"If I'd known, I'd have told you," said Kelly, her voice shaking.

Mary frowned. At their first meeting Kelly had appeared confident and self-assured, but now she saw that she wasn't much more than a girl, a girl young enough to be Mary's own daughter.

"My boss sent me on a wild goose chase," Kelly continued. "If I'd stayed in the White House, I'd have been able to warn you."

Mary shook her head. "You couldn't have reached me, remember? You didn't have the number. We were to meet here today. Don't you see? Even if you'd known about the broadcast, you couldn't have warned me." The girl looked so distraught she wondered if there was something else amiss. "Kelly, do you think they suspect you?"

Kelly looked up sharply. "Oh no," she said, "I'm sure they don't. My boss just feels threatened by me, that's all. He just wanted me out of the way. I thought if I got the security arrangements for you, it might help." She smacked her thigh with her fist. "I should have stayed with them."

"It wouldn't have made any difference," soothed Mary. She pulled Kelly close and hugged her the way she'd held her daughter when she'd failed one of her exams.

"I let you down," said Kelly. "I let you down and I let my father down."

"No, you didn't," said Mary. She helped Kelly sit down on the edge of the bed and then fetched her a glass of water from the bathroom.

Kelly sipped it gratefully. "They killed one of your people?" she asked.

Mary nodded. "Yes. A girl."

"Bastards," said Kelly. "There was a Brit there, a man called O'Brien."

"He's dead," said Mary.

Kelly shook her head fiercely. "No, he's in Shock-trauma."

Mary's mouth dropped. "Are you sure?"

Kelly nodded. "They're talking to him now."

Mary stood in front of the dressing-table mirror and stared at her reflection. That was twice that Cramer had escaped her. The man must have the luck of the devil himself. How the hell could he have escaped from the basement when the house burnt down? Especially after what she'd done to him.

Kelly held the glass of water with both hands. "They've identified everyone at the rehearsal in Arizona now," she said. Her grip tightened on the glass. "This Carlos, what's his role in all this? You didn't tell me about him."

Mary shrugged, trying to look as nonchalant as possible. "He helped us recruit the snipers, that's all. He's out of the country already." Kelly nodded and Mary knew she believed her. "How did they find out about Carlos?"

"Same way they identified you and Bailey, from the computer-enhanced photographs."

"Why didn't they include his photograph on the TV broadcast? Why did they only use me and Bailey? Why didn't they show the snipers?"

Kelly shrugged. "I'm not sure. My boss isn't telling me much at all at the moment."

"Do they know who the target is?" Mary asked.

"No," said Kelly. "They're working on a list of VIPs. It's over there, on the chair, with the security details. They're planning to flood the stadium with extra agents – I've got a map with their locations on it."

"Does that mean they think the hit is going to be there?"

Kelly shook her head. "No, that's going to be standard procedure at all the presidential venues for the next few weeks."

Mary picked up the sheets of paper and looked through them. "They're mostly British, I see. The targets."

"They're assuming it's either the President or an IRA target," said Kelly.

"Do they know where?"

Kelly shook her head. "That computer program I told you about hasn't come up with anything yet. Something about them not being able to identify the long shot."

Mary smiled tightly. "Or when?" Another shake. "Good," said Mary. "Then we can still go ahead."

Cole Howard knelt down by the side of Joker's hospital bed and unlocked the padlock which secured the chain. He tugged the chain and it rattled through the steel rails at either side of the bed. Joker slid the chain from around his waist and dropped it on the floor with a rattle like a ship weighing anchor.

"Better?" asked Howard.

"Much," said Joker. "Thanks."

The two men were alone in the room. The television set flickered silently in the corner, its sound muted. Howard had told the uniformed cop that the FBI would be responsible for custody of the patient and he'd taken his newspaper and left. Don Clutesi had gone to the FBI's field office in Baltimore to collect some clothing for Joker. Mary Hennessy had destroyed his shirt, and the rest of his clothes had gone up in flames when his car had exploded in the fire. Joker swung his legs off the bed and placed his bare feet on the floor. He tested them gingerly, shifting his weight gradually until he was standing upright.

"You okay?" asked Howard.

Joker nodded grimly. "A bit weak, but I'll be fine." He took a few unsteady steps towards the window. He walked like an old man, slightly stooped and with a discernible pause between each step.

"If it's going to be too much, you can get back in bed and we'll forget the whole thing," offered Howard.

Joker turned around and glared at the FBI agent, "I'll be fine," he said tightly.

Howard's cellular phone bleeped and he pressed it to his ear. It was Ed Mulholland. "Bob Sanger's given you the go ahead," said Mulholland.

"That's great, Ed. Thanks. I know you must have pushed for it," said Howard.

"Yeah, I've got to admit that he took some persuading," said Mulholland. "But I told him that you were prepared to accept responsibility for him at all times, and he agreed. But he's most definitely not to be armed, Cole, I can't emphasise that enough. He's to be there as a passive observer, nothing else."

"That's understood," said Howard.

"So what's your plan now?" asked Mulholland.

"Don's having a word with the Secret Service people in

Baltimore. They're handling the on-the-ground searches and I think we should leave it up to them."

"I agree," said Mulholland. "Bob Sanger's sending more of his people to Baltimore right now. There's no point in the FBI duplicating their work."

"Yeah, though we're going to stick close to the President at all venues in the Baltimore-Washington area where the computer projection suggests he's vulnerable. I'm going to talk to Andy Kim right now for a list. Then we're off to the ball game, the President's due there at six-thirty."

"Okay, Cole, keep in touch."

The line went dead and Howard called up Andy Kim's private line in the White House computer room. Kim answered on the third ring and sounded tired and harassed. Howard asked if he had put together a list of the appointments on the President's agenda where two out of the three snipers matched. A flustered Kim asked him to hang on and Howard tapped the phone against his cheek as he waited. The door to the hospital room was thrown open and the doctor who had treated Joker stormed in, his white coat flapping behind him.

"What do you think you're doing?" he asked. "Get back in bed right now."

Joker looked at Howard for support, and the FBI agent was about to speak when Kim came back on the line. Howard turned his back on the doctor while he wrote down a list of venues. When he'd finished he had seven locations, including the ballpark and the National Aquarium, the two places where the President was going to be that evening. "The Secret Service already has this list, Andy?" asked Howard.

"That's right, and we're working on others now," said

Kim. He sounded as if someone was listening at his shoulder.

"Are you okay?" Howard asked.

"I'm fine, Cole, there's just quite a bit of pressure here at the moment, that's all."

"How's Bonnie?"

"Dog tired," said Kim. "Look, Cole, I have to go, we're running a new program and I have to give it my full attention."

"Sure, Andy, sorry," said Howard. He switched off his phone and turned to face the doctor, who was if anything even angrier than when he'd entered the room.

"What the hell's going on?" the doctor asked Howard.

"We need Mr Cramer's assistance in a security matter, doctor," said Howard, slipping the phone back into his pocket.

"He needs bed rest," said the doctor, "he shouldn't be on his feet."

"I feel better," said Joker, sitting down on the edge of the bed.

"You're in shock, and your body still hasn't made up for the blood you lost."

Joker shrugged. "I'm not planning on running a marathon," he said.

"Any sort of movement is going to open up those wounds," warned the doctor.

"Doctor, this is important," insisted Howard; "if it wasn't, I wouldn't be taking Mr Cramer out of your care."

The doctor clicked his tongue in annoyance. He put his stethoscope against Joker's chest and listened. "Your heart seems steady enough," he admitted grudgingly. He pulled a sphygmomanometer from his coat pocket and took Joker's blood pressure. "Your blood pressure is on the way up, too." He looked at Howard severely. "I'd like to give him a vitamin shot, and what he really needs is a couple of days' bed rest, but I don't suppose I can stop you, can I?"

"No, doctor, I'm afraid you can't."

The door opened again and Don Clutesi came in, carrying a large brown parcel which he dropped on the bed. "There's a shirt and a sports jacket, and underwear. There's a pair of trousers, but I'm not sure that they'll fit. And I had to buy the shoes."

"Keep the receipt," said Howard, knowing how difficult it was to get anything past the eagle eyes of the FBI's accountants.

"I'll get the vitamin shot," said the doctor. "And I'd like to change his dressings before he leaves."

Howard looked at his wristwatch. "No problem," he said. "We've got plenty of time."

The Colonel parked his dark green Range Rover in the garage and pressed the remote control device which closed the overhead door. His back ached, the lingering soreness the result of several High Altitude Low Opening freefall parachute jumps he'd made over Salisbury Plain a week earlier. He rubbed the small of his back with his knuckles. Leading from the front was all well and good, he thought, but he was getting too old for jumping out of planes.

He took his keys and opened the two high security locks on the door which led from the garage to the kitchen of the four-bedroom stone cottage. The door looked like painted

wood but in fact it had a steel core and was impenetrable by
any means short of a bazooka. Immediately he opened the
second lock he pushed open the door and stepped into the
kitchen, closing it behind him. He crossed the tiled floor
quickly, opened a closet door and stuck another key into a
white metal box on which a red light was flashing,
neutralising the silent burglar alarm which was connected
to his local police station and which would have a carload
of armed police on his doorstep if it wasn't switched off
within thirty seconds.

He rubbed his back again and went through to his sitting
room where he opened up a large floor-mounted globe
which looked antique but which contained several bottles
of malt whisky and crystal tumblers. He poured himself a
large measure of an Islay malt and savoured it, breathing in
its rich, peaty bouquet as he walked over to a table by the
side of the fireplace where a chess game was laid out, a
problem he'd been working on for several days. He looked
down at the wooden pieces, his brow furrowed. The game
was the ninth of a series Bobby Fischer had played against
Boris Spassky in the summer of 1992. Fischer had opened
with the ancient 'Spanish Game', but using the Exchange
Variation. Spassky had resigned black's position after only
twenty-one moves but to the Colonel it was clear that he'd
really lost the game on his seventeenth move when he'd
moved his king. The Colonel had decided that Spassky
should have taken one of white's knights with his bishop
instead, but he hadn't yet decided where the game would
have gone from there. It was an intriguing strategical
problem and one that he relished.

The telephone on his hall table rang and he went over
and picked it up. The light on his answer machine was

flickering, indicating that he'd received several messages while he was out. The rich, almost plummy, voice on the line didn't identify itself, but there was no need. The Colonel knew who it was, and that what he had to say must be important for him to call him at home.

"The operation has been discontinued," the man said. "One of my operatives has been eliminated, one is missing, presumed inactive."

"Damn," said the Colonel quietly. "What happened?"

"Your man liquidated one at the house, for what reason I have yet to determine. The other operative followed the objective, but has since disappeared. The house was destroyed in a fire, your man is now in the Shock-trauma Unit of the University of Maryland Hospital in Baltimore and I am at a loss how to proceed further."

"So we've no idea where the objective is?" asked the Colonel.

"That's the position, yes."

"What is my man's status?"

"Injured, but not seriously. A request for information on his cover name has come through from New York, along with a set of fingerprints. It appears that he is sticking to his cover, but there is no way of knowing how long that will last. There is, of course, the question of what we do with him now. I do have other operatives in the area; they could tidy up the loose ends for us."

The Colonel smiled grimly. If Joker had discovered how he'd been used, he would be bent on retaliation, and an angry SAS sergeant, albeit one who was out of condition, was not a threat to be taken lightly. Joker's ire would be aimed not just at Mary Hennessy. "Does he know how he was being used?"

"I have no way of knowing, but if he has discovered that Five is involved there is a reasonable chance he will draw that conclusion."

The Colonel nodded. He looked out through a leaded window across rolling countryside, not unlike the hills of the Brecon Beacons where the SAS trained its men and honed their killing edge. "I will handle him," he said quietly.

"Are you sure?" asked the voice, though it contained little real concern; it was more a matter of ensuring that there was no misunderstanding, in case there should be ramifications at a later date.

"I'm sure," said the Colonel. "Thank you for informing me so promptly. I'll call you from the office tomorrow to clear up the paperwork. And I am deeply sorry about your operatives."

"They knew the risks," said the voice. "We'll talk again."

The line went dead and the Colonel replaced the receiver. It was true, the MI5 agents did know the risks, it was Joker who'd gone in blind, not knowing that he was being used as bait. The Colonel had gone through a lot of soul-searching before deciding to send his former sergeant to the United States, but in the end had decided that the ends did justify the means, and that Joker was expendable if the end result was the capture or elimination of Mary Hennessy. He doubted whether Joker would see it that way, though.

* * *

Carlos parked at the far end of the car park, facing the entrance to the huge Toys R Us warehouse, and switched off the engine. He settled back in his seat and looked at his wristwatch. When he looked up again it was to stare down the barrel of an M16 rifle. The pudgy finger on the trigger tightened and the weapon crackled and then the little boy holding it giggled. He put the rifle back to his shoulder again and aimed at Carlos' head. The gun was almost as big as he was. Carlos smiled thinly as the boy pressed the trigger a second time. The boy's father came up behind the boy and cuffed him around the ear.

"Don't point your gun at strangers, son," he chided. He apologised to Carlos and hauled the young would-be assassin off to a blue pick-up truck. Only in America, thought Carlos. They gave replica guns to four-year-old boys and wondered why they had the highest murder rate in the world. Carlos felt nothing but disgust for a society which treated guns as playthings. A gun had only one function – to kill, and it deserved always to be treated with respect.

Carlos watched the white Volkswagen turn into the car park and head in his direction. The driver parked, climbed out, and walked over to Carlos' car. Carlos leaned over and opened the passenger door for Khatami. Khatami eased himself into the seat. He made no move to shake hands; it had been clear from the start that their relationship operated purely on a business level, but he acknowledged Carlos with a curt nod of the head. Khatami looked much the same as when the two men had first met in the First Class cabin of a jet parked on the tarmac of a Middle Eastern airport: a small, nervous man with a pointed chin and an adolescent's moustache.

"Things are not going well," said Khatami. It was a statement, not a question.

"Not as planned, but we shall not fail," said Carlos.

The pick-up truck drove away, the barrel of the toy gun sticking out of the passenger window.

"The death of Rashid is a major problem," said Khatami.

"But certainly not insurmountable," said Carlos. "I've fired her weapon before, and I will do so this time. The operation can go ahead exactly as planned."

"I'm afraid not," said Khatami. "We had other plans for Rashid."

Carlos narrowed his eyes. "What do you mean?" he said softly.

"We have invested a great deal of time and money in this endeavour," said Khatami. "Do you think we would have committed so many resources simply to help the IRA?"

Carlos said nothing. It was a thought that had occurred to him, but he'd assumed that his paymasters were vindictive enough to want to help anyone who acted against their enemies.

"We had our own agenda," Khatami continued. "That is why we were so insistent that you use Rashid as one of the snipers. She was working for us. She had her own target."

Carlos closed his eyes and sighed as he realised how he'd been manipulated all along. "The President," he said.

"Indeed," said Khatami. "We knew that the IRA would have nothing to do with an assassination of an American president. They depend on American goodwill for money and support. But we needed their expertise."

Carlos reached up to grip the steering wheel. Mary Hennessy and Matthew Bailey were being set up to take the blame for the assassination of the President. And he, unwittingly, had been the one doing the setting up. He had betrayed them. And Dina Rashid had betrayed him. Was there no-one in the world who could be trusted any more? The answer hit him immediately. Of course there wasn't. Loyalty counted for nothing in the world of the 1990s. It was every man for himself. That had been proved to him once and for all when he'd been betrayed by the Sudanese in 1994, delivered to a French ministerial jet drugged and trussed up like a chicken. "Why didn't you tell me what you had planned?" he asked.

"It was enough that Rashid knew of our intentions. The fewer people who knew, the better. Your role in this did not depend on the nature of the target."

Carlos nodded. He understood. He had himself sent terrorists on missions without putting them in the complete picture. Sometimes they hadn't come back, but it was a price that had to be paid. It was results which counted, not the sensibilities of those involved. He understood what Khatami had done, but he still resented being used.

"You will be firing Rashid's rifle," said Khatami quietly. "Are you prepared to shoot at her target?"

Carlos felt his insides tighten. Khatami was asking him if he was prepared to assassinate the President of the United States. The enormity of what was being asked of him made him almost light-headed. But he knew that he could not refuse. Khatami was his only hope for a safe haven. Without his support Carlos would be thrown to the wolves. He quickly ran through the technicalities of the shot. The President would be in the sky box, which meant there would have to be two shots: the first to smash the glass, the second to hit the target. His marksmanship was up to it. Just.

"It would be an honour," said Carlos.

Patrick Farrell, Sr, was sitting at his desk going over the service records of a Cessna 172, which his company used to broadcast traffic information to several radio and television stations in the area, when his secretary told him that he had visitors. She showed in two men wearing almost identical black suits and sunglasses. They looked and acted almost like robots, sweeping the room with their shielded eyes, their lips together in neither smiles nor frowns.

"Can I help you, gentlemen?" Farrell asked, getting to his feet.

"Patrick Farrell?" asked one of the men, his impassive face impossible to read. Farrell nodded. The two men flashed their credentials and identified themselves as Secret Service agents. "We'd like you to come with us, Mr Farrell," said one.

"What's wrong?" asked Farrell.

"We'd just like you to come with us," said the second agent.

"And if I refuse?"

"We'd still like you to come with us," said the first agent.

"Can I call my lawyer?"

"There'll be time for that later, Mr Farrell," said the first agent.

"Am I under arrest?"

"No, sir," said the second agent. He held out his hand as if to guide Farrell out of the office.

Farrell looked over the man's shoulder at his secretary who was nervously biting her lip. "Get hold of my son and tell him what's happened," said Farrell.

The two agents looked at each other as if communicating telepathically. The first agent looked at the secretary. "I think you'd better come with us, too, miss."

Don Clutesi drove the blue Dodge to the Secret Service's Baltimore field office in West Lombard Street, about a mile from the Shock-trauma Unit. Cole Howard briefed Joker in the back of the car. The jacket Clutesi had supplied fitted Joker around the shoulders but was slightly short in the arms and was a garish plaid. Clutesi had explained that he'd borrowed it from the Baltimore police's Vice Squad and that it was the best he could do in the time. Joker wondered if Clutesi had deliberately chosen the most noticeable outfit so that he'd be a better target. The only thing easier for a sniper to hit would be a bullseye on the back.

Joker had continued to express surprise at the notion that one of the former Navy SEALs would go for a two thousand yard shot with the bullet taking a full four seconds to reach its target. He'd worked with military snipers before, both in Northern Ireland and the Falkland Islands, but never over that distance. It almost defied belief.

Clutesi stopped the car outside the Federal Building and dropped off Howard and Joker. He drove away in search of a parking place while the two men went inside and up to the

Secret Service's office. There Howard introduced Joker to Bob Sanger who the FBI agent explained was in charge of security arrangements for the President's visit. Sanger looked curiously at Joker's strange sports jacket over the top of his pince-nez spectacles. Joker felt that he ought to say something to explain his attire, but before he had the chance Sanger was shaking hands and ushering them to chairs.

Sanger handed a stack of faxes to Howard. "This is the latest from the Kims," he said.

Howard skimmed them. They contained lists of places where the snipers might be located. He showed them to Joker. "It's a big list," said Joker.

"Not really," said Sanger. "We'd be pretty much covering all those places anyway in advance of a presidential visit. We normally go through every building with a view of the President within a half-mile radius. All this does is extend our search area."

"They seem quite specific," said Joker. "He says the sixth and seventh floors of the Holiday Inn, but not below. That should make it easier."

"Yeah, that would be a help, but it doesn't mean we won't be searching all the floors which overlook the ballpark. We can't assume he's right, we have to look everywhere. I mean, we wouldn't stop searching the sewers for bombs just because we think a sniper is going to try to kill the President. We still send the Technical Security Division into the sewers, looking for time bombs, taking away trash cans and sealing manhole covers shut. We're talking about a hundred advance agents, and since we've put them all on red alert we're all working overtime."

Howard nodded and handed back the faxes. "It's still

okay for Mr Cramer and I to be as close as possible to the presidential party for the next few days?"

"I'm still not overjoyed about the idea, but I can't think of a good reason to deny your request," said Sanger. "I've photographs of Hennessy, Bailey and Sanchez here. They've been handed out to all our men." He pulled open a drawer and handed over three Secret Service identification badges, with metal chains so that they could be hung around necks. "Wear these at all times," he said. "If one of my men or the agents who come with the President from Washington see you trying to get close without one of these, at best you'll get your arm twisted." He frowned. "I thought there were three of you?"

"Don Clutesi will be here shortly. He's parking the car." He picked up the three badges and handed one to Joker.

Sanger stood up and went over to a closet. He took out three ballistic-protective vests, gave one to Joker and the other two to Howard. "I'd be happier if you all wear these," he said, almost apologetically. "Just in case. I wouldn't want you guys getting hurt."

Joker weighed his vest in his hands. It felt lighter than the body armour he'd worn in the SAS, and seemed more flexible.

"It's made of a special woven fabric, the trade name is Spectra," said Sanger. "They're supposed to be ten times stronger than steel but with a fraction of the weight. We get them from a company run by Ollie North. These are certified to stop a 9 mm 124 grain full metal jacket bullet at fourteen hundred feet per second."

Joker raised an eyebrow. "Impressive," he said.

"Yeah, they hardly show under a shirt, either," said Sanger.

"Do we get the dark glasses?" asked Joker.

"I don't follow," said Sanger, confused.

"The regulation shades. Do we get those, too?"

Sanger grinned as he realised that his leg was being pulled. "No, Mr Cramer, those you'll just have to buy yourself. Is there anything else you guys need?"

"Binoculars would be handy," said Joker.

Howard nodded. "We can get those from our field office," he said. He looked at Sanger. "The President's helicopter touches down at six, right?"

"Right," agreed Sanger. "I'll be at the ballpark an hour before Marine One lands. I'll meet you there, if that's okay with you."

"That's fine," said Howard.

The intercom on Sanger's desk buzzed and he depressed one of its buttons. A secretary told him that Don Clutesi was outside. Howard and Joker said their goodbyes and left Sanger working his way through the faxes.

Mary Hennessy drove back to the motel where she found Carlos and Schoelen cleaning their rifles on sheets of polythene spread out over a bed.

"How did it go?" Carlos asked.

"She didn't know about the broadcast until she saw it on television," said Mary. "There's some sort of power game going on between her and her boss."

"And because of that we were almost caught?" said Carlos. He picked up the barrel of Dina Rashid's rifle and held it like a conductor about to conduct his orchestra. "If she'd known about the broadcast, we could have left earlier, and Cramer wouldn't have killed Dina."

"That's true," admitted Mary. "But there was nothing she could do. There's something else – Cramer is still alive."

Carlos stood up. "That's impossible." Behind him, Schoelen had finished cleaning his rifle.

Mary shrugged. "He's in Shock-trauma, and the FBI are talking to him."

Carlos paced up and down the room. "How much do they know?"

"They know who we are, but they don't know when or where we plan to make the hit. Their computer simulation isn't working – because they can't anticipate where Lovell is going to be. It's throwing out all their calculations."

"So we go ahead?"

Mary nodded. "Security is going to be tighter, but if we're careful we can do it. Kelly has given me a full briefing on the security arrangements at the ballpark, so we have an edge." She opened her handbag and handed Carlos a stack of papers.

He flicked through them. "Okay," he said. "If you're sure." He looked at her, his deep brown eyes boring deep into hers, leaving her in no doubt that the responsibility for failure would rest with her.

Mary returned his gaze. "I'm sure," she said, quietly.

Carlos nodded slowly, then sat down and continued to clean the rifle. Lou Schoelen zipped up the sports bag which contained his Horstkamp sniping rifle and shouldered it. "I'll be going," he said. Schoelen went over to Carlos and shook his hand. "Good luck," he said.

Carlos looked at him with narrowed eyes. "Lou, this has

nothing to do with luck, you know that." He had an opened box of Ritz crackers by his side and he slotted several into his mouth, chewing them with relish.

Schoelen smiled. "Yeah, I know, but I'd like luck on our side as well." He waved goodbye to Mary and left.

Mary opened a drawer in the bedside cupboard and took out a packet of hair dye. She went into the bathroom, leaving Carlos sitting on the bed. Carlos finished cleaning the rifle and reassembled it. Mary came out of the bathroom, her hair wrapped in a white towel. There were red streaks on the towel, and the few strands of hair that Carlos could see were a dark red. She looked at him, saying nothing. Carlos wondered how she would react when she realised how she'd been used and that the IRA were being set up to take the blame for the assassination of the President. He smiled. She smiled back. "Bathroom's free," she said.

Carlos covered the rifle with the bedcover and went into the bathroom, carrying his wash bag. The sink had a red ring around it where it had been stained by the hair dye. He took out a can of menthol shaving cream and he spread some over his face, lathering it into his stubble and moustache. He used a disposable razor to remove the moustache, and then washed the remaining lather off his face. He looked very different without the facial hair, and by combing his hair in a slightly different fashion his appearance was totally altered. In the bedroom, Mary's hairdryer kicked into life as Carlos stepped into the shower and soaped himself clean. By the time he showered and towelled himself dry, Mary was sitting in front of the dressing table putting the finishing touches to her hair. "Red suits you," he said.

She smiled up at him. "Ilich, you said blonde suited me."

"And it did, Mary. It did."

He kept a towel wrapped around his broad waist as he picked up a dark pinstripe suit and a brand new white shirt, still in its polythene wrapper. He carried them into the bathroom and changed. "What do you think?" he asked Mary as he walked back into the bedroom.

She looked at him in the mirror. "Good. Every inch a businessman – all you need is a tie. And shoes, of course."

Carlos selected a red and blue striped tie. "Are you all right, Mary?" he asked as he fastened the tie. "You seem a little apprehensive."

"When I'm focused on what we're doing it doesn't worry me, but sometimes I relax and look at it from a distance, and it scares me," she said as she combed her hair.

"Fear is good, it keeps you on your toes," said Carlos. "It is those without fear who make mistakes and get caught."

Mary turned and nodded. "You're right, of course," she said. "What about you, Ilich? Are you scared?"

Carlos shrugged. "A little," he said. He grinned. "But if you ever tell anyone that I told you so, I'll have to kill you." He patted her on her shoulder to show that he was joking. "We must go soon."

"I know," she said. "You have the keys to the plane?"

Carlos laughed. "You sound like a doting wife, Mary. Is that how you treated your husband?"

"I suppose it was," she said, standing up and checking her outfit in the mirror. She had changed into a yellow wrap-around skirt, a white shirt and white pumps.

Carlos sat down on the edge of his bed and broke the rifle down into its main component parts, then wrapped them in a motel towel and placed them in a black leather briefcase. "I'm really impressed with the way you handled Bailey," he said. "He's a changed man. Now he actually seems to be looking forward to it. And did you notice how he's completely lost his stammer?"

Mary shuddered as she picked up her suitcase. "Yes, I noticed. Are you ready?"

Carlos slipped the box of crackers under his arm and picked up his briefcase and suitcase. "Oh yes," he said. "More than ready."

The FBI's Baltimore field office was in a cream-coloured brick building on an industrial park next to Route I-695. Cole Howard showed Joker into a small interview room, bare-walled with a couple of chairs and a teak veneer table. "Do you want a coffee or something?" asked Howard. He was carrying the bullet-proof vests in a nylon bag and he dropped them on the floor next to the table.

"Yeah, coffee would be good," answered Joker, sitting down gingerly. "I don't suppose you've got any Famous Grouse, have you?"

"Famous Grouse?" repeated Howard, his brow furrowed.

"It's a brand of whisky," said Joker. He moved his shoulder as if it pained him.

"I can get you some painkillers," said Howard. "Aspirin or Tylenol or something."

"That'll have to do, I suppose," said Joker. "How about a beer to wash them down?" He slouched back in the chair, his eyes closed. Howard stood and watched him for a few seconds, and then went out of the room to where the vending machines were. He realised he'd forgotten to ask how Joker took his coffee, but figured that he could probably do with the sugar, so he chose it sweet and white. When he got back to the room, Joker was still resting, his eyes firmly closed. Howard put the styrofoam cup on the table.

Don Clutesi came into the room carrying three Motorola two-way radios and three pairs of high-power binoculars. "You wouldn't believe the paperwork I had to go through to borrow these," he complained. "You'd think I was planning to steal them." He put them on the table next to the coffee.

"Have you got any painkillers?" asked Howard.

"Headache?" asked Clutesi.

Howard shook his head. "They're for Cramer."

Clutesi went through his pockets and came up with a small foil packet of four tablets. He tossed them down on the table. "Is he going to be up to it?" he asked.

"I'll be fine," said Joker, opening his eyes. He grunted as he leaned forward and took the packet of painkillers. He broke open the foil pouch, swallowed a couple of the white tablets, and washed them down with the coffee, a look of disgust on his face.

Howard picked up one of the two-way radios and showed Joker how it worked. "This will be operating on the Secret Service frequency, so don't use it unless you have something urgent to say," explained Howard. "You'll be able to listen in to what they're saying, too."

Joker nodded. He put the earpiece in his ear and slotted in its jackplug. "I've used similar equipment," he said.

Howard slipped off his jacket. He was wearing a leather

holster which he'd clipped to the back of his belt and he removed it, placing it on the table.

"Colt 45?" said Joker. "I thought you guys were switching over to Glocks or Berettas."

Howard took off his tie and unbuttoned his shirt. "I prefer the Colt. It's reliable, it does the job."

"It's heavy to carry around all day, though," said Joker. He gestured at the gun. "Do you mind?"

Howard looked at Clutesi and then back to Joker. "Go ahead," he said. He dropped his shirt on the table and picked up one of the vests. Clutesi helped him fit it while Joker took the magazine out of the gun and checked the mechanism. Joker looked down the sights and weighed the gun in his hands as Howard put his shirt back on and retied his necktie. It was a good fit, and once he'd put his jacket on the vest was barely visible.

"Have you used it?" asked Joker.

"Oh sure, we have regular training with firearms," said Howard.

Joker shook his head. "No, I meant have you really used it?"

"Sure."

"Fired it? At someone?"

"Well, yes, I've fired it, but only warning shots. If you use a weapon properly, you don't have to fire it. The threat should be enough."

Joker laughed bitterly. "Is that what they teach you at the Academy? For fuck's sake, Cole, a gun has one purpose and one purpose only. To kill people. Anything else is bullshit."

"So how many people have you killed, Cramer?" asked Clutesi scornfully.

Joker turned around slowly until he was facing Clutesi. The Colt was still in Joker's hand, and though Clutesi could see that the clip was out, he still paled. Joker looked at the FBI agent, his deep-set eyes like impenetrable black holes either side of his nose. "A few," said Joker coldly. "Quite a few." For a moment it appeared that Joker was going to say something else but then he shook his head, put the Colt back in the holster and handed it to Howard. Joker adjusted his jacket and scowled at Clutesi. "Are you sure this is the only jacket you can get?" he asked.

"I'm afraid so," said Clutesi, smiling brightly. Howard had the feeling that his fellow FBI agent was getting his revenge for the urine-filled bottle. "It's not so bad. It goes well with the jeans."

"How's your shoulder?" Howard asked.

"It's painful, but I'll be okay," said Joker.

"The vest fits okay?"

"Sure, it'll be fine so long as they don't go for a head shot," Joker replied, pocketing his two-way radio.

"Okay, let's get down to the ballpark," said Howard.

"What's the chance of us stopping for a drink on the way?" asked Joker. He saw the look of distaste on Howard's face. "For medicinal reasons," he added.

Lou Schoelen stepped out of the elevator on the fourth floor of the office building and looked up and down the corridor. The office he was looking for was three doors down on the left. A sign on the wall next to the dark blue door read 'Quality Goods Import-Export Inc'. Schoelen took out the

489

key Mary Hennessy had given him and unlocked the door.

The office interior was neat and bland: cream painted walls, cheap wooden furniture and metal filing cabinets, an IBM clone computer sitting on a desk. According to Mary, the office had been leased some six months earlier by one of her contacts in New York. The man made regular trips down to Baltimore, keeping up the appearance that the office was used, paying the utility bills and collecting any junk mail that arrived. The office had been selected on the basis of two main criteria: it overlooked the ballpark and had a window which could be opened. In the days of central air-conditioning, the latter had proven remarkably difficult to find.

Schoelen put his sports bag on one of the desks. He looked around the dummy office. It was impressive, and any casual observer would assume that it was a functioning business, with faxes and telexes in two wire baskets, a wall planner covered with marks and scribbled notes, and various well-thumbed directories in an old bookcase. He went over to the window and looked down at the traffic below. The car parks surrounding the stadium were empty: there was more than an hour before the game was due to begin. The stadium was in the shape of a horseshoe, the open end facing towards Schoelen and the tower blocks of the city centre. Through the gap he could see the bright green playing surface, and the sandy mound and diamond. At one side of the horseshoe was an advertisement for Coca-Cola, depicting a bottle of the soft drink which was several storeys high. Schoelen unlatched the window and slid it to the right. Immediately the throb of traffic and a distant ambulance siren flooded into the office, along with a wave of hot, moist air. He pushed open the window as far as it would go and checked the view of the pitcher's mound in the distance. Perfect. He closed the window, sat down at the desk and unzipped the sports bag, whistling softly to himself.

Rich Lovell drove the rental car to the airfield, while Matthew Bailey sat in the passenger seat, the peak of his orange and black baseball cap pulled low over his face. Bailey had a map of the area spread out over his lap. The airfield where he was due to meet Patrick Farrell wasn't the one where Farrell Aviation was based; it was a smaller, less accessible field to the north-east of the city, across the Bay Bridge, where the company owned a large hangar and a helicopter training centre. "So tell me, Matthew, how much are you getting for this job?" asked Lovell.

Bailey looked up from the map, his upper lip curled back in a sneer. "Money?" he said. "I'm not getting paid for this."

Lovell raised his eyebrows. "Not a cent?"

"Nothing," said Bailey. "I'm not a hired hand. I'm doing this because I believe in it. Because what we do will make a difference."

"A difference to what?" asked Lovell.

Bailey frowned. "You want the next turn-off," he said.

"You didn't answer the question," said Lovell. "How does killing this man make a difference? He'll just be replaced, right?"

"It shows that we're serious," said Bailey. "It shows the whole world that there isn't anyone we can't reach. The

Brits will have to listen to us. They'll have to give us our country back." He looked over at the American. "How much are you getting?"

Lovell laughed. "A lot," he said. "Enough to never have to do it again. Enough to never have to do anything again."

"Early retirement?"

"Sort of," said Lovell. "But I won't retire."

"Why not?"

Lovell glanced at Bailey. "Because I enjoy it. I enjoy the anticipation, the planning, the pulling of the trigger. It's what I do, and I do it well."

"That's the road," said Bailey, pointing ahead. "Six miles down there and then we hang a left."

Lovell nodded. "What about Mary? What drives her?"

"The Brits murdered her husband, and the Protestants killed her brother. And she believes in a united Ireland. That's something you'll never understand. You don't know what it's like to be a second-class citizen in your own country. Being a Catholic in Northern Ireland is like being . . ." He struggled for an analogy. "I don't know, I guess the closest comparison would be to being black in the South, with the whites always putting you down and pushing you around."

"And killing this one man will change all that?" He beat a drum tattoo on the steering wheel.

"Maybe," said Bailey.

"I don't think so," said Lovell. "I don't think it'll make any difference at all." He grinned. "But what the hell, I get paid anyway, right?"

"Right," said Bailey.

The men drove the rest of the way in silence, other than when Bailey gave Lovell directions. Eventually they saw the hangar. "Wow, it looks huge close up," said Lovell. "Like a giant white whale or something." He was looking at an airship which was to the left of the hangar, tethered to the ground with ropes. The blimp was more than a hundred feet long and emblazoned with the logo of a Japanese electronics company. Below the gas-filled envelope was a white gondola with windows all around it and two fan-shaped engines at the rear.

Lovell parked the car next to the hangar and took his bag out of the trunk while Bailey stretched. Patrick Farrell came over to meet them. He was wearing the same short-sleeved white shirt as they were, with black slacks. He shook Bailey's hand and the Irishman introduced him to Lovell. Farrell cast a predatory eye over Lovell's body as he shook hands and Bailey threw him a warning look.

"Are we ready to go?" asked Bailey.

"Yup," said Farrell. "The laser sight is under my seat in a bag. There are two personnel, a cameraman and his assistant. The cameraman's a big brute, I can tell you. Come on, I'll introduce you."

The three men went over to the base of the blimp. Four ground-crew in blue overalls were preparing to help with the launch. There were two doors to the gondola, one on each side, and each bore the aviation company's logo. A set of aluminium steps had been placed next to one of the doors and Farrell stood to one side to allow Bailey and Lovell to climb aboard. Lovell stowed his bag behind the pilot's seat and nodded a greeting to the cameraman and his assistant. As Farrell had said, the cameraman was massive, a big bear of a man with a wild ginger beard and hairy forearms. He was the last choice he would have expected for an assignment in an airship. As if to compensate for the man's bulk, his assistant was much younger and slighter, barely five feet six inches tall and with the lithe figure of a ballet dancer. They were both fussing over their equipment.

Bailey climbed into the co-pilot's seat and scanned the instrument panel. It was very similar to the standard aeroplane panel: attitude indicator, heading indicator, compass, airspeed indicator, vertical speed indicator, altimeter, slip and turn indicator, power indicators for the two engines, and magnetic compass. The airship was also fitted with DME and VOR navigation equipment, and an expensive Trimble TNL-GPS system which used twenty-seven navigation satellites orbiting the earth to fix its position to within fifteen feet. There was an extra dial which would allow them to read the speed and direction of the wind once they were stationary in the air, connected to a meter suspended under the gondola.

The controls were also similar to those of a fixed-wing aircraft, despite the difference in the propulsion system, with rudder pedals on the floor, power throttles in between the two seats and control wheels in front of the pilot and co-pilot.

A soft hand squeezed his shoulder and Farrell slipped into the pilot's seat. Lovell sat in a third seat at right angles to theirs and groped around for the seat harness. Farrell looked over his shoulder and asked the cameraman and his assistant to take their seats and strap themselves in for take-off. He put on his headset and motioned for Bailey to do the same.

He handed Bailey a plastic-coated checklist which the Irishman read through as Farrell expertly went over the controls and instruments, started the two rear engines and checked that his instruments were functioning correctly.

Satisfied, he gave a thumbs-up to the groundcrew and they released the tethering ropes. The airship rose slowly and almost vertically with a surprising amount of vibration. It wasn't like a helicopter, Bailey thought, it was more like a speedboat, growling and making his chest shudder.

Farrell increased power to the engines and pulled on the control wheel. The airship glided upwards, and Bailey felt the seat press into his back. Farrell's voice came over the headset. "Okay?" he asked.

"Terrific," answered Bailey.

"How about you take the controls while I speak to Baltimore Approach," he said. "Take her up to about five hundred feet and then level her off."

Behind Bailey, Lovell sat with his hands linked in his lap. He saw the cameraman's assistant looking at him and he smiled and winked.

Carlos smiled at the girl behind the reception desk, and signed his credit-card slip with a flourish. "Thank you, Mr Sharrard," said the girl, handing him a key. "Your room is on the seventh floor. I hope you enjoy your stay at the Holiday Inn."

"I'm sure I will," said Carlos, picking up his suitcase and bag.

"Do you need help with those?" she asked.

"Oh no, my wife and I can manage just fine," he said. He walked over to the elevator where Mary Hennessy was waiting, her newly-red hair tied back in a ponytail, a wide-brimmed hat on her head. "The seventh floor," he said.

They went up together and found their room at the far end of the building. Mary looked out through the window at a fire station and multi-storey car park while Carlos slid his suitcase into the wardrobe.

"Ready?" he asked.

Mary turned and nodded and they left the room and went back to the elevator. Mary was carrying a sports bag over her shoulder and she tapped it nervously as she waited for the elevator doors to open. There was no-one in the elevator when it arrived and they went down to the fourth floor. A trolley piled high with clean sheets, towels and bathroom supplies stood halfway along the corridor and as they walked by they saw a black maid making a bed. Mary stopped outside one of the doors and checked the number. "This is it," she said. She knocked on the door, but there was no answer. Carlos nodded and walked back along the corridor to the room where the maid was working. He knocked quietly on the open door and heard a tap being turned off in the bathroom. The maid appeared at the doorway, wiping her hands on her apron.

"I'm really sorry to bother you, but my wife and I have just stepped out of our room without our key," he said politely. "Do you think you could let us in with your pass key?"

"Of course, hon," she said, giving him a beaming smile which showed a gold tooth at the front. She waddled down the corridor, swinging a pass key on a chain. She saw Mary waiting outside the door, and smiled.

"I'm sorry about this," she said. "I feel so stupid."

"Oh, it happens all the time, hon," the maid said. She looked at the number of the room, then frowned. "Are you sure you have the right room?" she said. "I didn't think there was anyone . . ."

Her words were cut off as Carlos clapped his hand across her mouth. He dropped his briefcase on the floor and used his left hand to stop her thrashing about. She was a big woman but Carlos was strong and he leant backwards and tightened his grip on her mouth. Mary stepped forward and grabbed the key, ripping it off the chain. She inserted it into the lock, opened the door and then went to pick up the briefcase as Carlos half pushed, half carried, the struggling maid into the room.

Carlos pulled the maid down onto the bed like a cowboy wrestling a steer to the ground as Mary closed the door. The maid's legs were flailing around and Carlos was trying to get his left arm around the woman's throat, but he was finding it difficult. The maid's breath was coming in short gasps and her eyes were wide with fright, but she wasn't losing consciousness.

Mary grinned. "Come on Ilich, finish her off."

The maid thrashed her head from side to side as Carlos struggled to get his arm around her neck.

Mary shook her head in amusement and reached into her bag. Her hand reappeared with the P228 and its silencer and she aimed, almost casually, at the maid's chest, manoeuvring the weapon so that there was no chance of hitting Carlos. The gun coughed once and the maid's legs both kicked out together and a red stain appeared on her apron. Mary fired once more, to make certain, and Carlos released his grip on the woman's mouth.

"Get rid of the trolley," he said as he began wrapping the body in the bedcover.

Mary went out into the corridor and pushed in the laden

trolley. Carlos swung the body of the maid over his shoulder and dumped her in the bathtub, then put the trolley into the bathroom and closed the door. He walked over to the window and looked out. Less than half a mile away was the baseball park, and he had a perfect view of the pitcher's mound and the spectator stands behind it.

"Help me with the table, please," he asked, and he and Mary moved the dressing table until it was in front of the window.

Mary looked at her wristwatch. "I'll have to be going, Ilich," she said. She wasn't sure how to say goodbye. She knew that he wouldn't want her to wish him luck, and it seemed trite to just say that she'd see him later at the airfield. What they were about to do was of such enormity that it merited some words to mark the occasion, but nothing came to mind. She realised that he was looking at her with an amused smile on his face and for the first time she was flustered in his presence.

Carlos stepped forward and wrapped his arms around her in a fierce embrace, more like a wrestler's bear hug than a friendly squeeze. He kissed her on both cheeks, then pushed her away, his big hands on her shoulders. "We will succeed," he said. "We will both get what we want. What we need." His dark eyes bored into hers and she tilted her head down, feeling like a small child in the grip of her father. He put a finger under her chin and lifted her head up. "Go," he commanded softly. "And take care."

As she left the room, Carlos opened his briefcase and began assembling Dina's rifle. In the car park below, youngsters with bright orange flags were guiding drivers into parking spaces, while the sidewalks were thronged with baseball fans, chattering and laughing as they headed towards the ballpark.

Patrick Farrell switched on the Global Positioning System and read his position on the display as Matthew Bailey turned the airship to the north, over the Chesapeake Bay. At an altitude of only five hundred feet they could clearly see the waves curling on the water below. Bailey watched a yacht carve through the sea, an elderly man in a white crew-neck sweater holding the wheel with one arm and drinking a can of beer with the other.

Farrell had spoken to Baltimore Approach and had received permission to enter the Terminal Control Area around the main international airport. "Fly a heading of Three Five Five," Farrell told Bailey, "that'll take us over the city. You'll have to climb, take us up to about nine hundred feet to make sure we're well clear of any obstructions."

Bailey nodded and made the course correction and began to gain altitude. Down to his left, several miles away, he could see the burnt hulk of the house they'd stayed at, reduced to blackened timbers and fallen masonry, the grass around it rutted by the wheels of the fire engines and emergency vehicles which had long since departed. To his right were the twin spans of the Bay Bridge, ferrying traffic across the bay.

Bailey took a quick look over his shoulder. The cameraman and his assistant were preparing their equipment. The assistant had lifted a hatch in the floor of the gondola in which there was a mounting for the camera which would allow it to film directly downwards.

"We're right on schedule," said Farrell. "According to ATIS, the wind is below five knots."

"Perfect," said Bailey. Ahead he saw the tower blocks of the city centre, sparkling in the light of the late afternoon sun as it headed inexorably for the horizon.

Cole Howard found Bob Sanger on the second level of the main stand, checking security arrangements at the entrance to the sky boxes, where corporations paid huge amounts of money for the privilege of entertaining their executives and clients. Because the President and an entourage of VIPs were to be in one of the main boxes, the corporations had been required to submit a list of their guests in advance, and each visitor had to show the requisite pass and be checked off against a list held by the Secret Service agents. The managing director of a leading oil company and a woman who was not his wife had been turned away for not having the correct pass, and the oil company's public relations executive was trying to persuade Sanger to be more flexible. Sanger refused to budge. He explained patiently that the security arrangements could not be altered under any circumstances, and that if the PR man continued to make a scene he would be removed from the ballpark and would spend the next twenty-four hours in a cell.

Howard watched with great amusement as the man stormed off, threatening to take the matter up with Sanger's boss.

"What an asshole," said Sanger, as he walked over to Howard, Joker and Clutesi. "I don't think he realises that my boss is the President of the United States. What does he think? That I'd put his catering arrangements before the President's security?" He was wearing the regulation dark glasses, and Howard realised it was the first time he'd seen the Secret Service man without his pince-nez spectacles. The dark glasses made him look slightly sinister until he smiled. "So, how are the vests?" Sanger asked.

"The vests are just great," said Howard. "What time does the President arrive?"

Sanger looked at his wristwatch. "Ten minutes," he said. "Marine One will land in the ballpark, over there." He pointed and Howard saw that he had an earpiece in his right ear. "Our men will escort him and the First Lady directly into the stand. He'll greet the Prime Minister inside the sky box. After the anthem the Prime Minister will go down to the mound and throw the first pitch, then he'll be escorted back to the sky box. His own security team will be with him, and we'll have our own agents around them."

Howard frowned and reached into his pocket for the sheets of paper Kelly had given him. He flicked to the itinerary for the visit to the ballpark. There was no mention of the Prime Minister throwing the first pitch. It was a bad slip.

Sanger turned to look at the three men. "You've got your radios on, right?" All three nodded. "Okay, we use code-names over the air so that there's no mix-up. You'll hear the President referred to as Pied Piper."

"Pied Piper?" said Joker. "You're not serious?"

Sanger smiled. "That's his code-name. We started using it during the election and I guess no-one saw fit to change it."

"The President knows, right?" said Howard.

"Sure," said Sanger. "He's got a sense of humour. You know what George and Barbara Bush were? Timber Wolf and Tranquillity. Bit pretentious, huh?"

"I guess so," said Howard.

"Yeah, well, you'll hear the Prime Minister referred to as Parliament. The Fantasy Factory must have been working through 'p' code-names." He grinned ruefully at the jargon. "That's what the guys call the Service's Intelligence Division," he explained. "The top agent here will be Dave Steadman, he'll be arriving on Marine One with the presidential team. Once the helicopter lands, Steadman will be in charge and it'll be his voice you'll hear directing operations. Where do you guys plan to be?"

"We'll be down on the diamond when the helicopter lands," said Howard. "Then we'll follow you up to the sky box. I guess he'll be most vulnerable walking from the helicopter to the stand?"

"Actually, no. He'll be shielded from the tall buildings by the helicopter," said Sanger. "He'll be most vulnerable in the sky box." He gestured over at the buildings looking down on the ballpark. "We've got men on all the floors which Andy Kim says are potential trouble spots. Ed Mulholland has arranged for a hundred rookies from the Academy to help. We've got sixty around the ballpark and we're using them to monitor the buildings, too." Overhead they heard the thud of helicopter rotors and they looked up at a Maryland National Guard Huey, circling over the ballpark. "There are two National Guard Hueys up there, and a Police spotter helicopter. We've got snipers from the Baltimore SWAT unit in the Hueys, and on top of some of the taller buildings." He gestured around the stand. "We've brought in almost a hundred extra agents in plain clothes and they're scattered among the spectators."

He pointed to a long, brick building to the right of the stadium, many of whose windows looked directly down into the ballpark. "We've got snipers in there, too."

Joker looked over at the building. It was so close that he could see the faces of the people looking out. If they were offices, he could imagine a lot of people offering to work overtime on game nights. They had a perfect view of the ballpark, almost as close as some of the spectators who'd paid to get in.

"I can't stress enough how important it is that you keep the identification we've given you in full view at all times," continued Sanger. "I'd like you to also keep your FBI badges visible, too. And don't make any movement that could in any way be interpreted as being hostile to the President. Everyone's a little jittery today."

The three men nodded. "Okay," said Sanger, "I'll leave you to it. I've got a few more checks to make before Marine One touches down." He turned to go, and then stopped short as if he'd just remembered something. "Oh yeah," he said, "we picked up Patrick Farrell this morning. He denies all knowledge of Matthew Bailey, but we're putting the squeeze on him right now. If he knows anything, we'll get him to talk."

He smiled and walked off. "What is it with the dark glasses?" asked Joker. "How come all Secret Service agents have them?"

"Gives them an air of mystery," said Clutesi. "Makes them seem more than human. Sorta like your jacket." He grinned and wiped his forehead with his handkerchief. It was in the high eighties and humid.

Howard smiled. "It's more than image," he said. Through the earpiece he heard Sanger calling in for situation reports from agents on top of a bank building. "They can look over a crowd, and no one knows who or what they're looking at. Without the glasses they'd only have eye contact with a few individuals – with them, they can stare out a whole crowd. And if a psychopath thinks he's been stared at, he's not going to do anything stupid. That's the theory anyway." He reached into his jacket pocket and brought out a pair of Ray-Bans. He put them on, and grinned. "And if you can't beat 'em . . ."

Joker looked out over the ballpark. He put his binoculars to his eyes and scanned across the Marriott Hotel and the Holiday Inn to the tops of the tallest tower blocks in the distance. On one he saw two men in blue overalls with 'SWAT' stencilled on their chests in white letters. One of them had a rifle with a telescopic sight and a blue cap, with the peak pointed backwards. "Four seconds, you said?" Joker asked.

Howard looked through his binoculars. "That's for the sniper who was two thousand yards away," he said. "A shot from those buildings there would take less than a second."

"Where would the long shot come from?" Joker asked.

Howard pointed to a spot over the city. "That way, about four hundred feet or so in the air. I guess that would be a twenty-five storey building or so, and as you can see there's nothing that big anywhere near there."

Joker nodded, and scanned the crowds with his high-powered binoculars. "You really think Hennessy will be here?"

Howard shrugged. "Maybe," he said.

* * *

Matthew Bailey looked at the altimeter and saw that they were still at nine hundred feet. Directly below were several brick apartment buildings, their flat roofs peppered with air-conditioning units. Bailey had been surprised how easy it was to steer the large airship, once he'd followed Farrell's advice and begun to treat it more as a boat and less as an aeroplane. The constant vibration was a nuisance and he hoped that Lovell wouldn't find it too much of a distraction when it came to making his shot.

"You can start to descend now, we've passed over the tallest buildings," Farrell said through the headset.

Bailey nodded and rotated the control wheel slightly forward. The nose of the airship dipped down like a whale preparing to swim deep. Farrell was keeping a close eye on the GPS, and cross-referencing it with the DME and VOR, trying to pinpoint the airship's position until they were in the exact spot for Lovell's two thousand yard shot. Farrell turned round and nodded at Lovell. "Nearly there," he shouted over the noise of the two engines. "Now would be a good time."

Lovell smiled and reached down into his bag. He took out a small automatic pistol and shot the cameraman in the neck. The assistant looked up, his mouth open, and Lovell shot him in the forehead. Blood and brain matter peppered the window and the assistant slumped forward onto the camera equipment they'd been preparing. The cameraman had clasped his hands to his wounded neck and blood was dribbling through his fingers as his mouth worked soundlessly. Lovell put a second bullet into the man's skull and he fell sideways, his massive bulk sending a shudder through the gondola. Lovell flicked the safety back on the automatic and put it back into his bag. The cartridges he had used had specially reduced loads which resulted in comparatively slow-moving bullets, fast enough to kill at close range but slow enough to stay lodged within the bodies and not pass through the walls or windows of the gondola.

Lovell unfastened his harness and dragged the bodies to the far end of the gondola, where they wouldn't get in his way, and then knelt down and unpacked his rifle.

Bailey unbuckled his harness and slipped out of his seat, taking care not to unplug his headset. He pulled a green nylon bag from under Farrell's seat. Inside was a laser targeting device, normally used by hunters, which had been fixed to a metal frame and a telescopic sight. Bailey carried it over to the hole in the bottom of the gondola where the television crew had been installing their camera. Bailey slid their equipment to the side and fixed the laser into the mounting, attaching it with four bolts.

Mary Hennessy handed her ticket to the grey-haired man at the gate, took the stub he gave her, and pushed through the turnstile, taking care not to snag her bag on the chrome bars. The man's orange peaked cap was pushed back on his head and his forehead was bathed in sweat. The stadium was packed with fans, most of them dressed in colourful T-shirts and shorts, and the black and orange Oriole insignia was everywhere. The crowds were buzzing, and as Mary walked she heard good-natured arguments about the merits of the players, the teams, and whether or not the Prime Minister would manage to reach the catcher with his pitch.

She walked by food stalls where men in short sleeves were selling giant pretzels and hot dogs and the air was thick with the smell of french fries and onions. The lavatories were on her right. Kelly Armstrong was standing at the entrance wearing a pale blue jacket over a white dress. She gave no sign that she recognised Mary, but followed her into the lavatory. Most of the stalls were empty and Mary selected the one in the corner, furthest from the entrance. She put her bag on top of the toilet and undressed, hanging her clothes on the peg on the back of the door. From the bag she took out her orange and black usher's uniform and the orange cap with its shiny black peak. She slipped on the black pants and fastened her orange suspenders, then put on the shirt and waistcoat, and adjusted the cap. She fastened her transceiver and holster around her waist, then took out a compact and checked her appearance in the small mirror. She tore off a piece of toilet paper and rubbed away her lipstick. She had a pair of bifocals in the bag and she put them on. The combination of bifocals and no make-up made her look much older. She nodded at her reflection, then rolled up her original clothes and stuffed them into the bag.

She knocked on the stall door twice and heard Kelly say that the coast was clear. Mary slipped out of the stall and pushed the bag into the bottom of the trash bag by the sinks. She gave herself a final check in the grimy washroom mirror and walked by Kelly to mingle with the crowds. As she went she heard the FBI agent whisper "Good luck."

* * *

Lou Schoelen opened the office window and stood to the side as he looked at the ballpark in the distance. Four floors below, traffic was bumper to bumper as office workers headed out to the suburbs. Beyond the roads were the harbour-side shopping malls, and beyond them was the harbour, littered with small boats. Schoelen inserted the earpiece of his transceiver into his ear and switched it on. He clipped the radio to the rear of his belt, picked up his Horstkamp and knelt down by the side of the desk. He had put a large commercial directory on the desk and he rested the barrel of the rifle on it while he put his eye to the scope. He centred the pitcher's mound in the scope, then swung the rifle slightly to the left so that the crosshairs were centred on the chest of a man wearing a grey suit and sunglasses.

He tested the pull on the trigger, then slipped his finger out of the trigger guard and laid the rifle on its side. He looked at the large stainless-steel diving watch on his wrist and rocked back on his heels. The excitement was almost sexual and he took several deep breaths. High in the air above the ballpark he saw a large green helicopter, Marine One. He picked up the rifle and focused on the helicopter as it circled over the stadium, then aimed at where he knew the fuel tanks were. One shot and Marine One would go down in flames, taking with it the most important man in America. Schoelen smiled. It would almost be worth it, but that wasn't what he was being paid five million dollars for. He put the rifle back on the desk and watched the helicopter flare for landing.

* * *

"Incredible, isn't it?" said Cole Howard, the binoculars pressed to his eyes as he watched the door of Marine One open and fold outwards to form a set of steps.

"I'm amazed that something that ungainly can fly," said Clutesi.

The two FBI agents had left the main stand and gone down to the baseball diamond with Joker so that they could be closer to the President when he disembarked. Joker stood with his back to the helicopter, scanning the crowd for any faces he recognised.

As Howard watched Marine One, two Secret Service agents came down the steps, resulting in a wave of tumultuous applause from the spectators. Secret Service agents ran out and surrounded the helicopter, their heads swivelling from side to side, their hands never far from their concealed weapons. The radio crackled in Howard's ear and he recognised Sanger's voice, asking for situation reports from the men in the tunnel leading to the stand through which the President would be walking. Marine One had landed close to the tunnel entrance and effectively shielded the President from the buildings which overlooked the ballpark.

In his earpiece, Howard heard a voice say that Pied Piper was moving to the door of Marine One. The President appeared at the top of the steps and waved to the crowd. Howard heard an agent say that he'd seen a man reaching inside his jacket and there was a flurry of activity close to the tunnel with a trio of black-suited agents surrounding the man. It turned out to be a camera the man was reaching for. If the President was aware of the disturbance, he showed no sign of it. He walked down the steps, waving with his right hand and keeping a careful grip on the safety rail with his left. As soon as his feet touched the ground he was surrounded by half a dozen of the Secret Service's bulkier agents and they moved together to the tunnel like some strange fourteen-legged sea creature. Only when the President and his security team were safely in the tunnel did the First Lady appear, followed by several more Secret Service agents. The First Lady followed her husband's example and waved to the crowds before she descended. A second group of agents surrounded her and ushered her into the tunnel.

The crowd yelled and the rotor blades of Marine One began to spin, accompanied by the roaring whistle of its massive turbine. The huge helicopter lifted off, turned slowly in the air, and then flew up into the sky. It lifted up beyond the stands and the ranks of powerful spotlights which had been switched on, even though there was still plenty of daylight left.

"Come on," said Howard, and he led Clutesi and Joker towards the tunnel entrance. Joker jogged to keep up with the fast-walking FBI agent. "Sanger says we'll be allowed into the sky box, but he'd like us to keep our distance," said Howard.

"The box is enclosed, so it's unlikely that a sniper would try to shoot him through glass, isn't it?" asked Joker. "The glass would deflect any bullet."

Two Secret Service agents barred the way of the three men, their hands moving inside their jackets, until they saw their identification. They moved apart, their faces displaying no emotion.

"Yeah, that'd be the case if there was just one sniper," said Howard. "But we're talking about three. It could be that the first shot is to smash the glass, and it's the second and third which will be the killing shots."

They reached the sky box just in time to see the President shaking the hand of the Prime Minister. The two men were talking and smiling, though it seemed to Howard that the President was bored and only going through the motions. The First Lady joined them and began talking earnestly to the Prime Minister. A discreet distance behind the VIPs stood Sanger, his head turning slowly from side to side.

"Does your Prime Minister go in for sports?" Howard asked Joker, his voice little more than a whisper.

"Cricket, mainly," said Joker. "And he goes to the odd soccer match."

"I don't see his wife here," said Howard.

"She doesn't get too involved in affairs of state," said Joker. "Not like your First Lady."

Howard grinned good-naturedly. "Yeah, I know what you mean. Seems to me that we voted in a two-man team without realising it."

Secret Service agents were constantly moving around the President and his guests, and they were still on edge even though there were no members of the public within fifty feet. There were other security personnel around, members of the Prime Minister's bodyguard unit. They seemed smaller and less fit than the American agents, and not as well groomed. The Secret Service agents wore expensive, immaculate suits, brilliant white shirts and perfectly knotted ties which wouldn't be out of place in a bank's boardroom. The Brits wore suits, but they clearly weren't made-to-measure and their shoes were dull and scuffed. They did have one thing in common with their American counterparts, however – cold, watchful eyes, But while the Secret Service hid their eyes behind dark glasses, the Brits kept theirs unshielded and Howard had eye-contact with several of them as he stood by the door with Clutesi and Joker.

"Are these guys SAS?" Clutesi asked Joker.

Joker looked at the men standing guard on the Prime Minister and grinned. "No way," he said. "They're cops, not soldiers."

Through his earpiece Howard heard an agent he assumed was Dave Steadman calling for situation reports from his men around the stadium. The President pointed down to the pitcher's mound and said something and the Prime Minister smiled wryly. The First Lady said something to him and put a reassuring hand on his shoulder. They all laughed.

"He doesn't seem the happiest of campers," Howard whispered.

Joker shrugged. "He's got a lot of problems at home," he said quietly. "How are they leaving? By helicopter?"

Howard shook his head. "Motorcade," he said.

"That's risky, isn't it?"

"They're only going to the National Aquarium, less than a mile away. Sanger says they've arranged for a dummy motorcade to leave first by the main entrance as planned. The real motorcade will go ten minutes later through a back way. They're using a bullet-proof Rolls-Royce from the British Embassy in Washington. Sanger seems happy with the arrangements."

Joker nodded. He looked out through the window of the sky box. Secret Service agents were gathering around the diamond. "I think I'll go down and check out the ground level again," he said. "Is that okay with you?"

"Sure," said Howard. "Just remember what Sanger said

– no sudden moves, okay?" Howard watched Joker go.

"Isn't that your friend?" asked Clutesi, tapping Howard on the shoulder.

Howard's heart sank as he recognised Kelly Armstrong. "What the hell's she doing here?" he muttered under his breath.

Kelly walked up and greeted Clutesi and Howard. "I didn't realise you'd be here," she said to Howard.

"I was going to say the same," he replied.

"I wanted to talk to the Brits about their security arrangements," she said. "Why are you here? I thought the Kims had ruled out the ballpark."

"They have done, but we wanted to keep Cramer close to the President to see if he recognises anyone."

"Cramer?" said Kelly, frowning.

"The British guy we found at the house."

"You mean O'Brien."

"His real name's Cramer. He used to be with SAS."

Kelly looked confused. "Why didn't you tell me?" she asked.

"We only just found out ourselves," said Howard.

"And I really should have been told that you'd be here today."

"I don't see why. You have your job to do, I have mine."

"But if you thought the assassins were going to strike here, I should have been told."

Howard took a deep breath. "Like I said, we just wanted Cramer here to see if he could recognise anybody. He'll be sticking close to the President for the next few days while we continue to look for the snipers."

"I wish you'd stop hiding things from me," she said. "It's as if you're deliberately trying to make me look stupid."

"What on earth are you talking about?"

"You know exactly what I'm talking about," she retorted. "You've resented me being part of this investigation right from the start."

Heads began turning to see what the argument was about. Clutesi was watching the two of them, scratching his chin thoughtfully.

"That's not true, Kelly," said Howard. "Besides, I don't think this is the place to be having this discussion."

"Where would you rather have it? In a bar? The way I hear it, you function better with a few drinks inside you."

"That's not called for," said Howard quietly.

"Yeah? Once a drunk, always a drunk, that's what I say," she said. "We all know that if it wasn't for your father-in-law you wouldn't even be with the Bureau." For a moment it looked as if she wanted to slap him across the face, but then she turned on her heels and walked away.

Howard could feel his heart racing and he fought to contain his anger. "I wonder what's got her so riled up?" said Clutesi.

"She's just an evil bitch," said Howard.

"I don't think so," said Clutesi. "I think there's more to it than that."

Through the open window of his hotel room, Carlos watched the President's helicopter climb into the air and fly away from the stadium like a monstrous insect. Carlos linked the fingers of his hands and cracked his knuckles. In the distance he heard the first few bars of the Star Spangled Banner echoing around the ballpark. He checked that his microphone was clipped to the collar of his shirt and that his earpiece was firmly in place, then he carried the television set over to the dressing table. He took a pillow from the bed, placed it on top of the TV, then drew up a chair and sat down. The TV provided a perfect rest for the rifle, and the pillow would add extra stability and help dampen the recoil. Next to the television set he put the P228 and its silencer.

Lined up on the table were three gleaming brass cartridges. He picked up one and rolled the smooth metal between his fingers.

"Dina, this one is for you," he whispered. He kissed the cartridge and slotted it into the breech. The first shot to break the glass, the second for the President's chest. If there was time, a third. It would be the greatest achievement of his life: the assassination of the President of the United States. The IRA might take the blame, but the credit would be his. His heart thudded and he took a deep breath to steady his nerves. He had to banish all anxiety from his mind, he had to focus on the target, not the man. In the distance, he heard a deep, throaty voice begin to sing the National Anthem.

Patrick Farrell scanned the instrument panel and turned the blimp's nose slightly to the left. He looked at the altimeter. They were four hundred feet above the ground and Farrell was trying to put the airship in exactly the right position. He was using the GPS, VOR and DME equipment as primary navigation aids, but the final adjustment would have to be done visually by Bailey using the laser sight. During rehearsals earlier in the year they'd pinpointed an intersection of an alley and a road which was exactly two thousand yards from the pitcher's mound. If the airship was directly above the intersection, it was in the perfect position for Lovell's shot. Farrell was nudging the airship over the school, making small, precise corrections of the control wheel and rudders. He looked at the reading of the wind computer. Once he had the blimp stationary in the air, using the twin engines to hold it steady, he would be able to read the wind speed and direction and relay it to the snipers in time for them to make their wind corrections.

"Almost there," said Farrell in his headset. "I'll tune the radio to the general frequency."

Bailey looked over his shoulder and nodded as Farrell turned the dial to the frequency the snipers were using. Lovell was kneeling by the open window, his eye pressed to the scope of his rifle. He was as still as a stone statue, and Bailey could barely see the man's chest rise and fall as he breathed. Behind Bailey, a pool of blood was slowly spreading out from under the two corpses. He put his eye to the telescopic sight. Down below he could see the small red dot of the laser dancing on the roof of a black Cadillac. The alley was to the left of the dot and Bailey began calling out instructions to Farrell, guiding him slowly to the exact spot where Lovell would make his shot.

* * *

Marty Edberg clenched his knuckles and glared at the television monitor. The shot of the giant scoreboard was wavering as if the man operating the camera had Parkinson's Disease.

"Wendy," he said through gritted teeth, "tell Lonnie to get a grip on himself, will you? Tell him if he can't give me a steady shot I'll come out there and rip his throat out with my bare hands."

Edberg's assistant spoke quietly into her microphone and the picture on the monitor steadied.

"Thank you," said Edberg. On the main monitor, a bulky, cowboy-hatted country and western singer was putting every ounce of effort into his rendition of the Star Spangled Banner, and the picture was so sharp that Edberg could see the tears welling up in the man's eyes.

"Wendy, get me a close-up of the flag, and then we'll superimpose the singer on it," he said. His assistant spoke quickly to one of the cameramen and monitor number three soon had a tight shot of a fluttering Stars and Stripes. She moved one of the sliders and slowly brought up the flag on the main monitor so that it rippled like a ghost behind the singer. "Good," said Edberg approvingly.

The light on the phone in front of Wendy blinked and she picked it up. After listening for a few moments she handed the receiver over to Edberg. "It's the Secret Service guy, he wants to know why we don't have the airship pictures yet."

Edberg looked at monitor ten. The screen was still blank. "Tell him I'd like to know the reason, too," said Edberg. "Tell him we can't reach the blimp, we're assuming they're having technical problems."

Wendy relayed the message, then covered the mouthpiece with her hand. "He says he wants to speak to you, Marty."

Edberg glared at her. "Explain to Dick Tracy that we're in the middle of putting out pictures that are being watched by millions of people, and that I'll call him when I get the time. Just now, I'm busy."

His long-suffering assistant nodded. Edberg glared at the ranks of monitors. The shot of the score board was wavering again. Edberg put his head in his hands.

Cole Howard and Don Clutesi had moved to the far wall of the sky box as the President and First Lady made small-talk with the Prime Minister. As soon as the National Anthem began everybody stood to attention and faced the diamond, knowing that it was a photo opportunity that would have all the newspaper and television cameras pointing their way. Everyone looked appropriately sombre, with the exception of the Secret Service agents, who continued to prowl around their charges. Bob Sanger stood two steps behind the President. Through his earpiece, Howard heard situation reports being called in from around the stadium.

Howard saw Joker come out of the tunnel and stop dead at the edge of the diamond as if he'd just realised that everyone in the stadium was standing stock still out of respect. Howard smiled at the man's appalling plaid jacket. He looked across at Clutesi who was also grinning. Clutesi shrugged and Howard shook his head admonishingly. Howard saw that Joker was carrying a can of Budweiser and he groaned inwardly.

Howard surveyed the presidential party. The Prime Minister's own security team seemed far more relaxed than the Secret Service agents. He wondered when they had last had to deal with an assassination attempt. He recalled the IRA attempt to hit Number 10 Downing Street with mortars and the bombing of a hotel during a Conservative Party conference, but assassinations with firearms seemed rare in Britain. Maybe it was something to do with the fact that gun ownership was restricted there or that the people had more respect for their authority figures than the Americans had for their President. On television, he'd seen British politicians and members of the British Royal Family moving through crowds, seemingly at ease, with little in the way of security. At sports events, too, they generally got much closer to the public than the President ever did, closer even than American movie stars got to their fans.

Howard frowned as he stared at the pitcher's mound. He pulled his cellular phone out of his pocket and whispered to Clutesi that he was going out in the hallway. Clutesi had his hand over his heart as the anthem played.

Howard nodded to two Secret Service agents standing guard in the corridor, and moved away from them so that they couldn't eavesdrop. He tapped out Andy Kim's number in the White House and it was answered on the third ring by Bonnie Kim. She was surprised, and apparently delighted, to hear from him. He asked if her husband was there and she passed the telephone over to him.

"Andy, do me a favour. Can you call up the Baltimore ballpark and tell me what effect it would have if the target was on the pitcher's mound," said Howard.

"But I thought the President was in the sky box?" queried Andy.

"I know, I know, but I've just found out that the Prime

Minister is throwing the first pitch, down on the mound. Try it for me, will you?"

"Sure, Cole, sure. Kelly Armstrong sent me a copy of the Prime Minister's agenda but there's nothing on it about him being on the mound or I'd have done it already. It'll take a few minutes. Do you want me to call you back?"

"No, I'll hold on." Howard heard the National Anthem come to an end, and then in his earpiece he heard the Secret Service preparing to escort the Prime Minister and the First Lady down to the diamond where the manager of the Orioles was to present him with the game ball. "And Andy, please hurry."

Patrick Farrell looked down and made a slight adjustment to the power and turned the nose of the airship into the wind. The movement resulted in a sideways drift and he looked down and tried to line up with the corner of the road and the alley by following Bailey's terse instructions.

"Good, that's good," said Bailey through his headset. "Six feet more." On the ground below the airship, the small red dot moved inexorably towards the alley. Bailey lifted his head and saw Lovell still with the rifle to his cheek. Bailey wanted some sign from the sniper that everything was okay, but Lovell ignored him.

Bailey looked down through the scope again. The red dot was slowly moving across the pavement. "Steady," he said.

Farrell eased off on the power to the engines. The GPS display hadn't changed for some time, an indication of

Farrell's skill at manoeuvring the airship, but it was only accurate to fifty feet or so. The rest was up to Bailey.

"That's it, perfect," said Bailey. Farrell wiped the back of his arm across his forehead and it came away damp. In the distance, the pilot could see Secret Service agents gathering around the pitcher's mound.

Joker took a long pull at his can of Budweiser. It was too warm for his taste but he needed the alcohol rather than the refreshment. One of the Secret Service agents stared at him and looked as if he was about to say something, but Joker pointed to the ID hanging around his neck. Joker drained the can and tossed it behind him. The crowd roared and cheered as the Country and Western singer finished his rendition of the National Anthem. In Joker's ear a buzzing voice told him that Parliament was making his way down from the sky box. The agents around the mound visibly tensed.

Joker put his binoculars to his eyes and began scanning the crowds. He wanted to get Mary Hennessy so badly that he could almost taste it. He raised the binoculars higher and winced as it put his injured shoulder under strain. He was hot and the bullet-proof vest was a torture to wear. He considered taking it off because it covered such a small area of his body. He doubted that the limited protection it offered was worth the discomfort.

* * *

Cole Howard kept his cellular phone pressed to his left ear. The constant Secret Service transmissions in his right ear were irritating, but he knew they were necessary so he didn't remove the earpiece. He heard Sanger calling ahead that Parliament was leaving the sky box and he flattened himself against the wall of the corridor so that he wouldn't be in the way when the entourage went by on the way to the escalator.

Two agents came out of the sky box, looked up and down, and then headed towards him. Another two agents followed, and then Howard saw the Prime Minister and the First Lady. The Prime Minister walked slowly, a half step behind the First Lady, and he had a worried frown as if he was dreading the forthcoming pitch. Howard wanted to tell him that throwing the first pitch was a rare honour, one that most baseball fans would die for. The Prime Minister looked at him and Howard smiled, wanting to show some support, but the FBI agent's gesture was ignored and the Prime Minister's face remained a stone mask. Howard felt stupid, standing there with an inane grin on his face, and he turned the smile into a face-stretching exercise as if his eyes were itching.

"Cole?" It was Andy Kim on the phone.

"Yes, Andy?"

"Okay, this is a rough calculation, but I reckon that so far as the buildings nearest the ballpark are concerned, that's the Marriott Hotel and the Holiday Inn and the offices nearby, you'd be looking at two floors lower if they were aiming at the pitcher's mound. For the buildings a mile or so away you'd drop about four floors. Is that any help?"

"Yeah, thanks Andy. One more thing – does dropping

the target to the mound mean you get a match for the long shot?"

"Afraid not, Cole, There's still nothing anywhere near that position."

"Okay, thanks. I've got to go, I'll call you later."

Howard switched the phone off and went back to the sky box. Sanger was standing by the door. He nodded at Howard.

"Everything okay?" Sanger asked. "I see you've let the Brit off his leash. You know he's drinking?"

"You've got men in all the buildings overlooking the ballpark, right?" said Howard, ignoring the dig at Cramer.

"Sure, we did full searches and now they're on the floors that Kim recommended." Sanger's brow wrinkled. "Is there a problem?"

"It's not a problem, more a hunch. What if it's the Prime Minister who's the target and not the President?"

"We sent the details to Kim," said Sanger. "They're together all the time, so it wouldn't . . ." Realisation dawned. "Except for when he's on the mound."

Howard nodded. "Kim says he didn't know the Prime Minister would be there – he was assuming they were together all the time they were in the stadium. The difference is equivalent to two floors in the buildings within a half mile or so, four floors if they're a mile away . . ."

Sanger held up his hand to silence Howard and put his radio to his mouth. He began to call up his agents, speaking quickly and urgently.

* * *

523

Joker put down his binoculars and wiped his forehead with
the arm of his jacket. Sweat was pouring off his face and his
upper body was soaking wet under the vest. He desperately
wanted another beer.

"Parliament is in the tunnel," said a voice in his ear and
he instinctively looked towards the entrance where British
bodyguards were standing at attention. A gust of wind
lifted the jacket of one and Joker saw an MP5K Heckler &
Koch hanging from a sling in the small of his back. Joker
looked at the gun. It was a shorter barrelled version of the
submachine gun he'd used during his time with the SAS.
The wind dropped and the jacket fell back into place,
concealing the gun once more. He wiped his forehead again
and put the binoculars back to his eyes and scanned the
stands. He saw parents with children, young couples, old
men and teenagers, almost everyone wearing shirts or caps
with the Oriole bird logo. Most were eating or drinking, and
vendors ran up and down the aisles selling beer, popcorn,
burgers and soft drinks.

The stadium was all seating and was better organised
than any sports event he'd ever seen in Britain. He
remembered the Old Firm soccer matches he'd gone to in
Glasgow, Celtic versus Rangers, where the aggression on
the pitch unfailingly spilled over to violence on the
terraces. The animosity among the spectators was
compounded by the fact that Roman Catholics supported
Celtic and the Protestants backed Rangers, and the taunts
that were yelled back and forth had as much to do with
religion as they did with soccer. Compared with that, the
ballpark was a night at the opera.

A female usher flashed through Joker's field of vision
and then was gone, but something made the hairs on the

back of his neck stand on end and he panned the binoculars back, searching for her. He found her. She had red hair and glasses and was wearing what looked like an official uniform, but it was Mary Hennessy, he was sure of it. She was leaning against a metal barrier and staring down at the baseball diamond, a faraway smile on her face. Joker reached for his two-way radio and pressed the transmit button.

Mary stood at the front of the middle aisle on the second-level stand looking down on third base. She turned around, making sure that there were no other ushers nearby. So long as she didn't get too close, no one would realise she wasn't a regular member of the ballpark staff. According to the map Kelly Armstrong had given her, there were no undercover FBI agents nearby. At the top of the aisle she saw Kelly but she deliberately avoided eye contact. Mary wasn't sure exactly what Kelly thought she would achieve by being present, but she'd said that she wanted to be close by, to watch and, if necessary, to help.

Mary turned and saw the Prime Minister walk to the centre of the mound, holding the game ball as if not sure what to do with it. His security men were standing to the side, scanning the faces of the spectators, alert for any threatening signs, and beyond them were the agents of the Secret Service. The First Lady stood at the side of the mound, some twenty feet or so from the Prime Minister. Mary smiled. She wished there were some way she could tell the Prime Minister what was going to happen, so that she could see the fear in his face. In a fantasy that made her head spin she imagined shouting to him just before the bullets struck, telling him that he was going to die and cursing him as his chest exploded.

She bent her neck and put her chin down close to the microphone. The transceiver was clipped to the belt of her trousers in plain view. Many of the genuine ushers carried radios and it added rather than detracted from her authenticity.

"Check One," she said, pressing the earpiece into her ear to cut out some of the crowd noise.

"Check One," she heard. It was Lovell's voice.

"Check Two," said Mary.

"Check Two," said Schoelen.

"Check Three," said Mary.

"Check Three," said Carlos.

"Check Wind," she said.

There was a pause then she heard Farrell's voice. "One Nine Seven at Three," he said. Mary's heart lifted. The wind was negligible.

"One Nine Seven at Three," repeated Lovell.

"One Nine Seven at Three," said Schoelen.

"One Nine Seven at Three," said Carlos.

"With you, One," said Mary. Now it was up to Lovell. Mary leant against the metal barrier and watched the Prime Minister prepare to throw the ball. She frowned as she saw a man in a plaid jacket and jeans who was looking in her direction through binoculars. He didn't look like the rest of the Secret Service agents or the members of the British security contingent and Mary squinted, trying to get a better look at the stranger.

*　*　*

Rich Lovell centred the cross-hairs of his telescopic sight over the centre of the Prime Minister's chest. Lovell exhaled slowly, as he focused his entire being on the shot. In Lovell's mind the Prime Minister was no longer a man. He was a target, nothing more.

The Prime Minister took a step to the side and Lovell moved the rifle to keep him centred. Four seconds was a long time and Lovell had to be totally certain that the target wouldn't move while the bullet was in flight. The fact that there would be two more chances, two more snipers, didn't affect Lovell's judgment. He wanted his bullet to be the one that did the damage. He inhaled tidally, taking in just enough air for his body's needs. There had to be no excessive movement. He had long ago tuned out the vibration and noise of the two engines at the rear of the airship. Even though Bailey was crouched only feet behind him, in Lovell's mind he no longer existed. The heat and humidity were no longer factors. All that mattered was the target and the four seconds between it and the barrel of the Barrett 82Al.

"Do you see her?" asked the spotter. He had his binoculars fixed on Mary Hennessy, across the stadium.

"Got her," said the sniper. He was kneeling down with his Sauer Model 200 hunting rifle resting against the parapet around the roof of the office building adjacent to the ballpark. It was an expensive weapon, and the sniper had bought it from a sergeant who had retired from the Baltimore SWAT unit. It was a .308 Winchester calibre and with hand-loaded factory ammunition it could easily achieve 1/2 MOA. The woman was about three hundred yards away.

The spotter spoke into his walkie-talkie. "We have a clear shot," he said.

"Hold for green light," said the SWAT team commander.

The Sauer had a three-round magazine, but the sniper knew he would need only one shot. He was using soft-point bullets and they would rip a human chest apart. He nestled the cross-hairs in the woman's cleavage.

The man in the plaid jacket continued to scrutinise her through his binoculars, and Mary Hennessy instinctively knew something had gone wrong. She turned and looked up the aisle. There were two men standing just behind Kelly Armstrong, men in dark suits and sunglasses. They hadn't been there five minutes earlier. She looked to her left and saw two more Secret Service agents, moving down the aisle parallel to her.

Her heart began to race. She whirled around and looked at the pitcher's mound. The Prime Minister was preparing to throw the ball, the catcher squatting down and holding out a gloved hand.

She looked over her shoulder. The two men were moving down the stairs towards her, their hands moving inside their jackets.

"Sniper One, fire now," she said into the microphone. "Shoot the bastard now, damn you!"

There was no reply and she realised that the microphone wasn't working. She must have pulled it out of the socket of the transceiver when she turned. She reached behind her for the loose wire.

Kelly saw Mary Hennessy fumble for something at her waist. Something had alarmed her, and then Kelly realised what it was. Two men in suits and dark glasses were moving down the aisle parallel to her. Secret Service agents.

Kelly frowned, not sure what to do. "There she is," said a voice behind her, and she whirled around. There were two more agents behind her, one young and one middle-aged, so similar that they could have been father and son.

"Excuse me, miss," said the older agent, moving to get by her.

Kelly pulled out her FBI credentials and identified herself.

"Please let us by, miss, we'll handle this," said the younger agent. He put a hand on her arm and tried to move her. Kelly resisted.

"What's happening?" she said, wanting to give Mary every second she could.

"She's reaching for something, possibly a weapon," the spotter spoke into his walkie-talkie. Through the binoculars he saw the female usher groping behind her back. Up above her, moving down the aisle past a blonde woman, were two Secret Service agents. One of them had a pistol in his hand.

"You have a green light," replied the SWAT commander, "so long as there is no possibility of collateral damage."

The spotter could see that there was no one directly behind the woman. There were spectators on her left and right, but not close enough to be in the way. "Green light confirmed," he said. The spotter took the walkie-talkie away from his mouth. "Shoot the bitch," he said.

"It'll be a pleasure," said the sniper, his finger tightening on the trigger.

Todd Otterman stood in the corridor while the two agents from the FBI Academy ran the fibre optic lens under the office door. Many of the businesses in the tower block had agreed to hand over keys to the Secret Service for the duration of the presidential visit, but some of the smaller offices hadn't been contacted.

One of the FBI rookies was kneeling down and threading the cable through the gap, while his colleague looked at a small black and white monitor. The camera was one the FBI used for surveillance and it was perfect for checking those offices which were locked. Otterman and the rookies had been on the seventh floor in a travel agency whose manager had agreed to open his office late so that the agents could have a comfortable base while the game was on. They'd just been about to start drinking coffee when the call had come in to recheck the offices on the lower floors. Otterman and his two rookies had taken the fifth floor, another agent had gone to the sixth floor.

The agent scrutinising the monitor suddenly stiffened. He put a hand on his colleague's shoulder and shook him. Otterman went over and looked at the monitor. The picture was fuzzy but there was no mistaking the figure of a man kneeling in front of a desk, his eye pressed to a telescopic sight. Otterman could see that the man was preparing to fire – there was no time to call for back-up. He slid his automatic from its leather shoulder holster and signalled for the two rookies to stand to the side.

Joker watched the two Secret Service agents head down the aisle towards Mary Hennessy, and saw her fumble for whatever it was that was hanging from her belt. He heard one of the agents reporting that she was reaching for something and then he heard another voice giving instructions to a sniper. Off to his right he heard the crack of a high velocity round and then Hennessy staggered back, one hand clutching at her chest. A red stain appeared on her usher's shirt, and it reminded him of his days in the paintball arena in London. It was a perfect hit. This was different, though, and he knew Hennessy wouldn't be getting to her feet and complaining about being taken out of the game.

She fell back and sat down heavily on the stairs. Joker could see that her eyes were wide open as if surprised, and the hand on her chest was twitching spasmodically. A blonde woman in a blue jacket rushed by the agents and knelt at her side.

Joker panned across to the office blocks, trying to see where the sniper was. It had been a good, clean shot. As he scanned the sky something passed across his vision, something large and white with the name of a Japanese electronics company on the side. It was so unexpected that Joker thought that he'd seen an advertising hoarding at the far end of the stadium, but then he saw wispy white clouds and knew that he was still looking up high, above the buildings. He took the binoculars away from his face and shaded his eyes with his free hand, gritting his teeth as pain from his shoulder lanced across his back. It was an airship, hanging in the sky more than a mile away. He frowned as he remembered what Cole Howard had told him about the long shot, the sniper who was planning to shoot the President from two thousand yards away, and how there was nowhere the sniper could make the shot from in Baltimore.

He let the binoculars hang on their strap around his neck and spoke into the radio again. His earpiece was buzzing with agents calling in situation reports following the shooting of Mary Hennessy. "Howard, are you there?" he asked, interrupting the agents.

"Is that you, Cramer?" It was Howard's voice.

"Yeah. Have you seen the blimp?"

"Blimp?"

"The blimp. The airship. Over the city."

* * *

Todd Otterman thought about trying to kick in the door but dismissed the idea. There was no way of telling how strong it was, and the door was certain to be locked. He had two advantages: he had surprise on his side and he had a handgun. The sniper would have to swing his rifle through almost one hundred and eighty degrees to get a shot at the door. Otterman was breathing heavily and he could see that the two rookies were trembling. He motioned with his free hand that he was going to shoot out the lock, and that the two Academy rookies were to kick the door, then move out of the way.

They nodded and watched as Otterman mouthed a quick count: Three, Two, One, then fired at the lock. The metal screeched and the wood splintered and immediately the two rookies kicked at the door, close to the lock. The door flew inwards and Otterman stepped across the threshold, the gun held firmly in both hands.

"Secret Service!" he yelled. "Drop the weapon!"

The sniper began to turn and made no attempt to release his grip on the rifle. There was no way the Secret Service agent was going to take a chance with the President's life. He shot the sniper twice in the back.

Carlos centred his telescopic sight on the President's chest as he looked through the window of the sky box. He steadied his breathing. It would be so easy to pull the trigger without waiting for Lovell. He had a clear shot and the President was standing stock still, his eyes on the Prime Minister far below. Carlos was the closest sniper to the target and his bullet would take less than a second to blow the man apart. The difference in drop between the target on the pitcher's mound and the sky box would be minimal. It would be so simple to fire now. The anticipation was almost painful. He smiled to himself and blocked such reckless thoughts out of his mind. He had to stick to the plan. His plan.

Carlos was ready. He'd compensated for the wind drift based on the figures Farrell had given him, and he had already made allowance for the fact that it had been Dina Rashid and not himself who had calibrated the scope.

He heard something move in the corridor outside but he blocked out the noise. He had to be totally focused on the target. Nothing else mattered.

Lovell's voice in his ear almost caught him by surprise. "Target sighted," said the laconic West Virginian accent. "Countdown starting. Five . . . four . . ."

Joker looked across the field at the pitcher's mound, which was about thirty yards away from where he was standing. Secret Service chatter filled his ear again. The Prime Minister was drawing back his hand to throw, amid good-natured catcalls and whistles from the crowd. The First Lady was preparing to applaud. The Secret Service agents and the Prime Minister's own bodyguards were all concentrating on the crowd. None of them was looking at the airship. A chill ran down Joker's spine. He pressed the binoculars to his eyes and focused them on the gondola below the blimp. His hands were shaking and he fought to keep them steady.

The door of the gondola came into sharp focus. He was looking at a logo of a hawk and a propeller. The logo of Farrell Aviation. "Jesus Christ," said Joker, under his breath. He panned to the right and up and he saw a bearded man at the open window sighting down a rifle. Joker began to tremble. He wanted to shout a warning but he doubted that he'd be heard above the noise of the crowd. His mind was in a whirl as he tried to decide what his next step should be, then he saw the muzzle flash and in an ice-cold moment of clarity he knew what he had to do. He dropped the binoculars and began to run. Four seconds was all he had. Joker began to silently count them off. One thousand and one . . .

Carlos felt his heart race, like an engine out of control. He had the President dead centre in his telescopic sight and his finger tensed on the trigger as Lovell continued his countdown. It was an awesome feeling, knowing that Lovell's bullet was already in the air, hurtling towards its target at more than two thousand feet per second. In his ear he heard Lovell count: "One thousand and . . ."

To his horror, Carlos heard a key being inserted into the lock of the door to his room. It was followed by the whisper of the door against the carpet and Carlos knew that he had only seconds to react. A hotel employee would have knocked, it could only be the police or the Secret Service, and if he stayed at the window they'd shoot him in the back. The SEAL's bullet was on the way and Schoelen's would follow shortly. Carlos knew he couldn't wait. He squeezed the trigger and the sound of the shot echoed around the hotel room. He sensed a gun being aimed at his back and knew that if he didn't move he'd be dead. He dropped the rifle, grabbed the P228 from the table and rolled off the chair, firing twice at the doorway before he'd even looked to see who was there.

He continued to roll across the carpet, the gun coughing twice more, until he banged into the sofa. He brought up the gun, preparing to fire again. There was no need. There was only one person in the doorway, a tall, thin man in his late thirties who was sinking to his knees, blood streaming from his neck and chest. He was holding a Glock automatic, unfired. In his ear, Carlos heard: "One thousand and two . . ."

Carlos scrambled to his feet and pulled the body of the dead agent into the room. It left a smear of glistening blood on the carpet. He dumped the body by the bed, kicked the door shut and raced back to the open window.

Cole Howard watched Joker sprint across the diamond, towards the mound. "What the fuck's he up to?" asked Clutesi.

"Something to do with the airship," said Howard. Both men heard a Secret Service agent report that he'd just killed a sniper in an office block overlooking the stadium. Clutesi's jaw dropped. "It's happening," he said in disbelief.

The sky-box window exploded in a shower of glass. The guests began screaming as Secret Service agents rushed forward to protect the President. Clutesi's eyes were wide and he looked at Howard for guidance. Bob Sanger could be heard shouting above the screams and weapons appeared as if by magic in the hands of the agents as they surrounded the President. They hustled him away from the window, several positioning themselves between his body and the outside.

A warm wind blew in through the shattered window, and down below Howard could see Joker continuing to run, his plaid jacket flapping behind him. To Howard it appeared as if the man was running in slow motion. Howard looked up and squinted at the airship hanging over the city. His mind flashed back to Andy Kim's computer model. The long shot. "The airship," he whispered. "There's a sniper in the airship."

On the mound, the ball left the Prime Minister's hand.

Kelly cradled Mary's head in her lap. Mary's eyes were wide open but they didn't seem to be focusing. Blood was bubbling from a fist-sized hole in her chest. Kelly felt a hand on her shoulder and she looked up at the two Secret Service agents.

"Leave her alone," she spat. "Can't you see she's dead?"

Mary's hand clutched at Kelly's arm and the fingers gripped tight. Her mouth moved soundlessly, her eyes still unseeing. Kelly bent forward and put her ear close to Mary's lips.

* * *

Joker continued to count in his head as he ran. Individual, disparate images filled his head: a Secret Service agent, his mouth wide open, staring up at the sky box, a finger against his earpiece; the catcher, reaching out with his gloved hand, smiling behind his mask; the Prime Minister, looking ill at ease, his hair untidy from the effort of pitching; the First Lady, a wide smile on her face. Two thousand yards. Four seconds. An almost impossible shot under normal circumstances, but according to Howard they were up against a sniper who could pull it off. He heard glass smash somewhere behind him, somewhere high. Joker's heart felt as if it was bursting and his ankles were screaming in agony as they pounded into the ground. There was no time to shout a warning, no time to explain what was happening, There was only one thing he could do. One thousand and two . . .

Cole Howard dashed over to Bob Sanger and grabbed his shoulder. "The Prime Minister's a target, too. It's a double hit!" he shouted. Howard's spittle peppered the Secret Service agent's face.

For a second, Sanger was too surprised to react, but then the words sank in and he reached for his radio. "Get Parliament off the mound!" he ordered. "Now." The Secret Service agents had completely surrounded the President and were hustling him out of the sky box, their weapons held high.

Howard looked down at the diamond. The only man who was reacting was Joker.

* * *

As he hurtled towards the mound, Joker heard a call over the radio to get the Prime Minister out of the way, but knew that it would take seconds for his bodyguards to react. The ball thwacked into the catcher's glove and the Prime Minister raised a hand, acknowledging the cheers of the crowds. One of the Secret Service agents had turned towards Joker, his mouth open, and his hand inside his jacket. Joker didn't break his stride, he stuck out his arm and hit the man in the throat, hard enough to push him out of the way but not hard enough to kill him. The movement jolted his injured shoulder and Joker grunted. In his mind the count continued. One thousand and three . . . The Prime Minister was about twelve feet away, his hand in the air and his back to Joker.

Several of the bodyguards began to move towards the Prime Minister, but they were all further away than Joker. Joker could taste blood on his lips and he could feel that the wound on his chest had reopened. He looked up at the blimp, calculating the angle, knowing that the bullet was well over halfway to its target and knowing that there was only one thing he could do. He leapt into the air, throwing himself at the Prime Minister's back. Faces flashed by, two Secret Service agents groping for him with their hands outstretched, and Joker twisted in the air, screaming from the pain and because he wanted to block out the thinking part of his brain, the part which knew what was going to happen and which might try to flinch at the last second. Joker knew that the strongest part of the bullet-proof vest was the front and if he was to survive the impact he'd have to get his chest between the bullet and the Prime Minister. He screamed like an animal in pain, his arms out for

539

balance, his chest up, waiting for the explosion. One thousand and four . . .

Carlos swung his rifle, trying to pick up the sky box in the telescopic sight. The green playing surface flashed by, then a base, then the legs of running Secret Service agents. He trained the sight up and picked out the presidential sky box. The glass had shattered and he saw figures inside, but he couldn't see the President. He was too late. He cursed and trained the rifle back on the mound. There was a figure lying there, but it wasn't the Prime Minister. The man motionless on the ground was wearing a plaid jacket. Carlos took the scope away from his eye so that he could get an overall view of the diamond. The high magnification of the telescopic sight was fine for sniping, but its field of vision was far too narrow for general viewing.

Carlos blinked several times, trying to refocus his eyes. He saw the man in the plaid jacket spread-eagled on the mound, a Secret Service agent kneeling by his side. More agents were surrounding the First Lady, guns drawn, looking around to see where the shot had come from. The Prime Minister, surrounded by bodyguards, was being hustled to the tunnel. Carlos put the rifle back to his shoulder and aimed at the tunnel, hoping that he'd be able to get a clear shot. He found the group with his scope but he couldn't pick out the Prime Minister. Carlos put down his rifle. "Mary, what's happening?" he said into the microphone on his lapel. There was no reply. "Mary?" Still nothing.

"Sniper Three, is that you?" asked Lovell. "What's happening?"

Cole Howard gasped as he saw Joker leap and throw himself at the Prime Minister. His first thought was that the Brit was trying to tackle the man and bring him down, but at the last moment he twisted, like a high jumper going over backwards. Howard saw his arms flail out, then his whole body convulsed as if he'd received an electric shock.

Howard looked over at Bob Sanger, who was still talking into his walkie-talkie. He turned to Don Clutesi, who was staring open-mouthed at the diamond, where the Prime Minister was being engulfed by bodyguards. One of the Secret Service agents, a gun in his hand, knelt over Joker and opened his shirt collar. Howard gripped Clutesi's arm. "I'm going down," Howard said urgently. "Tell Sanger to get a chopper to pick me up."

"A chopper?" said Clutesi. "Why?"

"Just do it, Don," said Howard. He ran to the door, throwing his binoculars to the ground.

Rich Lovell had the back of a head in his sights, but he had no way of knowing whether or not it was the Prime Minister. Carlos had told him to keep firing, but Lovell knew it was useless. His target was four seconds away, and running from him. Even if the Prime Minister hadn't been surrounded by bodyguards, there was no way he could predict where anyone would be four seconds into the future.

"What's happening?" screamed Matthew Bailey as he squatted by the laser sight.

"I missed," said Lovell. "I don't know how, but I missed."

"What do you mean, you missed?"

Lovell looked up. "I had him in my sights, and I fired, and then at the last moment someone got in the way."

"You mean one of his bodyguards walked into the bullet?"

Lovell shook his head. "No, some guy threw himself at the Prime Minister. The bullet got him in the chest, dead centre. Now everyone's running off the field. I can't get a clear shot." He put his rifle back to his shoulder. The bodyguards had disappeared into the safety of the tunnel.

"Can you fire again?" Bailey asked.

"No," said Lovell.

"What about Carlos and Schoelen? Have they fired?"

"I don't know," said Lovell.

Patrick Farrell looked anxiously over at Bailey. "What do we do?"

"We keep calm for a start," said Bailey. "No one will know the shot came from the airship. Just take us back to the airfield." He got to his feet and headed back to the co-pilot's seat. "Keep talking to air-traffic control, tell them we've a problem with the camera and that we're heading back."

As Farrell put the blimp in a slow left turn, Bailey spoke into his radio microphone, a worried frown on his face. "M-M-Mary, are you there? M-M-Mary?" There was no reply.

The words came out slowly and Kelly had to strain to hear. "Did we get him?" asked Mary, her grip tightening on Kelly's arm.

Kelly looked down at the baseball diamond. The First Lady was being ushered to the tunnel, surrounded by armed Secret Service agents. A helicopter thundered overhead, its rotor wash tugging at their suits. More agents were pushing the Prime Minister into the darkness of the tunnel, out of danger.

Kelly cradled Mary's head in her lap. The blood had stopped bubbling from her chest, replaced with a pink froth. "Yes," Kelly whispered.

"You're sure?" gasped Mary, her eyelids fluttering.

Kelly saw the Prime Minister disappear into the safety of the tunnel. "Yes," she lied, "I'm sure."

Kelly felt Mary shiver and then relax. Blood dribbled from the corner of Mary's mouth and down her neck.

Cole Howard ran out of the sky box, past the President and his entourage of Secret Service agents amid a forest of Uzis and Heckler & Koch submachine guns.

He took the escalator, jumping the stairs four at a time. On the ground level he saw the Prime Minister and his security team heading in his direction and Howard unclipped his FBI badge from the breast pocket of his suit and held it aloft. "FBI!" he yelled, to make sure that there would be no confusion. The American and British bodyguards were all edgy, with their fingers inside the trigger guards of their weapons, and the Prime Minister appeared to be in a state of shock. An older Secret Service agent, a Uzi held aloft, was screaming at them to move faster and looking over his shoulder as if he expected to see pursuers.

Howard sprinted down the tunnel, shouting all the way that he was with the FBI. He had to squeeze by the First Lady and her bodyguards before he burst out of the confined space and into the huge stadium. He heard a public announcement reverberating around the arena, calling for everyone to remain calm. Howard could see spectators streaming towards the exits while others were standing in shock. Howard looked up. In the distance he could see the airship turning and heading away from the city. A deafening beating sound filled his ears and he tilted back his head. Directly overhead was a National Guard Huey helicopter, coming in to land. The downbeat of the rotors sent dust and sand whirling around Howard, stinging his eyes and making it hard to breathe. He ducked his head and put a hand over his mouth as the helicopter went by and landed about fifty yards away.

When he looked up the Huey was on the ground, its rotors still turning. Howard jogged towards it, bent double at the waist. Hands grabbed for him and half pulled, half dragged him inside and almost immediately the rotors speeded up and the Huey leapt back into the air.

* * *

Carlos pushed the maid's trolley to one side and checked himself in the bathroom mirror. Satisfied that there was no blood on his face or clothes, he picked up his briefcase, stepped over the body of the dead Secret Service agent, and let himself out of the room. In the elevator a pretty brunette with a name badge identifying her as an assistant manager smiled and asked if he was enjoying his stay.

Carlos returned her smile and nodded. "It's a fine hotel," he said. When the elevator arrived at the ground floor she held the door open for him and allowed him out first, wishing him a good day. They were always so polite, the Americans, thought Carlos as he left the hotel, swinging the briefcase. Overhead, a National Guard helicopter was climbing into the air.

Cole Howard yelled at the pilot to head for the airship, but his voice was lost in the roar of the turbine. A crewman in an olive flightsuit handed him a headset and showed him how to operate the microphone switch. Through the intercom system Howard explained that there was a sniper on board the airship.

In the back of the Huey with Howard were the National Guard crewman, a hard-faced Secret Service agent in a dark grey suit and ubiquitous sunglasses and a SWAT sniper in black overalls.

"What's the plan, can we shoot the blimp down?" asked the agent.

"Wouldn't it explode?" the crewman cut in. "Aren't they full of inflammable gas or something?"

"You're thinking of the Hindenberg; back then they were full of hydrogen," said the pilot. "These days they use other gases that don't burn."

"So we can shoot holes in it?" asked the sniper.

"I guess so," said Howard. The Huey was climbing rapidly and his stomach turned over. He took deep breaths, trying to quell his unease.

"I dunno about that," said the pilot. "Look at the size of it, it's as big as a whale. You could put a hundred holes in it and it'd still stay up for hours."

The Secret Service agent had his fingers pressed to his earpiece. "They tried to shoot the President," he yelled.

"He's okay, I saw him," shouted Howard.

"You sure?" said the agent.

"Really," said Howard. "Your guys got him out safely. He's okay." The agent looked relieved. Howard turned to the SWAT sniper. "What about the engines? Could you put a bullet in the engines?"

"I could try, but this isn't the steadiest of shooting platforms," said the sniper. "We'd have to get really close. And the closer we get the better a target we are for the guy on board. You've got to remember he isn't being shaken around as much as we are."

Howard nodded. He patted the pilot on the back. "Can you call up the other helicopters, get them to hover nearby?" he asked.

"Sure," said the pilot.

"Tell them there's a sniper on board, so they'll have to stay above it."

"Okay," said the pilot. Over the headset, Howard heard him giving instructions to the other helicopter pilots.

Howard looked around the cargo compartment. Behind

the crew member was a winch and a bright orange harness. Howard pointed at the weapon hanging from a sling under the Secret Service agent's jacket. "What are you carrying?" he asked.

"Uzi," said the agent.

Howard nodded. "I think I've got an idea," he said, slipping off his jacket.

"There's a helicopter heading this way," shouted Rich Lovell, pulling the barrel of his rifle inside the gondola and squatting on the floor.

"They can't know we're involved," said Bailey. "Just stay down out of sight. We'll be okay."

Lovell's right foot was sticking into the neck of the bearded cameraman and he pulled it away with a look of disgust on his face.

"What do we do?" asked Farrell.

"We keep on our present course all the way back to the airfield," said Bailey. "We land this thing, we tie you up, Rich and I drive to Bay Bridge. You tell them we hijacked the blimp and killed the camera crew because they put up a struggle. We fly off into the sunset."

"Maybe I should come with you; I'm starting to get a bad feeling about this."

"Whatever you want," said Bailey. With Dina Rashid dead, there would be an extra seat on the Centurion. "But they've nothing on you. All you have to do is to stick to your story. Tell them there was a gun on you every step of the way."

Farrell shook his head. "I don't think so," he said.

"There's another chopper coming our way," said Lovell. From where he was squatting he saw a two-seater Robinson R-22 police helicopter through the opposite window. "It's only a spotter but it's definitely after us."

"What do we do now?" asked Farrell, his voice unsteady in Bailey's headset.

Bailey wracked his brains. What would Mary do? "A spotter chopper isn't going to do us any harm," he said.

"But it can follow us until we land," said Farrell.

Lovell sneaked a look through the window above his head. "Shit, now there's another one. Another Huey."

Bailey looked over to his left. About half a mile away were two green National Guard helicopters. They were quite clearly heading towards the blimp. In the open cargo door of one of the Hueys Bailey could see a SWAT sniper, one leg resting on the skid, a rifle slung across his chest.

"Rich, can you stop them?" Bailey looked at the former Navy SEAL. He knew that the question wasn't if Lovell could, but whether or not he was prepared to.

Lovell stared at Bailey. He reached up and slowly scratched his beard as he looked down his long, hooked nose at Bailey. He nodded, once, and got up on his knees, sticking the barrel of the Barrett out of the open window. He sighted through the scope and tightened his finger on the trigger. Just as it seemed he was about to fire, he took his eye away. "What the fuck?" he exclaimed. "Would you take a look at that!"

Bailey and Farrell looked to the left. A man in an olive green flightsuit was sitting on the edge of the cargo hold, a bright orange harness looped under his arms. As the men in the blimp watched, the figure slipped off the side of the helicopter, kicked away from the skids, and dropped as the line paid out.

"What the hell's he doing?" asked Lovell.

The helicopter began to climb as the winch paid out its line and the figure swung from side to side like a hypnotist's pendulum.

"Who cares?" said Bailey. "Just shoot the fucker."

The wind buffeted Cole Howard as the Huey picked up speed. It rippled the arms and legs of the flightsuit with the sound of whips cracking and threatened to spin him in circles. Tears streamed from the corners of his eyes and he narrowed them to almost slits to cut down on the discomfort. He experimented with his limbs, seeing what position would minimise the spinning. He opened his legs and extended his arms and adopted the position he'd seen skydivers use on television. It appeared to work, the spinning motion stopped, though the air pushed against his arms and legs like a living thing. The Uzi swung on its sling and banged against his chest as it was tossed around but he ignored it and concentrated on maintaining a stable position.

He looked down and immediately regretted it. The city was falling away beneath his feet and his stomach lurched, the bitter taste of bile rising in his throat. He tilted his head back and swallowed and felt the acrid liquid slide back down to his stomach. Above him he saw the crewman, shivering in the doorway in pale green thermal underwear, one hand gripping the winch, the other in a thumbs-up.

Howard made a thumbs-up sign with his left hand but immediately began to spin to the right, so he thrust out both hands to the side to stabilise his position.

The winch continued to pay out. Howard had asked for the maximum length so that he could be as far away from the helicopter as possible, but the more the line extended, the more isolated he felt. He knew that the steel line was virtually unbreakable but he was all too well aware of how thin it was and that it was the only thing keeping him from falling to his death hundreds of feet below. Through his narrowed eyes he saw the blimp, side on and level with the helicopter. Howard began to experiment, he moved his arms in at the same time as he pushed his legs out, trying to hold the Uzi and at the same time remain stable. It seemed to work, though the new position had the effect of thrusting his head forward into the wind and he had to hold his head up higher to see ahead.

Rich Lovell refocused his telescopic sight on the man on the winch-line. He saw the Uzi across his chest and smiled thinly. The submachine gun was a fearsome weapon, one which was often used by the Navy SEALs, but it was only effective close up. At more than fifty feet, it was as useful as a peashooter. Lovell estimated the distance to be about seven hundred yards and he ran the calculations through the memorised charts in his head, figuring out how much the bullet would drop and by how much he'd have to compensate bearing in mind that his scope was set for a two thousand yard hit. The calculations were complex but he'd done them thousands of times before and it took him less than three seconds. He aimed low, took a breath, let half of it out, and squeezed the trigger.

As the bullet exploded from the muzzle, Lovell saw the man jerk upwards, out of harm's way, like a marionette in the hands of an inexperienced puppeteer. The sniper took his eye from the scope to see what had happened. He could see that all the line had been payed out and that the man in the flightsuit was now ascending at the same rate as the Huey. He put his eye back to the telescopic sight and tried to take aim again, but he was too late, the helicopter had climbed above the blimp and the huge gas-filled envelope blocked his field of vision. He looked around for the other National Guard Huey, but realised that it too had flown above the airship.

Lovell twisted around. On the other side of the blimp he could see the black and white police helicopter, hovering about a mile away. Lovell smiled. They clearly figured they were out of range, but the sniper knew better. He knelt down, took aim, and fired. He kept his eye to the scope as he mentally counted off the four seconds it took the bullet to arc through the air, and then saw the tail rotor disintegrate. The small helicopter immediately began to spin out of control as black smoke poured from its shattered tail gearbox. It lost height quickly, spinning faster and faster, and Lovell leant forward to watch it spiral down. It took almost twenty seconds for it to reach the ground where it smashed into a truck and burst into flames. Cars swerved to avoid the inferno, crashing into each other and mounting the sidewalks.

Lovell pulled the rifle back inside the gondola. He peered up, hoping for a glimpse of one of the Hueys that he knew were hovering overhead, but all he saw was the blimp envelope and the darkening sky. "Can you see them?" he asked Bailey.

"No," said Bailey through the headset.

"They know we're here," said Farrell. "What do we do now?"

"Just fly the fucking thing and let me think," said Bailey.

Lovell caressed the barrel of his rifle. Bailey wasn't holding up well and Lovell had a growing sense of impending doom. He'd have been a lot happier if Carlos or Mary had been in control. He looked down at the smoking wreckage of the helicopter. A parachute would have been nice, just step out of the door, pull the ripcord and float away. But he didn't have a parachute and until the blimp got a lot closer to the ground, he was in the hands of Bailey and Farrell. And they didn't inspire confidence. Lovell turned around again to look out of the window. A figure was hanging outside, about twenty feet away from the gondola, with a Uzi in his hands and his legs wide apart. Lovell swung his rifle around but he knew he wouldn't have time to get off a shot. His reaction was instinctive and had little to do with his chance of succeeding. The windows of the gondola exploded at the same time as he felt four quick punches to his chest. Lovell looked down and saw four small black holes in a neat line across his shirt, red holes with black centres like poppies. He tried to breathe but there was something liquid in his throat that bubbled and wouldn't let in the air and then he began to cough, heaving spasms that brought up mouthfuls of sweet, sticky blood that dribbled down his chin. The poppies grew and merged together into one red mass.

Lovell looked up. The figure jerked upwards again and

disappeared. A cold numbness spread out from Lovell's chest and his vision blurred. He sat back on the floor, his rifle between his legs. In his headset he could hear Farrell and Bailey shouting at the same time. Lovell tried to tell them that he'd been hit but his mouth was full of blood and he couldn't think of the words, they seemed to skip at the edge of his conscious mind like wild horses that didn't want to be corralled.

Lovell fell to the side. His head thudded down next to the cameraman and he found himself staring into the dead man's eyes. Lovell tried to push himself up but he had no feeling in his arms or legs. He heard Bailey shouting, but his voice was faraway as if at the end of a long tunnel. Lovell felt tired and he closed his eyes.

When the Huey lurched back above the airship, Cole Howard almost threw up. He began to spin and he let the Uzi fall back on its sling as he flung his arms out, trying to stop the dizzying movement. When he was stable again he signalled to the crewman to begin hauling in the line.

As he began to rise towards the Huey and its thudding rotor blades, Howard looked down on the huge airship below him. The rotor wash was flattening down the top of the blimp. It looked solid enough to walk on, but Howard knew it was an illusion. The airship was heading towards the inner harbour, away from the tower blocks. From below, the sounds of emergency sirens drifted up as fire engines and ambulances rushed towards the burning police helicopter. Howard had watched in horror as the crippled chopper had spun to the ground, knowing that he was powerless to help. He'd realised that the sniper must have been on the opposite side of the gondola so he had signalled to the crewman that he wanted to go down. When Howard had dropped level with the gondola he'd had the chance of shooting the sniper in the back, but he'd waited. He wasn't sure if it was because he'd wanted the man to have a chance, or if it was because he wanted to see the face of the man he was about to kill. Whatever the reason, he'd seen the look of surprise on the man's face before pressing the trigger of the Uzi.

Howard was turning slowly as he was winched up and he saw the second National Guard Huey hovering a few hundred yards away. When Howard drew level with the open door the crewman leant out and grabbed the line. Howard fumbled with his feet and found the skid, and then sat down heavily on the metal floor. He gestured to the crewman to give him a headset so that he could speak to the pilot.

"There are three men, I got one," said Howard. "They might be willing to land now. Can you talk to them?"

"I can try," said the pilot. Howard heard the pilot request the airship pilot to descend, but he was ignored. The pilot repeated his commands several times, but there was no response.

"He might not have the radio switched on," the pilot said to Howard.

"Or he might just be ignoring us," said the Secret Service agent. "Why don't we riddle the thing with bullets? It'll land eventually. We can just follow them down."

"What if they've got parachutes?" said the SWAT sniper. "They could be heading for a drop zone."

Howard nodded. The sniper had a point. Also, they'd brought down a police helicopter and probably killed the occupants. Howard doubted that they'd give up easily. "I've an idea," he said to the pilot. "Can you get the other chopper to fly on the opposite side of the blimp as a distraction. Tell them to be careful, though."

"Sure," said the pilot.

Patrick Farrell looked over his shoulder at the three bodies in the back of the gondola. Bits of glass were still falling from the window frame and wind was roaring through. "Oh sweet Jesus, now what the fuck do we do?" His hands were trembling on the controls. "Matthew, what do we do?"

Bailey was also shaking, his eyes darting around like a trapped rat looking for a way out. He peered down at the waters of the inner harbour. "How far could we jump?" he asked.

"Not this far, that's for sure," replied Farrell.

"What if we go lower? They're above us, they might not see us jump."

"Matthew, we're five hundred feet up."

"So like I said, go lower."

"If we go lower they'll go lower. They'll be radioing to the cops right now."

Bailey looked over at Farrell. "Have you got a better idea?"

"Tell them we give up. We haven't done anything, it was Lovell who fired the shots. He brought the chopper down."

"Fuck you, Farrell. You think they'll let us go just

because our fingers weren't on the trigger?"

Before Farrell could reply one of the Hueys began to descend in a slow hover, about six hundred yards to their right. In the open cargo doorway they saw a SWAT sniper, his rifle at the ready.

"Take us down," hissed Bailey, then he removed his headset and hung it up. He twisted out of his seat and looked around for Lovell's rifle. It was still in the dead man's grasp and the sniper had fallen on top of it. Farrell rotated the wheel forward and the airship dipped down. The bodies shifted as if they were still alive and a river of thick, treacly blood flowed across the floor towards Bailey's knee.

Some sixth sense made Bailey turn around. His mouth dropped. A man was rushing towards him through the air, his knees up and his feet forward, a submachine gun in his hands. Bailey began to scream. He saw Lovell's handgun lying in the bag on the floor and he grabbed for it, bringing it up with both hands. He pulled the trigger, screaming all the while.

The pilot of the Huey flared the rotor blades, bringing the helicopter to almost a dead stop in the air and swinging Cole Howard forward on the end of the wire. Howard braced himself for the impact as he surged forward towards the door of the gondola. He saw another man with a handgun and Howard pulled the trigger of the Uzi, sending a stream of bullets blasting across the gondola. As the Uzi kicked in his hands he felt a lancing pain in his shoulder.

What little glass there was remaining was shattered and the door was peppered with holes. The man with the gun disappeared and Howard let the Uzi hang on its sling so that his hands were free.

He slammed into the door so hard that the breath was driven from his body. The impact drove his knees against his chest and he clawed at the window frame for support. The nerves in his shoulder shrieked with pain, leaving him in no doubt that he'd been hit. The pilot of the Huey descended a few yards to take the strain off the wire. Howard managed to get his good arm through the shattered door window and he groped around for the door handle. In the seat opposite sat a pilot in a white short-sleeved shirt, a look of panic in his eyes.

Howard pulled open the door and hauled himself inside. He could feel warm blood dribbling down his arm under the flightsuit. There were four bodies to the rear of the gondola and he recognised one as Matthew Bailey. Bailey was on his back, his red hair matted with the darker crimson of fresh blood. One of the Uzi bullets had blown away a good-sized chunk of the side of his head. Howard kicked him with the toe of his shoe, but there was no doubt that he was dead.

"Take this thing down!" Howard screamed at the pilot. He slipped the orange harness over his arms, switching the Uzi from hand to hand, and then he threw the harness out so that the Huey pilot would know he was okay. The harness disappeared upwards as it was winched in. Howard moved to the front of the gondola and eased himself into the co-pilot's seat. He looked around for something to stem the flow of blood from his injured shoulder but couldn't see anything. "And hurry," he said.

"It wasn't my fault," whined the pilot. "They made me do it."

Howard pointed the muzzle of the Uzi at the pilot's groin. "Just get me on the ground," he said through clenched teeth.

Carlos walked quickly around the small plane, untying the ropes which were holding down its wings and the tail, and checking that the flaps and ailerons were functioning. He didn't bother visually checking the fuel tanks, but as soon as he was settled in the pilot's seat and had put his briefcase on the front passenger seat, he turned on the electrics and looked at the fuel gauges. Matthew Bailey had been as good as his word – both tanks were full. Not that Carlos required full tanks.

He started the engine and the propeller was soon a whirling blur. The airfield was deserted, but there was still enough light to see by. He looked at the wind-sock and taxied to the end of the runway which would allow him to take off into the wind.

The plane almost leapt into the air as if making light of its single passenger. Carlos kept the plane in a steep climb, flying it parallel to the Bay Bridge. In the far distance he could see the tower blocks of Baltimore city centre. When he was about halfway along the bridge he made a slow turn to the left, and continued to climb.

As he handled the controls, Carlos tried to work out where they had gone wrong and why the operation had fallen apart. It wasn't that he wanted to apportion blame, it was that he rarely failed and when he did it was always because someone else had let him down. He went over and over the steps in his mind, looking for the weak point. Not Mary Hennessy, of that he was sure. And Matthew Bailey had done everything that was asked of him. The snipers too.

Maybe it was just bad luck, plain and simple. Maybe the gods had just decided that Ilich Ramirez Sanchez would not be allowed to retire, to rest on his laurels and spend his old age with his wife and family. His luck had clearly run out the day he'd escaped from France. He was like a cat which had used up all of its nine lives. The displays on the radios in the control panel were blank. There was no one that Carlos wanted, or needed, to speak to.

He flew south, down the centre of the Chesapeake Bay.

Carlos thought about his wife and children. He wondered how they were, and if Magdalena had found the time to get the stereo repaired. They had a nice house, a house he could relax in, with several acres of well-tended garden behind a high stone wall.

He turned the plane to the left until the heading indicator showed that he was flying east. He remembered how his children had cried when he'd told them that he'd be leaving them for a while, and how they'd nodded seriously when he'd made them promise to take care of their mother. His own mother had cried, too, and she'd held him tightly as if knowing that she would never see him again. He remembered, too, how urgent Magdalena's love-making had been on his final night in the house, his suitcase packed and locked on the floor at the end of the bed.

There was no going back, Carlos knew. That had been the deal. If he had succeeded he would have had a sanctuary for the rest of his life, no matter what the international pressure. But if he failed, there was to be no link to his paymasters. In return for his silence, his family would be allowed to stay in their home. Carlos had made sure that whatever happened there was enough money in their overseas bank accounts to ensure that Magdalena and their children would never want for anything. Ahead of him he saw the blue vastness of the Atlantic Ocean, the sky above it beginning to darken as the sun dipped down below the horizon.

Carlos relaxed as he flew over the water. He'd given it his best shot. He had done nothing to be ashamed of. He looked down at the white tips of the waves some four thousand feet below him. A man could hide for a long time under the water, he thought. Maybe for ever. He opened the briefcase and took out the P228. He unscrewed the silencer and tossed it into the rear of the plane. There would be nobody around to hear the shot. He took his left hand off the control yolk and pressed the barrel of the gun to his right temple.

"Magdalena, I love you," he whispered.

The doctor put the finishing touches to the dressings and stepped back to admire his handiwork. "You're a very lucky man, Special Agent Howard," he said.

"I don't feel particularly lucky, Doc," Howard replied.

The doctor removed his rubber gloves and tossed them into a trash bag. "If the bullet hadn't glanced off your shoulder blade, and if it had exited downwards and not upwards, you wouldn't be sitting here now."

Howard was sitting on the edge of a hospital cot, stripped to the waist. He tried to stand but the doctor shook his head and held up his hand, Indian-greeting style, and told him to stay put. "You're not going anywhere," he said. "You've lost a lot of blood. You need at least a day in bed."

"I want to go home," said Howard.

"I gather home is in Phoenix, and you're in no fit state to be flying. You stay put, and that's an order."

"But my wife . . ." Howard began,

" . . . is waiting outside," finished the doctor. He nodded to a nurse who left the room and came back a few minutes later with Lisa.

Lisa Howard rushed over to the cot, went to hug her husband, then held herself back as she saw the dressings. "I won't break," Howard said quietly and she grinned and reached for him. There were tears in her eyes. "What are you doing here?" he asked in amazement.

"Jake called me and said I should get here. Daddy arranged a jet." She looked suddenly uncomfortable at the mention of her father, and Howard couldn't help but laugh.

"That's great," he said. "Honey, that's just great." He stood up and hugged her hard, squeezing her against him even though it hurt like hell.

"Honey, I'm so sorry," Lisa whispered into his ear. "About the golf clubs. About everything. When can you come home?"

"Tonight," said Howard.

"When he's stronger," insisted the doctor.

The door opened again and Bob Sanger appeared with Don Clutesi close behind. Clutesi was smiling. "Cole, how are you?" asked Sanger.

"Fine," said Howard.

The doctor sighed in exasperation. "Agent Howard, try to remember that I'm the one with the medical degree, will you?"

Howard grinned at Sanger. "Really, Bob, I'll be okay."

"Are you up for a visitor?" Sanger asked.

"This is my wife, Lisa. She's the only visitor I need right now." He kept a tight hold on his wife's hand as if afraid that she'd leave him.

"Oh, I think you might want to make an exception in this case," said Sanger, opening the door wide.

Two more Secret Service agents entered, checked out the room, then went to stand in opposite corners like trained attack dogs. Three more men appeared, and Howard sat up straighter as he recognised the one in the centre. It was the President, flanked by agents. Howard thought he seemed surprisingly calm, considering what he'd been through.

"Special Agent Howard, I just wanted to thank you for your actions today. I will be forever in your debt." There was no doubting the sincerity in the President's voice nor the concern in his voice. "Are you okay?"

Before Howard could reply, the doctor stepped forward. "A few days' rest and he'll be fine," he said.

The President nodded. "Good, I'm real glad to hear that. Real glad. If there's anything I can do, don't hesitate to call my office."

"Yes, sir. I will. But Mike Cramer is the one who you should thank," said Howard. "He's the one who saved the Prime Minister."

"I wish I could, Agent Howard," said the President. "If it wasn't for him I'd have a hell of a lot of explaining to do to the British Government. Unfortunately he seems to have disappeared."

Howard looked across at Sanger in surprise. "What happened?"

It was the doctor who answered. "We don't know," he said. "We were treating him here in Shock-trauma, the nurse left him alone for a few minutes, when she got back he was gone."

"Is he okay?"

"He has a bruise the size of a dinner plate on his chest and he won't be doing any hang-gliding for a while, but he's in no serious danger. The body armour wasn't even pierced." He smiled. "I think the manufacturers could use him to advertise their product."

"Is what I hear true, that the sniper was more than one mile away?" asked the President, his head cocked to the right.

"Two thousand yards," said Howard.

"If it had been much closer, the slug would have gone right through the vest, and him," said the doctor. "As it was, the bullet had slowed down considerably, but it was still travelling at several hundred feet per second when it hit him."

"That's absolutely unbelievable," said the President, shaking his head in amazement. "It almost defies comprehension. What Cramer did is just as unbelievable, diving in the path of the bullet the way he did."

Howard wondered what it was that had inspired Cramer to throw himself in front of the bullet. Then it came to him in a flash – Cramer hadn't been concerned about saving the Prime Minister so much as he had been about thwarting Mary Hennessy. It was hatred which had driven Cramer, not respect for the politician. Howard realised that the President was looking at him, waiting for him to say something.

"I'm glad you're all right, sir," Howard said.

The President flashed his trademark grin. "Agent Howard, you're not alone in that." He turned and smiled at Bob Sanger. "Maybe you should get this man on our team, Bob."

"Sounds good to me, sir," replied Sanger.

The President turned back to Howard. "Well, I suppose I must be going. I'm supposed to be taking the PM to the aquarium, but I don't think he's in the mood for looking at fish." He smiled and held out his hand. "I owe you one, Agent Howard."

Howard shook the President's hand. The flesh was warm and the grip was firm.

Lisa stepped forward as the President and his entourage left the hospital room. She looked as if she was going to say something but then changed her mind. Instead, she kissed her husband on the mouth, hard and with feeling. It was Howard who broke away first. Clutesi was grinning.

"Any news of Carlos?" Howard asked.

"Not yet, but he won't get far," Clutesi answered. "Kelly Armstrong was just asking me the same question."

"She's here?"

"Downstairs. They were treating her for shock but she was checking herself out when I saw her. She was with Hennessy when she was killed. She was covered in her blood."

"How come?"

Clutesi shrugged. "She was up in the stands when the SWAT sniper took Hennessy out." Clutesi stood by the window. He slanted the blinds so that he could look down at the road below.

"That seems like a hell of a coincidence," said Sanger.

Clutesi saw Kelly Armstrong leave the main entrance and walk purposefully down the road, her blonde hair swinging gently in the breeze. She was a real stunner, thought Clutesi, and from the way she swung her hips she knew it. There was something familiar about her, something that made the hairs on the back of his neck stand up. He'd seen her before at the same angle, looking down at her from a window. Clutesi clasped a hand to the back of his neck. A bar. She'd been going into a bar and he'd been on surveillance. It came to him in a rush and he slapped his hand against his leg. "Now I remember!" he shouted.

The Colonel came wide awake, all his senses alert. He turned his head to look at the bedside clock. It was three o'clock in the morning. He lay back and listened, allowing his mind to roam among the rooms of his cottage, trying to find the source of the noise which had woken him. The Colonel was a light sleeper, but he was never disturbed by the sounds of the countryside: barking foxes, hunting owls or sheep kicking over rocks. It must have been something else.

His nearest neighbours were a mile away, a working farm owned by a former Merchant Navy captain, and it wasn't unusual to hear tractors starting up at first light. But it was still dark outside, and if it had been a tractor or any other sort of vehicle, he'd have heard the sound for some time.

The Colonel sat up slowly. He slept naked and the sheets whispered as they slid down his chest. The road which led to his cottage was dotted with potholes and it was impossible for anyone to drive down without the vehicle rattling and banging. And for twenty feet around his cottage there was a layer of gravel chippings, several inches deep. It was impossible to approach the dwelling silently.

The house seemed silent. On the Colonel's right was an electronic panel linked to a security system which covered every door and window in the house, and which was connected to pressure sensors embedded in the road and at various key points in the garden. All the lights on the display glowed red, none was flashing. If any of the alarms were triggered, the system would automatically call his local police station and the police would arrive within eight minutes. Under normal circumstances the Colonel would have put it down to an unremembered nightmare, but something felt wrong. His insides were tight as if his body knew something that his mind didn't, and over the years he'd learned to trust his instincts. He twisted to the left and opened a drawer in his bedside table, where he kept a loaded Browning Hi-Power 9 mm automatic.

He slid out of the bed, switched off the gun's safety, and took a blue silk dressing gown from a hook on the back of the door. He pressed his ear to the door jamb and listened. Nothing. He eased the door open and slipped into the corridor, his nerves on edge. He kept close to the wall and tip-toed to the top of the stairs, keeping his left hand flat against the plaster, feeling his way.

He peered down the stairs into the gloom at the bottom of the hall, moving his head slowly from side to side to utilise peripheral vision as much as possible. With infinite patience he made his way down the stairs, keeping close to the wall and taking one step at a time so that the wood wouldn't betray him by squeaking. It had been more than fifteen minutes since he had woken up but still he had heard nothing other than his own footsteps.

Five doors led off the hallway at the bottom: to his study, the sitting room, a closet, the kitchen, and the main front door. The only one which was ajar was the door to the sitting room. He padded past the hall table and stood by the open door. If there was an intruder behind it, he would be at his most vulnerable when he stepped across the threshold. He listened intently, his head slightly down, focusing every fibre of his being on the room beyond the door. He heard a noise, a knocking sound like a foot brushing wood, from the far side of the study, close to the window. He raised the Browning, pushed open the door, and moved quickly inside, taking aim at the corner where he'd heard the noise.

There was no one there. His heart fell as he saw the single white knight lying in the corner where it had been thrown. He began to turn, but before he could move, the barrel of a gun was jammed against his neck and a hand clamped down over the Browning.

"Careless, Colonel," said a voice by his left ear.

Now available from Hodder & Stoughton hardcover

THE BIRTHDAY GIRL

By Stephen Leather

Tony Freeman first met Mersiha when she was a twelve-year-old killer with a Kalashnikov, fighting for her life in war-torn Yugoslavia. He rescued her from the heart of the brutal civil war and took her into his family where she grew up to be the perfect, all-American teenager – pretty, vivacious, intelligent. But with an agonising secret in her past.

Mersiha is fiercely protective of her new family. And when, on the eve of her sixteenth birthday, she discovers that two of her father's company shareholders have made him an offer he's not expected to refuse, she decides to help. Whatever the risks. The consequences of her interference are lethal – she has unearthed a dangerous conspiracy and the shareholders want revenge.

Turn over for the explosive opening pages...

Extract from THE BIRTHDAY GIRL

It all happened so quickly that it was only afterwards, after
they'd shoved the sack over his head and made him lie
down on the floor of the van, that Anthony Freeman
realised that he hadn't said a word to his abductors. He
hadn't begged, pleaded or threatened, he'd just followed
their shouted instructions as he'd half crawled, half fallen
from the rear of the wrecked Mercedes. He was still in
shock from the crash and he'd stumbled towards the van as
his captors prodded him with the barrels of their
Kalashnikovs.

It was like some crazy, surreal nightmare. Only
minutes earlier he'd been standing outside the Holiday
Inn, hunched into his sheepskin jacket and wondering
whether the far off rumbling sound was approaching
thunder or artillery fire. The Mercedes had arrived on
time, rattling along the road with its rear window
missing and its licence plates removed. The driver was
the man who'd picked him up at Split airport several
days earlier and driven him overland to Sarajevo, taking
the dirt road used by the Red Cross to ferry supplies to
the besieged city. Zlatko, his name was, father to six
children, three of whom had died in the conflict. He'd
refused to allow Freeman to help him load the bulky
metal suitcase into the boot. It had been Zlatko who'd
told Freeman the names of the abandoned villages they'd
driven by, some of the ruins still smoking in the cold
winter air, and it was Zlatko who'd explained that he'd
taken the licence plates off the car to give him a better
chance of getting through the many roadblocks. There
was no way of knowing in advance who was manning

the barricades and a wrong licence plate alone could be reason enough for a hail of bullets.

Zlatko had done everything possible to avoid the truck as it braked, and if he'd been a less skilful driver the crash would have been a lot worse. As it was, Zlatko's head had slammed into the steering wheel hard enough to stun him, and he'd been unconscious when the doors had been wrenched open. The kidnappers had raked his body with bullets from their assault rifles, the noise deafening in the confines of the car.

There were five of them, maybe six, all Freeman could remember were the black ski masks and the Kalashnikovs and the fact that he'd wet himself when they'd dragged him from the back seat, screaming at him in heavily accented English. He hadn't fought, he hadn't even said anything, he'd just evacuated his bowels and cowered like a child.

Freeman couldn't understand what they wanted from him. It wasn't as if he was in Beirut, where hostage-taking was a way of life. He was in Sarajevo; it was snipers and artillery attacks that you had to watch out for, no one took hostages. It didn't make sense. The sack smelt of damp potatoes and something was crawling across his left cheek but he couldn't get to it because they'd tied his wrists behind his back with rope. His damp trousers were sticking to his skin. He could barely breathe and the musty smell made him want to gag.

Freeman jumped as whatever it was that was crawling around the inside of the sack bit him in the neck. He tried to move, to ease his discomfort, but a foot stamped down between his shoulder blades and a voice hissed at him to lie still. He lost all track of time as he lay face down on the floor of the van. Eventually he heard his captors talking to each other and the van made a series of sharp turns and came to a halt. Uncaring hands grabbed his shoulders and arms and he was pulled out of the van. His cramped legs gave way and as he slumped to the ground the men cursed. More hands clawed at his legs and he was carried bodily.

He heard the crunch of boots on broken glass, then the slam of a door being thrown open. The footsteps became muffled and he realised he was being carried across a carpeted floor and then he heard the sounds of bolts being drawn back and he was hustled down a flight of wooden stairs. More bolts were drawn back and without warning he was thrown forward. His legs were still weak and he fell to the ground, his chest heaving from the effort of breathing through the thick, foul-smelling sackcloth. He heard the door crash shut behind him and the grate of rusty bolts and then he was alone in the cellar, more alone than he'd ever been in his life.

The doorbell rang just as Katherine Freeman stepped into the shower and she cursed. She stood under the steaming hot spray and closed her eyes, enjoying the feel of the water as it cascaded over her skin. The doorbell rang again, more urgently this time, and she knew that whoever it was wouldn't go away. Her car was parked outside and she'd left the tape deck playing in the sitting room so it was obvious that she was at home. She climbed carefully out of the shower stall and she quickly dried herself with a large pink towel. Downstairs the dog barked, but it was a welcoming yelp rather than a warning growl. Katherine checked herself in the mirror. She'd tied her shoulder length blonde hair up so that she wouldn't get it too wet in the shower and she shook it free. "This had better be important," she told her reflection. The last thing she wanted was to go downstairs and find two earnest young men in grey suits asking her if she'd been saved.

She pursed her lips and examined the skin around her neck. "Katherine Freeman, you sure look good for a thirty-five-year-old broad," she said, and stuck out her tongue. She threw the towel into a large wicker basket and picked up a purple bathrobe. The doorbell rang again as she ran down the stairs. "I'm coming, I'm coming," she called. If it was Mormons, God help them, she thought. Buffy, her golden retriever, was sitting by the front door, her tail swishing from side to side. "A smart dog would have opened the door," said Katherine and Buffy chuffed in agreement.

Katherine yanked the door open to find Maury Anderson standing on the porch. He was wearing a plaid sports jacket and brown trousers and his tie looked as if it had been tied in a hurry. "Maury, I wasn't expecting you," she said, frowning. Anderson said nothing, and Katherine suddenly realised that something was wrong. Her hand flew to her throat. "Oh God, it's Tony, isn't it? What's happened? Oh my God, what's happened?" Her voice rose and Anderson stepped forward to put his hands on her shoulders.

"It's okay," he said.

"He's dead, isn't he?" She began to shake and Buffy growled, sensing that something was wrong.

"No, he's not dead, I promise you, he's not dead. As far as I know he's not even hurt," said Anderson. His voice was quiet and soothing, as if he were trying to comfort an injured child.

Katherine pushed him away. "What do you mean, as far as you know? Maury, what's happened? Tell me."

4

"Let's go inside, Katherine. Let's sit down."

Katherine's robe had fallen open but neither she nor Anderson were aware of her nakedness. Anderson closed the door and held her arm as he led her to one of the couches which straddled the fireplace. He sat her down and then without asking he went over to the drinks cabinet and poured her a large measure of brandy with a splash of Coke. He handed it to her and she cupped it in both hands. She looked up at him, still fearing the worse. Buffy was pawing at Katherine's knee but she ignored her.

"Tony's been kidnapped," said Anderson quietly.

The statement was so surprising that it took several seconds for it to register. Katherine had been sure that her husband had been involved in a traffic accident. Kidnappings happened to politicians or millionaires, not the boss of a struggling defence contractor. "Kidnapped?" she repeated. "You mean the Mafia, or something?"

"No, not the Mafia," said Anderson. He sat down on the sofa, his hands clasped in his lap. "Terrorists are holding him hostage."

"Terrorists? In Italy?" Katherine remembered reading about terrorist groups in Italy who'd killed businessmen, shot them in the head and left them in their cars. Her heart raced.

Anderson took a deep breath. "He was in Sarajevo, Katherine."

She took a large mouthful of the brandy and Coke and gulped it down. There was a pewter cigarette case on the coffee table. She opened it and took out a cigarette. Her hand shook as she lit it and inhaled deeply.

"He was negotiating with the armed forces there."

"But he told me he was in Rome. He called me yesterday morning."

"I know, I know. He flew to Split and then drove to Sarajevo. It's a long story, but the upshot is that he's been taken hostage by Bosnian terrorists."

"What do they want?" Her voice was wavering as if she were bordering on hysteria.

"I don't know. All I've had is a phone call. They said we weren't to speak to the police and that we'd be contacted with their demands. If we call in the authorities, they'll kill him."

Katherine's hands shook so much that her drink spilled. Anderson took the glass from her hands. She grabbed at his arm. "What do we do, Maury? Tell me, what do we do?"

Anderson looked at her levelly. "That's up to you, Katherine," he said. Buffy whined and put her head on Katherine's knee.

"The FBI can't help us?" asked Katherine.

"It's out of their jurisdiction," said Anderson. "We'd have to go to the State Department."

"So let's do that."

"Katherine, Tony shouldn't even be in Serbia, never mind doing business there. There's a UN embargo."

"So? Tony's still an American citizen. The State Department has to get him back."

"There's a war being fought over there. It's a shambles. No one's sure who's fighting who, we're not even sure who the bad guys are."

Katherine stamped her foot. "God damn it, Maury, what was Tony doing there? What the hell was he doing there?" Her voice broke and she began to sob uncontrollably. She stubbed out the cigarette. Anderson took her in his arms and held her, tight.

"He was trying to help the firm," Anderson said. "We're

desperate for contracts, you know that."

Katherine sniffed. "Tony doesn't tell me much about the business," she said. "But I can't believe he didn't mention that he was going to Sarajevo."

"We didn't know until he was in Rome. The Serbs insisted on seeing him on their territory."

"Maury, this doesn't make any sense. I thought there was an exclusion zone or something around Sarajevo."

"Yeah, there is. He had to fly to a place called Split and then drive overland. The Serbs insisted, Katherine. We had to do it.

"We?" said Katherine. "We? What do you mean? I don't see you out there."

Anderson ignored the outburst. "We needed the contract," he said. "He probably didn't want to worry you. But we're having cash-flow problems and we had to take orders from wherever we could."

Katherine pushed him away. "But you said there was a UN embargo? Doesn't that mean we can't sell to the Serbs?"

Anderson shrugged. "There are ways around all blockades," he said. "There are middlemen in Europe who'll handle it. Everybody's doing it. Not so long ago the Russians sold $360 million of weapons to them."

"Yes, but we're not Russians," said Katherine. "We're an American company."

Anderson sighed. "Look, the Russians werre selling T-55 tanks and anti-aircraft missiles, serious weaponry. We're just talking about a few mine clearance systems. That's all."

"But you're saying that the authorities won't help us because Tony shouldn't have been there in the first place?"

"That's right," said Anderson. "But you're missing the point. We can't get help from anyone. If we do and they find out, they'll kill him."

Katherine closed her eyes, fighting the urge to slap Anderson across the face. "Damn you, Maury," she hissed. "What have you done?"

There were six guards taking it in turn to watch over Freeman, and over his weeks in captivity he'd made some sort of contact with them all. Freeman knew that the psychiatrists referred to it as The Stockholm Effect, when a hostage begins to form a relationship with his captors, but he also knew that there was a more fundamental reason for his need to communicate with his guards – sheer boredom. They allowed him no books or newspapers, no television or radio, and for long periods he was left alone, chained to a disused boiler in the freezing cold basement, so it was hardly surprising that he'd try to drag some reaction from them when they brought him food or came down to change the plastic bucket they made him use as a toilet.

Four of the men appeared to speak no English at all and communication with them was restricted to nods and gestures, but even their surly grunts were better than the hours of mind-numbing isolation. The fifth man's name was Stjepan, and he appeared to be the leader of the group. He was in his early twenties, thin and wiry with deep-set eyes that seemed to stare at Freeman from dark pits either side of a hooked nose. He spoke reasonable English but slowly and with such a thick accent that often he had to repeat himself to make himself understood. Stjepan told Freeman why he was being held hostage, and what would happen to him if the group's demands were not met. On the second day of his captivity, Stjepan had Freeman's aluminium suitcase brought down into the basement and demanded that he show him how to work the equipment it contained. Freeman had complied, though Stjepan's limited English meant it took several hours. The equipment was then carefully repacked into its case and taken back upstairs. Stjepan then explained that his people wanted another fifty of the devices, and that if Freeman's company didn't supply them, he would be killed. And the company had to agree not to sell the equipment to the Serbs. Freeman had protested but Stjepan had punched him in the face, hard enough to split his lip.

A Sony video camera was brought down into the cellar and Freeman was handed a badly-typed script to read. As he struggled with the poor grammar and inept vocabulary of the statement he realised that the punch had probably been planned in advance to give more authenticity to the video, but the thought didn't make it hurt any the less. Freeman asked if he could record a personal message to his wife and, surprisingly, Stjepan had agreed. When he'd finished Freeman was given a plate of watery stew and left alone.

While they waited for a response to the video, Stjepan was an occasional visitor to the basement, and Freeman gained the impression it was because the young man wanted to practise his English. There was no further violence, which reinforced Freeman's belief that the punch in the face had been for effect rather than to punish him, but Stjepan always kept his assault rifle close by and left Freeman in no doubt that he was prepared to use it.

During his hours alone in the basement, Freeman spent a lot of time thinking about his wife and son, and it seemed that the more he replayed the memories the stronger they became. He began to recall events and conversations that he had thought were long forgotten, and as he sat on the cold concrete floor he wept for the life that had been taken from him. He missed his wife and he missed his son.

He lost track of time after just a few days. The basement was without windows and illuminated by a single bulb which hung from the ceiling by a frayed wire. Sometimes it was on but usually he was in darkness. Electricity was as scarce as medical supplies in the war-torn city. His meals came at irregular intervals, so he had no way of knowing what time, or day, it was.

The wait for news of the Bosnians' demands seemed interminable. Stjepan said that the tape was being sent over to the United States because they wanted to deal directly with Freeman's company. Freeman knew that made sense: the US Government prohibited the sort of deal he'd been planning to sign with the Serbian forces and he doubted that they would want to negotiate with Bosnian guerrillas.

Once Maury Anderson heard that he was in trouble, Freeman knew he'd move heaven and earth to get him out. If anyone was to blame for Freeman's predicament it was Anderson and his insistence that Freeman fly to the former Yugoslavia to find new markets for the minefield clearing system they'd developed. NATO forces had turned him down flat, saying that they were developing their own system, and the only real European interest had come from the Serbian forces. A representative of the Serb military had made contact with Freeman in Rome and asked him to fly to Split for a demonstration. Freeman had wanted to refuse and had called Anderson in Baltimore to tell him as much. That was when his partner had broken the news of

10

yet another US Army contract that had fallen through. The workforce of almost two hundred men were depending on Freeman, and if he didn't come up with a European contract soon almost half of them would have to be laid off. CRW Electronics was a family firm, founded by Freeman's father-in-law, and Freeman knew every one of the employees by name. Anderson had put him in an impossible position. He had no choice but to go. Twelve hours later he was in a hotel in Split meeting a German middle-man who knew how to slip through the US trade blockade, for a price. Everything had been done in secrecy, including getting the equipment into the country on a mercy relief convoy, and Freeman had no idea how the Bosnians had discovered what he was up to. He'd asked Stjepan, but the man had refused to answer.

Stjepan was more forthcoming on his own background. Over the course of several days, he told Freeman that he had been fighting since Croatia and Slovenia declared their independence in June 1991, splitting the Balkans into warring factions. He was a Muslim and his parents had been killed by Serbs, though he was sketchy on the details. His sister, Mersiha, was also one of Freeman's guards and more often than not it was the young girl who brought his food and emptied his plastic bucket. Unlike Stjepan, Mersiha refused to talk to Freeman, and at first he assumed that she couldn't speak English. No matter what he said to her, she glared at him as if she wished he were dead, and some days she would put his food just out of reach and later take it way, untouched.

Freeman waited until Stjepan seemed in a relaxed mood until asking him about his sister. He wouldn't say much, other than that she had been particularly hard hit by the death of their parents, and that she could speak some English. Their mother had been a school teacher, he said. Freeman asked him why he had the young girl with him but Stjepan shrugged and said there was nowhere else for her to go.

Mersiha's black hair was tied back in a ponytail and her face was always streaked with dirt but there was no disguising her natural prettiness. Freeman knew that she'd be a lot prettier if she smiled and it became almost a compulsion, the urge to crack her sullen exterior and expose the real girl beneath. He greeted her each time she came down the steps, and thanked her when she put his food close enough for him to reach. He even thanked her whenever she emptied his plastic bucket, and he always used her name, but no matter how pleasant he tried to be, her expression never altered. Eventually he could stand it no more and he asked her point blank why she was so angry with him. His question seemed to have no more effect than his pleasantries, and Freeman thought that maybe she hadn't understood, but then she turned to him, almost in slow motion, and pointed her Kalashnikov at his stomach. The gun seemed huge in her small hands, but she handled it confidently and he watched in horror as her finger tightened on the trigger. He cowered away and for the first time he saw the young girl's lips part, not into the smile he wanted but into a grimace of hatred and contempt. "I hope they let me kill you," she hissed, and jabbed at him with the barrel of the gun as if it had a bayonet on the end. She looked as if she was going to say something else but then the moment passed and she regained her composure. She turned to go, but before she went back up the stairs she kicked his bucket to the far side of the basement, well beyond the reach of the chain.

The next time Freeman saw Stjepan he asked him why his sister seemed to hate him so much. Stjepan shrugged and in broken English said that he didn't want to talk about his sister. And he warned Freeman not to antagonise her. Freeman nodded and said he understood, though he wasn't sure that he did. He asked Stjepan how old the girl was and the man smiled. She'd be thirteen years old the following day.

As soon as she came down the stairs carrying a tin plate the next day, Freeman wished her a happy birthday in her own language, trying to pronounce it exactly as Stjepan had told him. She showed no reaction as she put the plate on the floor and pushed it towards him with her foot, covering him all the time with the Kalashnikov. Switching back to English, he told her that he wanted to get her a present but that he hadn't been able to get to the shops. Her face remained impassive, but at least she was listening to him and her finger remained outside the trigger guard. Freeman began to sing "Happy Birthday" to her, his voice echoing off the walls of his prison. She looked at him in disbelief, a worried frown on her face as if she feared that he'd gone crazy, then she realised what he was doing. When she smiled it was as if the sun had come streaming into the basement.